By Our Beginnings

By the same author

THE ROSE-GROWER
THE TRAVELLERS
HANRAHAN'S COLONY
THE STRAW CROWN
MY GRAND ENEMY
THE PASSING STAR
THE CASE OF KITTY OGILVIE
AN UNKNOWN WELSHMAN
DEAR LAURA
THE PAINTED FACE
THE GOLDEN CRUCIBLE

Jean Stubbs

By Our Beginnings

Mutato nomine, de te fabula narratur.
Horace

Change the name, and the story is told of yourself.

St. Martin's Press,
New York

St. Martin's Press, Inc.,
175 Fifth Ave., New York, N.Y. 10010
Manufactured in the United States of America

Library of Congress Cataloging in Publication Data

Stubbs, Jean, 1926-
By our beginnings.

I. Title
PZ4.S933By 1979 [PR6069.T78] 823'.9'14 78-21408
ISBN 0-312-11114-2

To the days of us

Acknowledgements

I thank Lovat Dickson and Teresa Sacco for suggesting, some years ago, that I should write about my Lancashire background: Adrian Leaman for his eloquence on social geography, and recommended reading: Leon Drucker for hunting down an 1829 edition of *Horse-Hoeing Husbandry* by Jethro Tull: Mr. Walter Bennett, historian of Lancashire, for a long and invaluable letter full of information – and Miss Chris Simons, journalist, for introducing him to me: Mr. J. R. Sutcliffe, General Secretary of the Lancashire Authors' Association; Mr. Keith Bishop, County Archivist, and the Lancashire Record Office: the staff of Helston Branch Library, Cornwall, for obtaining books with such interest and alacrity: Felix, for listening to, commenting upon, and living with the Howarths, past, present, and to come: finally to my forebears and their circle, who seemed to come forward in a grèat host when I began to write this book, saying 'Remember us?' – I did, I do, and I shall.

J.S.

Contents

By Our Beginnings

One

A man sat penning his future, by candlelight. In the thirty-fifth year of life, he was trying to express something of great importance to a woman and a world little known to him, though she had become such a familiar part of his inner self that he could hardly think her an acquaintance. He was offering all he possessed, which might mean little to her but much to him and had been sufficient until he met her.

Inside, the fire on the broad hearth, and two sleeping dogs, kept him company. Outside, the wind tuned up an orchestra of threatening sounds to which he did not respond, for his farmhouse had been built into the side of the hill, with stone quarried from its heart, and would withstand centuries of tempest. Time was of small consequence here, and life was simple. A man woke with the coming of day, and stopped work at twilight. When he was hungry or thirsty he ate and drank. When he was tired he slept. And when he loved, as Ned Howarth did, he wrote his lady a letter and hoped to begin a new dynasty.

Kit's Hill,
Nick o' Garth,
Lancashire

Martinmas, 11 November 1760

Dear Lady Miss,

Happen you remember me. I am Ned Howarth the farmer

that raises his hat to you every Market Day this three year past and once I had the Honour of taking your Arm and helping you and your Lady Aunt out of the Crush at Preston Fair and we have spoke about my Horse and the Weather and All.

My dear Mother as died just afore Harvesting this Year used to say as Folk was wed to the Place they was born in and thats how I am with Kits Hill. They say as theres been a Howarth farming Kits Hill since the Hill were there but I wouldnt Swear on Holy Book to the Truth of that though I Feel it in my Bones. Dear Miss since Father died and the Sisters was wed and left Home and Brother Will went to Sea and was Drownded and Mother Took Poorly along of all the Fret, Dear Miss, Kits Hill and me has Lost Heart as you might say. Betty Ackroyd do the Cooking and Hens and Dairywork and the little lass Nellie do the Cleaning and Martha Glegg comes up from Garth on Washday but it seems Poor Sort o Work compared to what it might be Which not meaning to Offend is the Point Im coming at.

Dear Lady Miss Im not Rich but Im not Poor neither and Kits Hill is a Grand Place and theres Plenty to Eat and a Laugh or two round the Fire of an Evening. I know that your Aunt is a Kind Lady but wouldnt you rather live in Your Own House instead of Hers and have the Ordering of Us? I know your not used to Farming Ways but your very Quick and Smart at Learning and you could fetch your Bits and Pieces with you and have a little Parlour if You didnt want to Sit in the Kitchen and do your Stitching and Read your Book and youd be so Welcome dear Miss. Dear Miss I know You are of Age though You dont look it Else I would have wrote to your Aunt but then She might have seen me Off. So I am Asking if You would do me the Honour to be My Wife and if You dont want me then I ask your Pardon meaning no Offence but we have spoke so Friendly like these Three Year Past and I should be Honoured if You and your Lady Aunt Call on me Any Day and Betty Ackroyd is a Grand Baker Else I will be Honoured to Call on You if that is more Proper but perhaps youd let me know One Way or Tother as soon as Convenient for I think the World of You Miss I do.

Your Humble Servant Ned Howarth*

Dear Mr Howarth,

I am very Sensible of the Honour you do me, and Grateful for the many Kindnesses shewn me, and since I received y[r] Letter yesterday I have Pondered and Prayed that I might make the Right Decision and so not Wrong us both. You are Too Good to trust to my Abilities without Proof of their Worth, and I fear you might soon Tire of my Ignorance in such Matters as are Naturally Incumbent upon her who is Mistress of Kit's Hill. I might Fail you, sir, and in so failing fail Myself, for I have some few Accomplishments of a Different Sort. Is it not Strange (all being Equal in the sight of God) that in this World we are Trained Up to Inequalities of every Kind? I could Commend myself into y[r] Safekeeping, yet would I Hesitate to Recommend myself as y[r] Wife . . .

On the title of *Wife* her pen paused. So far, so fair, she thought. But Dorcas Wilde could be independent only in spirit, and a future rested on her present judgment. If she left the known custody of her aunt she must accept the unknown custody of a husband. Whichever way the trap opened, she reflected, it would shut again.

'So that it does not close upon my fingers!' she remarked, and laid down her pen and chafed her hands together, for the room was cold despite a fire in the grate.

Then she read his letter again, with a smile for its homely phrasing, a delicate knitting of the brows for its spelling, and something softer of expression for the man himself. She had been guilty of charming Ned Howarth but not of soliciting

*Mr Howarth's personal eccentricities of spelling and punctuation have not been fully reproduced, but the substance of the letter remains unaltered. The original is in the possession of the Longe family of Millbridge, Lancashire.

this proposal. They were too unlike for matching, and he knew that and had yet been brave enough to broach the matter. She folded the letter carefully and slipped it in her pocket, where it reminded her by every shift and rustle of its presence that she was loved and wanted. She walked over to her bedroom window and leaned against the shutter, looking down into the street.

Her face was not vapid enough to be called pretty, for Dorcas was encumbered with intelligence and the Wildes' strong features. Her nose was slightly aquiline, her mouth decisive, her narrow eyes dark and brilliant; but a discerning person could take pleasure in watching her changes of expression. A smile would dissolve the severity, anger increase its haughty aspect, tranquillity reveal its peculiar beauty. She would grow handsomer with age, exchanging her present graceful carriage for a straighter back and a head held higher. She wore her own black hair, unpowdered and simply dressed. Her demeanour was modest, her voice soft, her wit sharp: a strange woman to catch a farmer's fancy, for he was as open and frank as a summer's day while Dorcas was all night.

One would have imagined that Ned Howarth's easy body, his wheat-gold head and good blue eyes, were better suited to a simple wench; though there was a warmth within and about him that attracted most women, and had drawn even the self-contained Miss Dorcas Wilde to exchange good-days. He was of the earth, yet as gentle as any gentleman should be and more chivalrous than many. A man whose mouth was tender, whose smile was unrestrained, who gave every appetite its due and was not ridden by any. In anger he grew red, and shouted, but his temper was quick and fair and soon forgiven. *Happen you remember me.* Oh, she remembered him with affection, glad that such men existed (though not for her, they were so very different). Musing in the white light of a winter afternoon, Dorcas knew what her reply should be.

For the old market town of Millbridge was a handsome example of man's progress in the art of subduing nature. The churches took care of his soul, the shops his daily needs, the houses his shelter, the inns his pleasure, the grammar school his education, and the poor his service. Above the town stood Kersall Park, rebuilt in 1655, to rouse his worldly reverence and cause him to doff his hat on Sundays as the Kersalls filed into their family pew. Millbridge was awake and thriving, conscious of its historical and economic importance in the valley. Its Fair charter had been granted in 1589, and every second Monday from Easter to Christmas the drovers came with their herds from miles around. In addition, there was a weekly market on Saturdays where you could see as much as £5000 change hands in as little as an hour. Here huckaback table linen from the Preston area was sold, stout dimity for bedroom hangings from Manchester, fustians from Blackburn, woollens and worsted cloth from Bury. Farmers' wives drove in to sell their butter and eggs and cheese. There was a Hiring Fair where servants might be purchased for a season or a lifetime. Millbridge was as compact, as busy, and as rich as a hive, while her prosperity increased.

Looking down the High Street Dorcas could see the crossroads where Middletown Street (once the Roman Way) ran at right angles. Beyond this junction lay the new corn market, and Lower Gate which eventually gave access to the new turnpike road running from Keighley to Kendal. Turning her head to the left she had a view of the market square, dominated by a coaching inn at the far end. This hostelry, for fifty years The Royal Oak, was re-named The Royal George when the first Hanoverian king ascended the English throne. Now the third monarch of that title was in the first year of his reign, and the landlord had mounted a new florid-faced and bewigged sign to show that he moved with the times. (But The Red Lion, a farmers' tavern at the back of the square, remained true to John of Gaunt's ancient symbol.) The spire of St Mark's church dominated the skyline, with the rectory chimneys just visible below it and smoking frugally on the frosty air. And had Dorcas chosen her bedroom at the back of Thornton House, instead of the front, she would have seen the long garden going down to the banks of the River Wynden, and had a fine view of the corn mill and the pack-horse bridge (which together had given the town its name). Within the last three decades the spinners and weavers had been allowed to ply their crafts in the row of cottages further downstream, and on summer evenings the sound of shuttle and wheel came faintly upon the ear. While, out of sight of gentlefolk, was a fulling mill and a dyehouse; and well away from their noses, tanners and leatherworkers plied their trade. A place for everyone, and everyone in his place, the Reverend Walter Jarrett always said, implying that the social order should not change – except, of course, in heaven, where it would instantly be reversed.

Here Dorcas Wilde had lived as companion to her Aunt Tabitha for three quiescent years, following the death of both parents. The air was harsher, the land poorer, than in her father's Gloucestershire parish, but genteel existence was much the same. A cup of chocolate at eight, dinner at one o'clock, tea-drinking between four and five, and a substantial supper at seven. Between meal-times a lady could study her book, ply her needle, take an airing if the weather were fine, and admire or deplore her face in the glass. Sometimes there was a musical evening, or a modest assembly with dancing and refreshment. Otherwise Dorcas played backgammon or piquet with her aunt, lit her candle, said her prayers, and retired to her bed.

. . . but wouldnt you rather live in Your Own House instead of Hers and have the Ordering of Us?

Along the Wyndendale Valley, with its muddy chain of villages and hamlets, life wore a different aspect. Here rose the Pennines in desolate majesty, where the wind ruled, and ways were steep enough to make a horse uneasy, and snow might trap the unwary traveller or some black precipice await his careless step. Swarth Moor, Bleak Low, Th'Stoops, Nick o' Garth. Single files of flagstones criss-crossing the moors marked pack-horse tracks, where caravans of woolmen had trodden and driven their loads from scattered farmsteads to the clothing centres, for centuries. Drovers had beaten out their wider way, grass-verged and worn by the passage of time and man and beast, which cut through from Yorkshire by Scarth Nick, and wandered down the sale to proud Preston which held the finest of fairs. While up on Garth Fells, out of the cosy bustle of village life and close neighbours, a handful of old farms raised stone walls against the elements and defied them. Their sheep and cattle were leaner than those in the valley, their crops less sweet and plentiful, their people hardier and more steadfast. These random fortresses, strategically placed in the war against nature, bore names that flew like pennons in the prevailing wind. Long Hay, Fox-holes, Shap Fold, Windygate, Kit's Hill. Kit's Hill. Spring came slowly here, with small cold flowers. Summer had hardly warmed the heather and cotton grass before autumn fetched down the leaves. Then winter closed its hands upon them.

I know your not used to Farming Ways but your very Quick and Smart at Learning . . .

Another life, another world, Dorcas mused. Her woollen gown smouldered rich and green against the painted shutter. Her face was ivory in the failing light. She was so sheltered, so motionless.

Phoebe Jarrett, the rector's daughter, appeared at the junction between Rectory Lane and the Market Square, wearing a mantle with a beaver-lined hood and beaver trimming, and experiencing some difficulty with her pattens.

'Does one wear a mantle and hood at Kit's Hill?' Dorcas asked herself, watching Miss Jarrett's teetering progress down the High Street.

She supposed not, for the wind would snatch at fashion. Farmers' wives wore coarse white caps and shawls, or strapped old bonnets onto their heads as though they were helmets to be worn against the foe. Farmers' wives had red hands and faces, chopped by the wind, and their clothes were meant to warm them rather than to set off to advantage a trim waist and a neat ankle.

'Not even a ribbon to grace them!' Dorcas remarked aloud, and rapped the bedroom windowpane with her knuckles to attract Miss Jarrett's attention. For they were both daughters of the Church, both spinsters in their anxious twenties, and friends of a shy and trusting sort. On an impulse, Dorcas threw up the sash window and called down softly into the High Street.

'Phoebe! Phoebe!' Making a pantomime of the fact that she wanted to speak to her privately, and they must not disturb Miss Wilde, who snored with her dog in the parlour below.

But even as she pattered downstairs and opened the front door herself, the voice of her aunt sounded the alarm.

'Agnes! Dorcas! What's amiss? Who's there? Why have you not told me? Agnes! Where's Agnes?' Who was this moment appearing from the kitchen at the end of the long hall, wiping competent hands on a clean apron. 'Agnes!'

Then she rang her handbell incessantly, and the spaniel Walpole began to bark and growl and make little runs at the parlour door, to show that he knew a burglar when he heard one.

'Oh, mercy on us!' said Dorcas drily, 'you would think I had been fetched home by the Constable. I so wished to speak with you privately, but now you must come and show my aunt your new mantle.'

Miss Jarrett would not marry now. Her father had needed her too long. Her future was assured until he died, and would then become a terrifying question for a faded gentlewoman to answer.

Dear Lady Miss Im not Rich but Im not Poor neither . . .

Dorcas cried, 'Come in out of the cold, Phoebe!' And over her shoulder said to the servant Agnes, 'It is Miss Jarrett, and she will take tea with us, so put on the kettle if you please!' Then beguiled her custodian by popping her head round the parlour door, saying, 'Look who has called to show us her new mantle, Aunt Tib!' Giving Walpole a little nudge with the toe of her slipper to silence him.

'Ah, now I see,' said Miss Wilde, setting down the handbell at last. 'Well, Miss Jarrett, Dorcas has been sulking in her room since dinner, so I hope you will instruct her better with regard to her duty. Sit there, where I can see you. Why have you bought such a garment? I hope it did not cost too much. Is it come from Manchester?'

It was quite beautiful, Dorcas reflected, to watch Phoebe bring this little bedlam to order. She enquired after Miss Wilde's health with a concentrated frown of concern, though the old lady would possibly outlive them all. She patted Walpole until he ceased trying to bully her. She settled her hoop and skirts and herself onto a prim chair, and assured her questioner that the mantle was a gift, not new at all, and exceedingly warm to wear. So Miss Wilde, cheated of this victim, turned upon her niece instead.

'Well, Miss, have you wrote your refusal?' And, before Dorcas could answer her, gave Phoebe an explanation. 'I should not like this noised abroad, Miss Jarrett, but some impudent jackanapes of a labourer has tried to make away with my money.'

'Indeed, ma'am?' said Phoebe, bewildered.

'Since you vowed me to silence on the matter, ma'am,' cried Dorcas, indignant, 'I should not have expected you to mention it.'

'I do as I please, miss, in my own house.'

'So I observe, ma'am, and wish that I were able to follow your example.'

'That you cannot, without you have your own money, miss.'

'Oh, ma'am. Oh, Dorcas.'

Then Agnes came in, carrying the second-best china on a silver tray, and the ladies had to speak of other matters until she had gone.

'I think only of your good, miss,' said her aunt, lifting the silver teapot.

Dorcas did not answer her, but turned to Phoebe, saying, 'This was the very matter on which I had hoped to consult you privately.'

'There is no need of privacy and consultation, miss. Tell the blockhead to go about his business, and get him a serving-wench if he feels so inclined.'

Dorcas again addressed her friend, while Walpole begged for a biscuit.

'I have this day received a – proposal – a proposal of marriage. From Mr Edward Howarth of Kit's Hill. You know how we have often spoke with him, and he is something of a favourite with your father. I believe his offer – though mistaken, though unexpected – to be genuine. But my aunt insists that he has designs on her property, through me!'

'The rascal knows very well,' said Miss Wilde, feeding Walpole and making a slop in the saucers, 'that all this will be left to Dorcas when I am gone, and so he makes the chit an offer.'

All this. The tall house and long garden, linen on high shelves and clothes in deep closets, old-fashioned jewellery in locked boxes, chiming clocks in silent rooms. All this, which Miss Wilde cannot take with her at the last, but would if she could, and clutter heaven.

Phoebe was smoothing her muff, head bent. When she did speak she had marshalled her few facts.

'But Mr Edward Howarth is a most gentlemanlike fellow, ma'am. Though not, of course, what one would expect for Dorcas. I know him pretty well by repute, and folk think highly of him. He is quiet-spoken and honest, and somewhat independent in nature and manner. I cannot believe he has designs of the sort you mention. Why, ma'am, did he not assist you from Preston Fair when you was took faint?'

'Aye, so he did,' cried Miss Wilde, vindicated, 'and now I am sure I felt his hand upon my purse. Did I not say so at the time, Dorcas?'

'No, ma'am, you did not. You said you was very grateful to Mr Howarth and wished we might receive him, but that would not be proper.'

'Besides, ma'am,' Phoebe said firmly, for between Miss

Wilde's obstinacy and Dorcas's persistence there was hardly room to speak, 'you are like to live many more years yet, please God, and you can always change your Will.'

Miss Wilde shook a silver spoon at her caller, for emphasis.

'Mark my words, Miss Jarrett. If Dorcas was to take this villain I should be burned in my bed!'

'Oh, fiddle!' said Dorcas.

'I do not follow your reasoning, ma'am,' said Phoebe, accepting a slopped cup of tea and a sugar biscuit.

But there was no reasoning to follow.

'He is beneath her entirely,' Miss Wilde continued, as though no one had spoken. 'A paltry fellow with his dunghill farm and his sheep and pigs and poultry. Why, what should Dorcas do there, pray? She has Greek and Latin, as well as the usual accomplishments. For her father (my brother Ambrose) having no son to teach, taught his daughter instead. So she is no use to herself or any husband. Neither fish, flesh, nor good red herring!'

Having thus dismissed three people at a blow, Miss Wilde contented herself with sipping tea and persuading Walpole to catch pieces of biscuit.

'I should be obliged if you would read Mr Howarth's letter, Phoebe,' said Dorcas. Not without a twinge for its lack of polish.

Which her friend did, and handed it back with a little smile.

'There is nothing but proper respect and proper feeling in this proposal, ma'am,' said Phoebe, addressing Miss Wilde, 'and Mr Howarth deserves no less from anyone that reads it. You may be assured that I shall not mention this matter – no, not even to my father, if that is your wish.'

She declined further refreshment, and made her apologies and farewells. Dorcas followed her into the hall pensively, and held her muff while she strapped on her pattens.

'But what shall I say to him?' Dorcas asked.

'I have had no experience of such matters. I presume you thank him for the honour, and decline as graciously as may be, with the hope that some other lady more worthy than yourself will make him happy. Yes, that should do very well.'

She was in quite a fluster with her gloves, imagining rejected lovers.

'And if I decline him, Phoebe, what then?'

'*If* you decline him? Surely you cannot contemplate . . . What then, you say? What would Miss Wilde do without you?'

'She would doubtless find some other female companion to humiliate.'

'You are disturbed, as is natural, and do not know what you say.'

'I am disturbed, certainly, but mean every word of it! Well, do not entirely hate me. I shall need a friend. Do you not like Mr Howarth?'

'Who could not like him? Aye, and esteem him?'

'And yet he is not good enough to be married?'

'Not to you, I think.' Firmly.

'But do you understand me when I say that in this letter, and in his presence too – what little conversation I have had with him – there is a warmth and kindliness to which a woman could respond?'

'It would not do for a lady, Dorcas.' Very firmly.

'Too poor to be married to a gentleman, and too fine to be married to a yeoman farmer! Oh, if only I had money I should not need to marry at all!'

'Do not think me indelicate or overbearing,' Phoebe whispered from beneath the beaver-lined hood, 'but I should have liked to marry, whether I had money or no. A clerical gentleman, such as my father. And I should so have cared for him and his parish and (do not think me forward!) for his children. Yes, indeed I should, and have been blessed. But I am very fortunate. Do not imagine that I complain!'

From the sepulchre of the hall Agnes asked, 'Should I light the candles now, miss?'

'Yes, if you please,' cried Dorcas, but Phoebe had not quite done with good advice.

Homely and sturdy in her second-hand mantle, the vision of the clerical gentleman fading before the reality of her walk home, she endeavoured to soften their spinsterhood.

'Better to enjoy a single blessedness,' she whispered, 'than the discontent that must attend an unequal match.'

Dear Miss I know You are of Age though You dont look it . . .

Dorcas embraced her friend gently, and closed the door upon her unassuming back.

'I will take a candlestick up with me, Agnes, before supper. For I have a letter to finish.'

. . . and yet I hesitate tc Recommend myself as y^{r} Wife

She had sat an hour before the page. Now her pen darted at the final sentences.

Sir, I am forced to speak plain, and trust you will not regard my Honesty as Immodesty. I have but Twenty Pound a Year of my Own, which was my Mother's, and some few Pretty Things that belonged to her. The Rest was all Sold Up, for my Father was a Man of God that Practised what he Preached, and so Diminished his Substance. I have no other Expectations. If you have heard Differently you are Mistook.

A True Wife sh^{d} possess the Necessary Qualities to act as her Husband's Companion throughout Life, and some Fortune with w^{h} to Endow him. I sh^{d} but Burthen you, sir.

If this Answer sh^{d} cause you some Distress, pray you Forgive Her who is the Unwilling Cause of it. God Bless and Keep you, Sir.

Y$^{rs.}$ Dorcas Wilde

Kit's Hill,
Nick o' Garth,
Lancashire

15 November 1760

Dear Lady Madam Wilde,
I believe I should have Wrote to You First and I Humbly ask your Pardon if I did wrong. Madam Lady I wish to have the Honour of your Lady Niece's Hand in Marriage which the

Lady Miss Dorcas has Told me is no Use since She has no Fortune nor Expecting None. I have Enough for Both and I am not asking your Lady Niece to Work as I have a mort of Servants and She shall live here as Fine as Fi'pence at Kits Hill and only have the Ordering of Us and be Genteel and Comfortable. If you would do me the Honour to See me and let me Explain I could make us all Easy and dear Lady Madam you would be Welcome at Kits Hill as a Queen when you wanted and I could send Tom to Millbridge to Fetch you in the Dog-cart.

Y^{r} Humble Servant. Ned Howarth.

'Is the numskull entirely mad?' cried Miss Wilde. 'Did you not refuse him outright?'

'You know that I did,' replied Dorcas, very pale, very cold. 'I understand this letter no more than you do yourself, ma'am. It would seem that his regard for me is greater than his desire to make off with your property!'

'You had best watch your tongue, miss, or you and I will part company. So he would make me easy in my mind, would he? And send Tom with the dog-cart when I wanted to visit? Why, miss, this country lover of yours is a proper wag! Were I accustomed to entertain labourers in my parlour I might send for him to keep us company. We grow dull together of an evening. Well, I shall write him a letter he will not forget. Fetch me my writing-case, Dorcas.'

'Aunt Tib,' said Dorcas, standing her ground, 'I am full five-and-twenty and I have been with you these three years. Daily, I doubt that we can bear each other's company another twelvemonth, and I have no desire to spend my life awaiting your death. So let us be sensible. Mark! I am about to agree with you, Aunt!' And she counted her accomplishments upon her fingers. 'I have a headful of Greek and Latin. Of what use is that unless I marry a scholar? I write a pretty hand. Should I then go to London and hope to find work as a female copy clerk? I do a little of most things well enough, such things as a lady's companion might hope to have mastered. What of them? You have no ear for music, no eye for art, no need for my knowledge of the globes or of mathematics, and you sew at least as well as I do myself! In brief, ma'am, I shall apply for some post as a governess, and trouble you no longer than I need.'

Suddenly she had a vision of her father, face alight, wig awry, smiting the chessboard in sudden exultation and crying, 'Checkmate, Dorcas! Checkmate, my love!'

Miss Wilde stirred uneasily in her chair, and motioned the stout spaniel away, for he was whining at Dorcas's tone and looking for comfort. When she spoke she was subdued.

'Well, miss, we are not to squabble over such a tupenny lover, I suppose?'

'I did not speak of Mr Howarth but of myself, ma'am. I cannot live so. I am not useful as I was to my father when my mother died. I am not easy and affectionate as I was when my mother lived. I am nothing to you, Aunt, that cannot be replaced. And I have nothing to keep me here.'

'That fellow offers you nothing,' cried Miss Wilde, catching onto the word as onto an excuse. 'He offers you nothing that a lady would accept.'

'He offers me everything he has. That is surely a great deal? But I was not speaking of him.'

'Oh, yes,' said the elderly woman, looking into the fire for counsel, picking up her dog for consolation. 'Oh, yes, you was, miss. Well, you are of age. I can't prevent you from making a gaby of yourself. But I shall not receive him in my house, nor acknowledge him, nor visit with him. And I shall alter my Will in favour of someone else!'

It was apparent that no other candidate had yet presented herself for this signal favour, and the knowledge was lonely. Miss Wilde stroked Walpole with a trembling hand, and he growled softly and stared into the flames with bright protuberant eyes.

'Well, cannot you see that I want my card table fetched up, Miss? And the cards, if you please. No, I shall not play with *you* this evening. Pray draw the curtains. I am more in a mood for patience than piquet.'

Millbridge was a levee of lights against the evening sky, and beyond them glimmered the necklace of villages and hamlets, and above the valley like single candles in the Fells glowed the outlying farms.

'I did not marry,' Miss Wilde was saying, shuffling the pack dexterously so that Walpole was not disturbed. 'I knew my duty better, as the only daughter of my parents. Do not assume that nobody asked for me. I had many an offer, for I looked as well as you, Dorcas – and I had property beside. Oh, yes, indeed. Before and after they died I was asked. But when I was my own mistress and could do as I pleased, and had Agnes – that I fetched out of the Hiring Fair when she was a lanky goose of thirteen, and trained up into a proper servant . . .'

She had lost track of the conversation, and paused, tapping the Queen of Hearts thoughtfully on the table, looking for the best place to put her.

'. . .and why should your father ask me to act as godmother to you, and name you after me – except that he would have you christened by the Greek version, instead of the Aramaic which is more usual. He was always an awkward fellow! But still we are good friends beneath the squabbles, miss, for we are alike, you and I . . .'

Now the young woman turned from the window in some surprise, but Miss Wilde affected not to notice, though her tongue was thrust slyly against her bottom lip in self-congratulation.

'. . . oh, yes, indeed we are. We like our own way, and get it very often, don't we, miss? We hold our heads high and expect folk to think well of us. We like to live comfortable and elegant, and wear our best silk of a Sunday, and choose new trimmings and ribbons from Miss Buckley's shop . . . Why, whatever persuaded poor Miss Jarrett to wear that beaver hood? She reminded me of nothing so much as a child caught in a bear's mouth!'

Dorcas smiled involuntarily, but said, 'Dear Phoebe, She

has a loving heart. I fear her virtues are less regarded than they should be.'

Miss Wilde's calculating hands hovered over her game of patience.

'A shrewd head would have served her better, Dorcas. But she is like her mother was. A washed-out snippet that worships God and Jarrett both, and will die of pleasing people. At least they will not say that of us! For we are too fond of ourselves. You was always a perverse child, Dorcas, and sometimes a secretive one, but you knew your mind and kept your head. And who did you get that from, miss? Not from your father, nor from your mother neither, else they would have lived longer and died richer!'

'From you, ma'am, evidently.'

Her tone was dry, amused. Yet she acknowledged the sorry truths her aunt could always find in the human predicament.

Miss Wilde snorted in triumph, and slapped a card into place. Her humour restored, she looked upon her niece with more favour.

'Dorcas, you will allow that I was never mean with you? Fetch me my leather jewel-box! I have a mind to give you a pair of earrings.'

'I thank you, ma'am,' said Dorcas coolly, 'but your gifts come somewhat expensive. I had rather know the reason before I put myself in your debt.'

'Why, you hussy, because I please to give them to you!'

'So that I shall not leave you?' asked Dorcas plainly.

Miss Wilde's grey eyes flickered. She laughed, short and sharp. Her tone became waggish, bullying.

'You shall get no earrings from Mr Howarth, that I promise you!'

'I need none, for I have my mother's and they will last me out.'

'Why, they are but amethysts, and these that I would give you are diamonds, you minx!'

'I prefer a coloured stone, ma'am, and mine are prettily

set.'

'Fetch me my jewel-box!' cried her aunt, so loudly that Walpole started from sleep. 'No, wait one moment while I send for Agnes. Agnes!' And she rang her handbell again and again. Walpole growled and slithered from her lap. 'Agnes! Why, where have you been all this while? Your face is red as fire. Have you a lover in the kitchen? Dorcas, go and see! No, help me up and I shall see for myself . . .'

Confused, Walpole took an indecisive run at Dorcas and attempted to bite her ankle.

'Oh, mercy!' cried Dorcas, parrying him with her foot. 'Sit where you are, Aunt. Agnes has no lover!'

'I were dozing, ma'am, in front of the kitchen grate,' said Agnes reproachfully. 'That's why I'm red and slow, begging your pardon.'

'Well, well. Go upstairs with Miss Dorcas, in case there's a thief in the house. Stop that noise, Walpole! (Look what you have done to him with your bustle and pother.) Be silent, sir! Agnes, take a candlestick, and you too, Dorcas, and if you see a man hiding in the bed-curtains then throw up the window and call for the Constable.'

The two women exchanged looks of understanding and commiseration, but followed her orders to the letter, and consequently returned quite safe. Meanwhile Miss Wilde had drawn up a small key by its ribbon, from the bosom of her corset, and sat waiting. With her formidable countenance, stocky figure, and hunched posture, she seemed more like a man than a woman: a man who had unaccountably worn a longer wig than usual, and chosen to put on a blue velvet gown instead of coat and breeches.

The great leather case was set down upon the card table, and the spaniel drew closer in hope of something to eat.

'That will be all, Agnes,' said Miss Wilde, dismissing her with a warning not to doze lest her cap catch fire. Then she sought to advise Dorcas before bribing her. 'Now, miss, you have a good home here. It is no hardship, to my way of thinking, to keep a pleasing tongue in your head, and read the morning paper aloud, and walk the dog, and eat four times a day. Besides, marriage is an unseemly business. Faugh! I always thought a woman well out of it.'

Dorcas did not answer, sitting in Grandfather Wilde's armchair, hands folded in her lap, listening and watching.

'I never could abide a man living in the house, though he were my own brother,' her aunt continued, unlocking the jewel-box. 'I would start up twenty times of a night, wondering if he had set fire to the bedclothes. And then they stamp about one's parlour, and stare so, and talk too loud, and fall against the small furniture. Walpole hates 'em!' She lifted the lid, now repenting of her generosity. 'But if you are so *rabid* to be married, why not try the Schoolmaster? I do not mind giving *him* supper, once or twice.'

'Oh Lord, Aunt Tib, we have been over this matter before. Mr Tucker is so shy of the ladies as to make them shy of him!'

'Dr Standish's impudent new-fangled doctor of a son, then?'

'So ambitious as to be looking for a fortune to found his hospital, I hear. And when he has the hospital he will not want the lady! You have forgot Millbridge's other eligible bachelor, ma'am. Mr Jarrett's curate must be all of one-and-twenty . . . but Phoebe should have first try at him, of course!'

'That's enough of your sauce, Dorcas. Here then, will these not make up for having some ugly dolt slobber over you, and put you in childbed once a year?'

'I was intending to go for a governess, ma'am,' said Dorcas lightly, 'and had not understood that such inconveniences were a part of teaching!'

She hooked the pendants into her ears, and smiled at her reflection in the glass over the mantelshelf.

'Oh no, you was not, miss,' her aunt replied shrewdly, watching her. 'There would be no advantage in such a post. Here, at worst, you can look forward to my property, or to ordering Mr Howarth, but as a governess you look forward to nothing – and you are too sharp for that, Dorcas. I know you. Come, girl, tell me if these sparklets are not worth one wretched lover!'

Dorcas removed the bright water drops and handed them back.

'They are not worth my little liberty of choice, Aunt Tib, though I thank you heartily. I had not thought you loved my company so much! Bear with me, if you please,' as Miss Wilde looked pugnacious, 'and understand me when I say that I am not anxious for marriage but for some life of my own.'

'Do you not think I felt so, at your age, Dorcas? Why, I watched your father walk away and would have run after him if I could. But I was left behind. What is there for any of us poor females but service of one sort or another? You should be kinder with me. I shall not live for ever. One day you shall be Miss Wilde of Thornton House, with a maid and a companion, no doubt. Then you shall do as you please. But for now we have only each other, and Agnes, and this old creature on the hearth.'

She locked the box and lowered the key to its hiding-place. The clock chimed ten gravely.

'I used to feel my life ticking by,' said Miss Wilde to herself, 'as though time passed but were never, somehow, spent. Now I do not mind. Except that I shall not like it to stop . . .'

Two

St Thomas's Day, 21 December 1760

No Howarth had ever troubled himself about the origins of Kit's Hill, nor been scholarly enough to ponder on its name. The neighbouring farms were so simply dubbed as to be self-explanatory: Long Hay, nearest the Craven area where crops grew plentifully; Foxholes; Shap (or Sheep) Fold; Windygate, closest to the Nick o' Garth. But Kit's Hill seemed outlandish, until you went back a few centuries to *kitte* or *cutte,* referring to its being cut out of the hillside.

For the farmhouse had begun as a four-roomed cottage with a rough ladder to the upper floor, and some early Howarths who had no choice but hard work and hard weather had survived in it. Then a kitchen and dairy had been added, and outhouses which grew into cattle shed, stables and barn. Later still there was a wash-house and brew-house. As each Howarth extended his land and his interests the home grew, and the farm buildings, and his ambition to better himself; until Henry Howarth bested them all at the end of the 17th century by recreating Kit's Hill round the original shell.

Formally planned it would have come into the class of manor-house, but the Howarths were practical and only added rooms as they needed them. There was a pleasing asymmetry about the place, as it wandered up solid oak stairs and sloped across bedroom floors, or stumbled down stone steps into the working quarters, or looked out of unexpected windows onto the fells. Kit's Hill was faithful to no pattern, and yet complete, and as individual as those who lived in it.

The stone-mason had been set free to embellish with art and finish with craft. Each opening was framed in sandstone, the quoins were of limestone, the windows mullioned and decorated with hood mouldings, all edges were neatly chamfered. Above the front door, used only for life's three occasions, he had set the surname and initials of man and wife. *H & J Howarth,* and the date of completion, *1690,* within carved flourishes of stone. So that they were chiselled out for immortality, Henry and Jennet Howarth, 1690, in their pride and prime, at Kit's Hill. And over all the great king-post trusses carried tons of stone-slate roof.

The house furniture had evolved from many winters' work, wrought by hands which would otherwise have lain idle. Idleness was a sin, as the Parson said, but they knew that out of hardship and experience. Down in the valley folk were soft, feather-bedded, with nowt to do but their daily work. Up here, men and women fought against the wind, which was more terrible and impersonal that the wrath of God at times. Howarth children lived or died at Kit's Hill, according to their ability to come to terms with the weather, and the aged and less vigorous battled against chronic bronchitis.

In winter their tasks were completed early, for it was dark by half past four in the afternoon, and sooner than that on a stormy day. Then the men worked indoors at the small forge, making and mending domestic equipment; or turned their hands to carpentry and supplied a clothes-chest or a bench. And in the evenings, when the only warm place was as near to the kitchen fire as a body could get, they whittled with their knives: a long-handled spoon with a rough flower or blade of wheat at the end, perhaps an animal or bird, or a doll's head for one of the children. Sometimes they created things of beauty, but even these were hard-wearing and useful because necessity and survival were woven into the fabric of their lives. They could not have told you this, being poor hands at speech-making, but they knew and lived it at Kit's Hill.

The climate and soil prevented good arable cultivation, most of the Howarth acres being on millstone grit, but a few fields stole into limestone country and these were fine pastures, akin to the lusher prospects of the Craven district. They nicknamed the most characteristic fields with wryness and affection. The poorest was known as 'Owd Barebones', the richest as 'Butter Meadow'. Closest to the Drovers' Road lay the 'Ha'penny Field' where the drovers rested their beasts for the night, and paid a halfpenny a head for that privilege.

Farming was mixed: mostly sheep, some cattle, some arable, some dairying. Ned Howarth reckoned his modest wealth in sheep, which provided him with flesh and fleeces to sell, and lambs to take their places. They were mutton in the home-pot, rugs for the floor, and even their skeletons could be useful: the slates of Kit's Hill were pegged by rib-bones.

The women's world was a daily one. They rose with early light in summer, and in the dark of winter, and lit the fire and cooked breakfast and fed the household. Only the carter and cattle-man were awake with them at that first hour, while the shepherd kept his own watch at all times. The dairy was theirs with its scrubbed slabs and flags of stone. Here they slapped and shaped their wedges of pale yellow butter, stamped with a beechwood mould; and formed their tart white crumbling cheeses; and churned thick cream. The farm-yard was theirs, the watchdog geese and heedless ducks, the bronze and blue cock lording his little brown hens. And the money from selling these products was theirs, to put out on such groceries as they could not supply themselves, to buy cloth from the packman and ribbons at the Fair. They kept the farm accounts, though they might have no more arithmetic than could be worked on eight fingers and two thumbs. They spun and carded the wool from their sheep, and mended and knitted and sewed by the fire of an evening. They bore their children, and bred them, and saw them grow up and grow away. So they lived, a day at a time, keeping the heart of the household beating steadily until their own stopped.

The men were bound to the cycle of seasons, and their world was told in years. The tools which delved and cut were theirs: plough-share, scythe and spade. The cattle and horses were theirs. They fed and groomed and harnessed the bulky oxen, the massive geldings. They milked the cows, and fed and shod their beasts, and nursed and birthed and castrated and slaughtered and skinned and fleeced them. They were the couriers from Kit's Hill to the world outside, shrewd buyers and sellers who would bargain with expressionless faces – and then pull out a leather bag of gold sovereigns to pay the reckoning.

Over and above the world of man and woman wheeled the cycle of birth, marriage and death. All Howarths were born in the parental bed, and suckled there until they could keep themselves warm in winter. They learned to walk on uneven floors that were obstacles to small unsteady feet. They fell and picked themselves up again, and ran out into the farmyard and made themselves known to the animals, so that a child barely as high as the hock would push the great brown leg to make the cart-horse move aside (which he did, good-naturedly). Marriage found the Howarths at their best, because Kit's Hill was made for large families, and a new unit brought fresh life. Then they grew old, though working to the last, and perhaps took to their beds for a few days with a cough that turned to pneumonia; or died, as one Howarth did, sitting at his table after a good dinner. The front door was opened for the funeral, and the dead went forth in an oak coffin carried on the shoulders of their sons, and their oxen pulled the cart to Garth churchyard.

No Howarth was ever satisfied, which was why he prospered. Each son who inherited Kit's Hill came to her with grander ideas than his father had, and he chose a wife who would help him. Some wives brought a little parcel of land with them, or a clump of sovereigns in a stocking; others were noted for their skills in dairy work or poultry-keeping; but all were good breeders with plenty of stamina, fit to produce the next generation.

*

It was St Thomas's Day, when poor folk came a-mumping, begging food and provisions for Christmas, and Kit's Hill was astir at five o'clock in the morning. First down was Betty Ackroyd the housekeeper, a woman of forty sturdy years, thickset and quick-tempered, red in the cheeks and fore-arms as though she had lightly broiled herself. She set to work at once with a pair of bellows, coaxing a weak flame from the carefully-mended ashes. For it was foolishness to let a fire go out entirely, and would necessitate a great deal of trouble with a tinder-box and twigs to get it alight again. So she puffed and blew, and grumbled to herself, until she was sure of the day's warmth and cooking. Then she hung the iron kettle from its hook and wiped her hands on her coarse wool gown.

Next into the kitchen came Nellie Bowker, yawning and shivering, a starveling of ten years brought up from the village recently. Upon whom Betty bent a gaze both sharp and suspicious, looking for guilt of some sort.

'Here's your lantern. Mind you don't let the candle go out!' Betty warned. 'And when you've done the dairy I'll have a sup of summat hot for you. Lap yourself up warm, now. It's raw outside.'

Even her kindness came forth as bullying. The child folded an old grey shawl across her chest, and Betty knotted the tails behind her waist, and gave her a push into the dark yard.

There Nellie stood for a moment after the back door closed, then began to make her way round the edge of the slippery yard, shielding the candle-lantern and warming her hands at the same time. She could hear Tom Cartwright talking to the horses in the stable. His breath hung on the air in pale chill clouds. The horses snorted and shuffled, communicating with him after their fashion, for Tom had been trained by Ned Howarth – who had been his father's carter until the old man died – and Ned was a better carter than he would ever be a farmer. So Tom talked as he filled the mangers, each with its special feed, and the animals responded. Then he would groom them all until they shone, and polish their harness until it winked, and Nellie would take his breakfast out to the stable because there was always something for a carter to do until his team went to work. 'If you canna eat your breakfast off floor by the time as you've mucked out,' Ned had told him, 'then it's not clean enough. So think on!' The stables were clean enough, and the horses knew it, and Tom had no trouble with any of them, not even Chestnut the brood mare who was difficult when in foal.

In the cow-shed on the other side of the yard, Joe Dickinson stuck his greasy hat well into Daisy's side and his hard hands brought forth milk in steady streams. Further on, his apprentice milker fumbled with Clover, who would shortly kick his pail and then kick him as he righted it. The shed steamed with damp, and the morning wind riffled through puddles and straw as they sat on their milking stools. Joe had walked two miles from his cottage, and Billy had come up from Garth. They were fortunate in that Kit's Hill fed all its workmen, living out as well as living in, or they would have had a bitter walk back for breakfast.

Nellie held her breath as she passed the bull's stall, though he was quiet in winter, but was bolder past the shed where four oxen were housed, for they were companionable creatures. Poultry did not fear her a whit, though the geese could be spiteful.

Discreetly at the end of the yard was the building known as 'Jericho': a simple structure, containing a long wooden seat with two large and two small holes set over a pit, and a bundle of soft hay by the door for the purposes of cleaning. The stench here was stronger than that in the yard, being enclosed, and no one stayed longer than necessary. Once a year the men cleaned it out by the bucketful, and tipped the raw manure on the fields. And adjoining it was the vast barn, a woodshed, and a small workshop containing a forge. So that these working places formed a wind-shield for the back of Kit's Hill.

The well had been sunk before the cottage was built, so it

now stood near the front of the house, which was fortunate for the occupants – or they might have suffered from water seepage from the cesspool. But it seemed a weary way round for Nellie Bowker, who must winch up each bucket of water and then carry it back again. Still, no one considered inconvenience, so she lugged the bucket round to the dairy, which was vast and cruelly cold, and began at the far end: tucking a folded sack under her knees, wielding the coarse brush and sand, wringing out her cloth in the icy water. As she progressed, flag by stone flag, she pulled her lantern towards her to light her way.

She heard the voice of the shepherd, and the deeper tones of Ned Howarth, and made as little noise as she could in order to catch the conversation. Sam Cartwright was a law unto himself, solitary in spite of his large family, a man of some eminence despite his poverty, and independent of everyone else though his hours of work seemed endless. A little wiry man with a shock of grey hair, he gave the appearance of being all smock and boots. His dog, Jette, was closer to him than his wife and possibly dearer. He had worked for Ned's father, and been trained as a shepherd by his own father, and his grandfather had worked for Henry Howarth. Usually he managed with a younger son who was learning the calling, but at certain times of year and weather he descended upon Kit's Hill to ask for temporary assistants.

'What's to do then, Sam?' asked Ned.

'I want to fetch sheep in from up the Nick, master, and put them into t' near fold. I can fair smell the snow coming.'

'Snow?' said Ned. 'Shall we be fast up, then?'

'There's neither man nor beast'll get down into valley tonight – or my name's not Sam Cartwright. And there's above a hundred sheep on them high slopes. Shall you come up wi' me?'

'Nay,' said Ned slowly, 'if we're about to be snowed up – and I've never knowed thee wrong – I've some business to do in Millbridge first. We'll find thee somebody. Get thee inside and fill thi belly.'

The shepherd eyed him shrewdly.

'Well, if tha's got summat better to do!' he said sarcastically. 'But I'm not laiking in t' kitchen all day. As soon as I've supped summat, I'm off.'

'Aye, well, better be sure than sorry,' said Ned, shamefaced.

The shepherd whistled up his dog, and the black and white collie came to heel and trotted softly after him. Ned hesitated, for he knew very well he should go, but he was in bondage. So he strode across the yard and looked in at the milkers. Joe grunted a greeting without turning his head, intent upon his vocation. Young Billy had just picked himself up from the ginnel, and was swearing at the muck on his breeches, and righting the three-legged stool. Clover's tail caught him across the shoulders with a redolent whip-lash.

'Bugger thee!' he shouted, almost in tears with frustration.

'Watch thi mouth!' warned Joe, who was a staunch puritan. 'I'll not have thee cussing an innocent beast. I'd kick thi breeches if tha milked me. Tha'rt like a blessed bell-ringer instead of a milker.'

Clover's near eye rolled menacingly at the lad, and he paused.

'Go to, Billy,' Ned advised from the doorway. 'If you're feared of her she'll make thee pay for it.'

'I'd sooner go for a soldier!' Billy shouted, and kicked the stool over himself, then righted it and attempted Clover again.

'Tha'd get a proper whip across thi back then,' said Joe, 'instead of a poor cow's tail. And a French bullet to trip thee in the muck. Eh, I don't know what young 'uns are coming to. In my day we was glad of owt.'

'We've all got to learn, Joe,' said Ned peaceably, and moved on to the dairy, where Nellie's awed triangle of a face stared up at him.

He nodded reassuringly and walked over to the stable.

'When it's light,' said Ned, 'saddle up Wildfire for me, wilta? I'm off to Millbridge.'

Tom's expression said more than he could have put into words. He gave a quick embarrassed duck of the head, and bent again to his grooming.

'And give him a good brush-up and shine, wilta?' Ned persisted.

'I allus do,' said Tom reproachfully, and fetched the body brush in strong arcs over Chestnut's hide. 'Whisha, whisha, my lovely lass,' he soothed.

Ned hovered in the doorway.

'Shall I get thee a lad to help out, Tom?'

'Nay, I'd sooner manage on my own.'

'I trained thee up, Tom. You could do the same for another lad. You and me got on like a house a-fire, and were company for one another.'

'Aye, I know,' said Tom, for those few years had gone and were most precious to him, and he knew they would not come back.

'Well then,' said Ned, feeling ineffectual, 'I'll be off.'

He could neither work nor rest. He was living on the fringe of life at Kit's Hill, looking in at the others who were keeping her going. He had lost his peace of mind and his application, and his discontent infected the household. They laboured conscientiously but resentfully because he was no longer one of them, and though he had confided in none all knew he was courting a lady in Millbridge. This set him apart as being both fool and traitor, for a man did not marry outside his class and his village. They would have been suspicious of a girl from Coldcote, half a mile from Garth, let alone a great town that most of them had never seen.

Nellie rolled the last churn into place. Joe finished milking Smiler, while young Billy scoured out the ginnel with a long broom. The back door of the house was flung open, and Betty Ackroyd shouted, 'Am I going to wait all night, or are you coming for your victuals?'

The men said something to each other which made them laugh boisterously, and guessing what the joke was, Betty shouted indignantly, 'Then it can go cold for all I care!' and slammed the door shut.

Nellie cast the contents of her bucket into the cobbled yard and followed the men shyly. She was wondering what sort of woman could hold Ned Howarth at arm's length, for he was rich and handsome and everyone spoke well of him. He had ridden down to her mother's cottage only three months since, to relieve her of the eldest of ten children, and sat like a king on his red stallion. 'I've heard as thi master's gone,' Ned had said compassionately. Mother had put her apron up to her eyes, crying, 'Aye, last month, Mr Howarth.' Ned whisked a fly from the horse's nose with his whip, and said, 'We can do wi' a little wench to help out. A shilling a week and all found.' Then Mother had thrust Nellie forward. 'She's nowt but two ha'porth of copper!' he had said, startled by the child's small and famished aspect. 'But she's strong, master. Strong and willing.' He had hesitated, then cried, 'Put her up in front of me, then, missis. It'll be one less for you, and her belly won't be empty at Kit's Hill!' Nor had it been, but Betty Ackroyd was a hard mistress to serve.

The heat of the kitchen burned Nellie's face in the same way that the iron churns burned her hands. She stared raptly at the fire which blazed up the wide chimney, and at the winking fire irons, and she drew up her stool as close as she dared.

'Tha'll get chilly-blisters,' Betty warned, and shoved a bowl of thick gruel into the child's hands.

The small beer had been mulled with a hot poker, and Nellie sipped and spooned in great contentment, and thrust her clumsy clogs to the flames to bring life to her feet; while the men sat up to the table, and Betty waited on them. It was agreed that young Billy should be lent to the shepherd, which occasioned some jocularity on one side and disdain on the other.

'Is master not coming wi' you, then?' asked Betty.

'Nay, he's got summat better to do than mind his own farm,' said Sam Cartwright laconically. 'I reckon he's off courting again!'

'Nay!' cried Betty, shocked and delighted. 'But she won't have him, will she? He were down in the mouth twice running. First wi' a letter from her, then wi' one from her auntie. Eh, I wish I could read. I do!'

Her audience agreed with her, and Nellie said, 'I heard him tell Tom to shine Wildfire up as soon as it were light, Miss Ackroyd.'

Betty wheeled on her, and the men fell silent.

'You keep a civil tongue in your head,' Betty warned, 'and keep it still. We want none of your Garth gossip up here. Tom, indeed! Mr Cartwright to you. And get up off your backside and take his breakfast to him. Look sharp!'

In tears, the child carried the pewter mug and plate of boiled bacon and bread over to the stables. Next to Ned she worshipped Tom, and could not think how she had offended. She had not known his surname until Betty told her, and repeated feverishly 'Mr Cartwright' until she had it by heart.

'Well, it's no use him cantering off at that hour,' Betty was saying in the kitchen. 'Millbridge folk lie abed half the day, I'm told. Eh, I never thought I'd thank God for Mrs Howarth's death, but I'm glad she canna see him making a fool of himself like this!'

'Nay,' said the shepherd, 'he'd never have durst ask her if Mrs Hetty had been alive. There's no other woman'd cross the threshold while Mrs Hetty ruled the roost!'

The latch lifted and fell. They hunched over their wooden plates, wiping thick slices of bread round the bacon juice, drinking small beer noisily from pewter tankards. They might grumble about Ned, or mock him in his absence, but his presence silenced them.

His face reddened by the wind, Ned walked over to the fireplace and rested his arm on the mantelshelf. After him came Nellie, wiping her eyes with her sleeve, sitting shyly to the rest of her gruel and glancing at his leather leggings with great humility.

'Come and sit thee down, master,' said Betty, ingratiating, winking at the others. 'Tha'll need summat as'll stick to thi ribs if tha'rt going up Scarth Nick this day.'

'I'm not going up the Nick. I'm off to Millbridge,' said Ned frankly, and scraped back his grandfather's high-backed chair, and took his rightful place at the head of the table.

'Nay, nobody told me!' cried Betty, eyebrows raised in innocence.

Ned looked shrewdly round his table at the averted and guilty faces, and smiled wryly to himself.

'Oh aye, they did!' he said quietly, and was not contradicted.

He had polished his best boots, and donned his bottle-green Sunday coat, and smoothed down his fair hair with goose-grease. Now he stood, fine and irresolute, in front of the hearth, and the child in her sacking apron dared not get on with her work.

'Have you fed them fowls, Nellie?' Betty called from the larder.

'Yes, Miss Ackroyd.'

'And made master's bed, and washed the dishes, and tidied up?'

'Yes, Miss Ackroyd.'

'Then why can't I hear thi scrubbing brush, Nellie?'

The child's eyes fixed imploringly on her master's face, but he was away in a world which did not include her.

'Do you want to be sent back to your Mam for idling?' cried Betty, louder.

Still Nellie stood dumbly, both hands clutching the clumsy brush.

'Do you want a good leathering with Master's belt?' Betty shouted.

Nellie stared woefully at the strap hanging on the wall, but even this threat could not overcome her awe of Ned Howarth. So Betty appeared in the doorway, and seeing the obstruction and being unable to do anything about it, fetched Nellie a slap that sent her against Ned's boots. The assault roused him, and he steadied the child's back with a square hand.

'Why, whatever do you want to do that for?' he asked, amazed.

'Well, why don't you get from under us feet?' cried Betty, angry with herself and him. 'Canna you see that hearth wants cleaning?'

'Then say up, when it's my fault,' he remarked, 'instead of clouting a little lass like that. What's up with thee?'

'Nay, what's up wi' thee? Your Mam'll be turning in her grave wi' your carryings-on. She will that. I don't know,' said Betty, beginning to cry, 'we're all at sixes and sevens since she's gone. I never thought as I'd see the day. Thirty year since she fetched me from Millbridge Orphanage, and I were knee-high to a grasshopper, like this 'un here – get on wi' your work and stop gawping, Nellie, it's nowt to do wi' you!' as the child stood frightened, staring from one to the other. 'Aye, thirty year. And I worked for her, slaved for her you might say, and always willing. Who stayed up wi' Hetty Howarth for four nights running, when she were at death's door, and never took her clothes off nor nodded off once? It were me, weren't it? Aye, and who laid her out lovely when she'd gone? Me again . . .'

'Say what you've got to say, but for God's sake say it!' Ned urged, weary of feminine logic.

'Why, your Mam thought as you'd marry Mary Braithwaite from Windygate, didn't she? There's but the one lass at Windygate, and no lads. So when Job Braithwaite passes on you can run the two farms together, can't you? And what's wrong wi' Mary Braithwaite? She's a right bonny lass as can stand up wi' any of us for dairywork.'

'Mary's a right good lass, I'll give you that.'

'She'll be a good breeder, and all. Her mother were a Gregson – Nellie! will you get on wi' your work or do I leather you? – and the Gregsons bred like, like I don't know what.'

'Aye, but they bred lasses, didn't they? Else they died, didn't they?'

'Howarths throw up plenty of lads. If you and Mary

Braithwaite was to get together we'd have a bit of life round the place!' She paused, thinking. 'Besides, we don't know where this Other were brought up, do we? She'll make a stranger of me in my own home. Mary Braithwaite knows us, and we know her. Aye, and who her father and mother was, and where she come from. She's one of us. But I'm telling you this, and you mark my words, this Other'll not fit in. Nobody wants her, bar you. And when she sees how we live she won't want us, neither. So nobody'll be suited. Take my advice and marry Mary Braithwaite, and I'll dance at your wedding as if she were the Queen of England!'

Ned said briefly, 'Save thi breath to cool thi broth! Have you got summat as I can take wi' me to Millbridge?'

'Nowt but a black pudding!' said Betty, unforgiving.

He was helpless against her hostility.

'I must take summat,' he pleaded.

'If you was courting the right lass at the right time you could take her a bunch of daffy-down-dillies,' said Betty. 'As it is you'll have to go empty-handed – not that she'd like what you fetched, any road!'

Nellie cleared her throat, for speech was a dangerous business. She tugged at Ned's big cuffed sleeve.

'There's a egg,' she whispered, and ducked under Betty's vengeful arm and brought it very carefully, in her small cupped palms. 'Speckled,' she said, 'for the lady's breakfast.'

'What I'll do to you!' Betty warned.

'You'll do nowt to her!' Ned cried, flushing up. 'Unless you want to hear from me!' He gave the child a reassuring pat on the cheek. 'Now, my little lass, fetch us a bit of straw from the stable. Clean straw, mind. And I'll lap it round this here egg, nice and safe. Then I'll be off.'

As he rode through the gate into the muddy lane he could see the distant figures of Sam Cartwright and two younger boys, with Jette at their heels. They were halfway up the Nick, and on the slopes above them the sheep were scattered like the coming snow.

Three

Millbridge was ten miles away: a rough one down into Garth, and nine muddy ones through the villages or hamlets of Coldcote, Medlar, Childwell, Whinfold, Thornley, Brigge House and Flawnes Green. So Ned had ample time to repent of his folly and turn homewards to common sense, but he was in thrall to Dorcas Wilde. His love was as honest as himself, his idea of married life hazy and benevolent. He thought how grand it would be to lift the door-latch at Kit's Hill of an evening, and find Dorcas warming her feet on the hearth. He delighted, shyly, in the notion of them lying together safe and warm in the big bed, listening to the wind fretting round the house. He considered them growing old together: he still attentive, she still gracious. He was zealous in preserving his image of her as a lady, and foresaw no duties heavier than her presiding over his table, or rocking their child to sleep. Now and again he threw in another picture or two, to lend this dream reality: Miss Wilde taking tea at Kit's Hill, Miss Jarrett visiting, Dorcas coming to market with him. So time passed pleasurably, and as Wildfire's coat and Ned's boots grew dirtier, and Millbridge drew nearer, he gained courage. He picked his way carefully along the miry lane by the Corn Mill, giving a friendly nod and shout to the miller. He rode over the pack-horse bridge and down into Market Square, and clattered along the cobbled High Street.

Thornton House had been built in the reign of Queen Anne,

and its stately façade suddenly doused his confidence. Even his untrained eyes saw a symmetry here, an ordered beauty which Kit's Hill lacked. Slowly, he got down and tied Wildfire to the post by the mounting block. More slowly, he removed his brown woollen cape and stowed it in the saddlebag. Slower yet, he walked up the freshly-scrubbed steps and lifted the knocker. The lion's brass countenance sneered at his best suit and newly-shaven face. He let the knocker fall feebly, and hesitated. No one had heard his soft appeal for admission. Glancing up at the windows, glancing down at the state of his boots, he lost heart entirely.

'Nay, I cannot!' he said to himself, and returned to his horse.

Two or three passers-by recognised him. He nodded in their direction, flustered, and pretended to be getting a stone out of Wildfire's hoof. The stallion, pitiless with his nonsense, jerked away and splashed a stream of muddy water across his breeches. Red-necked and scowling, Ned swore at him, and rage gave him back the courage he had lost. He made the steps at a run, took the lion by his ring, and assaulted the house with noise.

Miss Wilde was still asleep, but in the kitchen Agnes dropped the kettle, and in the parlour Dorcas clattered her chocolate cup on its saucer, and both met in the hall dismayed.

'Oh, miss!' cried Agnes. 'Would it be the Frenchies invading us, do you think?'

'Nonsense!' said Dorcas, temporarily restored by this dramatic notion.

'Then should I fetch the poker afore I open the door, miss?'

'Certainly not,' said Dorcas. 'I shall open the door myself – only you must stand behind me. Oh, mercy on us!'

For the house was invaded after all.

Ned looked as startled as his lady, but he was resolute, though bemused by the fragrant hall and fine furniture.

'Well, miss,' he said. 'I've come. I have.'

Agnes gave a soft shocked exclamation of disbelief. Dorcas hesitated only for a moment, and then took command.

'Will you not step inside, Mr Howarth? We can discuss your business in the parlour. My aunt is not yet downstairs, but she would wish me to offer you some refreshment. Perhaps a glass of sherry? Agnes!' as the servant's mouth opened in silent reproof. 'Agnes, you will please to fetch up the sherry, and a glass for Mr Howarth.'

'At nine o'clock in the morning, miss?' Agnes dared say.

'Nay, she needn't. I've had my breakfast. I never . . .'

'Do as I say, if you please!' cried Dorcas, incensed with both of them. 'Come this way, Mr Howarth.'

He was on trial and he knew it. He negotiated a long stretch of elegant carpet, frowning and sweating slightly, made his way towards the strongest chair in the parlour, lowered himself cautiously into it, and stretched out his muddy riding boots. Once established, he drew out a red cotton handkerchief and wiped his forehead.

A warm brown smell of horse and man conquered the china bowl of dried rose leaves. Suddenly, Dorcas became aware of the narrowness of her existence. Nevertheless, she made a show of arranging her hoop and skirts on a graceful chair some distance from him. Then she folded her hands and inclined her head to listen.

He knew nothing of women, beyond the matriarchal power of Hetty Howarth, the shrewish tongue of Betty Ackroyd, the plump charms of village girls who were or were not willing to be courted. He sensed that compliments would be out of place, even if he could frame them aright. He guessed that if Miss Wilde woke and confronted him he could be routed. He understood that Dorcas, though prepared to give him a fair hearing, would not help him. Then his temper rose with his spirits: the Howarth temper, brief and fiery, and often repented.

He said hardily, 'I'll come straight to the point, miss. I ask you to marry me and you say you've got no fortune. I tell you it don't matter, and offer to explain to you and your lady aunt. I ask you both to come and see for yourselves, and make you welcome. All I get is a note from Lady Wilde saying as you must choose for yourself. Now what else can a man do? I'm willing to learn if only you'll say summat.'

Very pale and composed, Dorcas replied, 'Mr Howarth, I respect and like you, but I know nothing of the life you offer. I am not willing to risk this present life for a person and place unknown to me. I cannot speak plainer than that, sir. My aunt is against the match, and will have nothing more to do with me if I consent to it. Nor, I fear, would any of my present friends. Is that not a great deal to ask of me, sir?'

Ned leaned forward, blue eyes intent.

'Are you saying as you're not against *me*, miss?'

His letters had been moving, awkwardly chivalrous, within her power to grasp. The man was a formidable reality, out of her power to manipulate. And for what was she fighting, after all? For the privilege of consulting Miss Wilde as to her health and whims? For the long days and longer evenings, all so like each other that she had ceased to count them lest she despair?

Her face was expressive of the struggle within her, and he pursued his objective. He was endeavouring to see himself as she must see him, to show her that his proposal (though eccentric, though socially unacceptable) was possible.

'I'm not a learned parson like your reverend father were,' said Ned quietly, 'but I can read and write, and I'm fast enough to pick up a hint or two. I might sound rough, but I don't think rough and I don't act rough.'

Dorcas sat irresolute, unable to dismiss or accept him. Now he was gauging her as he would gauge a mare of quality, for Ned knew far more about horses than about women.

'I carry that letter as you wrote me, in my breast pocket,' he said gently. 'It were a grand letter, Miss Dorcas, and you can pen it like I've never seen nobody do. But there's one bit as I treasure more than all the rest, and if you'll pardon me I'd like to read it to you.'

He drew out the sheet of paper, and quoted reverently.

'*I could commend myself into your safekeeping.*'

'I fear that you take this out of context,' said Dorcas sharply, 'and that you place too much store upon what was intended as an expression of esteem.'

But he was feeling more at home now, sensing her fear and temper and her pride.

'Nay, my lass,' he said comfortably, 'it's a deal more than that, to my mind. It means you could trust me wi' yourself, and trust is first and foremost – like truth. Aye, you can fancy somebody well enough, but fancy's nowt. Fancy flies, as my old mother used to say. But trust looks forrard, don't it? Trust means tomorrow, and next week, and next year.'

'I do not love you, sir, if that is what you mean. And so I tell you!'

'I'm not asking,' said Ned humbly, but with great dignity. 'Just give me a bit of time, that's all. Slow but sure, Miss Dorcas. That's the way. You be straight wi' me, and I'll be straight wi' you. A handshake means nowt unless it's met halfway.'

He looked at her so kindly and directly that her fear quietened. A warmth emanated from him that was part physical, part emotional. He seemed to encircle her, to restore a flow of feeling and well-being which had been stemmed since her parents died.

'That's better,' said Ned, smiling. 'Now you look like yourself again, Miss Dorcas. Give us a chance, wilta?'

It was not noise but instinct that woke Miss Wilde from dreams of possessions. Nightly she ferreted through lost treasures, and would often send Agnes up to the attic in the morning, to search for some long-forgotten trifle which had presented itself vividly in sleep. So Ned's summons on her front door had been the lid falling down upon her jewel-box, and she had stirred and grunted and composed herself again to sleep. Then she and Walpole raised their heads simultaneously, and crept out of bed onto the landing. The house seemed quiet enough, but the dog whined softly, and the woman sniffed an alien scent in the waxed hall.

So Miss Wilde had robed herself in an impregnable flannel morning-gown, buttoned from neck to hem, and was descending the silent stairs silently, with Walpole in collusion at her heels, when the lion announced yet another visitation.

'Oh Lor'!' cried Dorcas, starting to her feet. 'That will be my friend Miss Jarrett. We were to dress St Mark's Church with greenery for Christmas, and she promised to call early. I had forgot.'

Ned stood up in Miss Jarrett's honour, but said, 'I've not rode ten mile, wi' snow coming up on the Nick, and Sam Cartwright more or less fending for hisself, without I get a proper answer from you, miss.'

'How can I answer you?' she cried, almost in tears, for she did not want them to meet.

But here was Agnes with the tell-tale bottle of sherry sack and the glass. And there was Phoebe, open-mouthed and arm-in-arm with her father. While beyond them, sending Walpole into the company of hooped skirts and scarlet faces and apologies, stood Miss Wilde, crying, 'My nose led me here, sir. You stink of the farmyard. Now get you back there before I send for the Constable.'

The Reverend Walter Jarrett had dealt with people in difficulties, and with difficult people, for the greater part of his clerical life. Now he shrewdly judged and took command of the situation.

'How fortunate to meet together, Mr Howarth,' extending his hand, 'for that was a splendid leg of pork you sold us, and I should like to know where there is more of the same quality. Yes, indeed. Good-day to you, Miss Wilde, we had not thought to disturb *you* so early. We came to fetch Dorcas. Aha! sherry wine! I am indeed come at the right time . . .'

But Miss Wilde was not bound by good manners. She advanced on Ned, who stood his ground and waited.

'My niece is not for such as you, sir, so get you gone. You have been impudent enough. Why, Mr Jarrett, I swear this villain is after my money and will try for it though he live to be a hundred – which God forbid! What, sir? Courting Dorcas in broad daylight, when I am abed?'

'Lady Wilde,' said Ned courteously, not knowing how else to address her, though she was lady neither by title nor behaviour. 'I come, not knowing as you was – retired. For we was up by five o'clock at Kit's Hill, and the morning's half over by now – to our way of thinking. I come to set your mind at rest and to get a proper answer, which,' he added firmly, 'I will have. For there's snow coming down the Nick o' Garth, and I ought to have been there, God knows (begging your pardon, Mr Jarrett). But if you'd given me a chance, for Miss Dorcas is part willing to my mind, I could set matters right.'

'Oh, Dorcas!' said Phoebe sorrowfully, for the man was quite inept.

She looked at her friend in bewilderment. There had been a fine feel of communication between them, which an incident such as this confounded.

'Agnes!' cried Miss Wilde. 'Show this person out and do not allow him to enter my house again.'

'My dear lady,' said Walter Jarrett, in reproof, 'this is not necessary. I protest, I have known Mr Howarth and his family for some years . . .'

'He is after my property, sir, and will dishonour my niece. I must protect us since no one else will do so.'

'Nay, nay,' said Ned, relieved to hear the cause of her hostility. 'I want nowt but Miss Dorcas, and she can come on her own terms. I'll place my hand on the Holy Book and swear to that, if you want. Mr Jarrett,' turning to his only supporter, 'you know me and mine. We eat nowt as we don't earn, not a crumb. Sir, if I could 'a' dealt wi' a man it would have been easier. For I can neither say nor do owt right here, and I'm fair flummoxed. Speak up for me, wilta?'

Phoebe's brows drew together in consideration. The man was sincere, but socially unacceptable. Walter Jarrett's face expressed a number of conflicting emotions, since he could only live comfortably in this world by promising eternal bliss to people with influence. Dorcas gave a little gasp, sister to a sob, and walked over the window in despair.

'I believe, Miss Wilde, that you and Dorcas should hear this gentleman out,' said Jarrett diplomatically, 'and we shall retire, and call later.'

Ned's stature increased. His natural good humour returned. The furniture seemed more fragile, the scent of beeswax less persistent, in his presence. His body was strong and healthy, uneasy in its best clothes. He glowed with vitality in the sterile house, so that Phoebe went over to Miss Wilde and stood by her for reassurance, since they were spinsters by nature as well as circumstance.

'I'd be obliged if you'd hear me out too, sir,' said Ned, addressing Walter Jarrett, 'since I only want what's honourable and right. I'll sign owt and do owt as'll show I mean what I say. (Though a man's word is good enough, where I come from!) I love Miss Dorcas and have done for three long year. I've watched and waited, and I've seen nobody else come courting. Now I know that I'm not good enough, in a manner of speaking, but she's got nowt here – begging your pardon, Lady Wilde, and meaning no offence. She's got nowt and she could have summat. She *is* summat, and deserves summat, I know that. I can give her more than she's got, or likely to get, in this here house. I'll care and fend for her, and think how best to please her, until they lay me underground. I'll make out a paper so she's provided for if I'm took before her.

'Now, sir, I'm not here because I canna take no for an answer. I'm here because Miss Dorcas has given me the notion, though she mightn't know it herself, that it's only what folks think that stands between us. Sir, you preach that we should love one another, and that we're all equal in the sight of God. Now I know where I'm out of place, and I'll doff my hat where it's expected, but when it comes to what I am and what I care about I'll stand afore King George hisself and speak out. I'm speaking out now, sir. Miss Dorcas and me could do very well together, if we was let. She's bothered about what folks think. With respect, sir, they can think as they please. But she might not like that.'

Now he turned to address his lady's back, as she stared, afraid and angry and ashamed, into Millbridge High Street.

'Miss Dorcas, if you tell me to go about my business, and never see you again, I'll do that. I'll think and feel no less about you, but you'll never hear more from me. I give my word, and my word's my bond. But if there's a bit of hope, if we could talk and meet – proper-like so as nobody starts gossiping – then give us a chance.'

Even Walpole did not break the silence that followed. But he crept up to Ned's boots and smelled them respectfully and then sat by them, tongue lolling.

Then Walter Jarrett said, half-ruefully, half-gaily, 'I believe that Mr Howarth has set us all to rights, whether we like it or no! He should have his answer.'

Out of the tumult of herself, Dorcas cried, 'I shall not be told what to do a moment longer. Deuce take the lot of you!'

Then she burst into tears, warded off all friendly hands, and ran upstairs to incarcerate herself for the rest of that cold day.

At length Miss Wilde stirred slightly, and said in a voice unusually low and dispirited, 'Now will you go, sir?'

'Aye,' said Ned, 'I will, Lady Wilde.'

He surveyed the quiet circle of onlookers to this drama, and singled out Agnes as the best possible keeper for his gift.

'Would you be good enough to give this here egg to Miss Dorcas, my lass,' he asked politely, 'and tell her as it were new-laid this morning, and the only one? When she's stopped fretting herself she might relish it, boiled.'

He shook hands with Walter Jarrett, bowed low to Phoebe and Miss Wilde (who murmured, 'Don't let him touch me! Faugh!') and said, 'I can let myself out!' Unnoticed, Walpole pattered after him.

From her long window, pressed against the shutter that she might not be observed, Dorcas watched Ned mount Wildfire and then turn, astonished, as the stout spaniel wriggled and capered before him.

'By Gow!' said Ned, easy and good-natured, 'you're a sly one. I never saw thee sluther out! What's to do, then? I'm going where you canna follow, my lad. You'd best bide where you're suited. Aye, poor little bugger. Nay, dost know where my dogs are? They're up on't Nick, else watching the house and yard, all working for their keep. Flash wanted to come wi' me, but he'd be out of place here. He'll run ten mile and think nowt of it, following me!' He looked round for assistance, afraid of leaving Walpole to the mercy of the outside world. 'You'd drop dead, my lad. You're bred up to silk cushions, not catching coneys. What in hell am I to do?'

A scream from Miss Wilde announced his deliverance, and Agnes came running down the steps and gathered up the spaniel, who, for the first time in his life, had someone to bite with cause, and attempted to sink blunt teeth into the woman's arm.

'Stop that!' Ned roared, and Walpole ceased, and flattened his behind and wagged his tail incessantly. 'You want to fetch him a cuff across the nose when he does that,' Ned advised Agnes. 'Why, I could put an egg in any of my dog's mouths and know it were safe. Oh, and don't forget about Miss Dorcas, my lass, wilta?'

Dorcas shrank further back, but listened more closely.

'She's like to fret for a bit,' Ned continued, keeping Wildfire in check, 'and it ain't easy for her. See as she eats her food, wilta?' Agnes nodded, drawn to his warmth and surety, in spite of her misgivings. 'You'd best take that little chap inside where he belongs,' said Ned of Walpole, who was panting in his direction. 'Take care of Miss Dorcas, now.'

Dorcas saw him lift his head when he was alone, and sniff the air of Millbridge. He sat his red stallion as though they had grown together. She knew that he was quietly confident, that he had found himself again, and now directed his purpose towards Kit's Hill. A victory of sorts had been his that morning, and showed they were equal in spirit if not in station. She had, in one way, answered him by refusing to answer, and they both knew it. So he could click his tongue softly to Wildfire, and set the horse's head for home, with an easy mind. While she must sit alone at her window, in the barren house, and know that everything was being set in order here again: an order which would never change.

Four

Christmas Eve, 1760

The encounter had shaken them all. Agnes, being least involved, was the first to recover, and she wisely concentrated on restoring Miss Wilde.

Ordered to keep to her room, since she had been responsible for a gross breach of privacy, Dorcas made the best of her own company. Devoid of guidance, she set down the advantages and shortcomings of her single life at Thornton House, and compared and contrasted them with those she might expect as a married woman at Kit's Hill. Years ago her father, the Reverend Ambrose Wilde, had advised her on this method of solving a problem.

'For the act of writing down one's thoughts sets the mind in order. Then, with both facts and beliefs before you, you shall best know how to deal with possible events. You will note, Dorcas, that I say *possible,* for we are all at risk in life, and chance makes fools of us. (Which seems to be the finest reason for trusting Almighty God, since He is our only surety!) But be honest with yourself, and once you have chosen your path be resolute in staying to it, and never be swayed by opinion. Opinion, Dorcas, is more akin to prejudice than to judgement!'

Snow fell prettily upon the roofs of Millbridge, and put nobody to greater inconvenience than that of a well-aimed snowball. But it swept down the Nick o' Garth like a vast white bird of prey, and transformed the fells into an eerie wasteland. Sheep huddled together, patiently living out the cold. The men who had stayed at Kit's Hill shovelled paths to the sheds and dairy, and came silent and frozen to the kitchen for warmth. The others were cut off by snowdrifts and bided their time and lost their wages. And Nellie Bowker wept quietly to herself, for Ned had long since promised that she should go home for Christmas and take a basket of food with her, and the way to Garth was impassable.

It was Christmas Eve when Dorcas strapped on her pattens and picked her way delicately through the slush, to find her friend drinking tea pensively in the front parlour of the rectory. She was brought in with little cries of delight and concern, dripping water over the hall tiles.

'Oh, it is you, Dorcas! Oh, I did so hope – but did not dare call. Happily I am alone (well, not happily, for Papa is the best of company, but he will be out until supper-time). Louisa will fetch us another cup and saucer. Come by the fire, do. (Shoo, Puss!) And warm your feet. I hope you do not think I have neglected you, but Papa thought it best that I should not annoy Miss Wilde by calling. And the last time we met was such a . . . oh dear, Dorcas!'

'As though the house was broke open,' said Dorcas thoughtfully, examining the wet on her skirt hem. 'It is about that, and other matters, I should like to confer with you and ask advice of you.'

'Whatever is within my power, and according to my conscience, of course, dearest Dorcas!' cried Phoebe, confident in the outcome.

'I wish you to listen to something I have wrote, and speak as honest as may be, without fear of hurting me.'

A singular dignity about Phoebe's assent suggested that Dorcas was underestimating her powers of judgement.

'I hope I am always as honest as my father's daughter should be, my dear. At least wait until you have drank your tea!'

Louisa, one of a steady flow of country girls trained for

work at the rectory, brought in an extra cup and two more biscuits. Then, seeing that all was well, she curtseyed and closed the door quietly behind her.

'Your servants are a credit to you,' said Dorcas cordially. 'I hope I may do as well with mine, some day.'

'Let us hope that time will be many years hence,' said Phoebe somewhat pointedly, 'for I can think of no one more competent and civil than Agnes!'

Dorcas gave her friend a long rueful look, and attempted to leaven the atmosphere. Producing her little manuscript, she cried gaily, 'Now, one moment, while I unfold such a tract as Dean Swift might well have been proud to write!'

'I do not care for Dean Swift, Dorcas,' said Phoebe firmly. 'What little I have read of his writings I thought both coarse and unkind.'

'Oh, I swear this is neither. I was referring to his qualities of honesty and truth – though I do not compare myself with him, of course.'

'I do not care for his notion of the truth, neither,' said Phoebe, pink and obstinate, sugaring Dorcas's tea as if to sweeten the conversation.

'Well, this is a female essay,' said Dorcas peaceably, 'and open to any commonsensical advice you may think to offer.'

'And though I do not mean to take you up short, my dear,' said Phoebe, suspicious, 'if you have made up your mind to have Mr Howarth then why not tell me so outright? Not tease me with some clever thing you have wrote, and ask advice that you do not require!'

'Why, you are determined to quarrel with me!' cried Dorcas, aghast.

'What is this about a quarrel?' came the voice of Walter Jarrett from the doorway. And he walked forward to spraddle the hearth and dominate the talk, lifting his black coat-tails to warm himself, and smiling on both young ladies.

He was a handsome man in his late fifties, with sufficient intelligence to gain respect and not enough to trouble him. He would have been a bishop at least, had his income and connections matched his charm of manner. For his good-tempered way of talking, his ease in any class of society, made him popular with most people, and he was particularly fond of children so long as they did not trouble him. He would have made a better squire than a parson, but was born too late in his father's family for that position. And, having to decide between the Church and the Army, had chosen God as the lighter taskmaster.

'I thought you was taking tea with poor Miss Spencer, Papa!' said Phoebe, quite put out.

'Aye, and so I should have, but that she was took most unwell and had to send for Dr Standish. I must ask leave to join you both, instead!'

And he rang for fresh tea, and cake, and more coals for the fire, thus throwing out all Phoebe's small economies.

'Why, what is that great screed in your lap, miss?' Jarrett demanded of Dorcas. 'What have you been playing at now? A translation from the Greek or Latin? May I, without mockery, commend such an intellectual proceeding? Most young ladies would have smoothed their ruffled plumage with a visit to the dressmaker. Not so Miss Dorcas Wilde! She casts out her memory of the worthy but importunate Mr Howarth by communing with Homer. Well done, Dorcas!'

'I fear I am about to disappoint you, sir,' said Dorcas, looking at him with irony and affection. 'Far from consulting the illustrious dead, I have merely taken stock of my poor self. This screed, sir, is my very life, and contains my fate for good or ill.'

'Why, miss,' cried Walter Jarrett, laughing, 'what nonsensical notions have you been hatching in that busy head of yours?'

And he sat back in his armchair, and crossed his legs, and placed the tips of his fingers judiciously together.

'How do you know that they are nonsense when you have not heard them, sir?' she parried with spirit. 'They might be very good notions indeed!'

'Oh, all you self-willed young women are full of foolishness, until you marry and settle down,' he replied idly, 'but it amuses me to listen.'

'Oh, I had not intended to trouble *you* with it, sir. Poor Phoebe was to be both audience and critic.'

Her heart was hammering in her breast, but she endeavoured to hide her hurt and disappointment, and so she folded the document and slipped it into her long purse, smiling. Then she warmed her hands, and fell silent.

'So we are not to know your fate, miss?' said Jarrett more kindly, for he perceived that her visit was of great import to her. 'Why, we are eat up with curiosity. You cannot be so cruel!'

'Sir,' cried Dorcas, trembling, 'I came to speak with my friend, and thought she would deal gently with me, but I perceive that I am an object of contempt to her, and of jest to you. It was not always so,' clutching the bulky purse. 'There was a time, in my father's house, when I was loved and used well. That time has gone, but I thank God for it, and have borne my present ills the better because of it. But it is hard to feel that those early years were all I might expect of joy and usefulness.'

She struggled to preserve her composure, while Phoebe and her father sat silent and astonished. Displays of feeling were not usual in Dorcas, who cultivated a sprightly air, and tended to be acid rather than tearful.

'I ask your pardon,' said Dorcas, rising. 'I have been somewhat low in spirits of late. A cold room and one's own company are not conducive to merriment. Will you give me leave to come again, when I am more myself?'

The document was her only companion, and Jarrett looked on this and on Dorcas with considerable interest, and some compassion.

'We have been found wanting in our friendship, Phoebe,' he cried, 'and Dorcas would feel the better for a glass of cordial. Sit down, Miss Dorcas, and we shall talk together amicably and in all seriousness.'

But Phoebe, though obedient to her father's whims and wishes, kept herself a little apart. For Dorcas had been her strength, and was not expected to fail.

'Now, miss,' cried Jarrett, hearty over his glass of shrub, 'you have always had more of head than heart about you, though your heart is sound and good. I shall speak directly, as both friend and father. This business concerning Mr Howarth has made you restless, and that is natural enough, for every woman would prefer to have an establishment of her own. I am not so selfish,' said Walter Jarrett, who was very selfish indeed, 'as to wish to keep Phoebe to myself, were she to have a good offer. I say the same of you, whom I regard as another daughter. But as a loving parent I should inspect that offer closely. It should include sufficient similarity of taste, breeding, and interest. Preferably with a little money on both sides. This is why I have always believed that matrimony was the concern of the parents. They know what to expect, within reason, and unless there is some vast disinclination on one or the other side, these marriages turn out far better than your amorous matches. Let the Strephons and Chloes, and their like, sport in poetic glades to their hearts' content! But do not allow their sentiments to disrupt the significant undertaking of matrimony.'

Phoebe said uneasily, 'Only there should be love, Papa. Surely there must be love? You and Mamma loved each other, did you not?'

'Aye, aye,' said Walter comfortably, 'we were very well together.'

Perhaps the winter afternoon had shadowed the rectory parlour, for Phoebe said no more, and Dorcas mused in her corner, and the rector rang the bell and ordered Louisa to remove the tea-things.

Then Dorcas said with some of her old humour, 'It would appear that marriage is not made in heaven, but arranged upon earth, sir!'

At which Phoebe was a little shocked, but Walter Jarrett laughed.

'I thank you, sir, for your directness,' Dorcas continued. 'I shall be as frank in my turn. Could I but choose my helpmeet I should have just such another as my father was to my mother. That is, a man who would esteem me and care for me, someone with whom I could share sorrow and joy alike and know I could trust. For, now I speak so open (and hope you shall not hate me for it after), I do not trust my aunt. I feel that as she and I grow older she will plague me with her property, rather than placate me as she now does. Your parish has its share of rich and ageing spinsters, and what is their chief delight? To dangle a fortune before their relatives and swear to disinherit them! I have done pretty well so far, because I am still young enough to say her nay. But what in ten years' time, sir, when I am subject to her? Should I not then wish that I had accepted Mr Howarth?' Her voice shook a little as she pronounced his name, and saw their expressions, but she went on hardily.

'I must have a purpose in life, sir, and there is none at Thornton House. But there is purpose in Mr Howarth, and an honesty that cut me to the quick. For he was right, sir, when he said I feared what folk would think. And I could not but admire him for saying he would speak up before the King. If only I could have taken time and thought,' becoming agitated again, 'but it was as if the house was broke open. And I cannot stay with my aunt, sir, now. Indeed I cannot!'

'Well, well,' murmured Jarrett, uncrossing his legs as the fire scorched one of them. 'Well, well. Have you made up your mind to Mr Howarth, then, Dorcas? Nay, don't answer me on the instant. Let me speak first. You will lose all your friends . . .'

She was opening the purse and withdrawing her little document, half-crying, to show that he had no need to speak, for there at the head of the page were penned the words *I shall lose all my friends.* So he paused, and read, and glanced at her over the top of the page, as if to say that there were two she would not lose. But Phoebe, suddenly tired, said she must consult with Louisa about supper, and excused herself.

Every detail was set down, in a painstaking way which touched Jarrett. For she had endeavoured to counsel herself, and the result amounted to a personal philosophy, a declaration of faith. Jarrett read it through to the end, and handed it back with respect, though shaking his head ruefully.

'I deplore the conclusion, and admire the concluder,' he said, graceful to the last. 'How may I be of service to you, Dorcas? Apart, my dear, from marrying you both in Millbridge at St Mark's – which I refuse outright!'

'Oh, I did not hope for that, sir,' said Dorcas, recovering her composure, 'but is there no way you could marry us in Garth?'

'Why, miss, you want your cake and eat it!' he cried laughing, and was pleased. 'I know the Reverend Tom Redfern a little. I dare say he would be willing to allow me to assist him at – I forget the name of the church in Garth. Yes, that could be arranged, I believe!'

He spoke complacently, for who would refuse the rector of St Mark's in Millbridge? Then they sat companionably together, though both a little stunned at such an outcome, and Dorcas glanced at him with humility because she needed all his resourcefulness. Also she knew that Miss Wilde had promised a gift of silver for the altar, and might be capricious with her Sunday offerings if displeased. So he must balance his goodwill against his interests.

After a while, he said, 'Would you wish *me* to acquaint Mr Howarth with your acceptance of his suit?' And, as she inclined her head, added, 'It would be as well, miss, if I were to command you for a while. None of your arguments and sauce!' She shook her head, obedient. 'Well, I must get a message to Mr Howarth, and through him to Mr Redfern, and suggest that they start calling the banns as soon as may be. For it will be difficult to live with Miss Wilde during your engagement, and the less time that tongues wag in Millbridge the better it will be for all of us!' A shadow passed over Dorcas's countenance, for she liked folk to think well of her, and they would not. 'You could stay here with us,' Walter Jarrett added, 'but that would cause some scandal and ill-feeling, which is best avoided,' and he mused again, then said smiling, 'I wish Mr Howarth had chosen finer weather for his proposal; it will be cold work coming here and going there. Dorcas, I feel you should make the rectory your meeting-place – and do you not wish to visit your future home before spending the rest of your days there?'

She murmured something about taking it on trust, and was subdued.

'I believe it to be a large and prosperous farm,' Jarrett remarked, 'though I have not seen it. Mr Howarth is somewhat of a local squire at that end of the valley. The wedding may be a little rough. A mountain of good plain food, coarsely served. A quantity of good-natured noise and humour. And a number of pagan observances, all carried out with the zeal of good Christians!'

Phoebe, having run out of excuses, now came back into the parlour and took up her sewing.

'My dearest Phoebe, you shall be invaluable in this,' he cried, turning his head leisurely to be able to see her, resolved not to inconvenience himself. 'You shall act as chaperone. Dorcas will need to visit Kit's Hill – what an extraordinary title for a farm! – and Mr Howarth will be calling here a time or two before the wedding. I dare say you and Dorcas will be deep in ribbons and trimmings, will you not?'

Phoebe raised her faded head and looked directly at Dorcas. Then she looked away. Their friendship was shrinking from the wedding. It would fulfil its duties and retreat, and what the outcome might be no one could guess.

'We have spoke frankly,' Walter Jarrett continued, 'and as good friends, my dear Dorcas. I will speak once more, and then be silent. I have always thought you to be a remarkable young woman, though wilful and headstrong at times. Still, a little spirit in a woman is to be admired!' So he said, having chosen a submissive wife and produced a submissive daughter. 'It is a great pity your aunt did not think to bestow a dowry on you. A thousand or so would make all the difference, for you are an excellent match and would make a worthy wife in the right circles. Shall I not put this to her, using our present decision as a persuader?'

Dorcas flushed up, hesitated, was ashamed of the hesitation, and shook her head.

'I thank you, no, sir. I esteem Mr Howarth. I would not use him so.'

'A pity!' said Jarrett. 'Well then, my love, keep your quaint document by you to the last. There are trials in every marriage, and I fear you will be tested in a hundred ways. And when you are about to pack up your pocket-handkerchief and run away from Kit's Hill, read your *locus standi** and stay in your place!' And he laughed at his turn of phrase.

'I think it is dark enough to light the candles,' said Phoebe in a smothered voice, and hurried from the room.

'I shall escort you home, miss,' cried Walter Jarrett, already becoming faintly jocular about this eccentric match (which he would deny thrice and thrice again when needful, like some unrepentant Peter).

Phoebe came back with candles for the gloomy hall, and lifted her cheek to be kissed. And Dorcas bestowed a small cold act of contrition upon it.

Then Phoebe said, 'So you have made up your mind? Now all is changed, of a sudden, and will never be the same again. God bless you, Dorcas.'

Sitting by candle-light, waiting for her father to come home, Phoebe thought this would be the sorriest Christmas she had ever spent. She was sewing a baby's gown for one of the weavers' wives by the river, and now and then she wiped her eyes lest a tear mar the soft fabric. Into the material she had neatly stitched her dreams, one of which was a vision of herself and Dorcas growing older and closer together as they lost their dependent guardians, perhaps even sharing a small establishment in Millbridge. Now the stitches must take on another meaning, and she did not know what, so hemmed very

*The document referred to as *locus standi* by the Reverend Walter Jarrett was found among the papers of the late Charlotte Longe, and is in possession of Millbridge Historical Society.

fine and prayed for the weaver's baby instead.

Miss Wilde's head was cocked to catch the sound of her niece's return, and she barely greeted Walter Jarrett, who had both hands outstretched in friendship and sympathy.

Her first rage and fear had been succeeded by emptiness. Walpole, too, had passed from surliness to apathy. A visitor was better than nothing, but at the moment Miss Wilde would have welcomed battle. She motioned him, impatiently, to sit down.

'My dear lady,' Jarrett began, gauging her temper, 'I know you too well to prevaricate, so I shall not be tedious. As you feared, Dorcas will not listen to reason, and intends to have Mr Howarth whether her friends think ill or well of the match! There, that is the worst over. Now for the better part. We can save ourselves a scandal, ma'am . . .'

She was listening to the low voices of Dorcas and Agnes, conversing in the hall.

'. . . whether you stay friends with Dorcas or no,' Jarrett was saying persuasively, 'the immediate embarrassment will be spared you, ma'am. Finding Dorcas obdurate, Pheobe and I put our heads together over this matter, and we believe we have discovered a way. I have persuaded Dorcas to be married in Garth, so that Millbridge niceties shall not be offended. No one shall know of the wedding until afterwards. If you attend the nuptials it will seem an act of benevolence on your part. If you stay away we can plead your health and the weather. Phoebe and I believed we should be there, to give an air of seemliness to the occasion. And all folk can say after is that Dorcas was wrong-headed and ungrateful. There, ma'am, that is plainly spoke, but you was always a stickler for the truth!'

He sat back in Grandfather Wilde's armchair, well satisfied with his version of the proceedings, and said, 'Ha!'

The light step of Dorcas on the stairs grew fainter. Miss Wilde picked up her spaniel and stroked him, and he permitted this attention without snapping.

'My dear lady,' Walter continued, as she did not answer, 'it will be difficult enough for you and Dorcas to live under the same roof for the usual length of time – and this is not a usual engagement. So we thought it best that Dorcas should marry as soon as may be. Phoebe will act as chaperone, and Mr Howarth can call at the rectory about any necessary business. So you shall not be troubled.'

She appeared to be waiting for him to finish talking altogether before she replied. He crossed his legs and rubbed his hands, slightly uneasy.

'You may rely upon me, ma'am, to conduct every detail of this marriage with the utmost propriety, and with the least possible upset to yourself. I hope to get through to Garth in the next week – they are still snowed up on the fells, I believe. If you do not wish to speak to Dorcas I can act as intermediary. Of course, it will be awkward, but for your sake . . .'

'Yes, yes, yes!' she cried impatiently. 'Let us be done with this distasteful business. Get Dorcas wed, and out of my sight as soon as possible. I shall not attend the ceremony. And there is one other little matter you can look to for me,' as he nodded and smiled. 'You may call on Mr Hurst, my solicitor, this very night, and tell him to step round immediately.'

'On Christmas Eve, ma'am?'

'What matter when he does his business?' said Miss Wilde drily. 'He is paid for it. I mean to sleep safe in my bed tonight, sir!' He inclined his head and sighed. 'And since you are so conversant with my niece's affairs you can tell her my mind!'

They looked at each other very closely, and understood one another: he with misgivings, she with the knowledge that only her money was her power.

'You need not be afraid, sir,' said Miss Wilde in the same dry tone, 'I have not forgot my offer of a sacramental cup for the altar, and I shall remember your part in this matter. Agnes will show you out.'

So he walked home in the cold, without a shred of dignity to warm him, and found his daughter almost in tears because Mr Howarth had called.

'Deuce take the man!' cried Walter Jarrett, and cast his black hat on the floor, out of all patience with these people. 'Where is he?'

'Oh, Dorcas has made it so difficult for us,' said Phoebe trembling, 'for I have always seen him in the kitchen before, when he delivered the meat, but now I thought (as he would be Dorcas's husband) that he should go into the parlour. Did I do right? Oh, Papa!'

'Well, well,' he said, picking up his hat, 'we must bear with our friends, must we not? Send the sherry in and leave us, Phoebe.'

'And supper will be late, and (I had almost forgot) Mr Howarth has fetched such a feast for us . . .'

'A feast?'

'Why, yes, Papa. A great basket with a cheese (such a cheese!) and butter, and a goose that Louisa is feathering this instant, and fresh-killed pork, and cream you could stand a spoon in!'

Walter Jarrett's smile increased to a chuckle, and the chuckle broadened into a laugh, so that he flung open the parlour door and came in, hand outstretched, crying, 'I give you joy, Mr Howarth. I was wondering how to reach Kit's Hill in such weather, with my good news!'

The man's face paled and became exalted, and he shook Jarrett's hand with both of his. He could not speak, but stood swallowing and brushing his sleeve across his eyes. Then laughed at himself to excuse his weakness, saying he was fair flummoxed. But Jarrett, ready for all occasions, made him sit by the fire, and poured him a glass of sherry with his own hand, and gave him joy again to steady him, and asked how and why he had got here.

'It were the little lass Nellie,' Ned Howarth began, and took a cautious sip of sherry, supposing he must get used to such elegancies when he had Dorcas to wife. 'She were skriking in t' corner this morning, wanting her Mam, and all of a sudden I thought to myself that it were but a mile to Garth. So I got every man on the farm out there with his spade. Betty

Ackroyd kept us warmed and fed, and we dug us-selves out. It took nigh on all day, but they give us a free swig of ale at The Woolpack, and I left two of the lads there and I shan't see them again for a bit! Then I went back and saddled Wildfire, and put the little lass in front of me, and then I thought I might come to Millbridge and all, and I did.'

So he and Nellie Bowker rode in triumph, and he delivered her at the door of her mother's cottage, with a pair of boiling fowls and a lump of suet and three months' wages. Then on to Millbridge with his bounty, and the goose swinging head down from his saddle.

'To thank you, sir. Just to thank you for what you did. You spoke up for me, sir, and I shan't forget. Hoping you'll do me the honour to accept a few Christmas victuals, and there's more where they come from. You'll allus be welcome because of what you've done for me. I can rest easy in my mind, now, sir. I'll be off back.'

Of those three eventful interviews on that Christmas Eve in 1760, Walter Jarrett remembered this one with a tenderness that was alien to him.

'I had done nothing for the good fellow,' he would say, astonished, mellow with claret. 'Indeed, I had spoke against the match and would have stopped it if I could! Yet he meant well by me, and was grateful, and had brought me gifts and asked nothing of me. Asked nothing of me.'

'No, no, no, Mr Howarth!' Jarrett was crying now. 'You must take supper with us. Indeed, I hardly know how you made the journey. This is the least we can do! And what better time than now to discuss the wedding arrangements? Phoebe! Mr Howarth will stay to supper. Phoebe?'

But she was weeping quietly in her room, and said she could not come down, for the headache that had threatened her all day was now an open enemy. He made commiserative noises, and spoke to Louisa himself, asking her to help Miss Jarrett to bed, and then to serve supper directly for himself and his guest. For Jarrett must be off to midnight mass, and Mr Howarth to Kit's Hill.

So the two men ate and drank heartily together, and found good fellowship in food and wine as so many had before them, and toasted Dorcas's health. The rector was in jovial vein, but the courtier was reverent. Then Walter Jarrett began upon his Christmas offices, and Ned Howarth rode for home in the pitch dark and slush. He carried a message to the Reverend Thomas Redfern of Garth, to start calling the banns that coming Sunday, between Dorcas Cicely Wilde, spinster of Millbridge, and Edward Howarth, bachelor of this parish. . . .

The lantern, fixed to his saddle on a stick, bobbed ahead of him. The roads were quaggy as far as Garth, but the fells were white and pure and cold. It seemed to Ned, fuddled by claret and thanksgiving, that he mounted into a heaven of snow towards the candles that Betty had lit and set in every window facing the lane.

All was now well. No one had taught him Greek or Latin, nor educated him beyond a rough knowledge of his letters, but he knew (even in one of the great moments of his life) that Dorcas was not similarly exalted. He knew, because he loved and revered her, that she had made her decision in isolation from lack of choice.

'I must take care to not mither her too much, at first,' he said aloud, as Wildfire plodded through the gateway. 'I must let her find her way about, and take her own time. Who's there, then?' As another lantern bobbed towards him in the dark.

'It's me, master,' said Tom, out of the frozen night.

'Nay, you should have gone home, lad. I can rub the horse down myself.'

'You've had a bit of a long journey, like,' said Tom, and asked a question.

Ned swung down from the stallion, and patted his neck in thanks.

'Wish me joy, Tom,' he cried, holding out his hand, 'for I'm wedding Miss Dorcas Wilde of Millbridge, as soon as may be, and it's one of the best nights of my life, lad.'

They shook hands clumsily. Then Tom took Wildfire's reins from him, saying in sorrow and curiosity, 'Folk say as she's a bit high and mighty for us, master. Will she settle here, dost think?'

'Tom,' said Ned, dazed and smiling with his good fortune, 'I know nowt about women, but from what I know of horses I'd say she would – given time, mind! Dost remember this one, when she were a filly?' Patting a pretty little mare, who tossed her mane coquettishly. 'Nobody but me'd dare fill her trough. Sithee, Tom, she'd eat out of us hands now.'

And he put his arm round the lad's shoulders.

'Tha'rt right,' said Tom, marvelling. 'Hast had a drop too much, master?'

'I'll give thee a yea and a nay on that, lad. What's to do?'

For the back door had swung open, and Betty Ackroyd stood there with a shawl about her shoulders for extra warmth.

'Well?' she shouted. 'Is everybody but me to hear t'news?'

'Wedding's on!' cried Ned across the frosty yard. 'Tha can start baking, fit to feed all Garth, Betty!'

'Nay,' she said, in delight and regret, 'I never thought she'd have thee, not in a hundred year!'

'Now tha comes to mention it,' said Ned, amazed at the state of his legs, 'I allus thought she would in the end! Well, you can tell everybody, Betty, and wish me joy this Christmas, for it's the best Christmas I've ever had.'

'Is she coming to see us, aforehand?'

'Aye, as soon as she can. Miss Jarrett'll be with her, and mind your manners when they do come. I don't want to be turned down, along of you!'

He staggered slightly, crossing the yard, and Tom helped him and winked at Betty.

'You'd best get that store-house cleaned up, that leads off kitchen,' Ned went on, leaning on the door-post. 'She'll be fetching her bits and pieces with her, to make a little parlour.'

'Whatever would your mother have said to all this?' Betty asked, as he found his way to the fireplace, and stood there swaying, scarlet with cold and pleasure.

'I don't know,' said Ned factually. 'She's not here, is she?'

Getting Wed

Five

7 February 1761

'It takes a man,' said Betty Ackroyd bitterly, moving between the fireplace and the kitchen table, 'to fix his wedding in the middle of winter. As if I hadn't enough to do wi' Christmas, and then St Distaff's day, without baking and brewing fit to feed the five thousand! Did I tell thee?'

A little knot of neighbouring women, who always helped out with festivals, had joined Betty for the final hours of preparation. Nellie Bowker peeled a sack of potatoes and listened avidly to the female conversation.

'He come pawming home that night, wi' the parson's letter in his fist, and he says, "Wish me well, Betty, for we'st be wed in three week!" Three week! You could have dropped me wi' a stone! "Three week?" I said. Eh, I must have looked as gormless as he did! "Three week?" I said. "You must be daft. It'll take us three week to get the place ready, on top of all else. She canna walk into a midden. There's folk to be bidden, and food to be thought on – let alone cooked. And what about weather? What happens if we get another fall of snow like the last? We'st look a right set of fools sitting up by us-selves wi' food enough for an army!" '

'You can do nowt wi' them, once they get an idea in their heads,' said Sam Cartwright's wife, more to keep the conversation going than to contribute to it.

' "How many are we having then?" I asked him outright.

He looked foolish, I can tell you. Then he says, "All them as come to mother's funeral!" If I hadn't been nearer skriking I'd have laughed in his face. "You do well to talk of funerals," I said to him sharp-like. "There'll be another funeral coming up afore long, and it'll be mine. Run off my feet from morning to night!" Nellie! When you've finished a pailful of potatoes swill some water over them, to keep them fresh. Where were I?'

Across the width of the fireplace a long wheel spit turned, bearing six chickens. Another six waited, six more cooled. Four pounds of pease pudding were keeping warm in the bread-oven, and a vast plum pudding simmered in an iron saucepan. Potted meats and boiled bacon were ready for slicing in the larder, along with a saddle of cold roast mutton. There were jugs and basins of cream, and two twenty-eight-pound cheeses in the dairy. And Betty had churned sufficient butter to spread even the three-day baking of bread, which was stacked up against the larder wall keeping cold and moist. For the dairy and larder had been built into the hillside part of the farm, and were in a constant state of chilliness whatever the time of the year.

'Anyway, you told him!' Mrs Braithwaite suggested, feeling pretty sharp-tempered herself about this state of affairs, for she had expected Ned to ask her Mary, and took it very much amiss that he had not.

'I said, "You canna get wed in three week. Make it six and I'll think about it!" So he did. I'll say that for him. "Will any of them be baking or coming?" I said. "Nay," he said, "Miss Dorcas is wedding me in spite of them. Barring the Reverend Jorrick, as will be wedding us" (but that's another story!) "and his daughter Miss Jorrock, they won't show their faces!" I said, "Well, that's better than giving nowt and stuffing their faces wi' our victuals!" But he never thinks. So I've done the best I could, and hope all's well!'

She looked for a compliment here because the feast was abundant. She had made a wedding cake of dried fruit, sugar, butter and spices, held together by breadcrumbs and leavened with ale-barm. She had poured half of a quarten of rum into it, and they had wished and stirred before it went into the bread-oven overnight. Betty had wished that Dorcas might return to Millbridge very soon.

'Have we got enough, do you think?' asked Betty, with false anxiety.

There were pies filled with apples from the autumn, redolent of cloves and nutmeg: and custard tarts like open suns. Slices of Betty's own gingerbread (whose recipe she would not divulge) had been pressed out and dried in the oven, each imprinted with a rough eagle from the mould, and there were taffy sweetmeats for the children, with treacle boiled hard enough to stretch their little jaws.

From the cool vaults of Kit's Hill the men rolled casks of ale, and set them up ready for drinking. All the farm hands, and members of their families, had been co-opted into helping with the banquet. As Betty said, they would take it out in food after!

'But you'd think he could have waited until his mother had been underground twelve month, wouldn't you?' Betty demanded. 'We were doing this for her funeral, afore harvesting last year. Then they turned up, a week or two later, and had their harvest supper and all! I said to him. I said, "Dost know we've fed Garth three times over? When will they feed us, do you reckon?" '

'They don't think,' mused Margery Tunstall. 'Where is he now?'

'Gone down to Millbridge wi' Tom and the wagon. They're fetching her stuff up this forenoon. Wedding's at three, and up here after. It'll be dark. I told him. I said, "It'll be dark by then!" Big daft lummock! Billy! Make sure that trestle-table's chocked up wi' a flat stone, else it'll keel over when they lean on it. Nellie! If that brother of yourn don't keep turning that spit I'll thump him so hard he'll never turn another!'

'Fred!' Nellie shrilled, in imitation of her mother's voice.

The lad rubbed his eyes and mouth, and wound away like a small windmill. He had never seen so much food in one place in his short life, and the heat of the fire was soporific, but he meant to do his best.

The married women from the outlying farms had dressed the bridal chamber, after its scrubbing out and airing, and Betty had laid a fire in the grate. It would not be lit again until the birth of the first child.

'They'll warm each other up well enough!' she had screeched, and the women's high voices and open ribaldry so shocked Ned that he avoided them as though they were unclean.

The former storehouse, once a parlour leading from the kitchen, had been swept and left empty for Dorcas's possessions. A fire was laid in this little mausoleum also. Ned had given the stone walls a coat of whitewash, and pondered on the bare boards and uncurtained window. He hoped it would do.

'Are you putting a cloth on the top table, Miss Ackroyd?' asked Mrs Sowerbutt, thrusting her face round the kitchen door.

'Aye, I reckon. That's as it should be, isn't it? You'll find it on the first shelf of the big cupboard on the landing. Rest of us'll have to manage without. Any road, there'll be more muck than manners when we set the food up!'

'They're here!' shouted Billy, hands on hips, peering through the window.

Sure enough, there was the wagon jolting across the yard, carrying perhaps the most graceful cargo its rugged sides had ever enfolded. Betty Ackroyd pulled a shawl over her head and shoulders and came out to look, giving orders and cautions as though she had personally loaded it by herself.

'Have you got food ready, then?' called Ned, sarcastic.

'Near enough.'

'Near enough is far enough. Get thee inside out of the cold. We'st manage, Tom and me. We've managed all right so far.'

The kitchen helpers stood to one side, holding their skirts out of the way as the two men brought in Dorcas's dowry: a pretty gilded looking-glass, a fine clock in a walnut long case, a secretaire, an elegant day-bed, a small oval table finely inlaid, six dining chairs with slender legs and faded satin seats, and sundry boxes containing china, glass and books.

'She'll sort them out herself when she comes,' said Ned. 'Just sluther them into t' parlour, careful-like.'

'Hadn't you best get yourself changed?' said Betty. 'Or are you fixing on getting wed in your workclothes? How will them three be coming, and when?'

'Mr Jarrett is fetching the ladies in his gig, but they're going to t' parsonage. Mrs Redfern's taking care of them. Then we'll all come up together from Garth.'

'And how many'll be coming up?' Betty asked, arms akimbo.

'How should I know? Thirty or forty folk all told?'

'Nearer sixty, if I know owt. When Kit's Hill lays the table everybody in Garth thinks there's a plate for them! We'st be full of empty bellies and fawse smiles!'

'Nay, Betty, I'm wed but once in a lifetime. I'd never grudge a mouthful to nobody as wished us well. Let them come, my lass, let them come!' He looked round, and his fresh face and frank eyes were alight with contentment. 'Eh, you've done a grand job,' he said, putting his arm round her shoulders, 'and you're a grand lass, Betty.'

Suddenly her chin shook and she whipped up her apron to hide her tears. Mrs Wharmby came forward, saying, 'She's worked herself to death, nigh on. Nobody knows what us poor women go through! Sit you down, love, and have a sup of summat hot!' And she led the weeping Betty to a chair, whereat the female helpers all gathered round, commiserating with her and glancing indignantly at the men.

'I think we'd best get out o' t' road,' said Ned, bewildered, to his cohorts, 'and try the first cask, afore we get us-selves cleaned up.'

They stood about awkwardly, feeling that they were to blame, though they could not see why. Then they shrugged at each other, left the drama to the women, and drew a preliminary draught of ale. Sam Cartwright looked thoughtfully into its warm brown depths.

'That's good ale,' he said. 'Should we go and tell her?'

'No,' said Tom unexpectedly, 'we'st only get bawled out, whatever we say!'

'You've getten a fine day for t' wedding, any road, master!' said Billy.

'Aye,' said Ned peacefully, 'we have that.'

Kit's Hill sat in her hollow and looked out onto the Pennines. She had been made ready for the next generation, and how many generations she had known no one could count. The February sun was pale and clear on her old stones. Her thick windows gleamed. Her front door, decorated with sprigs of bay and rosemary, had its hinges oiled with goose-grease to make sure it opened easily when the bride was carried over the threshold. She was waiting, with Ned Howarth, for their new beginning.

The church of St John the Divine in Garth was a cross between a fortress and a barn, a community centre for its people, a refuge in times of trouble. The nave dated from the fourteenth century, the font was large enough to immerse a baby entirely, and horse-box pews kept out the draughts. Henry VIII's men had destroyed the rood screen, and Cromwell's men had smashed the stained-glass windows. But the hammer-beam roof soared proudly overhead, the pulpit was high and elaborate, and they were already talking about heating the building during the winter months. Certainly, St John's lacked the costly silver vessels and elegantly-worked altar-cloths that you would find in St Mark's. Her congregation was poorly or plainly clad. The difference between them lay in their need, for Millbridge folk paid lip-service to God whereas Garth folk put their trust in Him – and even forgave Him when the crops failed, putting this setback down to their sin rather than His omission. And outside, in tribute to the countless generations, lay the little clusters of tombstones and crosses bearing a dozen family names.

The church was packed by the time the wedding party

arrived, and somewhat noisy in anticipation. Anyone who could claim the slightest kinship with Ned, and they were many, had attended his marriage in expectation of food and fun. They had scrubbed their children, skimped their breakfasts, and brought a gift (whether as fine as a sycamore spoon or as humble as a barley loaf). Ned was slightly embarrassed, but almost elegant in his bottle-green wool coat and best drab-coloured breeches, his black leather shoes with metal buckles, and white stockings. Neither he nor Betty had managed the white cravat, but since Garth went open-necked all the year round they thought it very grand, though it sat somewhat awry and the knot stuck under his chin.

Behind him, various versions of his courtship were being fabricated and embroidered by the local wives. He heard Betty's voice, provoking old enemies, making new ones. Before him, the Reverend Thomas Redfern conducted a private prayer with his Maker, and congratulated himself on a strong mind and a puritan conscience. Mr Jarrett's diplomatic request to marry Dorcas had met with a robust refusal, much to that polished gentleman's astonishment.

'This is a Howarth wedding,' Tom Redfern had said, 'and this is my church, sir. I've served this congregation for forty year come Lady Day, and married and christened and buried every Howarth as showed his face here in that time. I christened Ned, and by God (forgive me, sir) I'll tie his knot, and hope to christen his son this time next year.'

'Miss Wilde,' Mr Jarrett had ventured, 'is without relatives, apart from an aunt who cannot come. She will have no friends here, sir, but my daughter and myself. It would be a kindness in you, at least, to allow me to *assist* in her nuptials. She has so little share in the proceedings (socially speaking) otherwise.'

'Miss Wilde will be Mrs Howarth within a half-hour of standing at the altar with Ned. That makes her one of *them,* sir. *Thy people shall be my people, and thy ways my ways.* If she has no relatives then you'd best give her away, and your daughter stand witness. You will both be made as welcome as Miss Wilde by my congregation, sir, for all that you're foreigners. The Howarths are the backbone of this parish, and good people. Plain and straight-spoken like myself, sir, and there's an end on it!'

'Except, Thomas,' said his gentle wife, filling Mr Jarrett's cup, and smiling to soften her husband's words, 'except that we shall be very pleased to receive Mr Jarrett and Miss Jarrett and Miss Wilde here before the service. They will have driven nine miles in the cold, and possibly the wet.'

'Of course, of course,' cried Tom Redfern, throwing up his arms, 'you're most welcome, sir, to what poor hospitality we can offer.'

'Perhaps the young ladies would care to make some change in their apparel, or to rest a while. They can surely avail themselves of the best spare room, love, can they not?'

'They can have owt,' said Tom, lapsing into his native tongue, 'so long as they leave me to my business and mind theirs!'

Dorcas had said, smiling with a wryness that was her habit, 'It seems fitting, Mr Jarrett, that they should take me over entirely. I do not mind, sir – but that you and Phoebe stand my friends.'

'Oh, Dorcas,' Phoebe had murmured, 'are you sure this is the right thing to do, my dear? It is not yet too late to change your mind!'

But Ned had said, 'Never fear, my lass. I'm for you, and bugger them as is against you – begging your pardon!'

Now he said to himself, waiting, and sweating slightly, 'Never fear!' as the noise mounted, and the people pressed and packed themselves into the pews.

Then there was a hush at the door, and here she was, the lady that all the fuss had been about, and fine as fi'pence in plum-coloured silk. With the tall clerical gentleman holding out his arm and walking her forward, like she might be the queen, and the other lady (not near as handsome, but very genteel) coming after.

Miss Buckley of Millbridge, sworn to secrecy, had re-trimmed Dorcas's best gown with velvet bows down the bodice and ruching across the skirt front, so that it looked to have come from London. The lace ruffles falling from Dorcas's plum-silk sleeves, the lace veil tied round her starched and pleated cap, were inherited from her mother. Phoebe now took charge of the black velvet mantle and hood (which they had steamed last night in the rectory kitchen to make the nap come up, and really it looked almost new!). Miss Buckley had re-lined the matching muff, and looped a handsome swathe of dark-red ribbon round it.

Beneath the trifling little cap Dorcas's face was so pale that even Phoebe had advised her to bite her lips and rub her cheeks, to give them colour. But her narrow dark eyes were bright and watchful: aware of the crowded church, Tom Redfern's obstinacy, Phoebe's concern, Mr Jarrett's elegance, and Ned's cravat. This was not his moment, and he knew it, but Dorcas made it hers. Smiling at the parson to ask his permission, to Ned to show that this was a wifely duty, she most delicately and swiftly came forward to rectify the ill-tied linen: a few moments later he appeared as immaculate as Mr Jarrett. A lift of Dorcas's slanting eyebrows, as the voices rose again in comment, caused Tom Redfern to bring his congregation to order, with much thumping of his red fist on the altar rail.

'That's better!' he said at length, nodding his head up and down. 'Now see as tha keeps quiet while the knot's tied!' This raised laughter, being an unwitting pun on the event which had occasioned their ribaldry. 'Shut up!' Tom shouted angrily, then as they quietened he added, 'and after the service I want none of the usual rommicking. It's a downright disgrace what goes on outside the church door – aye, and inside, when the parsons allow, which I never do! So think on. This is a sacred occasion. Let it be treated as such. Now, Ned, step forrard. And you, miss. Take her by the hand. Go on, lad, catch hold of her. She won't break, sithee!'

A man cried from the back of the building, 'Tha'll need to do better than that tonight, Ned!' And was sent out for his impudence.

Dorcas placed a small cold hand in Ned's warm one, and he ventured a squeeze of comfort. As the service proceeded his warmth reached Dorcas, and she let her hand rest there with a sense of safety. Her mother's ring had been re-made to fit her finger, since she set such store by it. As Ned slid it firmly and carefully on, she prayed that their alliance might be as considerate as that of her parents, and she smiled at him for a beginning.

As Tom Redfern had promised, Miss Wilde was Mrs Howarth within a half-hour. The service was brisk and plain, and the parson's private homily matched it.

'You'll find life rough-going more often than not,' said Tom Redfern, 'and many a hundred times you'll wish you'd never wed at all. You'll wish you'd stayed single and had nobody else to bother about but yoursen! That's the easy road, and leads nowhere in particular. What you've got to remember, when you're over your clogs in muck, is that there's somebody there to lift you out. One or t'other, it don't matter which. Never let the sun go down on a quarrel. Dunnot turn your face away when t'other's in trouble, whether they're at fault or not – none of us is perfect! Give each other a kind word, and a hug and a kiss now and again, and you'll be capital. I've been wed for thirty-four year, and I know I'm not good enough for her,' glancing humbly at his gentle wife, 'but she doesn't! So I thank God for that, and for her, every night on my bended knees. That's about it. All right, then. Give the wife a kiss, Ned!'

Uproar presaged the riots to come.

'Go on, parson. Your turn!' several shouted, as Ned kissed Dorcas's cheek and was roundly hissed for his modesty.

'You'll have to forgive them, lass,' said Tom Redfern, and saluted her on the other cheek respectfully.

'Now for it!' said Ned, and braced himself and caught Dorcas to him by the arm. 'I'll do what I can, but we shall have to meet them halfway-like!'

The youths at the lych-gate rushed forward shouting, 'Give

us thi garter, missis!'

'Oh, God Almighty!' muttered Ned, but had not allowed for his bride's wits.

'Which one among you won the race?' she asked clearly.

Their faces clouded. They consulted, one with the other.

'I know this custom very well,' said Dorcas, 'and you must all ride to Kit's Hill, and the one who is first there may claim my garter – and I shall give it with a good will. So be off with you!'

Billy was first on his shaggy pony, clattering up the track as though a demon drove him. Behind him came the mob, screeching and whipping their mounts, and hallooing so that the stones rang again.

Hetty Howarth's square little dog-cart awaited Dorcas, and in the shafts stood Bluebell, the quietest horse in the stable and one of the oldest.

'It hasn't been out much since mother's legs were bad,' Ned explained, helping his wife to her seat, 'but Joe Burscough, the wheelwright, did it up. Once the horse is used to it you can have it as your own trap, and go to market or a-visiting, what you please. Come up then, Bluebell! Eh, Tom! What's up wi' this horse? Well, I know she's quiet! I said quiet, not dead, lad! Give me a good stick out of the hedge, then. We'st be here all day!'

They were followed by a hail of old clogs (all economically picked up again), coarse jokes, and the firing of blunderbusses into the air to signal their departure. Ned clicked his tongue in disapproval, but Dorcas sat very composedly, for she had made the first of her decisions as a married woman, and intended to endure all with a good grace.

It was growing dark as the wedding trap rattled into the small courtyard at the front of Kit's Hill, and a fine rain began to fall. Yet bride and groom must wait until the whole company was assembled before they could dismount, so that all could observe the ancient custom of a bride being carried over the threshold lest she stumble and bring bad luck. Betty was waiting with the fire-irons (highly polished) and nipped smartly forward and held them out to her new mistress. Dorcas grasped them firmly, and thanked her graciously, thus setting the tone of their future relationship. Nellie Bowker had been entrusted (with awful warnings) to hold a hen so that it might cackle good fortune. This she did very well, for she was so afraid that she clutched the fowl too tightly, and it squawked exceptionally loudly before escaping with a plunge of its horny legs, and a casting of white feathers over the scrubbed flagstones. Then the wedding guests, amounting to over a hundred people (which did not include babes in arms) squeezed into Kit's Hill.

'I won't have them in t'kitchen while we're serving up!' Betty warned Ned. 'Now have I said? Have I?'

So they poured into the ground-floor rooms and sat on the stairs, and the more curious among them even inspected the bedrooms, and would later peer into the neatly-packed boxes which contained Dorcas's most fragile possessions. Four great trestle-tables had been set up for an expected sixty at most. Now they seemed frail and inadequate before this mass appetite. But Betty had the fire roaring up the chimney-back and ordered her little army of helpers as well as any general could.

Dorcas and Ned were pushed and pulled into the big parlour, and ensconced in the seats of honour. They had ceased to be people, and became symbols of the occasion. Now the bride was among Garth folk, and of them, they felt free to finger the silk of her gown and make remarks about her in her presence and give her advice.

Vast wooden and pewter platters of steaming chicken and pease pudding and boiled potatoes clattered down on the tables, and were cleared within minutes by a forest of reaching fingers. The men took out their knives, steadied joints of bacon and mutton and mounds of potted meats with one greasy hand, and hacked off slices for themselves and their families with the other. Women tore at fresh loaves and scooped the pieces into bowls of fresh butter, and ate hunks of cheese. Children scrambled on and off chairs, and in and out of laps, and dropped food on the floor and fought the dogs for it, and emerged merry and smeared from the contest. Desserts followed the main course, in equal abundance and greater disarray, and the heat and clamour increased as everyone swilled ale and the men rolled up another cask or two from the cellars.

They laughed and called across the rooms, and mothers suckled babies as they ate and drank, and infants slobbered and choked over Betty's treacle taffy. Billy and other youths were sick from too much strong ale. Some of them got to the yard in time, and others were scolded by Betty Ackroyd while Nellie sloshed a pail of water across the solid flagstones, and sprinkled them with sand.

Dorcas had brought her own silver knife, fork and spoon with her in her pocket, but when she saw the avid interest aroused by Phoebe's cutlery she kept them hidden for the time being. Her appetite, usually small, now vanished as this cornucopia of food poured from the kitchen. Yet she feared to offend, so sipped a glass of Hetty Howarth's elderberry wine and picked at a leg of chicken, and slid tidbits to the waiting dogs beneath the table. As the smell of unwashed bodies mingled with cooking odours her stomach felt queasy, but she continued to smile and answer good-wishers, and privately to hope that they would soon go home.

The two clergymen and their ladies departed early, having stayed only as long as politeness dictated. Dorcas and Ned came to the door to bid them farewell, and Dorcas stayed a little longer than her new husband, pleading fresh air as an excuse. She was protected by a sense of unreality, but as the wheels of the Jarretts' gig sounded faint and fainter she drooped for a moment, and could have wept to think they should leave without her. Then she turned resolutely and made her way back to the bacchanalia.

The darkness became intense, the hours passed, humours roughened, children cried and were smacked and cried again, and bounty turned to squalor. Dorcas's head and smile ached.

The men were drinking in earnest, the youths had long

since fallen asleep, the women rocked their babies and scolded their infants. Ned's colour was high but his eyes were steady, his fair hair only slightly ruffled. From time to time he looked for his wife, and nodded and smiled at her as if to reassure her that he was not swilling his gut with the rest of them. Then, when Dorcas could hardly keep herself awake, Betty came in with a bowl of sack-posset, and those who could still drink raised their tankards to the health of bride and groom. Dorcas sipped and coughed, and set down her cup with a hand that trembled in weariness.

'Now if you've done, missis,' said Betty 'we'll help you to bed.'

The wedding party had gone on too long. Outside, rain fell steadily and the wind blew. Inside, children stared with dull eyes and sucked their thumbs, women nodded stupidly over sleeping babes, men snored. Unwashed platters had been pushed aside, or stacked roughly on the floor. It seemed as though order could never be restored.

'What is to happen to them all?' Dorcas asked, bemused. 'Will they not go home?'

Ned rose from his armchair and came towards her. He was as dazed as she.

'Is it not time our guests went home, Edward?' she asked, in composed desperation. 'The children should be abed, should they not?'

'I dare say they want to see us abed, first,' he answered, 'but they're too far gone for that, most of them.'

'Aye,' cried Betty, 'they should see you abed and wish you well, and throw the stockings, and sing a song or two!' She stared round at the sorry spectacle. 'I told you what it would be like! Well, I'm not giving them their breakfasts and that's flat!'

'No, indeed,' cried Dorcas, seeing an opportunity of ridding herself of the drunken mob. 'You have done quite enough. So how shall we get them home?'

'There's not above me and Tom here as could drive a wagon down that track in the dark,' said Ned, thinking. 'The lads'd fall off their ponies, even if we put them on. How did we manage at mother's funeral, Betty?'

'She was buried when the nights was lighter, and they eat everything up by afternoon and went home, didn't they?' cried Betty, enraged. 'I told you to wait until summer, but you wouldn't listen!'

Dorcas saw that there was one final effort to be made.

'How many people will a wagon hold, Edward?' she asked, and counted heads and did a little arithmetic on her fingers. 'Then if you and Tom can take a loaded wagon apiece, you need but three journeys into Garth.'

Ned was not quick enough to find objections, but Betty always could.

'They don't all live in Garth, missis. Some live at cottages on the fells. And what about their horses, and that?'

'At least we can take the villagers safe home, and then there will be less for us in the morning. And their horses can be stabled temporarily, can they not, Edward?'

'Well, aye, I suppose they can. After a fashion.'

'The women surely do not wish to stay here with their children? We have nowhere for them to sleep comfortably. They will help us, since they are not drunk,' Dorcas added fastidiously.

'But then they'll all come traipsing up here tomorrow, supposed to be getting their horses, and supping our ale again instead!' Betty objected.

'That is tomorrow,' said Dorcas firmly. 'Let us deal with tonight.'

'She's right,' said Ned, dousing Betty's next objection. 'So let's get on wi' it. Who've I got as'll help me? Sam! Tom! Billy! Joe! Throw a pail of water over Billy's head, wilta, Nellie? Now then, Mrs Braithwaite and Mary, will you round up all them as live in Garth Bottoms? We'll take that lot first. Come on, you lads, we want lanterns lit. Tumble up, wilta?'

'But what about seeing you abed, then?' Betty cried, cheated.

'Oh, but you shall see us abed, and throw the stockings and sing a song,' Dorcas promised, 'when they have all gone. And that will be more fitting. For we are Kit's Hill folk, are we not? And this is Kit's Hill's wedding!'

The guests had infiltrated the deepest parts of the farmhouse. They were even found snoring on the marriage bed, and Betty beat them off with her broom. There were babies sleeping in half-opened drawers of linen, very comfortably. One couple were clasped in what had been a highly indecorous embrace before the ale stunned them.

'Look at that!' Betty cried, delighted. 'And her a married woman. I said that second child looked nowt like Malachi!' She saw Nellie Bowker gaping, and yelled, 'Be off wi' you!' Then to the man who stirred awake, 'Go on, cover it up. It's nowt to be proud of. Ah, you're a right turkey-cock in your cups, aren't you? And you, missis, pull your skirts down. I never saw the like, not in all my born days!' With relish.

Women and children were helped into the wagons first. Tom stood in the pouring rain, his lantern held above his head to light the slimy cobbles, while Sam and Joe packed the families aboard. Ned shouted through the wind, 'I'll go first, lad. Then you follow. Wi' two of us together we shan't lose our way!' And he saluted Dorcas as he mounted the first wagon.

Billy, very white and sick-faced, was herding ponies into the barn and tethering them. Nellie ran here and there with straw and pails of water, her head and shoulders tied up in a wet wool shawl. Betty was in her element, thrusting her broom into unlikely corners and rousting out celebrants. Her commentary did not cease, and beat against Dorcas's ears like another storm. The male Cartwrights were invaluable, bringing together a wagon-load of fallen youths, and stacking them neatly in rows to await transport. The female Cartwrights scraped and washed dishes, and collected the remains of the feast. Not to be outdone, Dorcas tidied her bridal chamber and lit the fire. The wagons were rolling back into the yard, and she drew a curtain aside to see Ned (who was looking round for her approval and not finding her). So she went downstairs to cheer the removal on.

Then she found her way into the bare store-room that would be her future private parlour. Tomorrow she would unpack and make herself at home here. In the meantime, she consulted her fob-watch, wound up the long clock, and waited to hear it chime (which it did most sonorously, drawing a little group of Kit's Hill folk to listen to it). None of them had seen such a clock as this, fashioned with figured walnut veneer and decorated with inlaid marquetry. And when Dorcas showed them that it told the day of the month, as well as the time, and had been made in the reign of Queen Anne, they felt they had something to boast of down at The Woolpack. So they huddled respectfully by the door, and stared at its fine face. A few books and ornaments had been rooted out by the curious, and then abandoned in favour of more food and drink. Nellie, tongue between teeth, helped Dorcas to put them safely back again. Only a little china cup had been broken clean in two, and Dorcas thought it would mend, and smiled at the awed child who held it out for inspection.

'Night's half-gone,' Betty remarked, and so it was, though the clock meant nothing to her, and she told time by the state of her digestion or exhaustion. 'Some of them'll have to stop!' she said regretfully, and toed one heavy sleeper with her merciless clog, and poked him with her broom. But still he slept, bubbling a little.

They looked at one another, and at their new mistress, and at the master who came in from his last journey, shining with rain but smiling and cheerful still. Kit's Hill needed scrubbing out, but was otherwise recognisable after her long orgy. Some food was left over.

'So we had enough, after all,' Betty remarked with satisfaction. 'Well, let's get thee to bed, master, and be done.'

An air of weary good-nature came over the small assembly. Betty put her best tallow candles in an old-fashioned wooden candelabra, and led the way upstairs. The women's party was decorous enough, as they made sure that Dorcas had no pins about her person when she got to bed. They marvelled at the delicacy and cleanliness of her underclothing, and the hoop, and her linen corset stiffened with whalebone, and passed them from one to the other in admiration. But in Ned's old room, just down the passage, the men shouted and laughed and scuffled over a lustier ceremony, as they held him down and pulled off his breeches. Then Betty mended the bedroom fire, and Dorcas was sitting up very fine against the pillows when the male party burst in with Ned on their shoulders, and flung him down beside her. He crept sheepishly between the linen sheets, and Sam Cartwright sang a very ancient ballad in a high reedy voice. The more bawdy lines were punctuated by shrieks from the women and guffaws from the men. Then they all joined in the chorus merrily.

A discreet sideways glance at her fob-watch told Dorcas that time approached the hour of three. In one corner of the bedroom unnoticed, Nellie Bowker cautiously stroked Dorcas's undergarments and sniffed the clean sharp perfume of lavender. She had not realised until now that anyone could smell of anything other than milk or manure. She watched the lady's mouth and hands, which showed tremors of tiredness or uncertainty. She had never seen anyone so grand. She thought the lady's nose very fine, with its high bridge and narrow nostrils. She marvelled at the rows of tucking and lace on her night-gown, and the starched frill on her night-cap, and the long braids of black silky hair, and the bright black eyes.

'Now for t' stockings!' Betty shouted, and snatched Ned's woollen ones from the chair, and sat at the end of the four-poster bed.

'Throw us them over, Nellie!' shouted Tom Cartwright, and the child started with nervousness, seeing that he wanted Dorcas's white stockings.

She looked to her new mistress for permission, and Dorcas looked back at her, comprehending an unusual sensibility in this starved girl. Then she smiled and nodded at her, to show that all was well. So Nellie brought them over, the frail threads clinging to her small chapped hands.

With a joint whoop, Betty and Tom threw the stockings backwards towards the bridal pair, and succeeded so well that Dorcas received an armful of homespun and home-knitted wool, and Ned had to unwind her hose from round his head.

'Right, we've done all us can,' said Betty, panting and triumphant. 'The rest is up to thee!'

'It must be nigh on day,' said Mrs Cartwright, mindful that her daily work would not wait upon the lack of a night's sleep.

'Well, all of you take your time,' said Ned, folding his wife's stockings carefully, 'and sleep as long as you can, and get done as best you can. We'st have a farm full of sore heads when we wake.'

They nodded, relieved, and made their final jokes and good wishes. Nellie cast a longing glance at Dorcas, and an envious one at the warm room.

'You may come and help me dress later today, Nellie – if Betty can spare you,' said Dorcas kindly.

Nellie clasped her hands together, unable to frame a proper reply. So Betty gave the child a shove.

'Well, go on. Where's your manners? Say "Yes, missis"!' she ordered.

'Eh, for God's sake get thee all gone!' cried Ned, exasperated at last, and raised a laugh without meaning to, and shook his head at his own stupidity.

But they closed the heavy door gently enough, and left the new Howarths to their prayers, and the company of the wind and the rain which threatened to endure all day.

'Art tired?' Ned asked unnecessarily, for Dorcas still sat up with her hands folded in her lap, and a smile that was mere courtesy on her lips. Her eyes closed now and again, and then opened quickly as though she reproached herself for inattention.

'Yes, I am tired. Are you not?' she replied. Her tone indicated extreme weariness, but still her spirit had strength enough to carry out the final demands though she was much afraid.

'Me? I'm knackered,' said Ned honestly. 'Shall us get some sleep, then? Bless you, I'm no stallion,' he continued, as she turned her head and looked fully at him. 'Nor am I brute enough to do owt now. You've had enough, and more than enough for one day. We've got all us lives to get to know one another. We've nobbut shaken hands, as you might say. It'd be daft to make a horse gallop afore it could trot. Dost want an arm round thee?'

Dorcas nodded and smiled, but could have wept with relief.

'I have always liked you, Edward,' she said (for she could not bring herself to call him 'Ned', and would have preferred 'Mr Howarth' but that he thought it too affected!). 'I was not mistaken, it seems.'

'Cuddle up, then. We'd best start somewhere.'

'I have never shared a bed before,' she explained, coming in a gingerly fashion into the circle of his right arm.

'I should hope not! Let me punce that pillow softer for thee. That's better. Now lay thi head on my shoulder. There, then, how about that?'

'How warm you are,' said Dorcas drowsily, for she felt the cold keenly and had shivered many a winter night in her solitary state.

'Aye,' he said, moving his chin so that her cap frill did not tickle it, 'I am that. Mother had the same constitution, as you might say. I've seen her go out in the freezing cold wi' nobbut a shawl over her head, when the rest was stamping their feet and clapping their arms behind their back to keep wick!'

'I often saw her with you, at the market. She seemed a – strong-willed person, Edward. Full of – character.'

'Strong? She'd make a man quail! Oh, she were soft enough, they say, when father wed her. She were a Sowerbutt, from Long Hay. A bonny lass wi' a good big laugh. But she changed as she grew older. My father were man enough in his own house, but we allus knew when mother wanted summmat. She got it, and all! Then, when he died, she took Kit's Hill over and let Betty do the housework. What mother said, we did. The sisters found theirselves husbands in foreign parts, north of Garth in the next valley. Brother Will couldn't take her tongue, and he went off to sea. That left me and her alone, and I were allus her favourite. So I could no more wed than I could fly! But I saw thee, Dorcas, three year since, and I knew then as I should wed thee somehow.'

A faint sound reminded him that his lady could breathe and sleep like any other mortal, and he smiled to himself, content.

'We've got a lot to learn about one another, thee and me,' he continued, for he was free now to speak as he felt, and not to mind whether she understood. 'Like parson said, there'll be times when we want to shut door behind us and forget we ever wed. I'm not saying as what I feel for thee is common-sensical. It isn't. You can make a fool out of me, and have done. But I know I don't want you any other road. It'll be a while afore you feel the same for me. But I'll tell thee this much. You'd never have trusted yourself to me if you didn't feel summat. You've been brought up very genteel, and right now you canna see owt but my lack of manners. But I'm here, my lass, and I allus shall be.' He moved his chin out of range of her cap flounce again, good-natured at this new turn of events. 'Eh, you're trussed up wi' frills and furbelows like Christmas poultry! But I know thee, Dorcas. I may not say much, but I miss nowt. I saw you today, and you never lost your smile. You'd make up your mind to go through, whatever it cost, and I like that. It shows guts. It's easy to smile when things are going right. It takes more to smile when they're going wrong. Like I said to mother, when she were near the last . . .' He smothered a yawn, and blinked two or three times to help his recollection. 'I said, "Is it hard?" She said, "Eh, my lad, I've done harder in my time." Aye, she were in a bad way, and still she said, "Dying's easy, son. It's living that's hard." And so it is. Many a hundred time I've thought as I'd break my heart over thee. Aye, I thought it would break. But it never did . . .'

It was beating strongly now, slow and steady beneath Dorcas's cheek. He touched her hands gently, for they had been cold, and found them warmer. She was fast asleep somewhere, with him and yet away from him, in some world of which he had no knowledge, into which he would never trespass. Around them, Kit's Hill slept, and the dogs snored downstairs on the hearth, and the cat watched over her latest litter with yellow eyes. The kitchen fire had been raked up and a cross marked in the hot ashes. The chimney-posts were made of rowan-tree wood, and carved with symbols to keep witches away. Beneath the threshold, Henry Howarth had buried pieces of iron, and behind the door hung a necklace of holed stones. So all was well. They had done what they could to withstand the powers of darkness. God must take care of the rest.

The sky turned from richest black to deepest blue. Now the cock crowed on the garden wall, and the clock chimed with him. Ned folded his other arm round his wife, and closed his eyes, because he held her as safe and fast as any man could in this uncertain world, and was thankful for that.

Th' Foreigner

Six

But the following night Ned fetched a bucket of water and a tin basin up to the bedroom. There he stripped himself naked, anointed his goose-fleshed body with Betty's home-made soap, and rinsed and towelled himself vigorously. Horrified, Dorcas averted her eyes and pretended to be saying her prayers, with the image of the man standing between herself and God. She had never seen anyone naked in all her life, and however tightly she might squeeze her lids together she still saw him: the gold hair on breast and belly and male organ, the whiteness of his body and limbs, the red-brown weathering of face and neck and fore-arms. Then he said his prayers quickly and jumped into bed. She followed him reluctantly, with a pleading glance for his undonned night-shirt.

'Now will you give us a kiss?' cried Ned, and bussed her soundly.

She was extremely worried, and clung to him so that he would do nothing more. This he understood, and soothed and talked to her as he talked to his mares. Then he began to explore her gently, and she allowed this, though very much ashamed of what he was doing and how she was responding. At last he entered her, which was most disagreeable, and she wept tears of atonement for the small pleasures that had gone before. And he bewildered her utterly by losing himself in thrusts and grunts of delight. Then pulled down her nightgown as though she were a child, and warmed and cosseted her, until she fell blissfully asleep and even stretched out her arm in the night to make sure he was beside her. A confusing experience, a confusing time.

Almost at once they entered upon the cold and frugal period of Lent. Daily, he rose from her side at five o'clock and left her sleeping, dressing himself as quietly as he could, glancing tenderly at the cap flounce just visible above the bedclothes, observing with wonderment and pride her little linen corset on the chair. At seven o'clock Nellie knocked softly, and entered with a pot of tea (which Dorcas had taught her how to brew, from the pound packet brought with her on her wedding day). The child's devotion was the only warmth shown to her, for Betty was openly hostile, and the men either shy of her or uncomprehending. Dressed and washed, with her hair smoothed beneath the starched cap, Dorcas descended into the unknown day with nothing to alleviate its dullness. For her enquiries as to calling upon her neighbours were met with contempt.

'Nobody goes calling here,' Betty said, stirring frumenty as though her life depended upon it. 'If you start calling on Mrs Braithwaite, else Mrs Wharmby, else any of the others on the fells, you're like to be asked to take the butter-churn handle. And you don't know how to do that, do you?'

'I could learn, if you would teach me,' said Dorcas, determined to be peaceable, in spite of Betty's tone.

'Nay, I've not time,' said that irascible woman, and added maliciously, 'and the master said as you was to live like a lady and do nowt. So you'd best get on wi' it!'

So Dorcas went into her little parlour, and sat at her secretaire, from which she could command a view of the kitchen through her open door, and a tangle of weeds through the window opposite. There, Nellie laid and lit the fire daily so that Dorcas should be comfortable. There, Betty pointedly served up her breakfast and her mid-day meal. There, Ned called in upon her, at odd times during the day thrusting his wheaten head round the door and grinning. Sometimes, he would close the door behind him and sit carefully on one of the slender chairs (with his neckerchief beneath him to protect the stain), and converse with her privately. Then, at six o'clock in the evening, master and mistress and servants would sit to a substantial meal at the kitchen table after Ned had said grace. By nine, they were all abed.

The first lambs came, and Ned went out daily to help the shepherd, and so did foxes and buzzards. One morning, Dorcas ceased to gaze on the tangle of weeds outside her window, and borrowed Hetty Howarth's grey wool mantle from behind the kitchen door (for her own was much too fine) and found a neglected garden. She traced its shape, borrowed a spade, and struck wood almost at once: old wood, damp wood, that had once been a great cart's wheel.

'That were Mrs Howarth's herb garden,' said Betty reluctantly, when asked. 'She were a one for simples, were Mrs Hetty. But when she took ill the garden were left to itself.'

'My mother had a herb garden in Gloucestershire,' said Dorcas, sitting at the kitchen table, 'and at the vicarage there was a little still-room where she made up her compounds. Indeed I have her book of receipts. She was always in the village, taking her pills and troches and ointments with her, to help and heal folk.'

'And what happened to her, missis?' Betty asked, curious in spite of her determination to ignore Dorcas.

'She found a knot in her breast, that grew,' said Dorcas, clasping her hands remembering. 'We had a good surgeon from Gloucester, and he took off her breast. My father was with her, and prayed throughout, and so did she although she was in anguish. She was hearty for a few months, then discovered a knot below the surgeon's wound, and then another and another. He dissected them from her, and still they grew. Until she died.'

The kitchen was silent, except for the hissing cauldron.

Betty said roughly but kindly, 'Well, the lady's with God now, missis.'

Dorcas wiped her eyes resolutely, and said, 'I shall take a turn in the herb garden until it is dark.'

But she found Billy, knowing that she could seek her way only through the young at Kit's Hill, for the older do not welcome change. He lent her a few crude garden tools, and when Ned came home she was still out there restoring his mother's cartwheel of herbs.

'I suppose she'll want to be opening up Mrs Hetty's still-room now?' Betty grumbled. 'That'll be another place to keep clean and warm! There's no end to it.'

'She must do as she wants,' Ned ordered, and Betty fell silent at his tone.

On the fourth Sunday in Lent Betty had brewed bagot, a good spiced ale which even Dorcas pronounced delicious, and baked Simnel cakes. For on Mothering Sunday the young folk in service had a holiday, and Nellie Bowker was to visit her mother bearing the appropriate gift from Kit's Hill and a few flowers plucked from the hedgerow. And with her went a message from Dorcas, and her first order as mistress of the house.

'We don't need nobody!' Betty cried indignantly, when Dorcas made her suggestion of another house-servant.

'I cannot agree,' Dorcas had replied firmly. 'I have watched you and Nellie work, and there is too much to do. She is but a child, and should rest and play a little as children do, instead of slaving from dawn to bedtime. I shall need her more in future, to train her up in other duties,' and as Betty continued to find objections, 'do you not see that it will be easier for you?'

'Oh, you want everybody to be easy,' cried Betty. 'Life's hard work for most of us, I can tell you.'

Then Dorcas hardened too and said, 'I shall require Nellie to bring one of her sisters with her when she returns on Monday, and that is my final word on the matter. If you have objections then raise them with Mr Howarth.'

'I can save my breath,' Betty muttered, 'to cool my broth!'

So on the Monday two children returned, hand in hand, Nellie full of importance and nine-year-old Sallie full of awe, to report to Dorcas in the parlour. They stood, noses running, pink with cold, scantily clad in cut-down gowns that had belonged to other people.

'And Mam says to thank you and say God bless you,' Nellie said hurriedly, trying to get the words out before she forgot them, 'and to say as Sallie might be a bit on the small side but she's strong and willing and to leather her if she don't do as she's told and thank you for the cake it were good.'

'There will be no need to leather her,' said Dorcas loudly enough for Betty to hear. Then she softened the implied rebuke. 'Now go to Miss Ackroyd and do as she tells you, Sallie. She will feed you well, for Nellie has grown since she came here. And thank Miss Ackroyd for the cake.'

'Go on,' said Nellie, 'what do you say?' Nudging the child.

'Yes, missis,' said Sallie, grinning with embarrassment.

'My name is Mrs Howarth,' said Dorcas, in the same clear voice. 'I should prefer to be called by my proper name, or else *ma'am* if you cannot remember it all at once.'

Betty's sniff of contempt could be heard in the parlour. But Nellie and Sallie bobbed an awkward curtsey apiece, crying, 'Yes, Mrs Howarth, ma'am!' and then went into the kitchen for orders.

Inside and out, the work of the farm was hard and unceasing. The men mended dry-stone walls, cut peat and wood, dug ditches, ploughed fields which they would plant and weed and harvest. They laid snares to catch predators, and kept farm tackle in good trim. Sometimes a wheel would break or a ploughshare falter, and then they took it down to Garth for Joe Burscough the wheelwright, or Will Eccles the blacksmith, who kept workshop and forge side by side for convenience.

The busiest times of the year were lambing and sheep-shearing and harvesting. Then Ned and his neighbours would take turns to help one another, since a single farm's resources were not sufficient in labour, and sometimes they would hire workers from Garth as well. Afterwards, all the women would prepare the Shearers' Feast or the Harvest Supper, in the farmhouse concerned, and there was dancing until late in the night.

Palm Sunday came, fragrant with small wild flowers, and pussy willows swung their silk tassels over the brooks. Then Betty baked great spiced buns to mark the crucifixion day, and a cross was set upon the sponging dough as well as on each bun. Betty swore that these sacred confections would never go mouldy, and possessed powers of healing. But since they were every one eaten while hot from the oven, no one could prove her right or wrong. On Easter Sunday Dorcas made her own contribution to the sacred festival, in the shape of hard-boiled eggs which she had coloured with onion skins, gorse and herbs. Her offer to show Betty had been refused, but she engaged the services and interest of Nellie and Sallie while Betty was occupied in the brew-house, and the eggs were little miracles of beauty. No one at Kit's Hill would break the shells for fear of destroying the pattern, but kept them until they discoloured and had to be given to the pigs. And, of course, they showed them round at The Woolpack.

Every Sunday, unless the way was blocked, the members of Kit's Hill walked down to church. They divided their watch, so that someone was always there to keep an eye on farm and house, between morning and evening services. Daughter of the church, Dorcas made the muddy journey twice, though she regretted the plainness of both church and parson. Ned attended but once that day, and entrusted his wife to Tom and a lantern at night, fretting to such an extent until they returned that Betty lost patience with him. Only necessary work was done on Sundays, except in harvest time when four of these rest-days were consecrated to bringing in the grain. They ate cold meats, so that Betty should not be guilty of the sin of cooking, and she knitted instead, wearing a clean white apron over her best black stuff gown. It was at this time that Dorcas began, unobtrusively, to teach Nellie and Sallie their letters, using the New Testament parables as her text. So they were instructed and interested at once. Then Ned would light his pipe in deep contentment, catching the eye of one of his family from time to time, and nodding and winking to indicate what a clever wife he had chosen.

Now it was April, and fine enough for Dorcas to go with Ned to market. In a tremble of excitement and apprehension, she pulled the grey woollen cloak over her finery, to protect it from splashing, and sat by her husband, eyes shining and head erect.

'She's glad to be going back, then?' Betty observed, as the wagon rumbled out of the yard. 'Do you reckon she might stop?' Sarcastically.

Her pleasantry was not answered, and she tutted once or twice to herself and tossed her chin, then went inside to bake the bread. The two little girls, left to her mercy for the day, prepared themselves for hardship.

Between them they hauled forth the sack of flour, ground by Garth's miller from home-grown barley, and ladled it into the wooden trough. Nellie carried in the earthenware jar of barm, saved from the last beer-brewing and keeping cool in the larder. Sallie brought in bundles of faggots, and stood by while Betty pushed them into the brick oven at the side of the hearth. One by one the bundles were prodded to the oven-back with a long-handled fork. Then Betty thrust a flaming stick into their midst, and banged the door shut.

Each container was marked with a protective cross, for bread is a symbol of life, and Betty crossed the dough before setting it to rise. Then they all had a sup of ale and waited for the oven to heat. The bricks changed from black to red. Betty flung a handful of flour against the oven door, saw it vanish in a shower of sparks, and said, 'Right!' to herself. The faggot ash was raked out and stored in a hole beneath the oven. Then Betty and the girls divided the dough into pieces, scored them with a skewer, and Betty put them in to bake while they made dinner for the men. The work was hot and pleasant, and the children sat on their stools an hour later, each chewing a warm crust and a piece of cheese. Bits of charcoal adhered to the crust, tasting burned and sweet and adding to the flavour. And afterwards Nellie brought in a box of hen and duck feathers to be baked while the oven retained heat. These, dry and free of insects, would be used to fill pillows and make mattresses.

The visit to Millbridge was not a success. Former acquaintances either pretended not to see Dorcas, or greeted her in passing with an embarrassed look and mumbled word. She saw her aunt's window-curtain lift and drop, and knew the elderly woman was watching her behind it. Phoebe wore a pink frown throughout the twenty minutes Dorcas stayed there, and was obviously hoping that no one else would call at the same time. Ned apparently left his wife to her own devices, bought and sold, talked and drank at The Red Lion tavern at the back of the market square, and was ready for home at four o'clock. But he had guessed what Dorcas's reception might be, and taken the precaution of providing a hunk of bread and cheese from his own luncheon, lest no one fed her. Pride kept her spine straight, and her smile steady, from Millbridge to Flawnes Green. Then she broke down and wept, and what with clicking to the horse and trying to comfort Dorcas, Ned had his work cut out. She was over the worst when they drove through Thornley, wiped her eyes at Whinfold, bathed her face in the stream at Childwell, smiled a little at Medlar, gave him a kiss at Coldcote, and was prepared to be grand all the way through Garth and up the fells to Kit's Hill, where she was welcomed with genuine relief by Nellie and Sallie, and with grudging words from Betty.

'Well, we got on while you was away. Only I haven't done your laundry. I haven't time. And with all the linen changing and that we'st have to ask Martha Glegg up for a wash-day. She's not due, you know, not for two month. I said, master, what wi' warming and cleaning there's a deal more work to do.'

'Then get bloody on wi' it,' said Ned, impatient lest Dorcas be chivvied by his people as well as hers. 'I'm not short of sixpence. Martha Glegg can come whenever Mrs Howarth wants her.'

So she did: a raw gaunt woman in her fifties, whose hands

were in a permanent state of soft pink wrinkles. She had borne ten children and lost five, had worn out three husbands and was even now contemplating a fourth. Her comeliness had long vanished, but there was an errant gleam in her bold blue eyes, and her talent for gossip helped her find work in the big farmhouses for miles around. After a wash-day you would see a little knot of lonely women collecting where Martha had been, now gleaning the latest news from a laundered housewife. Sometimes she created gossip, being fond of a drink at The Woolpack, and brave enough or careless enough to go where most women did not dare. So Martha was double-value for her money, and popular in spite of her occasional lecheries.

Dorcas had observed the two children, Nellie and Sallie, trotting round the edge of the yard to avoid the stinking, slippery cobbles over which cattle trod. She saw them, a little later, coming back from the well at the front of the house, each trudging slowly and weighted to one side by a heavy pail. They passed the kitchen window, walked past the end of the cow-shed, and into the wash-house where a fire was lit under the copper. Back they went again, with empty buckets, and repeated the process until the copper was full. They would fetch water for the rinsing, and sluice it away afterwards, in the same wasteful fashion. Dorcas put on her pattens and the wool cloak, and took a survey of the house-front. When she returned, she sat for some time in her parlour making small sketches and calculations.

Martha came up for her breakfast at six o'clock and was amazed to find the new Mrs Howarth waiting to greet her. (It had been all over Garth that Dorcas stayed in bed until noon!) A shrewd summing-up from those roving blue eyes was followed by instant diplomacy. Martha dropped a curtsey, seeing future work doubled and tripled if she watched her manners.

'Now, my lady,' said Martha, 'I've been washing for Mrs Wrigley of Medlar Hall Farm, and she wouldn't let nobody but me touch her linen. I do fine laundry, my lady. You could trust me with your lace and think no more about it. I can goffer your caps, and crimp your bands, lovely. I can starch fine enough to suit a queen. And I'll come any time you want, and take it back with me if it don't suit you to do it up here.' And she dropped another curtsey, and smiled so that Dorcas could see the gaps in her teeth.

Betty stood aghast at this treachery, for Martha had been her gossip for years, and she had taken her allegiance for granted. But Dorcas, perceiving that she dealt with a time-server, put her to question.

'How do you wash your lace, Mrs Glegg?' Smiling.

'In new milk, my lady. Soaked until it's clean again, then rinsed in fresh rain-water, and pressed between two pieces of linen to dry, and ironed with the damp linen atop of it after it's been fingered into shape.'

Dorcas inclined her head, satisfied, and went upstairs with Nellie to look out a few more delicate articles for the wash. Martha winked at Betty.

'Here's your breakfast,' said Betty, disgusted. 'Get it down you! There's plenty to be done. She can go through more bed-linen in three month than Mrs Hetty did in three year!'

'I'm used to the gentry,' said Martha smugly, and swigged her ale off at a gulp. 'You want to butter her up a bit,' Martha advised.

'When I want your opinion I'll ask for it!' said Betty, slapping fried salt pork onto her plate.

But Martha was one of life's material philosophers, and took bad and good fortune alike. So she sat at the scrubbed wooden table with the farm-hands, and gave them joke for joke, and drank with them tankard for tankard, and eyed young Billy (who wasn't a day above fifteen) in much the same way that an experienced horse-breeder eyes a young stallion.

Halfway through the morning Dorcas picked her way to the wash-house, from whence came clouds of steam and hearty singing. And there was Martha Glegg, working away like a team of washerwomen; with the two little girls rinsing the voluminous linen sheets as they came white from the lye and hot water, and walking further and further apart, wringing them as they went. While Martha buffeted the soiled clothes against the wash-stone, and punched them down into the boiling suds with a great posset.

'If we had a gleam of sun, my lady,' Martha shouted over the noise and steam, 'I could put these cottons and linens out to bleach.'

Dorcas saw that she was dealing gently with the woollens, and had already stretched the first clean ones on tenterhooks to prevent their shrinking.

'Where did you learn your trade, Mrs Glegg?' asked Dorcas, impressed.

'From working wi' the servants of fine folk, like yourself, my lady. My mother put me to Medlar Hall Farm when I were eight year old, to work for the washerwoman there. I took her place when she died, but I like my freedom, my lady. So I said as I would still do Mrs Wrigley's washing but set up on my own. I work for those as takes my fancy, my lady.'

She mixed a fresh solution of ashes, slaked quicklime and boiling water. Her skill and her interest were obvious. Dorcas looked at her narrowly.

'I go all over,' Martha continued, and the gaps between her teeth were tremendous, 'so if you want owt as you canna get in Garth I'll fetch it for you, my lady. I know all the pack-men.'

'You are very kind,' said Dorcas, smiling. 'I shall not interrupt you further, Mrs Glegg.'

The wash took two days, and Martha came up on the third to do the ironing. The washerwoman's treachery had not been forgotten, but Betty put it aside in favour of pleasant conversation and ale-drinking. She had finished her major tasks, to clear space in the kitchen for the clean clothes, and sat knitting a stocking for Ned and turning the heel deftly; while Martha set the flat irons on the hob, and sprinkled the linen with water, gossiping as she worked. She paused only to hold the iron a judicious distance from her cheek, as if listening to its heat. Then she would press it down firmly, and talk again, blue eyes roving from glossy sheet to absorbed listener.

There was a great clothes-rack in the ceiling at Kit's Hill, the size of a four-poster base, which wound up on a pulley. Across its sturdy beams the immaculate laundry hung for two whole days before Nellie stacked it in closets, and between its deep drifts Dorcas inserted sprigs of dried lavender. Martha Glegg put her wages of three sixpences in her pocket, and carried her skills and her gap-toothed smile to other customers, while promising to wash Dorcas's personal caps and undergarments once a month. And everyone was satisfied.

Then Dorcas suggested that they knock a hole in the laundry wall which was near the well at the front of the house, and put a door there.

'What does she want to do that for?' Betty enquired.

'So you can fetch water from t' well without walking all the way round,' said Ned, showing her the sketch. 'That'll save thi time and thi legs!'

'But we'st have two doors, then!' Betty objected.

'Aye! So little lass can fill her bucket in the morning, come through the new door into the wash-house, out through the old door, and straight into t' dairy to do her scrubbing.'

'*I* never minded,' said Betty outraged, 'and nobody minded *for* me, neither, I can tell you. But it's Nellie, Nellie, all the while now!'

'Don't be so daft,' said Ned. 'If it saves time and leg-work for her it saves it for you and all.'

'It'll take a mort of dirt and sweat to make a hole in *that* wall!' Betty promised.

'Aye,' Ned agreed, 'but it's worth doing, I reckon.'

These were small triumphs on a long hard road for Dorcas. Fortnightly, she steeled herself to go to market with Ned, holding the tenuous threads of friendship with Phoebe, keeping her head high against rebuffs. It was a continuous exercise in stoicism, a grievous limitation of her natural sociability, for she had lost her home in Millbridge and found none at Kit's Hill as yet. Her parlour was a little island, furnished out of the past; her innovations little steps into an unknown future. She attempted to make a friend of Mrs Redfern, and found her to be a gentle spirit, anxious to help anybody and to hurt nobody, which does not make for a particular companion. Also, there was a clerical shyness between them, for Dorcas preferred a High Church service and Tom Redfern was pugnaciously Low.

The odours, the hard and narrow living, the lack of grace, scraped her raw. She instituted a jug, basin and chamberpot in their bedroom early on. She had plans for a close-stool, as in Thornton House, but did not broach them as yet. She opened Mrs Hetty's still-room, as Betty predicted she would, and turned this into another place for her use and usefulness. Once, she sat and read her *locus standi,* and put it away again with sadness. For she seemed to be in the same predicament but in a different situation, and knew that this one must be endured.

Betty had been making tallow candles the evening before, in response to her new mistress's needs, and with much grumbling in a low voice. Candles were a luxury. They used rushlights themselves.

'And we've got bundles of them,' Betty remarked. 'All fresh-gathered last summer, and the longest and fattest bulrushes as I've ever seen, and dipped and dipped until they was thick enough to burn a half-hour. What's good enough for us is good enough for her, I reckon. But she must be burning candles day and night, as if master was full of gold sovereigns!'

The candles were cheap, being made of melted mutton fat, but the process took time and patience. Betty set up her candle-making battery, threaded a wick through one mould, knotted it at the tapering end, secured it to a wire stretched over the top, then poured in the smoking tallow. One by one, painstakingly, they emerged: dim of light, smelling of grease, and liable to collapse if the wick were not regularly trimmed.

'I suppose you was used to wax,' said Betty bitterly, and sniffed when Dorcas agreed.

The smell made Dorcas's head ache, and she extinguished the candle as soon as possible. Then the wind rose up against the May blossoms, and wound her headache into a tight band. She lay against Ned's warm chest and listened to his steady heartbeat, and wept as quietly as she could, and even laid her handkerchief between her face and his breast so that she should not wet his night-shirt. He slept on and she lay awake and wished the wind might blow her away, and then she should have no more trouble. Her mind was her enemy, first presenting an injustice to gall her, and then a responsibility to bind her. So, even as she pondered how to leave Kit's Hill, she remembered Nellie and Sallie sleeping trustfully on their straw mattress, and knew she could not relinquish them. She loathed the miseries which Ned had unwittingly inflicted upon her. In her mind she wandered from room to quiet room of the vicarage in Gloucestershire, and found her mother sewing at the little oval table, and buried her head in that loving lap and cried out her woes.

A particularly hard sob woke up Ned and he began lovingly to stroke her and hold her to him for comfort. He had no need to enquire the reason for this flood of sorrow, nor to speak. His face above her huddled body was set and sad, for he was helpless to alter what ailed her. He could only be there, and show her that he was with and for her. Until gradually she was soothed into sleep, and then he could sleep too.

But when she woke she smelled that atrocious mutton-fat candle, and the tea (so carefully carried in by Nellie, tongue between teeth) turned her stomach. Then Ned opened the window to call to one of his men, and the stink of manure made her retch. Every corner in Kit's Hill held a private scent of its own, and all of them were varied and vile. So Dorcas vomited all morning, and lay abed all afternoon; and cried because she knew she was carrying Ned's child, and there was no way out but onwards.

He sat with her after supper, and held a cold-water compress to her forehead, and spoke cheerfully of buying wax candles from the chandler's in Millbridge; and drew her attention to the bunch of wild flowers Nellie had picked and put in a mug by her bed; and renewed her courage and her spirit. So that they talked quietly and peacefully of the coming child, and she was able to kiss his cheek and lay her hand on his in thanks and smile at him.

To and fro. To and fro. She fretting, he steadfast, in this first terrible year when she was the foreigner.

Blackthorn Winter

Seven

Childermas, 28 December 1761

'If you please, ma'am,' said Agnes, red with apprehension, 'it's Mr Howarth begging the favour of a word with you, and he says as it's important.'

Miss Wilde had grown a little stouter, a little greyer, and a little harder in the past year. She was currently teasing a poor relative with promise of inheritance, and making sure that the lady paid for her future wealth with present servitude. Nor had she relaxed her hostility towards Dorcas, though she invited Miss Jarrett to tea regularly, and pumped her for information about the Howarths of Kit's Hill. So now she was caught between curiosity and resentment, and did not know what to do, but blamed Agnes while she made her decision.

'Have I not told you, time and again, Agnes, that I will not have that fellow in my house? Whatever persuaded you to let him in?'

'Ma'am,' cried Agnes, wringing her hands in her apron, 'oh, ma'am, if you could see him you'd be sorry. Oh, ma'am, it's Miss Dorcas, so bad with child that Mr Howarth's come for Dr Standish. Oh, ma'am, if she should die . . .'

Then Agnes flung her apron over her head and wept, so that Miss Wilde was silent with astonishment, and the lady companion looked from one to the other to gauge what her reaction should be. Even Walpole raised his nose from the carpet to observe this wonder.

'You had best put your face under the pump, Agnes, and restore your senses. Bad news, you say? Well, we are Christians, I hope. Fetch the fellow in. And you, Esther, should sit where you are and observe what happens when a woman is headstrong and ungrateful . . .'

. . . and will not comply with my wishes, she thought. This is what happens. It is a judgement. I was always right, only she would not listen. Now she will be punished.

'So you have got my niece with child?' she cried, as Ned walked in. 'Well, that is what you were after, was it not? How is she?'

Nearly a year of life with Dorcas had given Ned more certainty with people of Miss Wilde's station, but a thousand years would not have softened the impact of her hostility. He was shocked that she should gain satisfaction from Dorcas's torment.

'I've nobbut a few minutes to spare, ma'am,' Ned began, 'for young Dr Standish is coming back wi' me to Kit's Hill, when he's seen Miss Spencer.'

'Why, what is wrong with poor Miss Spencer?' cried Miss Wilde, aglint with malice.

'Nay, how should I know?' Ned answered honestly, then seeing that she taunted him with intent, he said angrily, 'I should think as she's got more money than sense, and no man of her own, so she wastes a good doctor's time complaining!'

'Indeed, sir? Indeed? You know a great deal about the female condition, that is obvious. You are quite a wag, sir, about us poor maiden ladies!'

'Begging your pardon, miss,' Ned added to the lady companion, whom he now saw for the first time. For she was not noticeable. 'Miss Wilde,' he continued, 'I've come to ask a favour of you, for I know as you're fond of Dorcas, despite all. She's very poorly, ma'am. It'd do her a world of good to see you, and the little dog and all,' for Walpole had recognised an old acquaintance, and got up somewhat stiffly, and come over to smell Ned's boots. 'I can take you both up as nice as ninepence in the trap. It's got cushions in it, and that. I did it up for her, and we brought it to Millbridge just the once afore she had to stop at home along of the . . .'

'Yes,' said Miss Wilde smoothly, 'I saw her going to market in it, and though she did not look like a farmer's wife, the trap looked like a farmer's trap. Mr Howarth,' smiling into his fear and trouble, 'your wife will doubtless survive her labour. Women do suffer at this time. But I should not be able to console her (though as a good Christian I should try) because I believe her to have brought this upon herself. I was sorry to think that any lady should trail after a man like any servant-girl, but Dorcas did. She has got what she asked for, and must lie on the bed she has made for herself. It is no use her sending for me, in her extremity. This is God's Will, Mr Howarth, and we must abide by it.'

He struck his thigh with his hat in violent disbelief.

'Dorcas never sent for you,' he cried. 'I come on my own account. I'm near out of my mind wi' this business. Twisting like a blasted coney in a trap to find ways and means of helping her. She's been in labour above thirty-six hour. Nay, I don't know what to make of you, nor any like you, as puts pride and bad temper above a bit of common kindness!' Walpole was jumping up at him, giving short delighted barks. 'I tell you something ma'am, however this turns out for Dorcas and me – she were right to leave you!'

Then he clapped his hat on his head and slammed the door behind him, prepared to wait outside on the steps until Dr Standish should come for him.

Miss Wilde, conscious perhaps that her role had not been as high-minded as she could wish, called Walpole to heel for he was scratching the door-paint frantically. But as loudly as she screamed at him he loudly barked again, until she snatched up her newspaper and struck him.

The blow did not hurt, but he stopped his noise and scuffle at the astonishment of it, and began to trot back. Suddenly he paused, his flanks heaved, his eyes bulged, and he fell upon one side making desperate efforts to draw breath, short legs jerking. Now Miss Wilde screamed in good earnest for help, for Agnes, for a doctor, finally even for Ned – who returned out of humanity, though he could do nothing. But he spoke soothingly to the animal, acting as a sort of humble Charon between one shore and the next ferrying the soul across, until Walpole gave a gasp of recognition, and died. Agnes and the lady companion drew back, uncertain how to behave or what to do, while Miss Wilde burst into a hail of remorse.

'Fetch her a drop of summat sharp,' said Ned wisely. 'I'll put this poor little bugger in t'back kitchen for now. Dost want me to bury him for thee? I've got time. I told them where I'd be when I called at Dr Standish's. If the little chap had some nice place, like under a tree at the bottom of the garden, it'd be a comfort to the old lady. What dost think?'

The three women arrived at a conclusion out of their separate counsels. When young Matthew Standish arrived he found Ned cleaning mud from the garden spade.

'Shall us be off, then?' said Ned, numbed. 'She'll have been waiting for us a good while. I'll not trouble Miss Wilde with a good-day.'

But Agnes came after them, and slipped something small and cool and polished into Ned's hand.

'For Miss Dorcas, sir,' she said. 'It's a comfort stone. If she gives it a squeeze when the pains come it'll ease her.'

Ned looked at the egg-shaped lump of smooth granite, bemused, and thanked her.

'Miss Wilde said to give it you, along of burying the little dog, sir. But she says she don't want no more to do with you, begging your pardon, sir. And I'm sorry as I can't fetch you a nicer message. Please, sir, how's Miss Dorcas – Mrs Howarth – settling down?'

He was in pain himself, knowing that his wife was a stranger in a strange house, surrounded by strangers, and bearing yet another stranger. He did not know how to convey the trouble they had suffered, culminating in this greatest trouble of all. Their world was one long winter, one deep bruise, but he tried to answer as Dorcas would have wished.

'She's capital,' said Ned. 'You should come up and see us when the weather's better.'

'Would you remember me kindly to her, sir, and tell her I said God bless?'

'Aye, I will, my lass. Thankee.'

'Lead on, Mr Howarth!' cried Matthew Standish, short and ginger and very competent, fresh from Edinburgh's School of Medicine. 'I'll come behind you on my own horse. You did well to fetch me. I am quite caught up in obstetrics. Of course, there is great prejudice among the midwives, and much superstition, but we are sweeping away these cobwebs, sir. Miss Dorcas – Mrs Howarth – is indeed fortunate. A few years ago, I'm afraid . . . well, well, let us ride as fast as may be . . .'

'I told him. Marry in Lent, live to repent!' cried Betty, brewing sack-posset, and growing more garrulous as she tasted it. 'I told him!'

'He weren't married in Lent,' said Nellie, one year older and bigger and braver, daring to interrupt the monologue.

'You wash them dishes and mind your own business. Then what does she do but have a little 'un at Childermas, and that's the unluckiest day in the year. Why couldn't she have had him at Christmas, instead of making us all miserable?'

'She canna choose for herself,' Nellie muttered disobediently, 'and it might be a girl, and all.'

'Then she's not satisfied wi' poor Cissie Pycroft, who's been tending her, but has to send for this doctor, ten mile off. I've never heard of a doctor coming to a childbed afore. They have to make do wi' Cissie in Garth, else go without or go underground! Why, Cissie's been birthing Garth and Garth Fells since I were first here, thirty year ago.'

Sallie crept up to Nellie, under the pretext of bringing more dirty dishes, and whispered, 'If Mrs Howarth dies shall us get leathered?'

'No, she just wants to worrit the master to death,' Betty continued, oblivious of her small slaves. 'Here, Cissie – why, where's Cissie?'

'She went back some time since,' said Nellie loudly, for she saw that Betty had fuddled herself.

'Then you take this up to her. She needs strengthening. Well, Tom, have you nowt to do in t' stable?'

He stood, tall and awkward and concerned in the doorway. He had come to ask for news, and this annoyed her.

'How's missis?' Betty mimicked sarcastically. 'Missis is laiking as usual, isn't she? Instead of getting on wi' her work like the rest of us.'

'Nay,' said Tom reprovingly, 'it's harder on women than on animals. You should know that, for all you've had none yourself. Well, tell her I asked about her, wilta?'

'I'll tell her,' said Nellie, catching up the bowl of posset. 'She'll be glad *somebody* cares.'

'That girl's getting above herself,' Betty warned, but Tom went out without answering, and Sallie hid in the larder until her sister should come back to provide a frail protection.

Unrecognisable, but for the spirit that forced her to survive, Dorcas sipped a little of the posset, and the midwife finished the rest. Nellie bent over her mistress's head and whispered comfort.

'Master'll be back soon wi' the doctor, ma'am. I've aired the baby's gowns and set them out like you showed me, and made up the cradle and all. Is there owt else I can do for you? Oh, and Tom asked how you were, and Sallie's asking every five minutes.'

'Thank you, Nellie. I wish it were done. I wish only to be done.'

'Aye,' Nellie said sympathetically, for she was the eldest of ten, and had watched her mother bear a child every twelve months, until father died. 'You'll soon be done,' said Nellie, placing a little rough hand on Dorcas's smooth one. 'Then you can sit up, like on your wedding night, and I'll brew you a pot of tea all to yourself, and slice a bit of bread and butter very fine, like you showed me. And you'll have the baby in your arms, and Kit's Hill'll go mad!'

'It is a cruel place,' said Dorcas, 'and has a cruel wind to match it that makes my head ache. One can but endure. Who is that sitting in the chair?' For she thought she saw her mother. 'Has she come all the way to see me?'

'There's nobody,' said Nellie, afraid.

Dorcas smiled, for her mother was there after all, and very much at home.

'I did what I thought best,' said Dorcas to her mother, 'but I fear the outcome is a poor one. Perhaps I misjudged my circumstances. One is but human, and therefore fallible. But I have kept faith.'

'What's up wi' Mrs Howarth?' Nellie whispered to the midwife.

'Her mind's wandering.'

'No, it is not,' Dorcas cried, for she wanted them to know the truth. 'My mind is very clear, though my body is weak.' Then she said, 'Oh, how I wish I had asked Phoebe to come. I should have told my husband to fetch her, too.'

A sudden commotion downstairs roused Cissie Pycroft, and she went with Nellie to the door to listen.

'It's the doctor, ma'am,' cried Nellie, thrilled to bear good news. 'I can hear him and Betty carrying on, like hammer and tongs!'

'. . . well, bleedings was good enough for Mrs Hetty, and leeches. I should know. I put four of them on her forehead regular, didn't I? And when they dropped off I put fresh ones on, didn't I?'

'How should I know, my good woman?' cried Matthew Standish, very loud and clear and cheerful. 'Now I am a surgeon by profession, and an excellent profession it is becoming. So you can put away your poultice of snails and woodlice, or whatever filthy concoction you are brewing . . .'

A subdued voice said, 'I were only stirring pease pudding, sir!'

'Come, come, we are wasting time. A bowl of water if you please.'

His voice fetched Dorcas from her half-world, and she lifted her head to greet him. Tears of exhaustion ran down her cheeks, but she put out her hand to clasp his, and thanked him for coming.

Matthew Standish then turned majestically on the midwife, delighting in the fact that he was an unwelcome intruder.

'Your name is Mrs Pycroft, I believe? Ah, yes. And you have had some considerable experience in midwifery? Well, Mrs Pycroft, as you can see, all your experience will not help Mrs Howarth now. So I must do what I can, and I should be obliged if you would assist me.' To Ned, who stood silent and afraid before the unknown woman in the bed, 'I shall not require you, sir. I suggest you take some rest and refreshment while we ease your wife. I thank you!' Ginger eyebrows raised.

When Ned had gone, Matthew Standish took a flask of brandy from his pocket and gauged his opponent's mettle. Mrs Pycroft, surly in defeat, brought up all her lore to aid her reputation.

'Well, I don't know why she's laiking. There's every door in the house unlocked, and the knots loosened, and a knife under t' bed to cut the pains. And Betty's made the groaning cake, and cheese and ale enough ready for all Garth to wish the babby well.'

'Now, Miss Dorcas,' said Matthew, ignoring the midwife, pouring brandy into a cup. 'I want you to drink this up, if you please, until the ceiling goes round. Let me know when it becomes a whirlpool. Mrs Pycroft,' turning on her again, genial and dangerous, 'the reason that Mrs Howarth's baby has not been born has nothing to do with knots and locks!' He examined Dorcas carefully. 'The infant is the wrong way round and cannot emerge, and the mother is exhausted. We must fetch the child out, for Miss Dorcas cannot help herself. How goes the ceiling, Miss Dorcas?'

'Very . . . well . . . sir,' Dorcas mumbled, and her head

rolled drunkenly.

'Good. Now, Mrs Pycroft,' drawing her aside and hypnotising her with hard light green eyes, 'you are about to observe medical history being made on Garth fells. Think of the honour! But it will not be a pretty business, and it will not be easy, and if you begin whispering about it I shall see you are put in the stocks for a liar, else hanged. Do you understand me, ma'am?'

'Yes, sir,' the midwife murmured, and dropped a curtsey.

'Then do exactly as I tell you. For you and I know (whatever our difference of education or opinion) that Mrs Howarth is as good as dying, and the infant most probably dead already. Do we not?'

'Yes, sir. I were feared of that, sir. That were why I did my best, sir . . .'

'Enough of your nonsense. Where is that bowl of water?'

But in turning to find it the bowl was tipped by his heavy coat-tails and spilled on the bedroom floor.

'Never you mind, sir,' said Mrs Pycroft, anxious to ingratiate herself with this terrifying gentleman, 'I've got a kettle a-boiling on this fire, sir. Should I fetch some cold water to mix wi' it, sir?'

'No, no, pour it over this instrument. We have little time. There, that will do!'

Mrs Pycroft's hands trembled as she scalded the French forceps, and he waved them to and fro to cool them. Not knowing, for all his cleverness, that Dorcas's life would be as much saved by this accident as by his skill and purpose.

'Now, Miss Dorcas,' he said kindly, for he saw that the sound of her maiden name gave her comfort, 'Mrs Pycroft is going to hold you down, very carefully, so that you do not move and hurt yourself, and we shall soon have you out of your trouble.'

Cissie Pycroft pinned her down, and Matthew drew back the covers. Then Dorcas was aware of something agonising, and heard a woman scream so pitiably that she thought, 'Poor creature!' as she bobbed just under the surface of consciousness.

'Oh, my sacred Lord,' cried Cissie Pycroft, glancing sideways, sickened.

The agony ceased, Matthew Standish said, 'Clear this away. It is done for. We have work ahead of us yet. Give her a rest.'

Dorcas felt her face being wiped gently with a cloth wrung out in hot water, and heard the doctor call upon her to bear down one last time.

'That is very well,' he said. 'Do you see, Mrs Pycroft, how the afterbirth has come clean away? Now, Miss Dorcas, be brave once more while I mend this wound of yours. Mercifully, you should not suffer so much when it is done directly.' And he brought out a surgeon's needle, and a length of silk.

'You're never going to stitch her up, sir?' whispered Cissie, aghast.

'Why, what else? Is she to drag herself about, and gape from now until Doomsday? Hold her legs apart so I can see what I am at!'

At last they let her be, and washed their hands, and she tried to remember what she should ask them, but was too weary and fuddled to frame the question.

'Now listen to me, Mrs Pycroft,' said Matthew, washing the forceps in the soiled water, and wrapping them in an indifferently clean cloth, 'the details of the birth must be kept from everybody. I want you to lay out the remains of the infant, and put it into a coffin as soon as possible. The face, fortunately, is pretty enough. Aye, a pretty little lass. Dress it finely and bind the wounds and limbs so that no one knows what lies beneath. In answer to any question you say that it was stillborn, and say nothing more. If you do I'll have your tongue cut out. Your word would never stand against mine. You know that, do you not?' She nodded, afraid, and sponged Dorcas's unconscious face again. 'And I shall come to see how Mrs Howarth progresses. If I find you anointing her with any of your sheep's dung remedies you shall hang for a witch! Nothing but the simplest herbal lotions and poultices. We are emerging into an age of light and reason,

Mrs Pycroft. Whether you emerge with us is doubtful, but by God I shall make sure you do not hinder us, you and your kind! Now do we understand each other, madam, once and for all?'

Mrs Pycroft understood, and no other threat would have been powerful enough to break her silence. So she made the infant seemly, and covered the bruises on its small skull with a frilled cap. The little face looked peaceful and pretty, the mouth was pursed in supreme resolution.

Now all the doors and windows at Kit's Hill were opened, though the day was grown dark and bitterly cold, so that the infant's soul could fly free. Nellie draped Dorcas's looking-glass with a cloth, and stopped the pendulum of the long clock. Billy was sent down to Joe Burscough's shop for a child's coffin, and given a note for the parson to come as soon as he could. Betty began, almost in a trance, to bake currant bread for the mourners. And down in the village, where no housewife had washed clothes or linen on that unluckiest day of the year, Josiah Sidebottom rang a muffled peal for Childermas. The sound carried upon the frosty air as an unconscious mark of condolence for the silent household.

Ned wept when they showed him his daughter, but Dorcas kissed the infant's forehead and neither wept nor spoke. Partly this was out of exhaustion, and the need to conserve what little strength she possessed. Partly it was out of faith, for the bout of birth and death had brought her close to her origins. She was privately convinced that her mother had taken the child into safekeeping, with her father's knowledge and blessing, and she could not have wished for better guardians. Then she lapsed into passive obedience, and a remoteness that was to last all winter.

Set apart by her trial and tragedy, she sat in her parlour and sewed. Her door was kept ajar for extra warmth and company. Those in the kitchen shaped their conversation for her ears, even though the discussions did not involve her directly. Kit's Hill was mourning, for the child had been one of them, and they were the less for her passing. Life had apparently exacted enough from Dorcas for the time being, and flowed on without disturbing her. She developed a fondness for Betty's gingerbread, which did much to mollify that cantankerous woman, who deigned to serve it up on a china plate and even ordered Nellie to brew a pot of tea for the missis.

Dearest Phoebe,

I thank you for y^{r} Thoughtful and Loving letter, and Beg to be Forgiven for my Delay in answering. Indeed I am still Weak and must be Obedient to Dr Standish a While yet, but when the Weather is Kinder I shall come to Millbridge and spend the Afternoon with you as you Invite me to do. Edward will Not accompany me since he does Business in the Market, but he has Offered to act as our Messenger in this Correspondence, being v. Kind as always, and Putting my Interests even before his Own. Our Grief has been Great, but we Trust in God and Commend our Sweet Infant into His Keeping, and Pray He will Bless us, for His Delays are not Denials.

Please to thank y^{r} dear Father for his Kindness in ordering my Books, and my Husband will Settle the Account when he delivers this Note. I am presently Delighting in the Commonsense and Practical Notions of Mr Jethro Tull, who has Invented a Seed-drill. He was a Lawyer with such Prodigious Abilities of Mind that he could Look Afresh at our old Ways of Agriculture and Improve upon them. I Purpose to be of Greater Use to my Husband in the Future, by means of Pursuing those Paths w^{h} are less Familiar to Him than to Me.

I know y^{r} Duties leave you but little Liberty, yet I could Wish it were not Such an Age since we last Met, but You shall see me Shortly. Pray Remember me Kindly . . . y^{r} Affectionate Friend. Dorcas.

Sam Cartwright was lambing in the cold and wet. His sheepdog ran hither and thither tirelessly, herding and discovering and reporting. She worked with her master at all hours, day or night. A rogue fox troubled the sheep with his ferocity and his cunning. Ned laid traps for him, hunted him, waited for him. But the fox ranged at liberty among Betty's chickens. Crows hovered over the breeding flock, scattered at the noise of Ned's blunderbuss, then continued their watch for the weak and small from a safer distance. There was birth and re-birth, as the shepherd slit the warm coat from a dead lamb and wrapped it round a living one, to foster upon the bereft ewe. Occasionally, there were lambs that could not be mothered out, and these he brought to the kitchen, bleating and nuzzling, to be suckled by means of a feeding cup with a linen teat fashioned round the spout. Then Dorcas, clad in a white apron, would care for them in lieu of the child she had lost, until they wobbled into the yard one morning and left her.

Dorcas was settling down. Matthew Standish had done well by her. The birth wound healed, and Ned was forbidden to exercise his husbandly privilege for a twelvemonth, giving her a space in which to find herself. She and Betty had tacitly decided to live under one roof with two authorities. In the kitchen and dairy Betty reigned. In the parlour Dorcas was queen. Her innovations seemed harmless. Why should Betty mind if the linen was often laundered, and laid away in lavender, or that Dorcas should open other rooms in Kit's Hill and arrange the solid furniture to greater advantage? What matter that Nellie had become lady's-maid and house-maid, and beeswax and turpentine scented the air? As far as Betty was concerned, the books which Dorcas studied kept her quiet and out of real mischief. Had she realised that revolution was pending she would have had good cause to cry betrayal, but Dorcas was much too clever to lose a war for the sake of winning small running battles.

A little rush, yellow with pollen, braved the snow on Scarth Nick. Winter winds ceased to flay the fells, and the grass grew green. The lower meadows were embroidered with wild flowers, and children plucked and ate the new hawthorn leaves and called them ‘bread and butter’. At Kit’s Hill the early-morning lanterns hung unused, their tallow candles guttered to a halt. And rising was no longer a purgatory of the flesh.

Warmly wrapped, Dorcas ventured into Mrs Hetty’s garden, and found parsley and chives coming up through the draggled weeds, the rosemary bush gallantly spiked, and a dozen other humble friends showing signs of life. So she fetched her garden fork and stayed out there in the pale sunshine, bringing the great cartwheel of herbs to new beginnings, until Betty sent Sallie out with a warning that she should not catch cold.

Setting down her teacup, Dorcas looked out her mother’s book of receipts for *Herbs, The Growing and Usage Thereof, for Domestic and Medicinal Purposes,* and made a little list of those she did not possess, resolving to beg cuttings from Phoebe. She wondered how long it would take to grow a fine hedge of lavender such as they had in Gloucestershire, and wrote ‘lavder rts’ on Phoebe’s list. Then she got down her father’s three volumes on *Life and Lore of a Country Parish* by the Rev. Ambrose Wilde, and resolved to read them again. So the afternoon passed very pleasantly and harmoniously, with not a cross word from Betty to mar it, and the sun coming in at the parlour window as both present blessing and future promise.

Eight

Here in Millbridge, thriving more vigorously than ever, the news was of poor Miss Spencer's latest bout with death (who had surely become her Familiar by now?); of young Dr Standish's new-fangled notions of physic and surgery, and how his old father was grieved by him (after spending all his money on a fine education); of the schoolmaster Mr Henry Tucker adopting young Jack Ackroyd, a weaver's boy, that he said was very bright and would make his mark in the academic world (and if the lower classes were to take such notions seriously, then where would the gentlefolk of Millbridge be?); and of Miss Wilde changing her will three times in a twelvemonth and refusing to entertain the notion of another spaniel (and she had put up a little stone near the laburnum tree, inscribed 'WALPOLE 1750–1761. Well done, thou Good and Faithful Servant', as though he were a human being, which made folk think her mind was failing!).

When gossip was done, tea was proffered, and Phoebe enquired whether Dorcas drank tea at Kit's Hill (though the packet was clearly visible in Dorcas's wicker basket). Then Phoebe's latest maid, being trained beautifully for service, inevitably caused a question as to Nellie Bowker's progress. Later, Walter Jarrett joined the ladies and asked Dorcas jocularly how she did, and tested her Latin in tags and quotations to see whether Kit's Hill had stolen this accomplishment also. But Dorcas, pupil of her father, still studied her texts for an hour before breakfast. 'You rise early then?' he cried, surprised. 'No, I rise late, sir,' Dorcas replied demurely. Oh, she enjoyed these mental exercises with him, but Phoebe's emotional probes hurt and tired her.

'You seem less lively than you were, Dorcas. Are you not well and happy now? You are well and happy, I hope?'

Then Dorcas felt lonely, because each day demanded so much courage and endurance. She dividen the virginal dreams of marriage which Phoebe cherished (even while her flesh shrank at the very notion of a man) and Dorcas knew that such dreams did not endure. Something was being grown between herself and Ned, something occasionally flowered, that Phoebe might have called happiness. But its roots were as grey and hardy as Kit's Hill, and a stranger could have been forgiven for thinking their life difficult rather than challenging. The truth would not have been understood, nor in Phoebe's case was it wanted, so Dorcas mollified her gentle tormentor with a social lie.

'I thank you, Phoebe, we are quite content,' and as her friend's face expressed disbelief, Dorcas added in truth, 'though the death of our infant is a quiet sadness with us. Folk say that time heals all things, but I cannot think our memory will be so brief.'

When she had gone she knew that Walter Jarrett would say, 'Dorcas always puts a good face on the matter, and makes do very well. After all, she is no worse off than she was with Miss Wilde, now that she has a few comforts and books about her!'

To which Phoebe would be sure to reply, 'Except, Papa, that when she was single her friends could hope that a proper gentleman (who did not mind a wife without a dowry) might marry her. Now what can any of us say, but that it is a pity she married at all?'

Dorcas's long convalescence, early accompanied by Mr Jethro Tull's book on *Horse-Hoeing Husbandry,* had given her time to observe and consider life anew. She had seen all but the milking cows, the horses, the oxen and the bull, slaughtered in the autumn because there was not enough fodder to keep them through the winter. The sheep made do as best they could, and the hardiest survived. Only Ned's most precious acres in the limestone area bore any crops. These were not great: pease, oats, barley, potatoes fairly recently. They were used for domestic purposes, and served up with the salt pork and salt beef. She realised that the wind, the poor soil, and the climate, were against arable farming such as she had known in her father's parish. Yet Mr Jethro Tull believed that his principles of opening up the ground, turning it into fine tillage, sowing seed in rows instead of broadcasting it, and giving each plant room and nourishment to thrive, would produce excellent results even in fields such as these. His seed-drill and his horse-hoe saved time and labour. He costed up his crops, balanced expenditure against produce, and proved his method soundly. His common sense appealed to Dorcas, his ingenuity aroused her admiration. She resolved to try her hand, with her husband's permission, on that scrubby three-acre desert known as 'Owd Barebones'.

Her approach was diplomatic. She said she had come across an idea in a book she had read, about a new vegetable that would keep cattle fed throughout the winter. She pointed out that Owd Barebones was already nibbled flat and lying fallow for a year. She offered to pay the cost of the seed herself, and to oversee the method and labour. Of the seed-drill and horse-hoe she said nothing until she had proved herself and Mr Tull worthy of these machines.

Fond-and-Foolish, as they nicknamed Ned, was a little taken aback at the notion of his lady concerning herself with turnip-growing. The kitchen garden he could comprehend (adding a personal vision of Dorcas in a becoming sun-bonnet, gathering fragrant herbs). But since his wife waited for an answer, face uplifted in silent appeal, he relented slightly.

'I can let thee have Billy. Joe says he's worse than useless at milking. But so fat as I know he's never ploughed owt in his life. If he makes a muck of it I'st be left wi' ground as the sheep can't crop. Dost follow me, Dorcas?'

'I will pay his wages, Edward, and if the Swedish turnips fail then I will pay to have the field smoothed down again.'

'Nay, keep your brass in your pocket,' he cried good-humouredly, and put his arm round her waist, and thought that a year was a long time to wait, and yet he was afraid to get her with child again.

She kissed his cheek, comprehending, but said, 'I should prefer to pay!'

'Well, have Billy then,' said Ned. 'He's done thi garden nicely, I'll say that much for him. Why not get his old grandad to work wi' him? He used to plough for us when he were younger. But I'm bound to strike a bargain wi' thee, my lass. They'll have to take the oxen when nobody else wants them. I'm not giving up summat for nowt. And what you do, you do on your own. No running to me when a drop of rain falls, or the fly gets at the turnips. Right?'

'Right!' said Dorcas, radiant in accepting the very terms she wanted.

Kit's Hill was agog at this fresh departure from the norm, and prepared to savour the ultimate downfall of the three pioneers. So one dirty morning, when nobody else wanted the oxen, young Billy and Grandpa Sidebottom yoked Pearl and Di'mond, and Gowd and Siller, at six o'clock, and ploughed Owd Barebones. Meanwhile, Dorcas had traced the Swedish turnip seed by means of a chain of letters: beginning with Mr Jarrett's London bookseller, and ending with a Norfolk farmer who sent seed from his own crop, and advised her to grow barley the year after, for it did uncommonly well.

Billy and Grandpa ploughed Owd Barebones again, and then twice more in a short space of time, because the weather was bad and the oxen unused.

'I never heard of ploughing in t' wet afore!' said Ned, forced from his silence at last.

'When else can they plough?' Dorcas asked a little sharply, for she knew that the land should be dry, and she feared her enterprise was hampered from the start. 'The oxen are in use as soon as the rain ceases. My men must plough in the wet whether they like it or no!'

Her acidity, and her saying 'My men', amused Ned. So he relapsed into a watchful silence again, and forbade his own men to comment on these curious agricultural methods in Dorcas's hearing.

Fortunately, the seasonal life at Kit's Hill was gathering momentum, and the labourers were too busy to mock the innovators. So the manuring of the field with ashes from Betty's kitchen fire passed almost unnoticed, though Betty's comments were scathing. Finally, on a drizzling May morning, they patiently sowed the few ounces of Norfolk seed by hand. One row was thinly planted four inches down, and a second row planted an inch from the surface, instead of casting seed far and wide. And they sowed it in ridge rows, six feet apart, and trod the ground hard when they had done.

'I can't make that out! said Ned, in spite of himself. 'You need pounds of seed, not ounces. And look at that space wasted, and look what a mort of work they've made for theirselves! Barebones'll be the right name for that!'

Yet he did not gainsay her, and by July the ridge rows were green with shoots. Under Dorcas's direction, Billy and Grandpa thinned and hoed them and kept the earth stirred about and between the plants, which came up a foot apart. They continued to hoe, and Dorcas saw how a horse might tread easily between the ridges, pulling his field-tool behind him, and do the work of both men in a short time.

But Ned asked if she had not heard the parable of the wheat and the tares. For all his labourers were laughing at this wanton expenditure of time and effort. Dorcas answered him somewhat coldly, and ordered her men to hoe on.

They hoed. The weeds which would have taken nourishment from the soil were persistently removed. The manure of ashes did not attract flies as raw dung would have done; and if the flies had come, then there were two seedlings instead of one to survive the attack.

In August, Billy was feeding the cows and pigs with lower leaves from the Swedish turnip plants, but nobody noticed particularly because all were engaged in the most neighbourly act of the rural year: harvesting.

Anxious, as ever, to keep up the good name of Howarth (and to make sure that there was food enough) Betty and her helpers baked, boiled and roasted for the mell-supper to be held in the great barn. Dorcas herself decorated the tables with sprays of flowers tied in ribbon, and sat in the place of honour at her husband's side when the last dressed sheaf was brought in to the accompaniment of much singing and merriment. The weather had kept fine, and an ox roasted in the lee of the barn for twelve hours until Ned cut the first slice.

Nothing was discussed that might offend anyone present, so religion and politics were forbidden. Harmless gossip and the intricacies of family trees were the favourite topics of conversation, and Dorcas marvelled at the knowledge of genealogy displayed by the women.

'Nay,' Judith Braithwaite would say, 'that were Mally Sidebottom's youngest by her third husband. She had five by owd Billy Sidebottom, and there's only Josiah left now (as rings the church bell). There was none by the second husband, Dick Glegg – all the Gleggs come from the other brother, Sam. And her first were a Burscough, and she had five by him and all, and Will Burscough is owd Billy Sidebottom's step-brother . . .'

As the ale disappeared, and stomachs and mellowness increased, some old fellow would sing a song far older than himself, and as they applauded him would say sombrely, 'Aye, well, that's right good of you, neighbours. But how many on us'll be here a year tonight?'

Then they would look round and fall silent, nodding, for life was brief and difficult, and who knew whether they would celebrate the next harvest at Kit's Hill, or which old faces would have disappeared, and what new ones come to take their place? Until Ned cried, 'What about another song, then? Let's have a merry 'un this time!'

The party would swing into a lighter mood, and clink their tankards boldly, for life must be lived with joy though known with sadness, and thanks be given to God that their bellies were full. And the parson sang louder than the rest, for his tenth share of the produce lay in his tithe-barn, and Ned was a good parishioner who paid up without a grumble.

September was the time for shows and sales and fairs, and everyone took a holiday. Then Sam Cartwright was seen without his stout linen smock and thick boots, striding alongside Ned like a gentleman farmer in waistcoat and breeches, to admire the result of his labours. And Ned bought a gilded heart of gingerbread and a knot of scarlet ribbons for Dorcas, and put his arms round her and gave her a full kiss on the mouth (as if she were his sweetheart instead of his wife, as Betty said sourly!).

'And when does thy harvest come home, my lass?' he enquired jokingly. 'I've seen t' leaves, but where's roots?'

'They shall be ready for the lifting in November, God willing,' she replied, smiling.

'God willing,' Ned echoed, for much depended on God at all times and in all seasons.

At Martinmas, two years after Ned had penned his proposal of marriage, every man at Kit's Hill turned out voluntarily to help young Billy and Grandpa Sidebottom with the Swedish turnips. Outwardly composed, inwardly quaking, Dorcas went with them: picking her way through the mud on pattens, a thick wool shawl under her wool cloak to keep off the raw cold.

The roots came out of the earth weighing between eight and twelve pounds apiece, and one monster turned Ned's scales at fifteen. They were dug up easily from the well-tilled ground, looking as clean as a washed clout, with no sign of rot. As row followed row, and they saw there was enough harvest from Owd Barebones to keep all the livestock all winter, the men whipped off their battered hats and gave a cheer for the missis. At her request they then gave a cheer for

Billy and Grandpa, who attempted to look as though such public acclaim were a daily event, and failed. Then they topped and tailed the swedes, and stored them as Dorcas (and Mr Jethro Tull) instructed: in cone-shaped heaps, with ten bushels to a cone, a thick layer of straw on the ground to protect them from mould, a three-inch covering of straw to keep them from the frost, and a round of turf to cap them. Later, many walked down to The Woolpack to boast, and fight, and deny that they had ever doubted the innovation – let alone laughed at it.

Surly but curious, Betty said that if folk could eat English turnips they could eat Swedish ones, and she actually boiled up a cauldron of these strange vegetables and mashed them with butter and salt. They emerged a pretty orange colour, and were sweet to taste, so that some preferred them to the English variety, and at any rate nobody was poisoned. The water in which they had been boiled was put in the pigs' mash. They noticed a slightly different flavour to the milk and butter, in consequence of feeding the swedes to cows, but no one could decide whether this was an improvement or not.

Later, at a propitious time, Dorcas produced her first farming account book* for Ned's information: so clearly set out and neatly printed that he could grasp it at first glance. The humble sum for labour made the profits seem vast, and there was the value of livestock saved besides.

'I can save still more,' said Dorcas smoothly, 'if you will lend me a horse for hoeing, and allow me to order (at my own expense) a hoe-plough to be made to these specifications by the blacksmith and wheelwright. For in one day, with a hoe-plough and one man's labour, you may save the work of two men in one week. Also the plough will delve deeper, and such delving keeps the soil moist and well-aired. I have made a drawing of such a machine, as best I could.'

Ned held it at arm's length, admiring and amused, for it

*Dorcas Howarth's farming accounts for Kit's Hill (1762–1800) are in Millbridge Record Office.

was a proper young lady's sketch with the shading nicely done, and no use to a craftsman as reference. So she fetched out her book and showed him the original, and he produced a very workmanlike sketch of his own, at which he seemed pleasantly surprised.

'Aye, well,' he murmured, as Dorcas praised him, 'it's not so bad, my lass. Any road, they'll follow it, and that's what matters.'

She was keeping the seed-drill for later, so did not mention it. Also, not being possessed of a mechanical turn of mind, she did not fully grasp how this machine would carve out its furrows and sow and cover the seeds as well. So she pondered while the hoe-plough was forged and whittled into being.

Kit's Hill turned on its dark side. Winter was coming, and Betty lit the rushlights earlier and earlier, and set the fire blazing up the chimney-back. Billy now stayed at the farm, being in such demand with Dorcas that he had carved a place for himself in the household. He played softly on his home-made reed-pipe. The sound was wistful and kind upon the ear, so that even Betty remarked upon the tune and asked its name.

'I make it up as I go along,' said Billy, and continued to flute his way through the little air.

'Then mind as you don't forget it!' Betty warned, unable to praise without scolding.

Nellie and Sallie were grating loaf sugar from a huge cone, and stoning dried fruit for the Christmas fare. Plum puddings would be boiling after breakfast tomorrow. Billy laid down his pipe and sneaked a handful of currants, winking at the two girls, who fell to giggling so that Betty turned round and upbraided them all.

'Here, mend this fire if you've nothing better to do!' she ordered Billy.

In her parlour, whose door was not shut except during times of personal conversation or personal crisis, Dorcas mused over Jethro Tull's principles of farming and observed the comedy in the kitchen. While Billy's back was turned

Nellie picked up his reed-pipe and deftly inserted half a dozen currants through the mouth-piece, laying it down again and looking at him innocently as he returned to his music. The harder he blew, and the redder his face became, the louder the girls laughed, until Betty thumped the pair of them, demanding what they were up to, while Billy rapped his flute on the table in vain.

'Here,' cried Betty, with rough kindness, for she was always fonder of men than women, 'give it me, wilta?' and she poked a knitting needle into the little cluster of currants until they parted, and then shook them through the holes onto the table.

Suddenly Dorcas saw how the seed-drill worked, and flew into the kitchen like a dark absorbed bird, and flew out into the night calling for Ned, without so much as donning her grey cloak.

'Eh, I don't know!' Betty muttered to herself, but Dorcas was not really an annoyance to her these days, and she grumbled out of habit rather than conviction.

In the flutter of his wife's explanations and comments Ned stood and listened carefully. Then bent to brush the caked mud from the mare's leg.

'So that's what you've been so quiet about?' he remarked. 'I thought as it were summat I'd done wrong! Well then, I can draw it up for thee, like the last, and they can get going on that one and all. We'st be keeping half Garth in work, the road we're going! And here's thy hoeing horse, my lass. She's above sixteen year old, but she'll plough a good furrow yet, won't you, my beauty? Eh, I do love a good horse. Sheep are nowt but a silly mob, when all's said and done. Not a bit of common sense among them. You can talk to a horse. This one had a twin sister as died. I remember them being foaled. My father weren't long dead, and I foaled them. Rosemary and Rue was their names, but Rosemary didn't last until nightfall. I skriked like a child when she died, and I were a man of twenty-five year!' Then with his unexpected quickness of perception he said, 'So what else have you got on your mind besides this here seed-drill? You canna want all this machinery for one poor field!'

She hesitated, for she could not bear to estrange him, but she had now chiselled a little niche for herself at Kit's Hill and felt that this was only a beginning.

'Oh, Ned, I should so like to borrow Scrat-acre for the turnips next spring, and then I can grow barley in Owd Barebones, for Mr Simmons of Norfolk wrote that he recommended barley in particular (though any crop benefits after turnips) and this means that Grandpa Sidebottom can still be employed as well as Billy, for otherwise he will lose his sixpence a day and he does so enjoy the work . . .'

'Here, here, half a minute,' cried Ned, outdistanced. 'What do you mean by *borrow*? I were asked to lend thee Owd Barebones for this year, and now you're planning barley for next year. If you put crops in two fields then I canna use neither of them until crops are over and done with. So say t' truth, Dorcas. You mean will I *give* you Scrat-acre as well as Owd Barebones. And I'd be surprised if that were all, my lass. You'll be asking me for Butter Meadow afore you're done!'

'Oh, no,' she cried, sorry and yet exasperated, 'that was not my intention.'

'Not yet,' he pondered, and stroked Rue's mane. 'I'll have to think about it. I'm not being sluthered quiet-like into summat as I might be sorry for in a few years' time. Besides, Scrat-acre comes by the stream, and though turnips like water they don't like drowning.'

'Indeed, you are right,' said Dorcas eagerly. 'The field needs draining.'

He left the horse alone then, and looked at her very straight and blue.

'Oh, you're a sharp one, my lass,' he murmured, almost to himself. 'Aye, I picked a sharp one when I picked you.'

She stood outfaced and lost, as though he had taken something important from her. He had seen this expression countless times in the past two years, and been saddened to think that in some way it sprang from their life together.

'Nay, I'm not quarrelling wi' thee, love,' he said, drawing her gently to him, 'only I'm not standing for no more petticoat government. I had enough of that wi' mother. Coming up on the sly . . .'

He meant secretively, but Dorcas translated the word as dishonourably, and cried, 'I am not sly!' incensed, and pulled away from him.

'Nay, but you don't let me know all that goes on!' said Ned, with truth. 'I know that you're book-learned and it don't worrit me. I'm proud on it. But don't use it agin me. Tell me what you've got in mind, and be straight about it. Don't wheedle me a bit here and a bit there, until I find myself up to the neck in muck.'

She drew further away, trembling with rage and dishonour.

'Would you have listened if I had spoke the whole truth?' she cried. 'I think not. Well, since you have a taste for it, I shall say on! I am not wanted here, except by you, and until now I was not useful. What am I to do with my life? I seek to help you, not to dominate. My mother helped my father in his parish, and her advice was considered always as that of a loving helpmeet. But I am to be judged by your mother, and thought to be a wilful and domineering woman. Very well, then, you have asked for my opinion and you shall have it, and I shall take myself and my twenty pounds a year elsewhere – before I die of the next infant!'

Ned's face changed colour at this, but she did not heed it.

'Farming was re-born some thirty years ago,' Dorcas continued, 'but here we do not know that. We pursue the old wavs. We waste our seed by sowing it broadcast, instead of planting it in rows. We do not plough the land properly, so it is not made light and airy. We do not hoe sufficiently, and weeds choke the plants we endeavour to grow. Your fallow fields are wasted fields. They could be sown in four-fold rotation of crops, each crop nourishing the next. Land such as Scrat-acre could and should be drained. All this squabbling over enclosures is foolish, except that the poor should in some way be protected. As long as animals continue to roam the same common pastures they will breed as they choose, and produce indifferent stock. Your habit of throwing raw dung upon the soil is monstrous, for it kills the seedlings and attracts the flies. It should be well ventilated and putrefied before it is spread, and in some cases vegetable dung is better.

'I have not yet had time enough, Edward Howarth, to pursue the study of agriculture closely, but I tell you this – I doubt if any Howarth has spent as much thought upon Kit's Hill as I have these two years. I did not come, as ignorant and silly creatures do, to change the house to suit myself only. I studied her, and sought to make her better than she was, yet much as she was. I thought how to marry myself here in truth, not in name only, and I found a way. The proof lies in those turnip heaps outside. But now you choose to block my way with pride and foolishness. You could be among the first farmers in England to try these new methods, and to succeed with them. But you would rather stay in a backwater than attempt to progress.'

Old Rue nosed round for her master's hand, and Dorcas fell silent.

Ned said, 'Have you done?'

She began to cry quietly to herself, turning away to the stable door.

He called out strongly, 'Have you done, then?'

She sobbed violently, and he held her very close, and chuckled until she laughed and cried at once and said she was sorry (but did not mean a word of it, as well he knew) and they were peaceable together again.

'I don't know,' said Ned, tranquil in his ill-lit stable. 'You fancy a woman. A lady I should say. And you get wed, and all hell lets loose on the pair of you, as if you'd done summat wicked. What dost think, my lass?'

She nodded, wiping her eyes on his neckerchief.

'Aye, since we got wed it's been one long blackthorn winter,' Ned mused. 'The time of year tells you that the world should be at rights wi' itself, and the blossom's out fit to make your heart ache, and then the bloody frost comes! It's been nowt but trouble and grief for us, my lass, but so long as we hold onto one another, and hold fast, we'st be grand.'

She had recovered sufficiently to lean against him, and to kiss his cheek in thanks.

'You can have Scrat-acre,' Ned continued. 'It's nowt but kingcups and quag! And if you're doing four-fold cropping then you'll want two more. I'll give thee Short Shrift and Striving, and they're a pair of buggers I can tell thee! But let's see what you can do wi' them. I'm never too proud to learn, but you must be straight wi' me and tell me what you've got in mind. I'll not be kissed and cheated, Dorcas!' She smiled and nodded, and kissed him again. 'I'll tell thee summat else. You'll have your failures, for there's not a farmer born as doesn't. And there'll be no miracles, sithee. But I'st stand by thee, and you must stand up for yourself agin me if I'm wrong. Give us another kiss, lass.'

They held each other close, and were quiet together for a minute or two. Then Dorcas said, 'My year of convalescence is nearly up, Ned. Shall you be glad of that?' Half-wistful, half-afraid.

But he was of the same mind, saying, 'I'm not so sure, for I might have lost thee. I'd sooner live like sister and brother than lose thee.'

'And yet we must not be faint-hearted in life,' said Dorcas resolutely. 'I wish to bear you children, and shall incur the risk gladly.'

'I'm feared,' said Ned honestly. 'I'd sooner have summat than nowt.'

'I should be glad for you, too, for it is hard on a husband,' she said quaintly, having no desire of her own to trouble her.

'I could get another wench,' he said, grinning, 'and save thee the worry! How about that?'

Her indignation was spontaneous, and made him laugh outright.

'Nay, there's no woman for me but thee, Dorcas. It'd be empty pleasure. And how about thee?' In his sudden fashion. 'Is there nowt in it for thee, barring a babby as might kill thee?'

She puzzled, saying, 'It pleases me to please you, Edward.'

He laughed again, but ruefully this time, knowing he had not reached her. Then, seeing her shiver, realising that she had been standing all this while in her house-gown, he began to scold her good-naturedly.

'Why, what are you doing out in t' cold without your mantle on? How many times have I told you? You could catch your death! What were they thinking of in t' kitchen to let you go? Kit's Hill's a long way from Millbridge, you know. Come on in the warm, and shape thee. I need eyes in the back of my head to keep up wi' thee . . .'

Rinderpest

Nine

Spring, 1763

So Ned's year of abstinence was ended and, though Dorcas had made up her mind to have more children, she privately thanked God as month followed month without a sign of pregnancy. Now in the spring of 1763 she cultivated her kitchen garden, rich in a variety of herbs and bordered with lavender, and wondered whether she might grow a lawn of camomile such as Phoebe maintained at the rectory. For the two young women had deep discussions about plants which could withstand the conditions at Kit's Hill, and there was much fussing in the rectory flower-room with roots and cuttings, and a great deal of wrapping in damp moss and newspaper to protect these future pioneers, which Dorcas carried home triumphantly in the trap. So she was musing on the prospect of hollyhocks, and planning for Billy to raise the dry stone-walling, when she saw her husband running and shouting and waving his arms like a boy.

'Jamie Blair's come. He's come after three long year, Dorcas. He must have bypassed us afore and gone into Yorkshire, else made his way down to London. Eh, we'll sit round t' fire tonight and hear tales such as you've never heard in all your born days. Come wi' me, lass!'

She came out onto the Drover's Road, delighted with Ned's delight, and slightly jealous that anyone but she should merit this attention. Through the Nick o' Garth a river of black sturdy cattle was flowing down towards Kit's Hill. On either side of the moving, bellowing column men flourished their whips and shouted, dogs barked and ran. At its head rode a long man on a tall horse, and by his side was a bonny lad upon a little pony.

Cupping his hands to his mouth, Ned hallooed a welcome until the crags rang again, and the man roared reply and flourished his woollen bonnet. Then he urged on his horse as fast as it could safely go, and the boy on the pony rode gamely after. Ned was off, yelling to Billy to open the gate into the Ha'penny Field, calling Betty to set the fire going up the chimney-back for they had company that night, and finally running to meet the closest friend he had. (So close that he reckoned him as a brother, and had not even confided his importance to Dorcas.)

Somewhat piqued, Dorcas stood regally in her sunbonnet and apron, and removed her garden gloves. Fascinated, in spite of her determination to stay aloof, she watched the two men laughing and clapping each other on the back and thought she had seldom seen such a pair of opposites. For Jamie Blair was a reckless fellow in his faded plaid, with a wild black beard and wild black hair, and a pair of deep blue eyes which had seen much of life and all of its weathers. Then she turned, sensing a presence at her side, and saw that the lad had ridden up softly lest he alarm her, and was observing this lady with her high nose and narrow black eyes, and waiting to make his obeisance whenever she should deign to notice him. He was a handsome boy, perhaps ten years old and big for his age, as dark as his father but gentle-faced. As soon as Dorcas looked at him he swept off his Scotch bonnet and held it to his chest in quite a foreign manner, and bowed his head.

'My name is Dugald Blair, madam,' he said in homage.

Dorcas enjoyed homage, so she was simultaneously struck by his courtesy and grace, and seized with an emotion she had not felt so far.

I should like to have a son, she thought. I should like to

have a son who rode upon his pony, and went with Ned on a tall horse.

'And I am Dorcas Howarth,' she replied, smiling, and put out her hand to welcome him.

The farm was now alive with people, for Ned was not the only one to love Jamie Blair. Betty ran out quite flushed, to exchange insults with the visitor under the guise of hospitality, and Billy was sitting excitedly atop of the gatepost in Ha'penny Field when the first cattle nosed in.

'This is my wife,' said Ned proudly, fetching the Scotsman to her, who was as courteous as his son had been, and bowed over her hand like any fine gentleman.

So that suddenly the spring day flashed alive, and Dorcas was laughing as she had not laughed in three years, crying, 'Come inside, Mr Blair. You are very welcome to Kit's Hill, and your son also!'

In the background another language was borne to her ears as the drovers counted their beasts into the field, and dropped a pebble in their pockets for every score that passed. 'Yan, teyan, tethera, lethera, dic, sezar, laizar, catra, horna, tic. Yan-a-tic, teyan-a-tic . . .'

They had all eaten hugely and well of mutton pies and fig pudding, and now Betty made up the kitchen fire again, and set the poker in it to mull the ale. The rank and file of drovers were in the barn, the cattle were grazing and manuring the Ha'penny Field, and the drove dogs curled into their dog pits.

'I must've looked out for thee a hundred times,' said Ned, drawing on his clay pipe, 'for we've had many a drover here, haven't we, Dorcas?' She nodded, smiling. 'But it were never the right one. Where in hell have you been, Jamie?'

The big kitchen could not have held one more listener if it had tried. Ned sat in the inglenook opposite his guest, but Dorcas had withdrawn her armchair from the glare of flames and light so that she might better watch without being observed. Servants and farm hands sat or stood where they might, and Tom and Billy fetched up a cask of matured ale, and Betty plunged the hissing poker into each tankard as Nellie and Sallie poured. Then all raised their drink and wished each other good health, and took a long sup and waited in respectful silence. For these were isolated people, bound to one place, ruled by the land and the seasons, while Jamie Blair followed the call of the road and saw the world and was more free in consequence.

The drover sat at his ease, puffing his long pipe, thrusting out a leg, staring into the heart of the fire. By the blue absorbed gleam beneath the eyelids, a shrewd onlooker would have guessed that this man was wholly self-aware and only waiting for the silence to last long enough. Then, when he judged it was time, Jamie stretched and sighed and took the stem of the pipe from between his lips, and looked round in apparent surprise at his audience.

'Aye, aye,' he began softly, 'we've travelled a ways this last three years, have we not, Dugald?' The lad stood behind his father, and peeped at Dorcas shyly. 'We have been down as far as the great city of London. We have been to more fairs in your English shires than you could count on all your hands. Twelve miles a day, when we were fortunate, and keeping a look-out for that wee clump of Scotch firs that meant we might put up for the night at some good farmer's house. Then on again, wi' a skirl of the pipes for the beasties that lag behind, and they step out grandly. Over the Border at Larriston Fells and down into Carlisle. Through Shap Thorn to Low Borrow Bridge and on to Kirby Lonsdale. Ingleton and Clapham to Long Preston and Hellifield. Aye, aye, an ancient route along the old line of the Galloway Gate. A slow pace of five to six miles a day, with many rests and short stages, and the Pennines glowering at you, that have names as wild as themselves! Scarth Nick! A devil of a cleft, a gey scairy place. Did I tell you about the time we drove to Brough Hill fair, and at the inns on the road there were fine pies the size of cart-wheels, with a rich wall of crust to them . . .?'

They all drew breath when he paused, and drank again and waited. This was the curtain-raiser to their evening's entertainment. The play would follow, and each would be drawn in to take part. Jamie Blair smoked and took counsel of the fiery coals, and spoke again. As was proper, he brought in the host as first player.

'Do you mind a near neighbour of yours, Mr Howarth, by name of John Robb of Craven? Why, he prevented one of the meetings by taking every last beast from me at Falkirk. Aye, in he walked wi' his bank notes, and out he walked wi' my herd! I think I may have one of his notes upon me now. Do you know him?'

'I know of him,' Ned replied, glad to make his contribution and retire, 'but I don't know him to speak to, no.'

'Ah, here it is. A pretty piece of paper. Would you care to see a Craven bank note, madam?'

So, correctly, Dorcas was the second player to be drawn into Jamie's drama, and she studied the paper with interest. A huge fat ox stood in front of a fine engraving of Bolton Abbey, the whole picture flanked by trees in full leaf.

'I thank you, Mr Blair,' said Dorcas, and passed it on to Ned.

Some day, she thought, we shall trade with bank notes. But her husband was not impressed by this innovation.

'I think nowt to it,' said Ned, as everyone craned forward to take a look. 'You could get this sopped in the rain, else tear it up by mistake. I'd sooner have a gold sovereign as I could try wi' my teeth.'

'But if you were dealing with so much as £30,000 at one time,' said Jamie, delighted by this unexpected lead, 'would you care to carry 30,000 gold sovereigns about your person?' The hum of exclamations checked him for a moment. 'Aye, £30,000, my good friends. Ordinary folk such as ourselves are lucky to save a shilling in a stocking, or slip a piece of siller under the mattress or behind a loose brick in the wall. No man thinks it worth his while to rob us! But what shall a man do that is as rich as John Robb of Craven? He'll lie awake o' nights, wi' his gun cocked at the ready, will he not? And his trunk full of sovereigns is therefore a great burden to an honest man, is it not?'

'Tha'rt right!' they cried, sorry for the woes of honest John Robb of Craven.

'But what can he do in these modern times? He can take his trunk full of sovereigns to a Bank, and receive a note of exchange, and put it safely in his pocket!'

'What if somebody picks his pocket?' said Ned, always practical.

'It is easier to hide a small thing than a great one,' said Jamie, knowing all answers. 'It is simpler to exchange notes than to carry gold. I see the number of Banks growing as I travel the length and breadth of England. I tell you what else is growing, my friends – the wealth of this country. And do you know why? Because of the Turnpike Trusts! May God forgive me, as a drover, for saying so, and dinna tell my men out there that I so much as breathed a word of it. For I loathe being taxed for every beastie I fetch through the turnpike, and my hand goes slowly, slowly,' here he illustrated the action so comically that they all laughed aloud, 'slowly into my breeches pocket to pay that wee bit tax, for the drovers have trod their own ways for hundreds (and maybe thousands) of years, and why should we be pushed aside by their damned roads? That's my mind spoken as a drover. But as a thinking man – and there's time to think along the way, I can tell you – I know that good roads mean better transport and faster travel. In another few years they'll be good enough for the drovers to use in winter, and then our months of hand-to-mouth living become work – and work becomes wealth!'

Now he stopped and drank long and heartily, and smoked his pipe and waited for a cue from some member of the company. Young Billy, clearing his throat, received a frown from Betty and a smile from Dorcas. He put trust in the smile.

'If I'm speaking out of turn, sir, I beg pardon, but has

nobody told you as we kept all our animals alive and fed through t' winter? I thought, being a travelling gentleman, as you might like to tell a tale about that to somebody. For I never heard of it afore. It were our missis here, as thought of it, and me and Grandpa did the Swedish turnips . . .' Then he sat down, rather red and sheepish at his eloquence.

'Indeed, indeed, Billy. It is Billy, is it not, though you have grown a foot since we last met! I have heard something of this from Mr Howarth, but Kit's Hill is not the first to follow these new methods of husbandry – though it is among the first. Dr John Rutherford of Melrose planted turnips in 1747, and the oxen fed upon them grew so big that the people were afraid to eat the beef! But I prophesy that before the end of this century only the most backward farms will slaughter and salt down their beasts in the autumn. Aye, laddie, stay wi' your master and mistress. Kit's Hill shall grow rich on book-learning and good husbandry, and become one of the wonders of this wondrous Age!'

He spoke with the tongue of a story-teller, but Tom Cartwright took his rhetoric for truth.

'Is that what you'll say to other folk, sir?' he asked hopefully. 'When you sit by their fire of an evening shall you talk of Kit's Hill?'

Then they all spoke at once, looking upon one another with new eyes, for they might become part of a story told by Jamie Blair in places unknown to them and far away.

'It'd only be fair to say as Mrs Howarth learned it from a book,' Nellie ventured, from behind her mistress's chair.

'Aye, Jamie, tell them about our Dorcas,' Ned cried, flushing with pride and pleasure, 'for there isn't another lass like her in King George's England, and mention our Betty's gingerbread and all!'

Then Jamie Blair was swamped by further suggestions, each one present now having some task or animal precious to him that must come into this tale. And the drover listened, smiling, for their lives were small and poor and had suddenly been exalted by a chance remark.

'I shall call this story *The Book Farm*!' he announced, and everyone roared again, delighted. 'Come, my bonnie lassie!' Smacking Betty's broad rump. 'Let us drink to the *Book Farm*! For the new spirit that is going to make England great is abroad even here, even in this quiet place. And give me a kiss with the ale, Betty, for I have been pining for you these three years!'

'Be off wi' you!' shrieked Betty, scuffling just enough to be seemly, and not sufficiently to prevent him from planting a hearty kiss on her red cheek.

'Aye,' Jamie continued, when they had all settled down again, 'there will be roads from village to village, instead of mud-tracks, and that means trade. Look how Millbridge has flourished since they made the turnpike road from Keighley to Kendal. Your packman will not be stumbling down a lane with one miserable donkey and two bundles of goods. He will drive a wagon full of fineries for the ladies, and call at Christmas as well as mid-summer. All the year round. And he will have to sell as cheap as he can, for good roads mean many choices. Betty, if you can buy what you want at Preston – aye, Preston I said!' As they murmured astonishment, and Betty looked proud for she never went further than Garth. 'If, I say, you can buy at Preston why should you make do wi' Johnnie Packman?'

'Well, it'll be a while afore they put a road down from t' Nick to Garth', I can tell thee!' said Ned, puffing away on his clay pipe, enjoying himself.

'But if you breed more and better sheep, it may be worth putting down a road of your own,' said Jamie. 'Oh, this is a great time to be born. We stand upon the threshold of miracles. Have I told you of this thing called electricity? Why, I saw a man at a fair ignite brandy by means of shooting a spark from his finger. And they have rods that set your hand a-tingle when you touch them, and they say this shock has curative powers.'

'Well, I'm blessed,' said Ned, and smoked in silence, brow furrowed.

'But your lady knows all these things, and is gracious enough to let Jamie Blair babble of them at her fireside!' Jamie finished, smiling.

They all stared at Dorcas, who sat composed but pink, for she had no wish to be brought out.

'I do assure you, sir,' said Dorcas, 'that though I may have heard something of these matters I have not had them so well explained before. Indeed, my view now seems a narrow one. It is as though I had been peeping through a chink in the door, and then someone threw it open so that I saw the whole instead of the part.'

This polished reply, reminiscent of her verbal matches with Walter Jarrett, caused her servants to nod among themselves. She was doing well tonight.

'But I am not so fortunate as these good people,' Dorcas continued, smiling, 'for they have heard tales of your journeys and I have not, and I know they will be glad to hear them again – as I shall be to hear them for the first time – and to learn from you, sir, with such ease and pleasure that the hours pass unnoticed!' She inclined her head in thanks, and he got up and made a bow. A gleam of understanding passed between them. 'Betty, will you please to pass the ale again? Nellie and Sallie, please to help Betty.'

'I have never driven turkeys,' Jamie Blair began, 'but I knew a man that did, and he told me they roosted in the trees at night along with other birds! Now geese drive very well, though their legs are short, and I have seen 20,000 geese brought to a Michaelmas Goose-fair, with the fresh birds driving the weary ones forward . . .'

He knew that Dorcas had subtly forbidden him to draw her out, and from time to time he glanced at her with interest, but she was always far off, gazing at the flames with bright dark eyes. So he spoke of ferrying cattle across high-running rivers on rafts made of logs, and the bullock boats that sailed between Scotland and Ireland, and the great journeys down into the South of England, and the call of the road. They listened, rapt and intent, travelling with him, until at last he tapped the ashes from his pipe and laid it on its side to show that story-telling was done and the night late. Then they yawned and stretched, and came forward one by one to shake him by the hand and thank him, for he would be gone by first light. Last of all came Ned and Dorcas, and stood for a few minutes more, speaking of this and that, until the girls lit the candles and showed the company to bed.

During the night the cattle had become separated while grazing, and the morning exit from the field had further estranged regular companions, so that they moved in a distraught tide and bellowed as they sought their families. Jamie and Dugald were mounted, eating a hunk of bread and bacon as they waited for order to come from chaos. Ned strode out, followed by his servants, and Dorcas stood in the doorway to watch.

'Well, don't be so bloody long next time, Jamie!' Ned cautioned, and wrung his hand and Dugald's hand. 'Take care, wilta?'

Then Dorcas came forward to add her thanks and good wishes, and to hope they would meet again soon. This morning they were all drained of energy, after the excitement and lateness of the night before. An indefinable sadness hung over the parting.

'You might come back this way?' Ned suggested.

'All things are possible,' said Jamie Blair. 'I shall not stay away for want of a welcome. Then we shall travel fast and light to Dumfriesshire, for after seeing many towns it's good to return home. Are we ready, then?' to one rough fellow in a shabby plaid. Receiving assent, he cried, 'God bless you, Ned. We'll be off!'

The river of cattle was flowing strong and smooth again. Dogs trotted yelping at its side. Drovers shouted and flourished their whips. At its head Jamie and Dugald rode out proudly. The people of Kit's Hill stood in silence, watching the caravan become small, hearing its sounds grow faint. Then Betty spoke with the voice of a Cassandra.

'Summat's gone and summat's coming,' she said soberly.

Her prophecy was to be remembered in the weeks and months ahead. For cattle plague, which had troubled many parts of the country the previous year, was this moment being trodden into the heart of the Wyndendale Valley. Jamie Blair's beasts, free of taint when he started from Rowanburn, had picked up the disease called rinderpest, and were leaving a trail of future devastation in their wake.

On Easter Sunday the first casualties were given out from the pulpit of Garth church, and Tom Redfern put every member of his congregation on oath to report all sick animals to the Constable or Churchwarden. He reminded them of the distemper which had raged throughout the county sixteen years before, when tenants in the Pendle district had been unable to pay rent because of their losses. He bade them think of others, especially the old and feeble and very young, so that none should starve while there was bread to share. (Here he looked hard at the yeomen farmers and their families, who could live upon their resources longer than poor widow women.) Finally, putting them under pain of his wrath if they ignored his orders, he dismissed them and went home to see if his own horned beasts were still healthy.

But this was a poor village, and what owner would report the sickness of any animal while there was hope of healing? The family cow, who provided what little milk they were likely to drink, who pulled a home-made plough through their strip of land, who lodged so close to them, was part of the household and as hungry and needy. Would they not pour homely remedies down her throat by means of a horn? (Urine mixed with a handful of hens' dung. Tar water. Ale boiled with soap and hartshorn drops. Rhubarb and weak gruel.) Even when these failed, and they must report her death and be counselled to bury the animal entirely, would they not try to save her hide? Oh, it were all very well for Parson to talk! He took his tithe from t' Howarths and Braithwaites and Sowerbutts and Wharmbys and Tunstalls, he did. Parson was well off, down here and up there! Bugger t' parson!

In June they sang psalms and asked mercy in Garth church, but the plague swept through the parish and decimated the ruminants.

In August Ned Howarth held a meeting of the fell farmers at Kit's Hill, and his neighbours came to listen to him because any voice in this terror was welcome.

All the women retired from the kitchen, leaving the five men to pour their own ale, and sat with Dorcas in the parlour. She kept the door slightly open so that they might hear the conversation.

'It's all or nowt,' said Ned bluntly. 'Either the five of us stick together or fall out. You can take your pick. Garth village is damned near done for, but up here we stand a chance and we can help them later on. This here disease, rinderpest, as you know,' though they did not, but Dorcas had thought it politic that he should say so, 'is like the croup and the runs in one lot. It gets their lungs and their bowels, and wherever they've trod or coughed or shit or spit, it spreads. So a dog running across our Ha'penny Field is carrying it. A cow going down the lane is carrying it. Now we're told by Parson, and he talks for the King in a manner of speaking, we're told what to do. But no bugger is doing it. That's why we'll all be on t' Parish afore Christmas, if we don't watch out!

'From now on, Kit's Hill is out of bounds to any beast of any sort from anywhere else. I can't speak plainer than that. Job Braithwaite!' The old man lifted his head and looked Ned in the eye. 'Job Braithwaite, you know what you mean to me and mine as friend and neighbour, don't you?' The old man nodded solemnly. 'Job Braithwaite,' said Ned sternly, 'if your favourite dog so much as steps on my land I'st shoot his bloody head off!'

Job's eyes flashed, and he began to rise from his chair. The company was in an uproar. Ned waved his arms for silence, and gave his old neighbour a reassuring nod. Then filled the jug from his cask of good ale, and poured out another round of drinks.

'*That's* what I'm talking about,' he continued peaceably, as they calmed down. 'It's going to be bloody hard, and if we don't stick together there'll be more trouble than cattle plague on Garth fells. Now, are we divided or do we stand?'

One by one they raised their hands in assent. Job Braithwaite of Windygate, Harry Sowerbutt of Long Hay, Simon Wharmby of Foxholes, Rob Tunstall of Shap Fold.

'Right,' said Ned, 'now I'll tell you what we're going to do here. All the animals that's left are being put through the smoke. I should advise you to do t' same. As soon as a beast starts sickening, that beast is killed stone-dead wi' a pole-axe so as the blood don't seep its sickness into t' ground. They say as you should bury the beast in a deep pit, and keep nor hair nor hide of it, and slash the hide so as it canna be dug up again and sold. The men as kill and bury the beast have their clothes smoked clean again. The stalls'll be smoked clean. The litter'll be burned. The feeding troughs'll be scrubbed out. But we're going further than that here, though you please yourselves. We're burning our dead beasts, burning them to ash that canna harm nothing and nobody. There's one more thing. We shall have to cut us-selves off from Garth until Parson gives us notice that the disease has gone.'

They all began to murmur again, and he put up his hand for silence.

'It makes sense,' said Ned. 'Every lane and track down to Garth must hold the disease, and Garth is full of it. That goes for all the other places between here and Millbridge – and there's nowt to go to Millbridge for, because they've shut the market. Tomorrow, with your good will' (he had got this phrase from Dorcas, and it sounded faintly archaic in his plain speech) 'I'll go down to Parson Redfern wi' this message from all of us. Then we hold off, and hold fast. What do you think to that?'

They did not like it, but could offer no alternative. Finally, Job Braithwaite, as senior spokesman, said his piece. He was as small and gnarled as one of the blown trees on Windygate, and as hardy.

'Well, Ned hasn't minced his words. No more did his mother and father. So we all know where we stand. I don't know as I'm book-learned enough to argue wi' him,' which was a sly dig at Dorcas, 'but I can say this much. I never knowed a beast as sickened to get better. So we may as well pole-axe them straight off, afore they infect t'others. Right, Ned,' facing him doughtily, 'I'll say the same to thee. If *thy* beast sets foot on my land from now on, I'll shoot its bloody head off!' As they all laughed and cheered, though ruefully, he added, 'Up here we're a law on us own. If what Ned says is right, and I don't doubt it, then we must keep the King's Law on us own, too. And, like he says, when rinderpest is done we'll help them in Garth – if there's owt left of us!'

So the motion was carried unanimously, and its instigator sat quietly in her parlour, nose a little higher than usual, eyes a fraction brighter.

Then the slaughter began, and no animal was spared once it faltered. The farmers took turns to guard the Drovers' Road, the tracks and footpaths, armed with guns. Any dog that ran astray on the fells ran there for the last time. The carcasses were burned, or buried in great pits, and those who killed and burned and buried walked through a smoke made of wet straw that was fired. They smoked the cowsheds and drove the cattle through them. And they kept faith with the King, the Parson, and themselves.

All through the autumn, the stricken village saw fires upon the fells, and marvelled at the destruction. Yet out of the death came a little life, and when the year reached its end the five farmers were counting their stock, and sharing breeders and stud so that they might begin again.

On a November evening, Dorcas sat in her parlour and cast up her accounts, and Ned sat by her smoking his pipe and thinking. Through the open door they could hear Betty bullying her maids into making Christmas puddings, while Billy played upon his wooden flute.

'I had not thought,' said Dorcas with dry humour, 'that I

should ever welcome the sound of Betty scolding! But I have learned since Easter that when she grumbles she is content. It is entirely the other way with me! By the by, we have done pretty well with the swedes and barley, but we shall not feel the benefit this year. The rinderpest has thrown out all our reckonings.'

Ned removed his pipe to say, 'Aye, my lass, but we've got enough to see us through. And when they come asking at the door we canna say no. It'd gripe my belly to think of a child going hungry while I had a turnip to give. Think on, and thank God, Dorcas.'

She laid down her quill, and meditated on his quiet face.

'Well, Ned,' she said briskly, 'as Betty prophesied, summat's gone and summat's coming.'

'Oh aye? What are you up to now, my lass? I'st give up farming and let thee wear t' breeches, I'm thinking!'

'I am with child again,' she said, laughing and crying at once, 'and I am not afraid, Ned. I am not one morsel afraid. Is that not wonderful?'

He could only say, 'Nay, lass. I never!' in bemused delight, while she clasped him round the neck and wept and smiled, and his pipe fell on the floor and broke. 'Nay, Dorcas. Well, I never!'

Th' Childer

Ten

Midsummer 1764

'My niece grows very fine, sir,' cried Miss Wilde to old Dr Standish, as he listened to her sound heart. 'I hear she has engaged your son as a midwife. Not an occupation, I should have thought, for a gentleman. Nor the choice of a lady. But then she was always headstrong and wayward. What a merciful thing that your wife (dear gentle soul, how I did love her!) was spared the knowledge of your son's peculiarity!'

Having pressed the good man on a sensitive spot she waited for an answer. Moneymakers were welcome in Millbridge, but the eccentric could only bring dishonour upon their relatives, and Matthew Standish made his father wince.

'Well, well, we must move with the times,' the old man said, with heightened colour. 'These young folk have notions of their own, dear lady, and perhaps they might be right. How should we know?'

'Fiddlesticks,' cried Miss Wilde. 'It is up to you and to me to prevent them from making fools of themselves. Tell me, how is poor Miss Spencer? When you bury her at last it will not be for want of your pills and draughts!'

'Poor lady,' Dr Standish murmured, 'what a martyr she is to science!' So she was, but how else could she have gained attention? 'Well, well, well.'

'And how am *I*, sir?' Miss Wilde demanded with some asperity. 'For I have not called you here to gossip about your other patients!'

'Dear lady,' said Dr Standish, and though his dignity might often be endangered his income would never fail, for he had such a manner. 'Dear lady, how shall I describe the condition of one who has the valiant heart of a Queen, and the delicate stomach of an Infant? Nothing will conquer you, ma'am, save that which conquers us all in the end. I feel that a light diet for a few days, and plenty of rest . . . what did you say you ate, dear lady?'

'Six pickled herrings,' said Miss Wilde shortly, because she could see them receding from her in the future, and was very cross in consequence.

Dr Standish spread his hands in regret, almost in disbelief that she should be vanquished by these sea monsters.

'Well, well,' he murmured, 'the delicate stomach of an Infant . . .'

Old sow, he thought. Greedy, guzzling, mean old sow of a woman. And he took his guinea with a sigh, for he knew that poor Miss Spencer would have him out of his bed in the early hours of the morning because he had visited at Thornton House.

'One moment, sir,' cried Miss Wilde, who had not yet her guinea's-worth. 'Is my niece's life in danger that she engages your son?'

'Mrs Howarth most certainly had an exceedingly difficult and perilous first birth, and of course the poor infant died, ma'am . . .'

'But really it is that your son and my niece have outlandish notions of midwifery, is it not?' He inclined his head regretfully. 'I hear he has inoculated her against the smallpox, too. And others. Though they are keeping pretty quiet about it, and I am not surprised for I never heard of such a thing. I told Mr Jarrett the other day, and said he should preach against it, but he has not done so. And Miss Jarrett purposes to visit my niece at Kit's Hill now, though she has behaved in a very proper fashion so far.'

'Parish matters, perhaps, my dear ma'am?' Hopefully. 'A

polite call?'

'Oh, parish stuff!' cried Miss Wilde angrily. 'Nobody in their right mind calls at Kit's Hill. It is ten miles off and will take a day to get there and back. I dare say she will even stay the night! Do not attempt to conceal things from me. I know that Dorcas has visited at the rectory.'

She brooded over her wrongs.

'The human heart and spirit demand medicine too, dear ma'am,' Dr Standish ventured. 'You are too much alone. Your pleasant companion . . .?'

'Sent about her business!' said Miss Wilde with infinite satisfaction.

'You would not consider another pet, perhaps? A cat, for instance?'

'Some can be faithful to memory, sir,' said Miss Wilde, and her hard eyes moistened for a moment, remembering Walpole.

'Well, well, well,' said Dr Standish, awaiting release.

She rang the bell for Agnes. She had bought a modicum of time and attention, and both were begrudged though paid for in gold. There was only one atom of satisfaction left to her.

'Oh, Agnes,' she cried, as the middle-aged maid returned from showing the doctor out, 'Agnes, Dr Standish forbids us to eat pickled herring in the future. He informs me that they are particularly unwholesome.'

'They didn't hurt me,' said Agnes, somewhat pitifully, for she had relished her two with a slice of wheaten bread and butter.

'That is because you have a more robust constitution than me. We buy no more herrings, mind!'

'Very well, ma'am,' said Agnes sadly.

She carried secret consolation back to the kitchen with her. Old Dr Standish had promised she should be first to hear when Miss Dorcas was safely delivered, and only yesterday Miss Jarrett had most kindly borne away a little crocheted cap for the baby.

Phoebe Jarrett could not think how this change had come

about, but one morning in June she had said to her father at breakfast, 'I believe I should visit Dorcas, Papa, for she cannot come to Millbridge for a while!' And he had replied in his jocular fashion, 'Then you had best stay overnight, my love, since it is quite a journey and you will have a deal of news to exchange!' So she had entrusted a message to Ned, who was coming to market alone at this stage in his wife's pregnancy, and a few days later received her friend's joyful reply.

. . . and I shall send Billy for you with the Trap. I Beg you not to Consider returning the Same Day, but to stay for At Least one night, if your Father can spare you. Kit's Hill is uncommonly Elegant these days, and the Guest Room overlooks my Flower Garden. Oh when I think of All I have to Shew you since you Last came here I am quite Transported! Dearest Phoebe, Best of Friends! . . .

So that she felt ashamed, and wept a little as she packed her nightgown. Then she remembered the glory of early strawberries, and wiped her eyes and went out to pick them. Then there was Agnes's cap to pack, and two small gowns which she had thread-worked herself, and an ivory ring (which had been hers) for the baby to cut its teeth on, and altogether not enough time to prepare for such an excursion as this promised to be.

Sharp at nine o'clock Billy drove smartly up to the door of the rectory, and was puzzled where to bestow all Miss Jarrett's belongings. For gifts and remembrances had mounted, as news of her visit winged round Millbridge, and there were many who sent messages of goodwill. They would not have uttered Dorcas's name three years ago, and still would not approach Ned, but Miss Jarrett seemed a suitable intermediary and time softened prejudices.

The summer morning was fine and cool and blue, and Billy bowled along at a spanking pace through Flawnes Green, Brigge House, Thornley, Whinfold, Childwell, Medlar, Coldcote and Garth. An extra flick of the whip as they turned up the track so that the horse should not falter. Then higher and higher into the Pennines until the whole of the Wyndendale Valley lay below them, and the river wound its silver ribbon round toy villages all the way to Millbridge.

Kit's Hill was sunning herself in the pleasant air, with smoke spiralling from her kitchen chimney. Sheep were grazing in a long scatter almost up to Scarth Nick, and green turnip tops waved in the home fields, rank upon hoed rank. Grandpa Sidebottom now lay in Garth churchyard, and Billy headed Dorcas's men. He pointed out one of his deputies to Phoebe with the handle of his whip, and she saw young Jacob Eccles leading horse and hoe-plough between the swedes.

A shout from the yard, as Tom Cartwright saw the trap jogging up the hill, brought Dorcas to the back door. She was clad in a loose wrapper and great with child, but her muslin cap and dress were bright with cherry ribbons; and though her eyes had that curiously vulnerable look of pregnant women her face was serene. There were tears, of course, as the two friends clasped and kissed, and then laughed at their own foolishness. There were introductions all over again to Betty (now in a mild mood since her mistress was in check). Then Nellie came forward and dropped a curtsey (a tall slim girl of fourteen, very proud of her pleated mob cap and white apron), followed by Sallie (smaller and shyer, but pert enough when Betty was absent). An inspection of the guest room, after Phoebe had availed herself of Dorcas's close-stool, brought forth the compliment of 'most elegant, most convenient', and Dorcas promised that she should smell the night-scented stock through the open window when she retired. A survey of the farmhouse occasioned such a volley of praises, and such a throwing up of eyes and hands, that Dorcas shed a few more happy tears. Then Nellie poured tea beautifully in the little parlour, and served up a fresh batch of Betty's gingerbread, very brown and crisp on a china plate.

Every gift was unwrapped and examined, every message repeated and talked over, until noon. The day was growing hot and neither of the ladies could contemplate anything to eat but bread and butter, but Betty dished up pork pie and pickles for the house-folk and sent the same to the fields where the men worked. Ned appeared briefly but courteously, to welcome Miss Jarrett and see how his wife did (and Phoebe observed that he was very tender with Dorcas, and seemed much improved in his manner!). Then he returned, for at this time of year they were rounding up and dipping some three hundred sheep, and the men worked until they could no longer see their hands before their faces.

The kitchen garden caused Phoebe to unpack several small moist parcels, and to plant their contents under Dorcas's direction. It was too far to walk to the four fields, which were cropping turnips, barley, bearded wheat, red clover and rye grass, but Mr Tull's pupil pointed them out with pride. Then the ladies ate Millbridge strawberries for tea, with sugar and cream (and Betty and Nellie and Sallie had one apiece to taste), and more bread and butter and some watercresses from the stream. After which Dorcas had to rest on her day-couch and struggle with indigestion as they talked, until Phoebe noticed her pallor and asked if she wished to retire.

'It is the strawberries, I believe,' said Dorcas, reluctant to break the conversation. 'I have such a cramp. Come, let us walk a little together. The early evening is warm and pleasant. We shall not take harm, but I would advise a shawl.'

She moved awkwardly because of her burden, and Phoebe slipped a sturdy little arm round her to assist. As her feet touched the floor Dorcas cried out in surprise and fear. 'Oh, the waters have broke!' And as Phoebe stared uncomprehending, 'Oh, fetch Dr Standish as fast as you can. Send Billy on a good horse, and help me upstairs if you please. Oh, this was not expected for at least a fortnight!'

The little commotion brought Betty and the girls to the parlour door. Whereupon Betty issued her own orders, which did not so much countermand those of her mistress as run alongside them and confuse the listeners.

'Nellie, whip your apron off and go for Cissie Pycroft! Sallie, put that big iron kettle on t' fire and set the bellows under it! Miss Jorrock,' to poor Phoebe, who was standing bewildered with her arm about her friend, 'you sit yourself down. You don't want to get yourself upset wi' summat like this, being a maiden lady. I know what to do . . .'

'Should I fetch Mr Howarth, and all, Miss Ackroyd?' Nellie asked, cap and apron in hand, ready to run anywhere.

'No, you do not,' cried Betty. 'I had enough trouble wi' him last time. We want no men under us feet. Thank God there's plenty of daylight left. We can get the missis well on afore they come pawming and fretting. Off wi' you!'

Dorcas straightened herself slowly, saying, 'I thought it was the strawberries, and did not like to say so because they were such a delicacy. I must have been in labour these two hours, and I do not think it will be very long. Betty!' For she had learned to ignore the housekeeper's orders rather than argue with them, 'Betty, please to send Billy on a good horse to Dr Standish, and if Mrs Pycroft comes then that is well enough. Phoebe, I beg you, please to help me upstairs.' Then she paused, and hung her head and communed with the pain for a long minute while they waited in awed silence. They were all women, and though they might never bear a child, or might not bear one for years hence, they comprehended instinctively that they were ministers to a great mystery. 'I had forgot what it was like,' said Dorcas steadily, 'but it is very near. Phoebe and Betty, if you please!'

'Get running!' said Betty to the girls, and took Dorcas's elbow with as much tenderness as she could. 'You heard what we said? Doctor and Cissie!'

Phoebe supported her friend on the other side, and patted her hand, trembling. Before they were halfway up the oak stairs they heard Billy clattering out of the yard on Wildfire, with Nellie holding on behind. The sound of the bucket being lowered into the well proclaimed that Sallie was drawing enough water to furnish a nurseryful of babies. The three women moved slowly on, pausing reverently for the pains, which Dorcas received with a concentrated frown, and a gasp as they passed their peak. Carefully they removed her clothes, keeping their faces averted as much as possible so as not to embarrass each other or Dorcas, and slipped an old cotton nightgown over her head. Then Phoebe sat with her, handfast, while Betty prepared the bed for the birth.

'Are you afraid, Phoebe?' Dorcas asked gently. 'Betty will stay with me if you would rather sit in the parlour. I do not fear anything. It is strangely familiar now, and not as hard as last time.'

'Aye, I'll stop wi' her,' said Betty cheerfully, for drama brought out the best in her. 'I've watched over more births and deaths than you've eaten milk puddings, I'll be bound, Miss Jorrock!'

'I shall not leave my friend,' said Phoebe with dignity, for her principles stood firm whatever the opposition might threaten, 'and my name is Jarrett, if you please!'

A laugh was turned by pain into a sob, as Dorcas registered the conversation. Then she allowed them to heave her slowly into the bed.

'Pray do not quarrel,' she entreated. 'We have work enough to do, and need each other's help for that.'

There was a brief and tranquil space, as Betty and Phoebe looked ashamed and then smiled, and Dorcas smiled back.

'Sallie'll set his little clothes out,' said Betty graciously. 'I know you'd sooner she did it than me. Else Miss Jarracks might like to do it while I lay the fire. We wasn't expecting this for a week or two. Now are you all right, Mrs Howarth?'

This was the first time she had addressed Dorcas by her married name, for Mrs Hetty had reigned supreme until then.

'I am pretty well for the moment,' said Dorcas, pleasantly surprised, 'but when the pains begin again I shall need you, for I think the infant will be born before the doctor can reach us.'

'Then I'll lay t' fire!' said Betty, and looked through the window, without much hope, for signs of Nellie and Cissie Pycroft making their way up the track on foot; and hurried downstairs.

Glancing now and again at Dorcas, Phoebe shook out the

little garments and smoothed them and laid them on the chair by the fireplace, where the new mother might see them and take courage for her trial.

'Phoebe,' said Dorcas suddenly, 'it has begun again. Sit by me, and hold my hand!' Then she cried, 'Oh, God have mercy!' and bore down upon the pain.

Phoebe's heart hammered, but she wiped the sweat from Dorcas's face and encouraged her as best she could, afterwards surreptitiously rubbing her own crushed fingers.

'On the mantel-shelf,' said Dorcas, comprehending, drawing breath, 'there is a comfort stone. Will you put it in my grip, if you please? And when the next pain comes I will clutch that instead. But place your hand upon my arm, and then I know that you are with me. I thank you. The stone is very cool. My aunt sent it to me, but I was too far gone to use it before. How is she?'

'I fear she is lonely,' Phoebe ventured, 'but Papa says she will not be helped, and it is her own doing.'

'I have been lonely,' said Dorcas, looking a long way back. 'It is not easy. I have wrote to her, but she did not reply.'

'Forgive me,' cried Phoebe, weeping. 'I have been cold and unkind to you and Mr Howarth. I should not have judged. You were better and wiser than I!'

'A brief misunderstanding,' said Dorcas, gracious with those three bitter years. Then she bore down on the pain again, crying, 'Oh, I shall die!'

Then Sallie was there with a kettle of hot water, and Betty scattered her faggots on the hearth, exclaiming, 'You'd best get out, the pair of you, because we shan't be laiking long!' and turned back the covers.

But they stayed, though Sallie was only thirteen, and Phoebe very frightened, and helped Betty as much as they could.

Dorcas did not trouble them long. A dark crown appeared between her legs, then an ancient face screwed up with puzzlement, and lastly in one glorious bound the child came forth trailing a silver cord, and yelled as he hit the bed.

'Oh missis,' cried Sally, 'it's a lad, missis!'

Phoebe, hands over mouth, was crying, 'Oh, how terrible, and how beautiful. How terrible and how beautiful.'

But Betty, red and satisfied, said, 'I've fetched up the kitchen knife and a length of twine, for that's all I've ever seen Cissie Pycroft use!' Which made them all laugh, though Phoebe broke down shortly afterwards with the excitement, and had to be assisted from the room.

So the experts were not needed after all. Mrs Pycroft arrived in time to join the celebrations. But, on hearing that Dr Standish was expected, resolutely declined to do more than wish everyone well: such was the fear he had instilled in her superstitious soul. He rode into the yard about nine o'clock, congratulated Betty, pronounced mother and child to be in excellent health, and stitched up the inevitable birth wound (whereat Dorcas gasped again, but was too happy to mind much). Then Kit's Hill went mad, for a new line had begun. The infant's every cry was greeted like a lion's roar, and praised to the slates on the roof and the sheepbones which pegged them there.

Recovering, finding herself among the legendary ushers of this great occasion, Phoebe plucked up sufficient courage to bid Dr Standish call at the rectory on his way back, and inform her father that she should not be home for a few days. After which she prayed in her room, but finding herself unrepentant went back to the junketing, and drank such a glassful of Hetty Howarth's elderberry wine (now a very respectable vintage indeed) that she fell asleep on Dorcas's day-bed in the parlour, and was forgotten until next morning (when she had such a headache!).

'*He's* going to be a topsy-turvy one!' Betty shouted, as she fetched out the Groaning Cake. 'He turned me upsides-down I can tell you! I'd clean forgot about the supper wi' him coming that quick. (Nellie, cut Mrs Wharmby a slice of cake.) First I knew were Eli Sidebottom at kitchen door. "Wheer's victuals?" he said. Eh, he's ignorant, he is, you'd never think he were Billy's uncle. (Sallie, fetch that jug of ale here and pour a sup for Mrs Sowerbutt.) "Eh, Eli," I said, "Mrs Howarth's had a little lad, not long since. Run back and tell t' master!" (And a slice for Mrs Braithwaite, Nellie.) "A lad?" he says, gawping at me. "Nay, I never!" And he run back. In a minute Master come running like a fool, waving his hat. (Pour a sup for Mrs Tunstall, Sallie.) We was at sixes and sevens, and these two got the supper started, didn't you? (Have another slice, Mrs Cartwright.) Then Cissie Pycroft come panting up track, poor body. Then when we was all eating Doctor rode up on his horse. Eh, I couldn't tell you the trouble that little lad caused, God bless him!'

For William Wilde Howarth was to become Betty's prime favourite: his virtues extolled, his shortcomings overlooked, until the day he and she parted company. His passion for gingerbread sprang from his early alliance.

'Then somebody said – I forget who, I think it were your Tom, Mrs Cartwright – anyway somebody said as it were Midsummer Eve. Well, we'd meant to tend to that, but wi' Mrs Howarth coming on so quick we'd clean forgot! I sent Nellie to pick the fernseed, but it's still in t' pewter plate. Mr Howarth wants t' Bible, to write the lad's birthdate in, else we should have collected the seed on the Good Book, Lord knows . . .'

It was Tom, for in exaltation of the Eve he had tucked protective sprays of rowan in the horses' bridles, and nailed another spray over the stable-door. Old Joe performed a similar operation with his cow's tails, and hung a yellow circlet of St John's wort over the entrance to the cowshed. Then Nellie collected green birch and bedecked Kit's Hill like a bride.

In the village, each one looked to some favourite herb to safeguard them against witchcraft, and cherished their fennel and rue, their vervain and trefoil and orpine. And though they would have been horrified to consider themselves as other than good Christians, they observed these pagan rites with as much reverence as they took the Holy wafer between their lips of a Sunday, and drank the sacred wine. So at this magical time of year, when the sun must be honoured and given strength, they lit huge fires outdoors, and danced solemnly round them in the direction that the sun moved. They kindled branches and singed the calves and foals for protection, and drove their beasts through the failing embers, and placated gods thousands of years older than Christ.

This midsummer eve Garth fells had two celebrations on hand, and paid just tribute to both. Until well past midnight, Dorcas sat up in bed like a queen, with her son in her arms, and received well-wishers bearing gifts. Many brought the ancient tokens of egg and salt for fertility and safekeeping. All had some homely joke for the occasion, and several prophesied a great future for William Wilde Howarth because he was born on such a propitious night.

Betty said several times, 'We don't do things by halves, here. That poor little lass were born and died on Childermas, and we heard t' church bells as plain as if they rung for her passing. Now the little lad's come they're lighting bonfires for him all over England!'

The midsummer fires leaped on every hill along the Pennine chain, and down the Wyndendale Valley, and over to the other side, in places remote from their sight and knowledge. So that they felt the devout dancers and hallowed flames were part of their own rites, and of this private rejoicing.

Now, as embers turned to ash and all good folk went home to bed, Ned Howarth carried the great black Bible upstairs and sat with his wife and son in peace.

'I'd sooner you wrote it than me, Dorcas,' he said. 'It'd look fancier than in my big fist.'

'Certainly not,' Dorcas replied. 'It is fitting that you write the names.'

So he rolled up his sleeves and trimmed his quill pen, and dipped it in the ink, and sighed.

'Ned, did you ever put Tabitha into the Bible? I did not think to ask.'

'I hadn't the heart,' he said quietly, 'and I didn't want to fret you wi' it. So in the end I did nowt.'

'Then put her in now, if you please. Mr Redfern blessed and baptised her. She is a part of us, although we did not know her. I should not like her to be left out.'

'Tell me what to put, then, wilta?' he said steadfastly, and wrote large and clear, with his tongue caught between his teeth for better concentration.

No. 1 Tabitha Cicely, infant daughter of Edward and Dorcas Howarth, was stillborne, ye night of 28 December 1761.

He wiped his sleeve across his eyes, then dipped his pen resolutely into the ink again, and waited for his wife's dictation.

*No. 2 William Wilde Howarth, borne about 7 of the clock in ye evening it being ye Midsummer Eve, 23 June 1764.**

He paused, and read out this entry with satisfaction. He bent again to his task and added reverently, *Thanks be to God.*

*The Howarth Family Bible is lodged in Millbridge Museum, by courtesy of the Howarth family of Kit's Hill, Garth Fells.

Eleven

All through the summer Dorcas and the child lived slightly apart from the world, enfolded in a smile. Her glossy black head bent over his comical black fuzz, her arms encompassed him. She would allow no one but herself to attend to him, and he demanded her attendance with total self-absorption. He sucked lustily at each small breast, falling away into sleep, and when he woke again the milk came as sweet and abundantly as before. He was a part of that flesh from which he had been so recently and so easily separated. There had been no rupture, as with the first baby, no chill memory of suffering to trouble them both. They gave and received of each other without stint, with a tender satisfaction. Dorcas would carry him in her arms round the garden, and talk to him by the hour, and he seemed to comprehend her through his squinting dark-blue eyes. His smile wavered forth, but Betty said jealously that it was wind, and he was fed too often and too much! No one listened to her. She grumbled out of habit, waiting for the time that Dorcas would need her help with the boy.

Ned trod shyly into the bedroom or parlour, fearful of disturbing this tranquillity. Clumsy as he looked in these feminine surroundings, he could hold the infant as gently as any woman. Though later he would toss him in the air and tousle him, to the child's delight and the mother's terror. Now he stood on the edge of their lives, somewhat wistful at being left out, and hoping to share.

Then Dorcas, sensing his estrangement, would let him stay while she fed William, and when the baby had taken his fill she put him in Ned's arms, and watched them both with deep contentment.

'I'st take thee to feed horses before so long,' Ned would say, holding out a finger for the boy to grasp. 'Then we'st have to find a pony for thee. Buttercup looks to be in foal, so thee and t' little cob'll grow up together. I'st get Jacob Grundy of Coldcote to make a proper saddle for thee. Eh, Dorcas, look at that grip, wilta? I think the lad'll make a boxer!'

'Indeed he shall not,' Dorcas declared. 'He shall be Master of Kit's Hill when we are gone. His future is assured.'

'Well, let's hope he takes after his mother in the farming line,' said Ned, grinning. Then, thoughtfully, 'So you're not thinking of making a scholar of him, then?'

'I hope that all our children will know their letters, Ned, but William is the inheritor and has a property to care for, do you not agree?'

He bent forward and kissed her cheek, and the infant shouted with pleasure as he was caught between them, and laid hold of his mother's hair and his father's ear.

'Don't set your heart on owt, Dorcas,' said Ned, when they had untangled themselves. 'Our Willie should've farmed Kit's Hill, not me. Folks have minds of their own. I'm not crossing the lad if he wants summat different. And if he takes after either of us he won't let nobody tell him what to do!'

To save carrying the heavy hooded cradle up and down stairs, Ned made a portable bassinet from his mother's old wicker market basket, and this was set by Dorcas's day-bed in her parlour. They dozed of a warm afternoon, mother and child together, and the sun coming through the muslin curtains, and the steady tick and chime of the long clock, became part of that first magical summer. So that, decades later, William would be recalled by certain lights and sounds to an ineffable happiness which sprang from an unremembered source.

Each morning, Dorcas woke, knowing that something wonderful had happened. The first cluck or sneeze from the oak cradle gave her the answer, and she would reach over and fetch William into their bed. He was a comfortable baby to rear: a big, sunny-tempered boy with a healthy appetite and an excellent digestion. So he slept and sucked and looked round at his world, and grew.

The christening party taxed everyone except William and Dorcas, who remained in their celestial trance throughout. Garth village, still pinched from loss of livestock, seized this occasion as an excuse to fill their bellies. For the approaching winter would reap their old and young and feeble, and any crust was a temporary respite. So they packed the church, and claimed kinship or good friendship, and rode or walked up the long track to the bounty of Kit's Hill, and brought their shrunken children with them.

Betty, infuriated, set a bar across the dairy door so that no one might be tempted to steal, and kept the food in the kitchen where she could dole it out personally.

'Fetch up the small beer!' she shouted to Tom and Billy. 'Don't you go ladling and teeming the best. And you two girls, watch that nobody slips a loaf under their shawls. Cut the bread thick and spread it thin. Do you hear?'

But Ned, shocked by the forest of starved hands reaching forth, spoke sharper yet. Though he knew very well that his heart was bigger than his supplies. Even the Reverend Tom Redfern was heard to complain that his living was nearer dying.

'I know folk say that the parson takes his tithe, whether they've got owt or nowt,' he grumbled into his ale. 'But I tell thee this, Ned. A tenth of nowt *is* nowt, and that's what I've had this sixteen month or more!'

Whereupon Ned ordered Billy to put a cask of their best ale into the parson's gig. Then Betty burst into tears of vexation, flung her apron over her head and swore she would leave (though she had nowhere to go). Ned, looking for

Dorcas to make all well, found she had abdicated to the parlour and closed the door, preparatory to William's feed. But Phoebe, as godmother, smoothed matters over and made herself amazingly useful. She also spoke for a long while with Mrs Tom Redfern about parishioners and their difficulties. So that Betty said Miss Jessup should come again, and welcome.

The leaves fell, first gently, then whipped by a driving wind that heralded autumn. The new crops of beets and potatoes were brought in, together with those old friends the Swedish turnips. The barley and pease were sound. Now Dorcas was speaking of St Foin, which had been called Everlasting Grass or French Grass (after the country from whence it came). The poorest ground, wrote Jethro Tull, would produce these tall red-flowered stalks with their burrowing tap-roots, and bear a crop forty times more profitable than meadow-hay. Now Dorcas's little green leather marker stayed between the same pages of Mr Tull's book and collected dust, while she cosseted her maternal harvest of William. Ned let Billy superintend the home fields, until his head showed signs of swelling with too much authority. Then he reminded the young man that Mrs Howarth would be right vexed if any of her former orders were ignored or altered. So Billy stepped back into line, and gave himself no more airs (save on his wooden flute in the winter evenings).

They filled the barn and barred the door. They fetched all but the hardiest sheep down from the Nick, and penned them in folds. They shut up the pigs and cattle, and stabled the horses. They mended the roof of Betty's fowl-house. Then they went indoors where the fire roared up the chimney-back, and made ready for the dark time of the year. The men leaned forward and took a twisted wood shaving from the handy box, and lit it from a flame for their pipes; the girls spun and carded wool and Betty knitted; while Dorcas sat in her high wooden arm-chair by the fireside and read aloud.

Her shadow pitched forward across the white-washed wall as she bent over books familiar to her since her childhood. They had enjoyed *Gulliver's Travels*, though Dorcas had to edit a few of Jonathan Swift's expressions as being unfit for mixed company. The legends of Greece and Rome had come to an untimely end, since her listeners were plainly ill at ease with foreign pagans. Mr Fielding and Mr Smollett had been put aside at the beginning. The Reverend Ambrose Wilde had chuckled aloud in his study over Tom Jones and Roderick Random, but considered them too coarse for a young lady's reading. Now in her maturity Dorcas regarded them as indecorous for public reading. Nor would she introduce her simple audience to the covert delights of Samuel Richardson's novels, for she found him to be a terrible sensualist. But the adventures of Robinson Crusoe were popular from the moment of his shipwreck, and they were beginning his curious history all over again.

Dorcas had made her place among them as mistress of Kit's Hill. Mrs Hetty lay in Garth churchyard like an old memory rarely invoked, while her successor ruled with a soft tongue and a hard head. Kit's Hill was responding to this new steward, and she to it, as though they sensed a common durability against the enemies without. The wind no longer drummed Dorcas into a sick headache. She lit many candles to confront the dark. Against the gaps between flagstones and doors, where draughts threatened the room's warmth, she stuffed long ropes of rags covered with some bright remnant of her wardrobe. The green velvet snake uncoiled by the parlour doorsill was much admired, and did his duty nobly. One by one, in order of use and merit, she had curtained the windows with heavy home-spun wool, dyed to her requirements in Millbridge. The worst gusts of winter could only revolve within the folds, or perhaps cause them to belly outwards for a moment, and draw forth a remark about poor souls at sea and those who had no shelter from the storm. Now at the heart of the house, her parlour sat in quiet grace. They came here for orders or advice or comfort, wiping their feet first: looking shyly at the handsome walnut long clock, at the awesome knowledge of books within the glass-fronted secretaire, at small china ornaments of no use and great beauty. No one in the world (which to them meant Garth and the fells) had a missis like theirs. At The Woolpack they were inclined to boast.

Outside Kit's Hill, Dorcas had gradually made herself known to her neighbours and to the villagers in Garth. Her very foreign-ness was against her at first, as well as a high-bridged nose, a particular way of holding herself erect, and a precise manner of speech. These peculiarities brought forth all the people's surly independence, and were subjects of derision behind her back and hostility to her face. Still, she had been bred to community service whether they or she liked it or not. So she maintained an obstinate dignity which finally impressed them. Her practical nature and common sense won their respect. She was considered eccentric, but they did not mind her.

The birth of her son changed her, caught her up out of herself and her concerns, swept her onto some strange emotional shore and for those first rapt months stranded her there. But Dorcas was too well aware of other people's necessities to be blind to his: too fair to hold him when he moved away from her. So his diet and liberty increased. William crawled all over Kit's Hill and made friends with everyone. His father tossed him in the air, and tickled him until he shouted for mercy. And his mother's early bliss was over and would not return.

Dr Standish had again exhorted Ned to leave his wife alone for a twelvemonth, to give her time to feed the infant and regain her strength. Ned did not mind the exhortation, but the doctor's offhand manner choked him and the doctor's little lecture roused his temper.

'. . . for you have only to look around you,' said Standish, 'to see the results of incontinent lust. Women pulled down with children and ill-health, suffering premature death! If I had my way I should horse-whip any man that had more than five children, and had any of them closer than two years apart. So, though it is hard, I grant you, for a healthy man to contain himself, there is no other way. I do not wish to hear from Kit's Hill sooner than I need, sir!'

'Very good,' said Ned, somewhat shortly, 'but I'll lay a bet you change your tune when you get wed, sir!'

'Not a bit of it, my good fellow,' said the ginger gentleman coolly, 'and certainly not if I were to marry a lady of your wife's quality. For any female fool can breed, but a woman of spirit and intelligence should not be troubled with such a dangerous business too often!' Then he said, smiling, 'Good day to you, Mr Howarth!' very civilly, and left a small cold doubt behind him. Ned tried to invest all his joy in the baby, at which he failed, for no man thinks an infant wholly enjoyable.

As William pulled himself to standing position by the aid of skirts, breeches, coat-tails, and the legs of furniture, Dorcas looked to her husband for love-making and found him unaccountably reticent. She picked up her books, and put them down again. The driving need to make something of her life at Kit's Hill had been satisfied. For the moment she was content to manage the home fields and William. Yet these were not enough, though they filled her waking hours. She drove to Millbridge and was temporarily lightened by the bustle and talk, but Millbridge was not the answer. Nor was a visit from Phoebe, which everyone enjoyed more than Dorcas did. For Phoebe's role as godmother, her acceptance at Kit's Hill, and her old friendship renewed, made her complete. She was indeed very content, which Dorcas was not.

Staring out of her parlour window into the wet morning, Dorcas felt that she stared into the sad mist of her own soul. Prayers, normally a source of strength and consolation, fell onto stony ground. God gave no answer to her perplexity, though she admitted that He had not been asked a particular question. But her people noticed her depression, and Betty naturally spoke of it to Ned.

'What's up wi' Mrs Howarth then, master? I think she's broody, myself. You want to put your mind to it, and give her another! I can take care of the little lad. (Willie Howarth, keep your fingers out of my dough trough! You naughty boy, you'll give yourself a belly-warch eating it raw!) Yes you get yourselves another. This'un is fifteen month old if he's a day, and no sign of a brother nor sister. What way is that to carry on?'

'There were nobbut four of us!' Ned reminded her.

'Nobbut four living. Your Mam had ten, and knew her duty!'

'You mind your kitchen, and leave me mind my own business!' said Ned, so sharply that she gazed at him, and then bent to her work flustered.

His year was long up, but more than Matthew Standish's advice lay between himself and Dorcas. A lesser man than Ned Howarth would have looked elsewhere, if only in fancy. Or he might have vented his frustration on his wife, knowing by this time how best to offend her. Instead, he withdrew into himself as Dorcas did: like two people that sit together, but sit back to back in glum companionship.

She spoke at last, her colour higher than usual, saying that she was now well recovered, and Willie ran the risk of being spoiled if he should be an only child for long. Though she herself (she ran on, as he did not answer) had been alone, and her parents had been the stricter with her because of it, though always fair and just . . .

Ned knotted his hands between his knees and took counsel of the small parlour carpet, which gave him no advice. Suddenly he reddened from neck to forehead and slapped both thighs in forcible disgust.

'Nay!' he cried, so loudly that Dorcas feared they might hear him through the closed door. 'Nay, I'm not to be used like a bloody ram that's fetched to the ewe whether she wants him or not. To be put on and took off again, like a mucky glove. What man could stand it, or woman neither!' He looked straight at her as he spoke. 'How would you feel if I bore wi' you, instead of giving you a proper hug and kiss now and again? What would you think if you was told to let me be, because I were better than you and shouldn't be fretted wi' you? Nay, it's past all telling what I've had to put up wi', and for long enough, God only knows (nigh on five year!). You've had your own way, time and again, and you've done what you wanted, but you've never showed owt for me beyond a bit of liking. I should have let you be from the start! Whatever made you have me in t' first place? I thought it were women as loved, and men as learned it off them, not the other way about. You should have set your cap at that Dr Standish, wi' his fancy notions and his fancy education. You could have lain safe enough wi' him. You wouldn't be bothered in a month of Sundays!'

She had grown whiter as he grew redder, and sat facing him with her hands fast in her lap, and very still. Her quiet attentiveness quietened him. He had unburdened himself of his first rage and hurt. Now he spoke as he thought rather than as he felt.

'Nay, I run after you like a fool and badgered you to death. It were my fault. Only I did hope as you'd feel a bit more for me in time. Then I thought as you were cool-natured, and that's how you'd be wi' anybody. But when our Will come I saw different. Eh, my lass,' rising clumsily, and putting the chair away from him as carefully as he could, 'I've seen thee give that babby many a smile and a look (I don't grudge him, never think that of me!) as I'd have given sovereigns for. I've watched thee lover him by the hour, and touch him as if he was made of fine china. But for all your fancy manners, Dorcas, you make me feel like nowt. And perhaps I am nowt – but it's bloody hard, and so I tell thee!'

He could not speak more. His throat swelled and his eyes filled, and he fairly pushed his way out of the parlour to avoid her gaze and presence. She sat for an hour, weeping silently, since affection and goodwill had not been sufficient. Then she sat drying her eyes and grieving over what he had said. Much later, Betty knocked at the door and asked if there was anything she wanted. Receiving no reply, she ordered Nellie to make a pot of tea for the missis, and not to speak to her or seem to notice anything.

There were no tales read by the fire that evening. Ned told

Tom to go out, and took over his work in the stables: grooming and pondering. The boy slept soundly in his truckle-bed. And Dorcas sat hour after hour, as her household moved smoothly round her, and candles were lighted and curtains drawn, and supper brought in and taken out uneaten. Until at last Betty raked the ashes together, and went slowly and heavily up the stairs to bed, leaving two wretched people awake in Kit's Hill.

In the silent house Dorcas moved into another dimension, and her mind ranged freely over her childhood and youth. She had understood at an early age that her choice of partner would be limited, since her education and upbringing outmatched her circumstances. Still, her father and mother had made a match, without much money on either side. So there was always hope, which should not be allowed to sway common sense. There was self-respect, to prevent her making a sorry union out of desperation. Better to be unmarried than ill-married.

Unawakened by man or imagination, confined by manners and training, she had not been troubled by the flesh. Her closest relationship with a man, until Ned married her, had been with her father. Given free choice, she would have preferred such another: the interplay of like minds, love without demand, mutual tastes, and no carnal desire. At the mature age of twenty-two she had been set adrift by his death, only to find herself marooned on Miss Wilde's barren shore. In a way, she had set sail again by arranging her own marriage with Ned, believing that a clear head and a brave heart would be more successful than any amorous adventure. She had reckoned without his loving passion, and was now run upon the rocks.

Ned had been driven in by the cold at last, and sat shivering over the warm ashes of the kitchen fire, with the dogs at his feet. He glanced up and then away as she hesitated on the parlour threshold, mumbled something about not bothering her, and tried to thaw his hands by spreading them over the faint heat and crouching closer to the hearth.

'It is just past two o'clock,' said Dorcas softly. 'Have you not eaten? No, nor have I, and I am hungry now.'

Her heart was sore, and she was somewhat afraid lest he show his anger again, but she moved quietly about the kitchen, applying the bellows to the fire until it blazed forth, setting the iron kettle to boil. She fetched cold meat from the larder, and bread and butter and pickles. She drew a tankard of ale from the cask in the corner, and mulled it for him with a hissing poker.

He, conscious of her service, grateful that she did not try further conversation, accepted his supper with gruff thanks. She, sorrowfully aware of his wounds and her own, sat silent while they ate and drank together.

Then he said, awkwardly rubbing the dog's head, 'It were my fault, I reckon. I should have let you be, Dorcas. It's not in my mind to tell thee how to love me. Perhaps fine folk do it different. I allus thought they felt the same, whether they wore velvet or kersey, but I were wrong. Well, there's nowt we can do but make the best of it. If you want another babby to lover you can have one. If you want to live like brother and sister then we will. I canna say fairer than that. It's not what I wanted, but it's what I've got. We must make the best on it, my lass, and I dare say as we're no worse off than most.' So he spoke stoically, endeavouring to mend matters. Then the candle-beam set him musing in another direction. 'Eh, I mind how I sat at that table and wrote thee a letter. I thought then that if you'd have me I should never want for owt!'

He could have found no better way to dry the tears that were stealing down her cheeks, or to rouse her fainting spirits, or to steel her heart. When she replied, her tone was as dry as a lawyer's, and as inflexible.

'I do not like to think that what I have done amounts to nothing,' said Dorcas steadily. 'It was a great deal, for me, and cost me dearly, and was the best that I could do for any husband that I got! You are insulting, sir, to put aside near on five years of loving goodwill in such a manner!'

'I'm not blaming you, my lass,' said Ned uncertainly.

'Oh, but indeed you are. You have attacked my true affection, my honour and my intentions!'

She refilled his tankard and set it down with such emphasis that it slopped over.

'Why, however did I do that?' asked Ned, confused and aghast, for he had but voiced his injuries and thought himself ill-used.

'Why, sir,' cried Dorcas, 'you construe my affection as falseness. For what kind of woman uses her husband only as a means of getting herself with child? Indeed, if you had borne an infant you would not speak so lightly! I was like to die with the first, and so I should have but for Dr Standish. Then you impugn my honour by suggesting that I thought of him as a husband, that I set my cap at him! You are a villain to think so, sir, and a greater villain to say so!'

'Here, here . . .' Ned protested, for she was turning his arguments inside out and they looked a different colour from when he used them.

But she would go on. He was not the only one to nurse a wound or harbour a resentment. She blew her nose and wiped it, resolutely.

'I have had my own way, you say? I have done what I wanted? What, sir? With your property and with your servants and with your daily life?' She gave a short sarcastic laugh such as he had never heard before. 'My intention was to make you more easy than you were before, to watch over your interests and to improve your household. But you impute my care to selfishness. Why, this should be enough to hang me, sir!'

'Nay,' murmured Ned, now wholly bewildered, 'I never said owt like that.'

'Then you accuse me of lavishing attentions upon our infant. I had thought this usual among mothers, sir, but you correct me. And still we are not done! My very manners come within the scope of your judgement. For they do not spring, as I was taught, from true consideration. They have no grace, no lightness, contribute no pleasure, bring no harmony to life. No, no, they are an affectation as false as all my other vices. Why should you wish for tokens of love from such a creature as I appear to be? I should be flayed in the market-place! No, do not waste yourself on such as me, sir. You are too good for my poor understanding!'

Then she fell silent, and so did he, for neither of them recognised themselves or the other by this time. The dogs prowled uneasily between the two of them, and nosed their hands for comfort.

They had given tongue to old and new grievances, and a strange peace came upon them as though they were absolved of sin, and might begin anew. Ned stretched and yawned and looked shyly at her. Her imperious profile became gentler. She sat half-turned towards him and smoothed her wedding ring.

'It weren't as bad as all that, were it?' said Ned tentatively.

She shook her head and played with the ring.

'I don't allus put things the right way,' he said, and his old humour was back, his mouth was tender.

She looked down and smiled, looked up and laughed.

'Nor, apparently, do I!' she cried.

'Calling me *sir*,' Ned said reproachfully, and she laughed again and glanced at him sideways, and turned the ring round and round on her finger. 'And you're not sorry for it, and all!' he grinned.

His pride in her, his love for her, was creating her again. She touched his cheek with her hand. Their kiss was soft, mutual, and they smiled at each other afterwards. Then she came and stood closely by him, in the warm circle of his arm, and began to unpin her hair in an abstracted fashion.

Soon, a long black lock tickled his face, but Dorcas seemed not to notice and continued taking down her silky coronet as though she were in a trance. Ned touched the lock as delicately as any gallant, and carried it to his lips, now looking at her frankly and meaningfully. She leaned over him, closer and closer, until he caught her deftly round the waist and pulled her onto his knee. She was smiling, very dark and soft, and kissing his mouth. Soft and dark, as she had never been with him before, had never felt with him before, so that they both wondered at the event.

Afraid to break the spell between them, he was careful not to move too roughly or quickly, careful not to speak lest his voice be too loud. Careful. Careful as a lady's maid with the fastenings of her clothes (which had been a mystery to him, but were no longer unknown). He accomplished even the unlacing of her corset with no more than a concentrated frown to mark the achievement. She helped him unobtrusively, deftly, so that it seemed all his own doing, until she was standing young and flushed in her lawn shift. Pretty as a girl, for all that she was nearly thirty.

The dogs scattered as Betty's rag rug was taken over for a bedding, and stood ears pricked in amazement at this unaccountable coupling. Soon over, for the wait had been a long one. Then Dorcas and Ned lay tranquilly, with the fire warming them, and had another leisurely courtship and another coming together. So they spent the night in loving and sleeping, sleeping and loving, while the dogs snored disconsolately in a cold corner of the kitchen, and the cat watched them with yellow eyes. The sound of the cock crowing fetched them wide awake, guilty as thieves about to be caught. They nipped up their clothes, chased after Dorcas's scattered hairpins, and fairly ran upstairs to be safe in their room before Betty got up. Then lay in each other's arms, muffling their laughter lest they be overheard: adults and children and lovers, all at one time, in their bed together at Kit's Hill.

Twelve

Lammastide, 1 August 1766

'Charlotte Sophia?' cried Betty, enraged. 'I've never heard of such a name. That little lass should be called Harriet, after your Mam!'

'Ah well, that's all you know,' said Ned good-humouredly, for the birth had been easy enough, and Dorcas was sitting up and eating her dinner soon after. 'Have you not heard of our Queen of England, then? Her that married King George the same year as me and Dorcas was wed? Well, her maiden name were Charlotte Sophia of Meckleburg Relish, or somewhere. Dorcas did tell me. So our little lass'll be called after a queen, and if that isn't good enough for you it's good enough for us. So put kettle on and make Mrs Howarth a brew of tea, and stop splothering!'

'Charlotte Sophia! We'st never remember a mouthful like that!'

'Well, Dorcas'll know what to call her for short. She all knows. Is that kettle on or is it not?'

'They shall call her "Lottie",' said Dorcas, 'and they will get used to it. We cannot be the only parents who name their daughter after Queen Charlotte. Indeed, it is probably quite the rage in London. I do remember there was a crowd of "Carolines" while King George the Second reigned, for I knew three!'

'I tell thee summat,' said Ned without rancour. 'I should

have been a doctor. That Standish rides up when there's nowt to do, and drinks our ale like a good 'un, and takes his guinea and all!'

'Yes, but he has inoculated William against the smallpox, and will do the same for Lottie in time. And there is always the surgical attendance, which Mrs Pycroft is not qualified to undertake.'

'Aye, well, you know best,' said Ned. Though he didn't give a fig for the smallpox, which had marked half the villagers in Garth at one time or another, and came round as commonly as the pedlar.

He was very easy in his skin these days, as was his wife. They talked and smiled together, and were an invulnerable alliance. For in certain matters Dorcas's word was law, and in others Ned had full say. Anyone making an enquiry was directed to the right partner, and must make do with the outcome for there was no redress.

'I have been thinking about godparents,' Dorcas continued, and broke off to caution William not to hurt his sister. He was unsure of this new arrival, and had been known to poke it unkindly while imagining himself unseen. 'Since Phoebe is William's godmother we shall not ask her again. My aunt will not speak to us. I am not close to Mrs Redfern. So I had thought of Betty, who would be pleased, I think. There should be one other, and I would have asked Mrs Cartwright, but . . .'

But she had died of her thirteenth child that spring, and laid in the churchyard with her infant at her draggled breast.

'Betty'll be fair set up wi' that!' said Ned, pleased. 'What about asking Judith Braithwaite, else one of the other wives on Garth fells?'

'I know them all equally well,' said Dorcas, 'and should not like to offend others by choosing one. What do you think to Agnes at Thornton House? She is a good woman and feels so kindly towards us.'

'Aye, I like Agnes. Whatever you think best. Only shouldn't the little lass be called Betty Agnes after the godmothers,

Dorcas? That's only right.'

'It is usual,' said Dorcas firmly, 'but since our daughter is named in compliment to the queen I feel they cannot object.'

'I know one that will!' said Ned, in truth.

'Agnes, Agnes! Who is talking to you in the hall all this while? Come here at once, I say!'

Greyer, older, harder. So hard now that she outmatches her diamonds; so old that she dreams of death and plans to cheat him as long as she can; so grey that she has taken to wearing a glossy black wig, which ill assorts with her complexion.

'Begging your pardon, ma'am, but it were only Mr Howarth come to see me on a special errand, like.'

'What errand? Is aught wrong with Miss Dorcas or the baby?'

Agnes wrung red hands in her immaculate apron, and yearned for an acceptable answer, but could only tell the truth.

'Mr Howarth kindly brought a message from Miss Dorcas, asking me to stand as godmother to the little lass, ma'am. Charlotte Sophia, ma'am.'

'They are after my fortune again,' said Miss Wilde, seeing the plot quite clearly, though anyone else would have been puzzled to do so. 'What else did he say to you, to put you off your guard, Agnes?'

'Mr Howarth said very kindly as he'd send the trap for me if you was willing, but only if you was freely willing, and they'd fetch me back the same day, ma'am. If you please,' said poor Agnes hopefully.

'You mean you have accepted this impudent request?' Miss Wilde cried, threatened from all sides.

Agnes shed tears, and wrung her hands, but nodded steadfastly.

'And suppose I was to give you your notice?' asked Miss Wilde.

Agnes took a deep breath, for Dorcas had thought of this

contingency.

'If you please, ma'am, I've been with you over thirty year and I don't want to go nowhere else. But Mrs Howarth says if there's any difficulty then she'll offer me a place at Kit's Hill any time, begging your pardon, ma'am.'

Miss Wilde stared, mouth half-open, wig slightly awry.

'So that is what they are after,' she said to herself. 'They will part us before they rob me!'

She saw herself alone in the house, with the pale reaper hiding behind the bed-curtains. She was quite undone.

'What nonsense!' she cried at last, vigorously. 'When have I ever ruled over your religious feelings, Agnes? Why, it may be the saving of the child to have a decent godmother!'

'Oh, ma'am,' said Agnes, red with concern and relief. 'Oh, thank you, ma'am. I were only asking if I might.'

'I shall be pleased to set you at liberty for the day of the christening. You must be fetched back before dark, and I do not wish to see anyone who brings you, nor speak to any member of that family.'

'No, ma'am. Thank you kindly. And I'll tell you all about it after!.

'You know perfectly well that I forbid even a name to be mentioned!' cried Miss Wilde, who would wait up until Agnes got back and insist on hearing every detail. 'Ah,' she cried, enlightened, 'I have thought of such a good notion. Miss Jarrett shall keep me company while you are at the christening!'

But they had already forestalled her, for Phoebe called round that very afternoon to add her persuasion and offer her services, so that Agnes should be free to go.

'Well, this is a pretty pickle, Miss Jarrett,' said the old lady. 'They are to call the child by a queen's name, and have two servants as godmothers! Still, the girl will be brought up to milk cows and suchlike. So I dare say it is very proper and fitting when one thinks of it. And how is that ploughboy to whom you are godmother? What did your father think of you, I wonder, to lend your name to such a proceeding?'

'He bade me do as I thought fit, ma'am,' said Phoebe, pink and slightly waspish, 'and according to my Christian conscience. For my papa is a man of principle, ma'am!'

'Is he indeed?' Miss Wilde mused. 'A man of principle. Well, well, that should be a great comfort to us all, should it not?'

Poor Phoebe wondered how she was to survive an entire day of the old lady's company, and sighed to think of the difficulties Dorcas brought upon her friends. For had she not wondered, when she heard this latest notion, what folk would think? And though she knew that Agnes was her equal in the sight of God, and superior in many ways, Millbridge might consider it odd that she and Phoebe were on the same footing as godmothers. Which Miss Wilde knew very well, and would probe more deeply by and by, and thoroughly fluster this rebellious goose from the rectory.

Thirteen

To the children it seemed that Kit's Hill was the world, and all the rest attendant on it. So that Garth became the house's church and village, the outlying farms its special neighbours, and Millbridge its private market. Round Kit's Hill blew the wind which could not harm them, though it prowled and sought outside like a pack of wolves, and they would lie in bed together and laugh to hear its roar and plaint. They were safe here, living between the generosity of their father and the steel of their mother, safer than they would ever be again. Their world turned round them daily and made obeisance. Faces lit when they appeared: with humour for William, with love for Charlotte. The animals were theirs, to scold or fondle. The land was theirs, stretching to the ends of the earth like a great kingdom. The kitchen was theirs, to coax delicacies from Betty, and company from Nellie. (For Sallie had married Billy when she was seventeen, and they lived in the village with Billy's mother.) The parlour was theirs, during certain hours, where they could marvel at the magical centre. Here reigned their mother, whom they loved with a mixture of awe and delight, for what she did not know she could guess, and they found this most disturbing. Wise and formidable as a witch was their mother. Yet not a witch, or else the villagers would have ducked her until she died of drowning, like old Mother Cheetham (up and down, up and down, until she looked like a wet cat). Their father could be gulled, and sometimes was, but if he discovered the treachery his anger was deeper than Dorcas's and lasted longer. He loathed liars and charlatans, whereas Dorcas punished such transgressors coolly along with gluttons, sloths, peacocks, shrews, and those who showed too great an interest in their nether parts. To her all sins were alike. To Ned's way of thinking, man or woman or child stood or fell by their integrity.

'And it's a funny thing,' he said once, having smacked William soundly (not for stealing a pie but for lying about the theft), 'that none of them seven Virtues is the Truth, and to me Truth is the guts of living!'

Charlotte, weeping in the corner with William out of sympathy, registered this judgement in her mind for ever. William would remember his mother's considered reply.

'I do not gainsay you, Ned, and yet I like courage more. Truth stands fast, but courage spurs forward. Yet the one cannot shine without the other.' She looked directly at William. 'It was both untruthful and cowardly to lie about your theft, William. That is three sins at once. You show great promise! And now you must go to bed directly. I shall take him myself,' to Ned, 'for if he is allowed to loiter then Betty will give him more pie (to compensate for his punishment) and that will hardly form his character!'

'Then I shall go to bed with Willie!' cried Charlotte, for she had shared the pie, though innocent of its theft.

'Nay, my little lass,' Ned began, stricken by the child's loyalty, 'there's no call to punish thyself for nowt.'

But Dorcas said, 'If Charlotte wishes to go to bed early, for any reason, of course she must go!'

Which made Charlotte cross, because she had hoped to play the heroine without suffering the penalty. She kissed her father goodnight several loving times, but only touched her mother's cheek with her lips. Whereas poor Willie, as affectionate as he was greedy, kissed and sobbed over both parents equally, and said his prayers that night in such a hail of remorse that Charlotte was not surprised when the heavens opened and rain fell for three whole days.

Between 1768 and 1771 the cattle plague had run through England like a forest fire. William lost his puppy and his pony, and many other animals dear to him. The ruthlessness of these times impressed him deeply, though he was hardly four when they began and only seven when they ended. Quick to comprehend, he discovered a dark and bloody aspect to life. No need for the Reverend Tom Redfern to beat his fist upon his Sunday pulpit and scour them with the wrath of God. Older gods than Jehovah strode the lowering hills, and smote the innocent without cause. Their pagan wills were made manifest in the grave face of Dorcas ordering slaughter; in Ned's set mouth as he swung down the heavy pole-axe on defenceless skulls; in the wild bleating and bellowing of animals whipped through the stinging smoke; in the murderers' garments from which the blood-sin could not be fumigated; in forbidden ways where soil might be tainted with plague, and a straying puppy punished with annihilation; in the stench of singed hide and roasting flesh from the sacrificial pyres which rose to heaven.

Then the trouble passed, as all trouble does for a time; and children forgot whole years of darkness, but remembered the day they went to Millbridge in their mother's trap.

Released from their long incarceration, Dorcas drove her mare gingerly down Kit's Lane and paused at the top of the track leading to Garth. From here, on this fine May morning of 1772, a gentlewoman with some knowledge of landscape could enjoy the view of the River Wynden flowing gracefully down its valley to the white town, and impart a little of its rural beauty to her children.

Dorcas was feeling well and looking handsome. Her face, once unfashionably firm and composed for a girl, had mellowed into distinction. She now appeared to have been far more comely than was actually the case. Behind her in the freshly-painted trap, her children were her looking-glasses. William, glossy as a blackbird and tall for his seven years, had his father's stalwart frame. Charlotte pleased both parents (as was her nature) by having her father's wheat-gold hair and her mother's narrow dark eyes and fine features. All three, in spite of the recent years of worry and deprivation, were plainly but elegantly dressed. As a daughter of the church, Dorcas had long since learned how to look well (but not too well) on a small allowance. Much thought and good cutting went into each yard of cloth. Dorcas studied and adapted the paper patterns obtained by Phoebe, and would put out work for sewing, but she herself trimmed the garments and covered the buttons to give them a particular finish. She cut William's hair long and close on his neck, and cleanly-curved round ears and forehead. Charlotte was put to the torment of curling-rags, but submitted meekly and emerged an angel. So they were a personable family, faces turned obediently to the green valley below, as Dorcas's whip pointed out this and that feature. A click of her tongue, a touch of the whip, and off they went again: the mare's hind-legs spirting up off the track with a saucy flick of the hooves.

'Firefly's a dancer, mamma!' cried William, who noticed everything.

The mare tossed her silky mane and jogged her gleaming haunches, and flicked her hooves as though she heard him. The children laughed together. Then Charlotte's small hands reached for a branch of flowering blackthorn, and William stood up in the trap and imperilled them all to get it. So that Dorcas had to speak sharply, and they subsided for quite ten minutes until Garth was upon them.

Here, known to all and envied by most, they were besieged with begging or thanks. One ragged child ran barefoot behind them for nearly half a mile, beginning with praise and ending with abuse as the trap outran his powers. Then he fell away, shaking his fist and swearing, until noise and dust subsided and only the reproach remained.

'We cannot feed them all,' said Dorcas in explanation.

The children were silent, ashamed of their sufficiency in the face of want.

'The poor are always with us,' Dorcas added, knowing this was not good enough either. Then she cried gaily, 'Oh, look at Scarth Nick up there on the sky-line! And do you not notice how the wind has dropped since we reached the valley? Soon we shall be in Coldcote where Jacob Grundy lives, who makes saddles for us . . .'

They lifted their young faces to the grim cleft in the hills, with its grimmer signpost above it; and saw the scattered sheep below, and the grey roof of Kit's Hill with its chimney smoking steadily in the clear air; and shouted that they saw Nellie pegging washing on the line, and Sam Cartwright and his son walking with the dog at their heels, and the horse and hoe-plough led by Billy through Short Shrift field.

At Medlar they passed Martha Glegg with a basket of white linen on her head, and she waved and called to them, laughing. The gaps in her teeth were wider, her body stouter, her laundry as peerless as ever. At Childwell they saw children playing hopscotch in the dirt (marking their course with a stick, and hopping and marking). The children shouted and cheered as the little black trap bowled along the rough road in great style, leaving them behind in a cloud of dust. Between there and Whinfold rose the bleak place known as Swarth Moor, sparsely covered with pale coarse grass; and Dorcas told them that this was once a forest, and had ancient tree-roots in its peaty soil. The land, poor enough to chill any farmer's heart, normally stretched out for miles, empty of any human being. But today William stood up, again setting them at risk, and shouted that something was happening. So they stopped by the side of the road, and saw a little group of men busy boring into the ground. They had erected a triangle of three larch poles with a rope and pulley in its midst, and were working a hand winch to remove the rods. The Howarths watched for a time, and conjectured without success before driving on. At Thornley they caught up with the packman and his donkey, who gave them a wink and a wave and saw them grow small in the distance. At Brigge House they stopped to admire the old Hall from which the hamlet took its name. It stood upon the hill, somewhat like their own house, but was very dark and grand with little twinkling windows. Dorcas said that the Brigges had tricked the Roundheads more than a century ago, by hiding a priest in a secret room. Then on again, over the hump-backed bridge, to Flawnes Green, where Charlotte indicated that she must find a convenient place to stop, and William demanded to see the blacksmith.

When the ladies rejoined him, he was standing arms akimbo near the forge, his face as bright and quick as the leaping flames, watching the smith and his apprentice work in rhythmic strokes. The ring of the small hammer was followed by the deeper note of the sledge. Sparks rose and melted like magic as they fashioned the incandescent iron. Stroke by stroke, and stroke on stroke, until a warning tap on the anvil marked time for the sledge to stop. Then the smith wiped his face and neck and smiled at them, while the apprentice applied himself to the bellows.

'It is time we were on our way, William,' said Dorcas, and inclined her head courteously to the blacksmith.

Charlotte peeped round her mother's skirt, wondering if hell was like the smithy, and this dark giant the devil in scant disguise.

'Tell me, sir,' cried William directly, 'must a man be very strong to make a smith, if you please?'

The blacksmith smiled wider and wider, and his teeth were large and white in his bearded face.

'Strong, my lad?' he cried. 'Why, would'st call this strong enough?'

He picked up a plank of wood, full two inches thick, and pushed the tip of a nail neatly into it.

'Now wheer's my hammer gone?' he cried, jovial of countenance, though they could see the tool right by him.

Then, like lightning he brought the palm of his hand down upon the nail and drove it deep into the wood. They gasped in horror, but he laughed and held up his hand to show them no damage was done. Then they laughed too, in admiration and relief.

'Strong enough?' he repeated. 'Why, dost want to be a farrier, lad?'

'I think I might, sir,' said William, who was judicious, 'when I am grown.'

'Come back a-Monday, then. Move them iron weights. Hold a horse still for me. See if tha can lift this lad off the ground – and I'll think about it!'

'I am not yet eight years old, sir,' William informed him, thinking Monday somewhat soon to accomplish these trials of strength. Then, lest he lose his chance, added, 'but my name is William Howarth of Kit's Hill, in Garth.'

The smith came forward and shook him by the hand, and William saw the sweat upon his broad chest and the places where sparks had burned him, and he marvelled at the hardiness and shining might of the man. There was a special odour about him, of warm leather apron and scorched hoof. And though he looked a black and curly bull of a fellow, there was kindness in his eyes and voice, and the vigour of his handshake promised liking.

'I am named Aaron Helm, lad. Nay, never *sirrah* me, for I'm a plain man. I'll tell thee how I became a farrier. When I were a lad of fourteen I weighed nigh on fourteen stone. I'm nigh on eighteen stone now, in my prime as you might say, and not an ounce of it fat. I built myself, William Howarth, pound by pound, wi' boxing and weight-lifting. I can bend a bar of iron wi' these,' holding out his great hands. 'Tha wants good shoulders to make a good smith. Eat thy victuals, William, crusts and fat and all. Run and jump and pull and push wi' all thy might, like a good 'un, and tha'll do! But mind this, my lad,' and he caught the boy by his arm and shook him gently, 'never use thy strength against the weak. Never smite a woman, and if there's cause to correct a child – fear it wi' thy looks sooner than beat it. There's not a man in Flawnes Green as'd dare show a fist to his wife. He'd be over that anvil double-quick, sithee? There's not a man in Flawnes Green as'd hurt a child, or he'd answer to me for it. Dost know what I mean, lad? Good. Then go thy ways, and take care of thy mother and sister. And good-day to you, my ladies!'

He nodded at Dorcas, smiling, and winked at Charlotte (who had that moment dared to peep out, and immediately whisked back). Then he set to again with the aid of his apprentice (who seemed something short and light of a blacksmith's requirements) and the two hammers began their question and answer. *Ding? Dong! Ding? Dong!* Until, in the distance, over the sound of the trap wheels, William was sure he heard the final warning on the face of the anvil. *Tap!*

The last part of the journey was the best, for Millbridge sprawled far beyond her assembly of handsome houses and broad streets. They drove by the side of the river now, past the long-windowed cottages in Weaver's Lane where whole families spun and wove their lives away together. They glimpsed the tall chimneys of Kersall Park through its fine trees. Ahead of them lay Mill Fields and the big wheel of the corn mill dripping water in the sunlight into the pool. Then they rattled over Mill Bridge into the square Market Place, turned up the Lane, and ground over the gravel drive to the front door of the rectory, where they were greeted excitedly by a Pomeranian dog and Aunt Phoebe.

In the smother of hooped skirts and barks and incoherent exclamations, William stood politely to one side as his mother had taught him, then came forward doffing his black hat with its grey velvet trim, and bowing so that Aunt Phoebe smothered him too (which he bore with a strained smile and great good-nature). Then the Reverend Walter Jarrett came out, and kissed Dorcas and swung Charlotte up in the air, and gave William the sort of business-like nod and handshake that men exchange when they understand one another. Then the maid came out to collect up the dogs, and bear the ladies away to take off their cloaks and use Aunt Phoebe's chamber-pot.

They dined on soup and roast mutton, with tansy pudding and egg custard to follow. William ate his plate clean, as he had been bidden by Aaron Helm, but his mind was with the bidder rather than the repast. He yearned after such manhood, dreamed of lifting impossible weights, of knocking down innumerable opponents, of bending bars, and smiting nails with the flesh of his hand. He felt the heat of the forge upon his skin, heard the ring of sledge on anvil, saw sparks rise and fall in a glittering fountain. Pf! One of them had burned out on his strong bare chest. He did not mind it, not a bit!

'William!' cried his mother for the third time, laughing. 'Aunt Phoebe wishes to know how you like your tansy pudding?'

Mr Jarrett said, smiling, *'Tacet, satis laudat!'*

His silence is praise enough.

To which Dorcas replied swiftly, *'Quam diu se bene gesserit!'*

So long as he behaves himself properly.

'Are you teaching your son Latin, Dorcas?' Mr Jarrett asked.

'Oh, yes. He has been learning these two years or more, and does well enough in translation, but is by no means so learned as to converse with us.'

'But what shall Latin avail him?' Jarrett asked, kind but curious.

Dorcas concealed a certain private ambition which was as yet unripe.

'Why, sir, what has Latin availed me? Except that I act as tutor to my children!'

Phoebe, always mistaking verbal play for possible battle, hastened to intervene. As always, her charity surpassed her wisdom.

'Perhaps William may find his vocation in the Church, Papa. Only,' turning to her godson, 'you will have to be *very good,* William, to become a clergyman like your Uncle Jarrett!'

Smiling at the boy's embarrassment, Mr Jarrett said ironically, 'Oh, I do not think *goodness* has a great deal to do with being a Churchman!' Which made Dorcas smile and Phoebe cough and frown. 'But *Latin*,' Mr Jarrett continued, wiping his lips with his napkin and enjoying his own wit, '*Latin* is certainly compulsory!'

'Papa, William is but young and will mistake your merriness for truth!'

'I believe that young William has inherited his mother's ability to look most amiable – while ignoring one's advice!' said Walter Jarrett slyly. 'So I am not afraid of being misunderstood, only of being ignored. Now, sir,' to the enquiring young face, 'how should you like to see the ground being cleared for the new canal this afternoon, from the end of the town? It will run all the way from Leeds and eventually finish in the city of Liverpool. What do you say, sir?'

'Oh, yes, if you please, sir!' cried William, for he knew very well that his mother and godmother and sister would be deep in feminine talk.

So it was, about three of the clock, that Miss Wilde (putting aside her muslin window curtains so she might see her neighbours better) observed the reverend gentleman, immaculate in his black and white, escorting a handsome lad in a wide-brimmed hat down the High Street. As they passed she rapped upon the window-pane peremptorily with her knuckles, crying, 'Who is that boy, Mr Jarrett, if you please?' To which he replied pleasantly, 'This is your great-nephew, Miss Wilde. William Wilde Howarth of Kit's Hill!' And while she gaped and put her hand to her throat, the lad swept off his hat (though as startled as she at this sudden disclosure) and cried, 'Your servant, ma'am!' Whereupon she let the curtain fall and sat for half an hour without so much as ringing the parlour bell. Then roused herself and summoned Agnes, ordering her to wait at the front door and stop them as they returned home.

'For I had expected a bumpkin,' Miss Wilde explained with her usual frankness, as Mr Jarrett ushered William ahead of him into the sacred presence, 'but I see he is quite a gentlemanly fellow!' Staring through her eye-glass at William.

'So why does my niece visit you at the rectory with her children, and leave me out of her reckoning?'

'Perhaps, ma'am, Dorcas felt she was not entirely welcome,' Walter Jarrett suggested, and William saw him suck in his cheeks after that remark, as though it were a bonbon and tasted very good.

'Then she is mistaken,' said Miss Wilde grandly. 'I was about to take tea. Tell her that I wish to see her at once. She may bring Miss Jarrett with her, and we shall all drink tea together and Agnes will find us some cake and make us a toast.'

'Oh, ma'am,' said Agnes pitifully, for their baking was not due until the morrow, and they had not a fire on which to make the toast.

'Miss Wilde,' said Walter Jarrett, 'I fear your good Agnes will be quite put out to find refreshments upon the instant. Allow me to invite you to take tea with us at the vicarage, ma'am.'

'Certainly not,' said Miss Wilde. 'Dorcas must come to me. Your mother must come to me, William Wilde Howarth of Kit's Hill. D'you hear me, boy?'

'Yes, ma'am,' said William, bewildered but watchful.

'The boy has good sense, I can see,' said Miss Wilde. 'Off with you!'

But Walter Jarrett had a few words with Agnes in the hall which stabilised her colour (turning as it was from white to red and back again with all these different arrangements). Then there came such a procession down the High Street as made folk stare. For Dorcas and Phoebe and Mr Jarrett were carrying a covered plate of delicacies apiece, and laughing and smiling as though it were a party, with the children dancing alongside. There was a moment (William felt it) when the parlour door opened and niece and aunt came face to face. A moment's pause. Then Dorcas held out her hand first, and the old lady tried to rise from her chair to show that she welcomed the gesture, and eleven years of silence was broken.

Agnes spread copies of *The Wyndendale Post* beneath the

children's chairs so that their crumbs should not spoil the carpet, for Miss Wilde would not hear of them taking tea in the kitchen as Agnes had hoped. And a very strict hour they had of it, being asked questions as though they were on trial, and fed to bursting point because they dared not refuse Miss Wilde's borrowed cakes.

The old lady made only one major error, in referring to Ned as 'that fellow'. Whereat Dorcas grew very cold and upright and answered, 'My husband is very well, I thank you, ma'am!' and Miss Wilde glanced at her covertly for some time afterwards, as if to make sure she did not go away again. A little later she remarked upon the pretty colour of Charlotte's hair, saying, 'That will come from her Papa's side of the family, for none of us Wildes was ever anything but Crow!' and saw Dorcas's smile with much relief.

'Am I a crow then, ma'am?' William asked mischievously, for he knew himself to be an instant favourite, male though he was.

'You, sir?' cried Miss Wilde, delighted at his impudence. 'Why, you are a rascal and a scamp, and so I tell you!'

Her treatment of Charlotte was correct, almost perfunctory. Perhaps she sensed that any effort to cajole or dominate Dorcas's gentle daughter would be met with hostility. Whereas William could plainly take care of himself.

In the privacy of the hall, while the rest made their adieus, Agnes tied Charlotte's little face into her bonnet, and fastened her mantle and laced her boots, with devotion. Then she gave her a hug and a kiss and a penny for her pocket, saying, 'Dunnot spend it all at once!' in a joking fashion. But Charlotte answered seriously, clutching the shining coin, 'Indeed I shall not, I thank you, ma'am!'

Then William strode bright and dark into the hall, with a shilling from Aunt Phoebe in one hand and a half-guinea from Miss Wilde in the other (though he hid them like a gentleman when Agnes offered him a penny, too). This, Dorcas, who observed all things, observed closely. She had seen a side of William that day which was previously unknown to her, and resolved both to encourage and to watch it. For he was very clever and naturally charming, and this could be good or bad according to his intent and application.

Miss Wilde lifted the curtain to watch them wend their way up the High Street in the deepening light, and roundly blamed Agnes.

'For you should have reminded me what o'clock it was,' cried peevishly. 'They will be driving part of the way in the dark, and who is to know if some sturdy beggar will not wait in the hedge, and attack and rob them?'

The same thought had occurred to Ned as their appointed hour for homecoming passed. So he saddled his horse and took his brass blunderbuss and lantern, and was in Medlar before he heard the wheels of the trap bowling towards him; very nearly getting the whip across his head and shoulders as he hailed Dorcas.

'Here, steady on!' said Ned, amused and astonished at this vengeful little stranger. 'By Gow, I rode out here to defend you lot. I should have let you be! What's to do then, that you're so late?'

But first he must hear Dorcas explain that she thought for a moment he was a robber. Then he must see how William would have squared up to this fictitious scoundrel. And then Charlotte insisted on riding home in front of him instead of staying with her mother. Piece by piece, the afternoon was unfolded in all its marvels: the horses trotting quietly in unison.

'My aunt is no favourite of yours,' said Dorcas in apology, 'and you have cause for quarrel, but I pray you allow me to see her from time to time, and take the children with me.'

'Eh, my lass,' he said, as easy with Miss Wilde as with any horse-fly that could be whisked off and forgotten as soon as it had stung him, 'I care not, one way or t'other, so long as you're satisfied. Aye, and as long as I don't have to sit in her parlour and make conversation, I don't give a . . . ha'penny.'

Which reminded the children of their gifts, and Charlotte dropped her penny in the ditch while pulling it from her pocket, and Ned took several minutes to find it.

Every candle-stick in Kit's Hill had been pressed into service, and every window facing the lane welcomed them home. Now the stars came out in company, and the moon to show them all their business.

'It were like that,' said Ned, pointing with his whip, 'eleven year since, when I rode up from Millbridge on Christmas Eve to tell them as you was going to wed me. Art sorry, my lass?'

And did not need to wait for her answer.

A Young Spark

Fourteen

William Wilde Howarth lived as water moves: always finding his own level, altering his tempo to suit the circumstance, seeming to be at home in any place. He used two languages (besides Latin, at which he was quite adept). In his mother's and sister's presence or when visiting Millbridge, he spoke in a genteel fashion: among working folk he slipped into the rich brisk dialect of Lancashire. Yet there was nothing of the hypocrite about him. He kept everyone contented so that they might let him be. Within himself he waited, preparing to reach some great conclusion as yet unknown to him. He believed implicitly in a personal destiny, though he confided this to no one. He felt that life intended him to achieve something, and kept himself open to every opportunity for advancement. He had flashes of intuition, rare, but clear as signposts. On that significant day in 1772 he had met two people who he instantly realised were of great importance to him: his great-aunt and the blacksmith. They remained curiously linked in his mind, an unlikely pair of patrons. With this unusual perception he also knew that he did not belong to Kit's Hill as his father did; that there were other people and other places ready to receive him, and that they would be revealed by time and purpose.

Meanwhile he learned his lessons from Dorcas, showing so much quickness and understanding that his mother believed she had a scholar on her hands. Simultaneously, watching his son with the horses, Ned congratulated himself on having another carter in the family. But old Will Eccles, the blacksmith of Garth, seeing the lad spend all his spare time hanging round the forge, said, 'That young 'un is a born farrier!'

Once a week Dorcas drove to Millbridge, now visiting her aunt as well as Phoebe, and doing her shopping as well. Her 'elopement' as the gentlefolk chose to call it was almost forgotten. She met former acquaintances at the rectory and Thornton House, and since they had also mellowed they had more in common. As Ned increased in prosperity, and his youthful good-nature became ease of manner, he was regarded as a gentleman farmer. This mattered not a farthing to Ned, but since it pleased Dorcas he bore with the inconvenience of exchanging formal bows and small smiles with the ladies, and engaging in a few moments' talk on market days.

At the tea-drinking, Charlotte was content to play with other children or to sit demurely while the ladies conversed, but William fidgeted. So finally he was allowed to walk in the garden, or down the High Street (pressing his nose against the window-panes of Miss Shawcross's sweet-shop). Later, he extended this privilege as far as the Grand Trunk Canal and observed the Irish labourers at work. He explored the windind side-streets of the town, loitered near groups of businessmen discussing progress, hung outside. The Red Lion if his father chanced to be there, heard the local gossip from the ostlers at The Royal George, watched the stage-coach leave for distant places.

His new pony, a dark bay with a curly mane and tail, gave him more scope for travelling. He rode ahead of his mother's trap proudly, making sure the road was safe. When the women-folk were deep in patterns he went to the rectory stables and claimed his mount again.

Looking up from his anvil, one fine cold November afternoon, Aaron Helm recognised the long dark lad on the fell pony, and set down his hammer.

'William Howarth, isn't it?' he cried, and came over to

shake hands. 'And what can I do for thee? Does she want shoe-ing then?' looking at the pony's feathered heels.

'Oh, no, sir,' dismounting eagerly, face alight, 'and if she did then I could shoe her well enough. I came to see you, sir, about taking me on.'

'Taking you on, my lad? I don't recollect speaking of that!'

'Yes, if you please, sir, you said, if I could hold a horse still (which I can, sir) and if I could move iron weights (and I can shift them pretty well, sir) and if I could lift your apprentice (which I think I could, if he would let me, for I have practised on Jacob Eccles). I have eat all my crusts and fat, sir, as you bade me. And I punched a boy upon the nose until it bled, for he was tormenting his sister (only she will follow me about, sir). And I have took care of my mother and Charlotte, and rode ahead of them this morning to make sure the way was safe. And I am full eight years and five months old, sir, next week!'

Aaron Helm stared at his bright face for quite a minute, then roared with laughter so that the pony started.

'Take thee on?' Aaron cried. 'Why, lad, that would be as an apprentice, and is business between thy father and me, and you'll need to be all of fourteen afore then. Didst think I were serious, then?'

'Yes, sir,' said William, abashed.

Aaron Helm put his right arm round the boy's shoulders.

'I love thee for it, lad,' he said, 'I love thee heartily. Nay, why am I laughing? I should be punced for misleading thee. How can I make it up to thee, William Howarth?'

The boy came from dismay to delight in an instant, crying, 'Oh, let me stay an hour and help you, sir. But where shall Molly go?'

'Tether her to that post on the Green, then she can feed her while she bides,' said Aaron. 'Didst say you could hold a horse? Here, Josh, give him Owd Clem while I shoe him!' Turning to William, 'Is that 'un big enough for you?' William nodded, and stood by the mighty draught horse fearlessly, while the owner smiled and went off. 'Is your father a squire like, William?'

'No, sir, he is a farmer, but the land is our own. Kit's Hill sir.'

'He's given thee a good pony, any road. Jack! Blow the fire, wilta? Hold him steady, William. Dost know why he's called Owd Clem? Why, along of the blacksmiths' patron, St Clement! I named him when he were a colt, and he's never been nowhere else but this forge!' All the while he was shoeing the old draught horse, who did not need William's soothing for he was a regular customer, as great in years as in girth. But Aaron judged folk by what they did rather than what they said, and was observing the lad's easy way with him.

'Aye, it's St Clement's day next week, then we have a holiday and a supper and a song or two to cheer us on. I'll take care of him now. Canst fetch me that box, William?' Watching him lift and carry it, though scarlet to the temples with effort. 'That's right, lad. You tell truth, then?'

'It is best not to lie,' said William judiciously, 'for then I might be found out.'

'Is that what thy father tells thee?'

'No, sir. He says I should tell the truth because it is right.'

'And you've been lifting Jacob Eccles, then?'

'I can but get his feet off the ground, sir, and set him down fast again.'

'Tha'rt a good lad,' said Aaron. 'Never sirrah me. Canst talk plainer?'

'Aye, I can,' William replied, with the phantom of a smile on his mouth.

'We'll do well together, thee and me, lad,' said Aaron, and placed his hand on the boy's shoulder and shook him gently, smiling in his black beard.

Millbridge Grammar School had been founded in 1567 when Sir Richard Kersall bequeathed land to the value of ten pounds per annum, to found 'a fre gramer skoyle' which should endure, he hoped, for ever. Built in the reign of good

Elizabeth I, along with a dozen others in the country, it had enjoyed a quiet reputation among the town burghers for nearly two hundred years before Henry Tucker decided to make it famous. A brilliant Classics scholar, fresh from Cambridge, he chose this obscure post deliberately, and set out to prove that a northern market town could match the ancient seats of learning for opportunity and education. He believed sincerely, even obstinately, in the value of a daily rather than a boarding school, since it combined the best qualities of parents and teachers. He believed that intelligence was not the prerogative of the well-to-do, and could be found and nurtured in all classes. He discovered what many a visionary had done previously, that Millbridge was anxious to be famous but not to pay for that privilege. There was a dearth of academic young minds, and he realised he would have to compromise his ideal for a boarding and day school in order to house his rare plants. He suggested that the burghers take pupils into their own homes, for a consideration, and act as Elizabethan foster-parents did. But Millbridge associated payment and guests with lodging-places, and resolutely declined to be Elizabethan. He asked the authorities for money or a new building, to extend the school. They were full of a fine scheme for improvement of transport, and fended him off with great praise and vague promises. During this time of frustration Henry Tucker encountered the enigmatic soul of William Wilde Howarth.

The interview had come about by reason of Dorcas's pride in her son, Miss Wilde's concern for his upbringing, and Ned's belief that Dorcas knew best. In fact, for once, Dorcas was unclear as to her goal. She wanted William to be a rightful inheritor to Kit's Hill, to know what he was about; and at the same time she wished him to have the education her father would have given him. So when she was questioned as to its use (by Mr Jarrett first, and Betty Ackroyd last) she replied, 'Why, he will meet people who can help him in later life. The world changes so, and he must know what to expect!' To herself she thought, 'He will be a gentleman farmer, like Lord Kersall's youngest son that directs Kersall Park Farm!' And with this she had to be content. Sometimes the means are right, and the ends obscure.

With his usual fatalism, William went through his paces for Henry Tucker and thoroughly convinced and charmed that gentleman. Perhaps he would have been less charming, had he known the nature of Mr Tucker's feeling for him. Henry was devoid of tender emotion for the opposite sex, whom he regarded as a necessary nuisance which produced grammar school pupils. But he had nursed an interest in Miss Dorcas Wilde, who would have proved such an excellent partner in the school, and now a house-mother for those boys who must come from foreign places. Only, the absence of a dowry had been an immovable obstacle. Now she offered to place her son in his care, and William appeared to be exactly the sort of son he would have liked. So he smiled on him drily, while ascertaining that the boy would be living with Miss Wilde, returning home once a month for the week-end, and taking vacations twice a year at Kit's Hill. Miss Wilde had offered to pay all expenses, Dorcas and Ned supplied the scholar.

'A wise decision, Miss Dorcas!' said Henry Tucker sentimentally, for to him she was always five-and-twenty. 'I look to William to take a lead here. I expect him to gain external honours, to be one of our future great men in the world. This is an age of reason, of enlightenment!' Then briskly, 'We shall expect to see him on the first day of the coming term. You begin a new life then, William!'

Yet Mr Tucker was not one of the boy's mentors, and he knew it. But Millbridge Grammar School was a necessary step in his future. He bore with the one, and took the other gratefully.

'I shall miss him,' said Ned suddenly, smoking his pipe in Dorcas's parlour. 'We allus stopped at home when we was lads, you see.'

She put out her hand in sympathy, because this was his son.

'You shall see him on market days, Ned. He can meet you

in Millbridge.'

'Aye, and I know it's for his own good,' said Ned resolutely. Then, 'But I shall miss waking up in t' morning and knowing he's under t' same roof.'

Charlotte wept quietly in private, and publicly said how pleased she was that William should go to school. Betty argued on whichever side she happened to fancy that day, and blamed everyone indiscriminately. Dorcas, torn between her natural feelings and her ambition for him, was quieter than any. She wondered too how William would deal with Miss Wilde, though his evenings would be devoted to learning, and the old lady indulged him fondly.

'He will go to St Mark's church of a Sunday, and take tea with Phoebe and Mr Jarrett,' she mused, 'and Agnes will not mind if he has a friend to tea with him in the kitchen of a Saturday. And yet it is a narrow life for a young boy. One does not know what to do for the best.'

It would be some time before William found his life restricting. He was a hero at Thornton House (keeping burglars at bay) and at the rectory where his pony Molly was stabled. Dorcas's tuition was ahead of the grammar school requirements for a ten-year-old, and he had a clever mind and a quick grasp of learning, so he sunned himself in praise. And he excused himself to his aunt, his godmother and his schoolmaster, so that they were not aware of the amount of spare time he devoted to Flawnes Green.

He did not tell lies, as he said to Aaron Helm, because he might be found out. But he did not tell all the truth, and he was a master of insinuation, so that no one could say he told them such-and-such and yet they were led to believe it. He pursued his studies at school and at Thornton House, and attended church and took tea with Phoebe, and played backgammon or piquet with Miss Wilde in the dark of the evenings, and kept everyone contented with him.

Then his free spirit soared forth, and off he went on Molly to Flawnes Green, to lay the foundations for his apprenticeship. Jack was there, silent and good-natured. Aaron was there, loquacious and mighty. The forge was there with its bed of incandescent coals; and there was the dark anvil, and the smell of scorched hoof and hot leather, and the ring of the bright hammer as it rose and fell.

William would return bearing fiery marks of labour and physical endurance. Then Agnes cleaned the tell-tale shoes and breeches, rubbed bruised leaves of St Peter's wort on his arms and chest where the sparks had spat, and found him a freshly-laundered shirt; so he could present himself to Miss Wilde for a Saturday evening of backchat and backgammon, combed and elegant. Agnes never questioned his motives, though she must have suspected that all was not as it should be. She loved him with a dumb devoted love, which accepted and did not judge, and helped him to cover his small wounds, and prayed he would not be found out. Betty would have done the same, though scolding him. There would always be some woman in William's life who succoured and defended him, and he held them in tender regard, always.

Millbridge was in an uproar. Lord Kersall and the heads of council in the town had held meetings in secret for quite some time. Seeing the profits to be made from the Leeds–Liverpool canal, which circled coyly past, they came to the conclusion that it would be worth their while to cut a branch canal that reached Kersall Park. For his lordship had discovered coal in his demesne, and proposed shipping it down to the hungry limekilns, since limestone was one of the county's prime shipments.

All over England the waterways were being tunnelled and cut for national transport, which would make goods quicker to sell and cheaper to buy. Many a hand had been set to a contract, or written out a banking order, to begin a new canal project. Some notions were foolish, most were useful, all hoped for great gain and none was shy of competition or chicanery.

Miss Wilde had managed to remain majestically unaware of the grand canal being hacked beyond the southern end of

Millbridge, but its branch would run alongside the river and rob her of some garden, and she was aghast.

'What of my hollyhocks?' cried Miss Wilde to the heedless council. 'I shall fetch the Constable! I shall write to King George and Queen Caroline! Where is my solicitor? What is our Member of Parliament thinking of, to allow such a thing?' (He had shares in the canal.) 'Oh, and they will dig up Walpole, that was buried under the laburnum tree by the river, for he so enjoyed the water, when he was let!'

The council, scenting profit, pressed compensation upon the High Street houses whose gardens were to be curtailed, and went ahead with their plans. The new labourers were brought in: Irishmen whose occupation had already given them their nickname. Navvies, they were called, since they made navigation canals, and an aura of disapproval surrounded this term. For they were the wildest men quiet Millbridge had ever seen. It was a different wildness from that of the drovers, who were bound up in their long journeys and the care of their beasts. Starvation lay behind these strangers, and temporary work before them only as long as they had their full strength. They did not belong anywhere, were going nowhere, simply living the moment savagely. Landless and dispossessed, they had been let loose on society by the unrestrained flood of new enterprises.

They swelled the poorer houses at the wrong end of Millbridge, and many a widow thanked God for the year of 1774 which transformed her into a landlady. The Ram tavern in Middletown Street overflowed with drinking and fighting, and the surplus adventurers took their trade up to The Red Lion, which had known nothing worse than an argumentative farmer since it was built some centuries before. From here they reeled into the Market Square at night, roaring abuse and songs of ill-repute all the way down the High Street. One or two rough fellows might rap on a lighted window or thump a handsome door-knocker, to show their contempt for law and order and all householders. In vain, maiden ladies shrieked and fainted, and made use of more smelling salts in a month than they had in a year, the navvies cared not twopence for any of them. The Constable, preferring a quiet life, was never to be found when needed, but would take a quantity of notes the following morning. The council made many speeches and protests, without attempting to interrupt the course of the branch canal. Indeed, the men were always at work the next day, apparently none the worse for their drinking, and ready to spoil any garden before them with mangling picks and spades. The overseers yelled and swore them on in this work of destruction. Borders crumbled, trees toppled, old walls were beaten down, and the cutting emerged crudely from the debris.

Left to himself on a golden afternoon, William took off his jacket and hung it from a short branch of the laburnum tree. He rolled up his shirt sleeves with an air of great purpose, and spat twice on each palm. Then he began to dig with his spade (emulating the navvies, for he envied them their shoulder muscles). Miss Wilde had ordered him to remove Walpole's bones and tombstone to a safer place. Only, after some thirteen years no one was exactly sure in which spot Ned had buried the little dog.

Now the old lady appeared, walking slowly, one arm supported by her maid and the other requiring the help of a silver-headed cane.

'I was not there,' she was saying pitiably, 'but you must have noticed, Agnes. Mr Howarth did say under the laburnum tree, did he not?'

'Aunt Tib,' said William firmly, resting on his spade, 'the garden will be destroyed far beyond this point, so it does not matter if I dig around the whole afternoon, ma'am!' For he was determined to work in peace, since he had been robbed of his Saturday in Flawnes Green. 'I should prefer you to stay indoors, and Agnes also. This will be no place for ladies in the next hour or so. I do not wish either of you to see anything that might distress you, if you please.'

Agnes concealed a smile, but Miss Wilde turned obediently for the house. It had taken her seventy-and-seven years to become fond of a member of the opposite sex, but in William she found her match.

'Why, what a scold it is!' she complained proudly.

Down by poor Miss Spencer's house the gang of labourers was digging and embanking Millbridge's latest contributions to the Age of Progress. William heard them swearing on the summer air, but did not mind their raucousness. He had heard as much on the farm when a horse got stuck in the mire. He was sorry, yes, truly sorry, that this pretty flowered grove would be mutilated. Yet the canal promised an excitement which would never be found among pinks and pansies. There would be locks and lock-keepers, barges and bargees and their patient horses, tow-paths, red-brick warehouses crammed with goods from all over England. Salt from Cheshire, ironware from Birmingham, pottery from Staffordshire: an ever-growing supply and demand, fulfilled by horse and barge and stretch of still water.

His spade struck something resistant, which was yet fragile enough to have broken. Clearing the soil reverently away with his hand, William lifted Walpole's skull aloft, and looked through the empty eye sockets.

Our Dick

Fifteen

1774–1775

'You are not with child, Miss Dorcas,' said Dr Standish, 'of that you can be certain. Nor is there any growth or obstruction that might cause an illusion of pregnancy. Are you not close on forty? Why, so am I! Well then, I think it likely that you approach your climacteric. You cannot expect to feel well, though the discomforts will be temporary, and when it is done you will have no fears of unwanted children. It is remarkable how an intelligent woman, in reasonable health, improves in her mind when this barrier is crossed. Many dwindle, of course, since their reason for being has vanished. Indeed, I congratulate you, Miss Dorcas. There was a time when I feared you might succumb to a farm full of lively brats! Such a waste. Ah, I am no favourite among the husbands with my views, I can tell you. No favourite in Millbridge, either, and yet I will cure them – which vexes them properly!'

He rattled the change in his breeches pocket and smiled at her, quite unrepentant of his reputation. He accepted his half-guinea for consultation.

'Remember me to Mr Howarth, if you please. And a very good-day to you, Miss Dorcas!'

There had been no more children since Charlotte was born. At first, for the requisite twelvemonth they bore with abstinence and semi-courting. Then Ned applied the technique of his lustful youth, withdrawing as he was about to ejaculate, for he knew this to have been successful. Certainly, Dorcas did not conceive. After a long interval they had hoped for another child, but one miscarried during the lean years of cattle plague. They then began the same cycle over again.

'I don't know how they do it,' said Betty to Mrs Howerbutt, 'for they're warm enough together. I should know, my room's next door to theirs! Shall I tell you what I think? I think all Mrs Howarth's blood's gone into her brains, and she's got nowt left to nourish owt else!'

'It will be supper-time,' said Dorcas absently, hands on hips, admiring the splendid harvest of hay in the loft, the first day's reaping.

She had had her failures, as Ned predicted, but on the whole Mr Jethro Tull now took second place only to the Almighty at Kit's Hill.

'We should go in with the others,' said Dorcas, but wished to gloat a little longer over these riches, forced from ground so barrenly named.

One by one they had succumbed to her husbandry. Owd Barebones, Scrat-acre, Leavings, Mis'ry, Short Shrift, Striving: named with exasperation and humour, with a stoical acceptance of their faults. Now they gave up turnips and St Foin, barley and beets and potatoes and clover: reluctant wealth-bearers. Beyond her powers still were the undrained fields nearest to Garth, and the steepest climbs of the Nick.

So she leaned against her husband in comradeship, for this was their harvest, and he put his arm about her waist as tightly as he used to when they were courting.

'And how are you, then?' he asked tenderly, for she had suffered with headaches and occasional fits of weeping, which was unlike her.

'Oh, I am well enough, Ned. Only I wish I might have had another son for you. Indeed I do!'

For she began to doubt whether William would ever farm Kit's Hill. It was an eventuality which had occurred to Ned some time before. So he answered the unspoken concern.

'Eh, Dorcas, let be. Kit's Hill'll take care of herself. She allus has done. She'll be a farm, my lass, long after we're in Garth churchyard.'

'Do not speak of death,' said Dorcas, at the end of creating life within herself.

'How long have you been – clear, lass?' asked Ned indicating with a movement of his head that he spoke of her condition.

'Six months or more. Yes, not since Candlemas.'

'I should think you're over wi' it, then?' said Ned, with a practical glance round the barn. 'I tell you what, Dorcas, let's go up into t' loft and pleasure us-selves proper!'

She had been on point of weeping, and was now shocked and delighted.

'Up wi' you!' said Ned, urging her onto the ladder. 'We're neither of us as young as we used to be. We haven't got all t' time in t' world, and we shan't be rommicking in us grave – that's for sure and certain. We canna stand agin death, but we can give him a run for his money!'

She turned round to look at him, and caught an expression on his face that was neither lusty nor merry. He had divined her mood and was setting his love and his will against it. A middle-aged farmer of little education but great heart, with a pair of strong arms to hold her and a mighty spirit to sustain her. He would outface old age and the ills of the flesh, would renew her when she flagged, and love her until he died. Ned. One square brown hand in the small of her back, pushing her up the crazy ladder, grinning at her protests.

'Oh, I am glad I married you,' cried Dorcas suddenly, 'and I have never told you so!'

'You didn't need,' said Ned, as they went down into the hay, 'I allus knew!'

'I've never seen nobody suffer like that,' said Betty, as Dorcas sat in the kitchen, too ill to take the final steps into her parlour. 'Here, Mrs Howarth, I'll fetch you a drop of cold water and a flannel, to hold to your forehead!'

'I tried to make her stay in bed, but she would come down,' said Nellie, concerned. 'She's poorly nearly all the while now. Up one day and down the next.'

'She don't eat enough,' cried Betty, taking the opportunity to scold Dorcas while she was too weak to talk back. 'Mind you, the change is a funny thing. It took me with the hot flushes. Flush up, I would, from head to foot. As if folk had said summat shameful to me! Here you are, Mrs Howarth. Bathe your face in that. It's fresh water, fresh-drawn. Aye, one minute you sweat, and then you feel dizzy, and another time you're feeling sickly . . .'

'I have mentioned it to Dr Standish,' said Dorcas, cooling her forehead, 'but he seems to think that this is normal – as far as normality goes, of course. Forgive me if I leave the kitchen, but I cannot abide the smell of hot food. Nellie, please to help me into the parlour – and then I must close the door. Do not think me rude, I beg. I cannot help it.'

'Nay, I'm as sorry as you are,' said Betty. 'What shall I do when our Lottie comes in? Give her some dinner? And then not bother wi' her schooling,' just a shade bitterly, for education was not one of her favourite topics, 'not today. I'll tell her to go and play her, shall I?'

'As you think best,' Dorcas murmured. 'I am of no use to anyone today, and least of all to myself.'

'Well, dunnot fret!' Betty called after her. 'There's none of us so good that we canna manage without them!'

'She don't mean half what she says, ma'am,' said Nellie, seeing the irritation and despair on Dorcas's countenance.

'No, but how *well* one has to be to put up with her!' Dorcas remarked.

The day went on without her, and she stayed in this curious haze of unreality, content to be carried along with the rest of the household. Ned looked in once or twice, and Nellie guarded her privacy and offered various refreshments though they were all refused in favour of plain water. Dorcas worried about Nellie, from time to time, unmarried at an age when women usually had a gaggle of children round their skirts. She had thought that Tom Cartwright might well have combined the role of husband and carter, but he too remained single. Sallie, of course, had married Billy as soon as she could persuade her mother to forgo the wages, and now lived in Garth and had borne a child each year for the last five years. Billy no longer played on his flute in the kitchen at Kit's Hill, but came to and from the village daily. Dorcas suspected that he did not play his flute at home either, for Sallie looked as old as her mother, and though Billy was youthful he seemed careworn.

'I must ask Nellie!' Dorcas murmured to herself, and woke to find the young woman bending over her.

'Ask me what, ma'am?'

'Why you and Tom have not married,' said Dorcas sleepily, 'for I know you care for each other, that you truly care.'

'Eh, my dear ma'am,' said Nellie, troubled, 'why should us spoil our lives? Look at our Sallie. Look at our Mam! If our Dad hadn't died she would have give birth to ten more beside the ten she had. It's no life for poor women, ma'am. Tom wouldn't have me mauled wi' childer, and I dunnot want to see him pulled down wi' care like Billy. And we like us places here. We're part of Kit's Hill. It's not *all* we want, ma'am, but we could spoil what we've got. Look at Tom's Mam dying of her thirteenth. She were scarce on thirty-nine year old. She were only fifteen when Tom were born. Our Sallie, she got wed as if it was picking daisies. Look at her, ma'am. She's lost all her teeth, and she's sickly, and she's down wi' another one. Nay, never ask me why we haven't wed, ask why so many do!'

Dorcas's colourless face, and her own eloquence, startled her. She busied herself about the parlour, picking up the patchwork quilt which had slid to the carpet, smoothing her mistress's pillow.

'I beg your pardon, Nellie,' said Dorcas. 'I did not think.'

She would have said more but was too sick and weary to frame the words, let alone order her thoughts. She heard the parlour door close, and slept again. Her dreams were hot and confused, tumbling one upon the other in wild array, like a horde of painted fools with meaningful faces. She was aware of each member of her household bending over her in turn, discussing her condition and what they should do. And the faces in her dreams watched those human faces with amusement and scorn, because they knew the answer.

'I'll carry her upstairs,' said Ned. 'If she's no better tomorrow I'm sending for that Standish. You don't think it's the spotted fever, do you, Betty? She shows nowt o' t' signs, barring the fever itself. It canna be the small-pox, for she were done against that. Here, Nellie, take them covers as I lift her, wilta? By Gow, Betty, she weighs no more than a bloody feather. Has she had nowt to eat?'

'Pickings!' said Betty, but without hostility. 'Nellie, fetch the warming pan for Mrs Howarth. Eh, I don't know. A brick wrapped in flannel were good enough for your Mam, master . . .'

No one listened. She was grumbling to keep her spirits up.

'I'll see to her,' said Ned, as the women gathered round Dorcas. 'Nay, there's no life in her. No life at all.'

The faces opened in silent gapes of laughter. They shook with delight, shimmered and swam with merriment, and floated solemnly into place again; as though Ned were their entertainment, and they his knowing audience.

'I'd best help you, master,' said Nellie firmly, and then as he shook his head, carrying Dorcas up the narrow stairs, she whispered, 'the missis has got her corset on, and it'll take me to get it off, with her being helpless-like.'

'Got her corset on? In this condition? You must both be daft!' he cried angrily. 'I don't hold with them things, any road. Come on up. I thought you'd have had more sense, Nellie, than to listen to her.'

'You know as well as I do, master,' the young woman whispered fiercely, 'that missis'd have her corset on if she was laid in her coffin!'

'She soon will be if she goes on this road!'

'Lower your voice!' Betty shouted up the stairs. 'I can hear you all over the house!'

'Oh, shurrup, wilta?' cried Ned, beside himself with anguish.

Dorcas opened her eyes, and he stopped and looked into her face intently.

'What can I do for thee, lass?' he asked. 'I'm flummoxed.'

'Will you please to tell Betty,' Dorcas whispered, 'that when Mrs Pycroft calls tomorrow I should like to speak with her?'

'Aye, whatever you like, love. What can I do now?'

'Mrs Pycroft,' whispered Dorcas, 'may know of a particular herbal remedy for this condition.'

'Well, don't go listening to a lot of daft tales,' Ned cautioned. 'That Standish didn't hold wi' her notions.'

'Not with her superstitious nonsense, certainly,' the whisper went on, 'but she has homely receipts that are not harmful, and often do great good.'

'All right, love. Here, Nellie, help me off wi' her things, wilta? Nay, don't stand there wi' a face like the backside of a donkey! I've seen her corset many a time in the last thirteen year. Don't give me any of your young-lady looks!'

'Is it not strange,' the whisper said to itself, 'that whenever I am unwell they always quarrel?'

Then Dorcas gave herself up to the motley, for they knew more than anyone in the world and would shortly enlighten her.

Downstairs in the kitchen Betty said, 'Cissie Pycroft is not expected to come up here. She never comes, bar weddings, births, deaths and christenings. She's no gossip of mine, and she hasn't been made welcome, neither!'

'Well, that's what Dorcas said.'

'She's wandering,' Betty decided. 'Take no notice. She'll have forgot all about it tomorrow. If you've got plenty of brass to throw about you'd best send for that Doctor. Eh, I never could abide a ginger man, and that bit of a sneer on his mouth an' all . . .'

Dorcas was brought downstairs the following morning, so weak and full of tears that Ned saddled his horse after breakfast and rode off to Millbridge. The women kept the parlour door open so that they might watch her and do their work at the same time. The youngest of Nellie's sisters was being trained for service, and stood on a stool by the table, her small red hands plunged into the bowlful of turnips. She was snivelling quietly over something Betty had said to her.

'Dunnot grieve, love,' Nellie whispered, 'you've got me here, and it's none so bad. There's plenty to eat, and a blanket at night. You're older than I were, when I first come, and I had nobody because I were the eldest and Mam needed my wages. Dunnot grieve, love. Dunnot grieve.'

'And think on!' Betty ordered, catching the comforting murmur. 'You're the fourth we've trained up from your family, and the only one wi' any sense is Nellie. There was your Sallie, all set up, and she had to throw it away. Then we took your Margery, and she did the same. And look at them! We'st be training up from your house until Kingdom Come, and get nowhere. So when some lad tells you a lot of daft rubbish, and tries to put his hand up your skirt, you give him a good 'un on the jaw . . .'

'Leave her be,' said Nellie, quiet but firm. 'You've said enough this morning. I dare say you don't mean it, but it hurts just the same. Was you never a little 'un yourself, and trying to please folks and doing wrong in spite of yourself?'

Betty opened her mouth, and closed it again, contenting herself a moment later with saying, 'And keep your noise down, else you'll disturb Mrs Howarth!'

Her face was saved by the appearance of Cissie Pycroft, knocking on the kitchen window with her knuckles.

'Why, whatever's to do?' said Betty and Nellie together, as the old woman came into the kitchen. Then, 'Eh, sit you down and warm you. You look fair clemmed. Have a sup of ale, do!'

'I saw Mr Howarth going through the village,' Cissie explained, 'and he said as I were expected. What's to do, then?'

'Well, fancy sending you up here on a day like this!' said Betty, indignantly. 'He were on his way to fetch that Doctor Standish!'

Whereupon Cissie Pycroft looked paler and colder than ever. The December frost had nipped her nose and fingers, her eyes were rheumy these days, and a trickle of water stealing down her worsted stockings proclaimed that she was not always in control of her bladder.

Dorcas opened her eyes, and called softly, 'Is that you, Mrs Pycroft? May I speak with you privately for a moment?'

Betty indicated by winks, nods and sundry screwings of the mouth that Dorcas was unwell in head and body, and nudged Cissie in her thin ribs not to take any notice.

But Nellie said, 'Mrs Pycroft will be there in a minute, ma'am. She's right clemmed. Let her have a sup of ale first, ma'am,' and as Betty began to whisper to the old woman, 'That'll be enough, Miss Ackroyd. We don't gossip our business all over Garth.'

Dorcas registered all this, waiting patiently in her silent landscape. For the motley had vanished in the night, and she was deserted.

'Eh, that were good!' said Cissie, as restored as she would ever be, for she was nearer to Garth churchyard than anyone else present. 'Shall I go in, then?'

She asked Nellie, not Betty, and Dorcas noted this also.

'Aye, go in!' said Betty, cross and a little frightened, for her authority was sliding away from her and she was elderly.

So Cissie, smiling and gasping, and pulling her shawl over the inadequacy of her clothing, crept into the parlour, saying in a false voice, 'Why, whatever's to do, Mrs Howarth? . . .'

Nellie closed the door behind her, and Betty turned round from the fire crying, 'Why did you shut door? We canna hear what they say!'

'We'll wait until we're told, shall us?' said Nellie firmly.

'You're getting above yourself!' Betty warned.

'Miss Ackroyd, I shall never fail, I hope, to show respect

for you, but you must do the same for me – and for others, and all. As long as this kitchen is yours I'm your servant, but I'm the master and mistress's servant afore that. They asked Mrs Pycroft to come up, and that's nowt to do wi' you. I hope I've made myself clear and you'll take no offence.'

The child clattered at her work, to show she could not hear. After a while Betty said, 'You'll take my place, then, when I'm done for?'

Nellie said, 'We'll work together for many a long year yet, Miss Ackroyd, only you mustn't go over Mrs Howarth's orders.'

But to her pans Betty spoke without consolation, 'Aye, you'll take my place when I'm done for – and I've got nowt else.'

In the parlour the old woman crept and fawned, afraid, until Dorcas said, 'I need you to advise me, Mrs Pycroft. I cannot help myself, if you please!'

Then Cissie drew nearer and began to look, and her eyes sharpened and her body creased to cringe. She lifted Dorcas' hand and peered into her face and smelled her breath, and asked many questions. How long since? How much? Did she sweat at nights? Then, asking permission, she examined Dorcas's body, prodding and testing and questioning.

'The master has gone for Doctor,' said Cissie Pycroft, hesitating.

'I have asked for *your* advice,' Dorcas replied, 'and I shall pay you for your trouble.'

Cissie looked at her, and was reassured. She ventured a smile, then a chuckle. Finally her cracked hoarse laughter rang round the little parlour and startled a faint resonance from the long clock – which struck the hour of ten in protest.

'Why, it's plain as day, missis. You've been caught on the change! Aye, you thought you was all right, didn't you?' And she winked most lewdly. 'You thought you was safe! Eh, you're not the first and you won't be the last, missis. Think back, and think on!'

'Of course, I am with child,' said Dorcas to herself, and

remembered the day that the harvest was brought in.

'You've been sick now for a threemonth,' Cissie continued, 'so you should be near the quickening, and then your sickness'll stop. Quickening comes halfway. I tell them to count four month for'ard and take a week off, from when they feel the babby move, if they're not sure!' She laughed again, until she remembered that the dreaded doctor was probably already on his way, then she drew her shawl round her rags and made a rough curtsey, and waited. 'I'll be going along now, missis. You won't be wanting me, missis, but if you drink dried pepper-mint leaves brewed in boiling water you'll find it keeps the vomiting away. Else spear-mint leaves, if you haven't the other . . .'

'Please to send Nellie to me,' said Dorcas gently, 'and warm yourself by the fire, and ask Betty to give you more food and ale.'

So it was a good day for Cissie, as she hurried down to Garth Bottoms with a fully belly, a shilling in her pocket, and an old gown of Betty's over one arm. She was safe in her cottage long before Ned rode by with Dr Standish, and she laughed again as she watched them from her refuge. Someone had brought a few sticks and left them by the door, and she made a fire. There were small kindnesses in the world still, hard and cold though it was, harder and colder though it grew. But she had looked first upon so many faces in Garth, as they entered life, that she was assured of little charities: a coarse loaf of barley bread, a pig's knuckle, an egg. They would lay her out, at her latter end, as she had laid out so many – the young and fair, the old and ugly. The woollen winding sheet was in the bottom drawer of her chest, sweeter in its sprigs of rosemary than the sour flesh it would embrace. But for now she had her fustian gown, her fire, and the the shilling unspent still. A good day for Cissie.

Dorcas began to mend as soon as she knew the cause of her complaint. It was as though her confused body had not known whether to shed life or nourish it but, being told, decided to make the best of matters. A week or so later she woke in the middle of the night and stole downstairs, warmly wrapped against the winter chill. She was so hungry that her hands shook as she lit the tallow candle and peered at the larder shelves, and she slapped the dogs away impatiently as they nosed her heels. She could have wept with frustration as she heard someone else in the passage, and turned to see Betty blinking at the doorway.

'Eh, are you all right, Mrs Howarth?' she cried, with such concern that Dorcas's anger vanished.

'I am so hungry,' she confessed, 'that I came down to find food. Oh, I could eat these dogs I am so hungry!' and she laughed and cried at once.

'Well, I never,' said Betty, her face creased with delight, 'you've taken the right turn, missis. Here, sit you by the fire and let me get you summat tasty. What do you fancy? There's rabbit pie, and the pigs have been killed and salted down, and there's a collop of beef . . .'

'Oh, cut me a slice of beef, a thick slice, and fry it for me. And have you pickle?'

'Eh, I'm not sure you should have pickle, in your state. Still, they say as what you fancy does you good! There's some turnip and potato here from supper. Shall I fry that up an' all?'

So it was, at three o'clock in the morning, that Dorcas ate such a dinner as she had not tackled in her life. Betty sat with her for company, and dipped her crust of bread in her warm ale (for her teeth were few, and those few blunt) and marvelled at the appetite before her.

'Well,' she said, as Dorcas put her plate aside, replete and a little ashamed, 'you did yourself a bit of good wi' that, missis! You're carrying a lad, and that's for sure. A Kit's Hill lad. And we could do wi' one, couldn't us, missis? Our Willie won't stop here. No, he won't. He's for the world, as you might say. I told the master when he said he were calling him "William", I said, "The Williams never stop at home, master!" So you mind that you call this 'un by name of Edward, else

Richard – that were old Mr Howarth – else Henry, as was his father before him. I hope as I live to see our Willie settled, I do. He'll be Prime Minister afore he's done. You'll look back on this night and remember what I said, missis, though you might not believe me now . . .'

She said, setting down her mug on the wooden table, and pushing herself stiffly to her feet, 'I'll tell you summat, someday, missis. When it's the right time. Well, I'll be off to bed. I'm glad as you're better.'

'I thank you, Betty,' said Dorcas, touched by the woman's rare humility.

But Betty had not done. Suddenly she blurted out her trouble.

'I know my faults,' said Betty. 'I know I'm not easy to get on with. I've had hard life, and it's made me hard too, I dare say. Nellie tells me off now and again.'

She could not express what tormented her, standing before Dorcas, grey head bowed and shoulders rounded. Her rough hands played with the fringe of her thick shawl.

Then she said, in such a full voice that Dorcas was hurt for her, 'You won't turn me out, will you, missis?'

'I never heard of such a thing,' said Dorcas, and made herself speak very sternly to save Betty's pride. 'I had thought you were our friend for life. A part of the family. A part of Kit's Hill. Do you think so little of me, and so little of Mr Howarth, that you would entertain such a notion?'

Betty's relief was so great, and brought her so near tears, that Dorcas scolded her cleverly until she recovered herself.

'I must be getting old,' said Betty at last. 'I never thought owt like that afore, I must say!' She smiled uncertainly at Dorcas, saying hopefully, 'And we've had us good times, haven't we, missis? When our Willie and our Lottie was born . . .'

'. . . and now,' said Dorcas gently, 'now, this morning, talking together like good friends, like old friends.'

'Aye,' said Betty, comforted. 'Aye, you're right. I don't know what come over me, I'm sure. Only you get feared as you get older. 'You'll be old yourself some day. And all of a sudden you've got nowt to offer life, and life's got nowt to give, and you get feared.'

'You have no need to fear,' said Dorcas stoutly, into the void. 'There is nothing to fear!' And she stared down chaos, afraid.

The life within her trembled and softly exploded, like a shower of burst soap bubbles, and then she believed what she said and smiled most radiantly.

'Well, he earned his guinea that time, I must say!' Ned remarked, as Matthew Standish trotted wearily back to Millbridge.

Dorcas had suffered throughout the day and well into the night, while her husband and children sat in numbed silence downstairs. Now, weak and shaken, but alive, she lay asleep. In the hooded cradle by her side, the boy dozed and snuffled and sneezed, ridding himself of the birth mucus.

'We're calling him Richard after my father, and Edward after me, Betty,' said Ned. 'What do you think to that.' She approved. 'I'd best put him into t'Bible while I'm at it,' Ned continued, 'and then I can show her when she wakes up.' He paused. 'What o'clock were it when he were born?' he asked. 'Dorcas is particular as to the times.'

Together they arrived at a reasonable moment, and Ned wrote carefully, tongue between teeth. He was savouring a victorious match with Dr Standish, who had arrived downstairs, bitter with the struggle, crying that Dorcas was fortunate to be alive, that the child was fortunate to be alive, and that there were to be no more infants – upon pain of death.

'Well, there shouldn't have been this one, if you was right about her having the change!' Ned had replied sarcastically. 'And if you *are* right, then do we have to wait a twelvemonth to find out, or do we wait longer? Oh, I see, a twelvemonth after her monthly shows stop. I've often wondered where you got that twelvemonth from! It seems to be the answer to owt!'

'Hark at the rain and wind!' said Betty suddenly, listening.

'Aye. We'st have a bad harvest this year, short of a miracle – and there aren't so many of them round!'

She said without rancour, 'I've noticed, many a time, that when there's nowt to feed on – there's another motty open, waiting to be fed.'

'Nay,' Ned soothed her, finishing the inscription with a flourish, 'never let it be said in this house as a child were unwelcome. As long as God sends mouths we'll feed them somehow, Betty. When I canna share my crust they may as well lay me underground.'

No. 4 Richard Edward Howarth, borne towards eleven of the clock, ye night of 29 May, 1775. By God's Grace, both alive and well.

Apprentice

Sixteen

1777

'William is upstairs in his room,' said Miss Wilde lifelessly, 'where he has been since Mr Tucker sent him home yesterday. I let you know the news as soon as I could. You are so far off. As if I have not had trouble enough.'

She had been weeping, and her cheeks were stained. Her hands trembled as she clasped the silver-headed cane, and brown spots of age stood out against the frail white skin. Her wig sat on her head in youthful mockery.

'We shall wish to hear William's statement, of course,' said Dorcas gently, 'before we come to a conclusion, aunt. Perhaps Mr Tucker has acted hastily.'

'He was never hasty in his life,' said Miss Wilde, 'but I should not like you to be hard on the boy. He is a good boy to me.' Then she recollected her manners, saying, 'But will you not take some refreshment, Dorcas, after your journey? Agnes is brewing the tea.'

'I thank you. I should like to take up tea for William and myself. My husband thinks it best we take separate counsel with our son.'

She spoke formally, to give weight to Ned's opinion in the eyes of her aunt. He answered frankly and honestly as was his wont.

'Aye, lass, you go first. I'll sit in t'kitchen wi' Agnes.'

'You may sit with me, sir,' said Miss Wilde, very dignified

and correct.

'I'll sit wi' pleasure,' Ned replied, 'but I'm no great shakes at talking.'

'Nor I, sir, today. We can sit in a companionable silence. I suppose?'

So Dorcas left them together, a strange pair in the front parlour, and trod the familiar stairs with a familiar heaviness. William had been housed in his mother's old room, and she knocked on the door softly and called his name.

'Come in, if you please, mamma,' said a muffled voice, and she beheld him choked with tears and put out her arms to comfort him.

'Is my father angry with me?' he asked, wiping his eyes, drawing apart.

'He will be angry if you have spoke an untruth, but is waiting to hear your version of the incident,' she said, hurt by his independence.

William's brightness had been dimmed. He had lost his air of alertness, his gloss. A sorry blackbird, and a silent one. His mother stood by the painted shutter, as she had stood nearly seventeen years ago, and looked down into busy Millbridge.

'What have you to say to me, William?'

He had been rehearsing his reply, as she would have done, and put his case with considerable expertise.

'I have nothing to say, mamma, that will not grieve you – and for that I am sorrier than I can tell, for I wish to please you, but pleasing is not enough!' She glanced at him quickly, lips compressed. 'Mamma, I am no farmer though Kit's Hill is my home. I am no scholar either, though I can learn and delight in learning. What you wanted of me, when you put me to the grammar school, I cannot guess. I feel that if I had continued with my early promise you would have found a way for me, out of Kit's Hill. So my farming would not have been of first importance to you. But I have found another, and the man who will help me to it. I want to be a blacksmith. This is my quarrel with Mr Tucker. I did well enough at school, but my interests are elsewhere. He has taught me how to learn, and for that I honour him – but I have not been learning what he wanted. Now I am found out, and he has cast me off in a manner I find strange. He has treated me with an extravagance of feeling, a disgust in me as great as was his pride. And yet he speaks of equality and reason and progress. That is my case, mamma.'

She said, through lips that barely moved, that were colourless, 'What of the magazine you ordered through Mr Jarrett?'

'I am sorry,' said William, flushing, 'that I had no other means of finding what I wanted. This seemed of a piece with your own interests.'

'It is all seeming,' said Dorcas drily, 'You have managed to dissimulate without exactly lying. That takes a talent for which I have no admiration.'

William said, as he would say many times in life, 'But if I must seek my own truth, and can find no other way, but by a half-truth, is that not better than living a lie?'

Dorcas was shaken, and would have fought for him had he wanted something near to her own heart, but would not fight for a farrier.

'Mr Tucker says he will not take you back, and I see that you would not go back if he did! You are near on thirteen, William, not a child. The life of a blacksmith is a hard one. You will have no time to combine work and study as you do now, and once you are apprenticed there is no turning back.'

'I have not turned back since I was eight years old,' he said. 'I know what I want, mamma. I would I could persuade you of it.'

She kissed his cheek and passed out of the room without speaking. He felt heart-sore when she had gone, because he loved her and wished to please her, and was so like her in his stubbornness.

Ned was a different matter, sitting determined and angry in the pretty room with its dimity hangings.

'Never mind telling me a fancy tale,' said Ned, 'what were you up to ordering books on your mother's list, and sneaking off wi' them?'

'I was permitted . . . mother let me have books for special study. I needed something for my own interest. I ordered *The Gentleman's Magazine*. It's full of information of every kind . . .'

'Just a minute!' The hardworked hand raised up to silence him. 'What do you mean by "needed"? That your schoolmasters told you to get it?'

'No, father. I needed to know what was going on. Not Latin and Greek and History. I'm not a scholar. I can't live in the past. I want to live now, and for the future. Father, did you know that the iron master, Mr John Wilkinson, has ordered an engine that works by steam from Boulton and Watt? And they are going to build an iron bridge, father, the first in England – the first in the world . . . and in Shropshire they have been smelting by coke for years and years, not charcoal. My mother would like to read it, too, and I was going to bring my copies home with me to show her. Oh, you should see it, father, for the marvel of wealth it contains. I was transported. I felt that the whole world was in those pages, waiting to be grasped!'

The bright face and glossy head, the pouring out of words, silenced Ned's wrath, for the lad looked so like Dorcas.

'Well,' said Ned, 'it weren't right to go your own way, but then it weren't exactly what you call wrong, neither. So we'll say no more about it. But that Tucker's right vexed, I can tell thee!'

William stood by his father and touched his arm hopefully.

'I want to be a blacksmith, father,' he said simply.

All his love for the boy rose in Ned's throat and choked him. He shook his head from side to side, more in thought than in denial.

'I want to leave school, father, and be apprenticed to Mr Helm of Flawnes Green. He wants me, too. Please, father, make it right with my mother.'

'Nay, this'll break her heart,' said Ned gravely. 'She's set on making summat of thee, lad.'

'But I shall make something of myself if I am let,' cried

William. 'I am so clear in my mind about this, father. She will listen to you.'

Ned had come to bring William to justice, and Dorcas to lead him back into Mr Tucker's fold (for she could have persuaded the irascible man). Now Ned found himself turned into an emissary between mother and son, and was puzzled.

'I tell thee what,' said Ned, after a long pause, 'let's take thee home. It's not far off your summer vacation, and we need help on the farm. I might fetch her round afore the winter, you never know. But you've got a year's wait any road. I tell thee summat else, lad! Keep from under her feet, and be seen studying thy books now and again, and keep thy mouth shut! Right?'

'Right!' said William.

Then he held back tears and flung his arms about his father's neck, in relief and thanks, crying, 'And may I have *The Gentleman's Magazine* still?'

Aaron wiped his face and neck reflectively and sat down on a rough stool near the door, that he might see his visitor better.

'Draw up that other stool for thyself,' he said. 'So tha'rt Will's father, arta? I've seen thee now and again, passing through like, but never to talk to. Else I'd have asked thee a question or two, myself!'

'He seems to have played us all off, one agin the other,' said Ned, but without reproach. 'I've come to see thee because he wants to be 'prenticed. He'll be fourteen, come midsummer '78. His mother's been fetched round to the idea, and that weren't easy, I can tell thee. But Will's keen, and I'm keen, and I can't say fairer than that.'

The motes danced in the early autumn sunlight, the blacksmith wiped his face with an air of thoughtfulness and some regret. Ned sat comfortably in the smithy, and nodded in a friendly manner to the two apprentices.

'Will hasn't been here since April,' Aaron said, as though this explained something.

'Well, he had a bit of trouble like,' Ned replied, and gave

the gist of it.

'I wish he'd have told me,' said Aaron. Then, 'For I thought as it were a bit of fun wi' him, you see. He were full of tales (full of work, too, I'll say that for him, and I've never had a better lad helping out, never!). But you saw his jacket and shirt?' Confiding, one working man to another. 'And he said he were at the grammy school, and living wi' his aunt in Millbridge and had to get back in time! Well, I added one and one and made three – as you might say – and I thought to myself, "This is a lad as'd go a long way if he were born to it, but he's a scholar. So don't you be surprised, Aaron, if he don't turn up one fine day. Then, in a few years, you might look up from the anvil and see him standing there, a fine young man back from Parliament and glad to visit an old friend!" Oh, he said time and again as he wanted to be a smith, but I thought he were for another walk in life, altogether.'

'Well, he's not!' said Ned, wondering where this preamble led.

'You see,' said Aaron, 'he didn't turn up for six month, nor sent word.'

'We had to get his mother round,' Ned explained, 'and he's been treading eggshells since April. He dursen't move, I can tell thee!'

'Then I'm sorrier than I can say, for he's been like the son I never had. But you can see as this is only a blacksmith's shop. I can take one 'prentice wi' comfort, and two at a squeeze. When Jack left me two year ago I got another lad. Then this 'un,' pointing to a youngster somewhat older than William, 'this is a Flawnes Green lad, and his mother were widowed at Easter, and he's allus been handy. She come to me wi' the sovereigns in her palm, and begged me have him. I can take no more, Mr Howarth, and it'll be five year afore the elder is a journeyman.'

'By Gow!' Ned said, as though the wind had been knocked out of him. Then, laughing ruefully, 'Eh, he's too clever by half. He were so busy playing one off agin the other that the

Almighty's had a bit of game wi' *him!*'

'Joe!' Aaron shouted. 'Fetch me and Mr Howarth a sup of ale, wilta?'

'Dorcas'll never stomach him working for Will Eccles in Garth, that I can tell thee for a start. So what's to do?' asked Ned.

Aaron took a long and leisurely pint of ale to think of an answer.

'I'm a Methody,' said the blacksmith at last. 'You've heard of them?'

'Oh aye?' said Ned uncertainly.

'I were converted seventeen year ago when John Wesley first preached in Lancashire. I've walked miles to the Meeting-houses – which are like to your church. I've had stones throwed at me, Mr Howarth, and rogues lying in wait to beat and rob me. But the Lord makes the flesh withstand the stones, and giveth a mighty fist with which to smite the ungodly!'

'I can see t' fist,' said Ned respectfully, 'but Dorcas won't like the Methodys neither. Her father were one of them high churchmen wi' low wages.'

'Why should a man be paid owt to give God's word?' asked Aaron.

'Nay, waste no breath arguing wi' me,' said Ned decisively. 'All I do is pray of a Sunday, pay my tithe when it's due, respect Parson and tell truth. I know nowt about religious argument.'

Aaron smiled, then said, 'Dost object to Quakers, Mr Howarth?'

'What are them?' Ned asked, bewildered by heretics.

'Much like Methodists. Nonconformists. I travelled about a bit afore I settled in Flawnes Green, working and preaching as I went, and made many friends in the sight of God. They had a name for me, and all. The Forger of Iron and Souls, they called me. Aye! Now then, to our Will. There's a family of smiths in Birmingham of the Quaker persuasion. Scholes is the name. Nigh on six or seven brothers all in the iron trade, one road or another; and better men and better smiths you'd never hope to meet. He might find a place wi' them, if I said a word for him. And afore you open your mouth again, let me tell you this. If he'd come to me he'd only learn smithing. If he goes to Birmingham he'll have an education as you couldn't buy in twenty grammy schools!'

Then he began to talk, and Ned to listen (so that he could repeat all this information to Dorcas).

'This here family, by name of Scholes, is throwed as wide as Our Lord's net, and kept as sound and well-mended. They've got business connections all over t' country. Forges, foundries, ironmonger's shops, iron works, mines. Their 'prentices live wi' the family like sons. When the 'prentice-ship's over they'll find them work wi' another branch, if they want it. Menfolk and womenfolk travel the country once a year, preaching the Word and visiting. There's allus some-body staying wi' the Scholeses. When I were there I met a relation of Abraham Darby the iron master, from Shropshire, and a gracious woman she were.

'You'll never hear a harsh word spoke, let alone a swear word, but you'll hear the truth and be expected to tell t' truth. The food is hearty, but not fancy. Everybody works hard, but not beyond their strength. They sleep in good beds, but not soft 'uns. They're well-clad, but sober-like. Anybody can speak their mind, from th'oldest to youngest, but they must put their mind to what they speak. There's books a-plenty to read. There's conversation as seems to come from the four corners of the earth. The brother I know best (the one I'd like Will to go to) is Bartholomew Scholes. Now he reads out of the newspaper to the family over breakfast, so that they take in politics wi' their daily bread.'

Ned supped his second tankard thoughtfully, trying to think what Dorcas would say to all this.

'How are they different to us – to me?' he asked.

'They believe as all men are equal in the sight of God,' said the blacksmith, and Ned nodded agreement to this. 'They won't take their hats off to anybody, high or low, even the

King and Queen – except at the Meeting-house, in God's presence.'

'Dorcas won't care for that,' Ned murmured.

'They speak each other plain. Aaron Helm and Ned Howarth. No misters, no missises, no lords and ladies, no titles.'

'Nor that, neither.' Discomfited.

'They pay no tithes to the established church.'

'I'm surprised there's not more of them, then!' Jokingly.

'They take no oaths, since a man's word should be the truth.'

'I like that. I agree wi' that!'

'They have been persecuted and thrown in prison, robbed and insulted, and yet they'll bless the hand that clouts them. And if they was put in a barrel tomorrow, they'd shout Glory through the bung-hole!'

'I admire their spirit,' said Ned, though his own was faltering, 'but the lad's mother isn't going to like the idea, and so I tell thee.'

'Nay, life's easier for them now than it's ever been. They're allowed, now, in a manner of speaking. There's powerful folk among them, too. Folk big enough and rich enough to speak up in high places. If Will learns his business from them he won't be a poor man. For they fix a fair price on their goods, and never bargain. Their word is trusted, and their work prospers. You tell your wife this, and all. The Quaker women are respected, and reckoned equal with the menfolk, and they have their own marriage service – and the women dunnot have to say they'll obey, neither. I'm not sure how I feel about that, myself! I think it takes a rare woman to equal a man's reasoning.'

'I know how I feel about it,' said Ned humorously, preparing to drive back home. 'I'd be right glad to be equal wi' any woman. They can all get round me! And as for obeying, I've never done owt but please Dorcas ever since we was wed! They've got good sense, them Quakers, to face facts! Eh, but I tell thee what,' shaking his hand heartily, 'I thank thee,

Aaron Helm, for being good to my lad. I'll let thee know what the wife thinks. And, eh up a minute! If you think so much o' t' Quakers why was you a Methody?'

The blacksmith answered him directly, 'I'm not as peaceable as them, and I left the biggest difference to the last afore I told thee. They won't fight, not for themselves, nor King nor country. They allus turn t'other cheek (as Our Lord said we should, I don't quarrel nor argue wi' that!). But I canna do it. If a man raises his hand against woman or child I'll thrash him for it. If England wants me to go to the war, then she can have me. I'll fight for her, Americans, Frenchies and owt. I canna turn t'other cheek, Ned Howarth, and so I tell thee!'

'Aye, well, if you turn t'other cheek,' said Ned philosophically, 'they're like enough to punce that 'un and all! I feel the same way, myself, mind you.' Aaron nodded slowly, opening his eyes very wide, lifting his brows very high, in assent. 'I'll keep in touch,' said Ned, 'and thankee.'

Late in September, when the harvest had been gathered and the tithe paid, and everyone was deep in sheep sales and fairs, there was a shout from Eli Sidebottom, who was mending a drystone wall.

'Drovers!' The cry echoed round the hill, 'Drovers, drovers, drovers . . .'

'Open t'gate, Billy,' said Ned. 'This'll be the last of them afore winter comes!' And he shaded his eyes, for the sun was warm and kind, and looked to the black river of Highland cattle flowing through the Nick. Then he stared again, and shouted, and began to run.

'Dorcas! Dorcas! It's Jamie Blair, by Gow. It's Jamie!'

She was running, too, for he had not come since the rinderpest of 1763, and fourteen years of living lay between them all. The long man on the tall horse lifted his woollen bonnet in reply, and brought himself sedately down the steep path, while Ned and Dorcas waited arm-in-arm to greet him.

'Well,' said Ned, when they were face to face, 'Well, Jamie!'

For he was grey now, and white where the beard met the cleft of his chin, and the blue eyes had looked on a lifetime. 'Tha'rt welcome,' said Ned, and held out his hand, for he knew that Jamie Blair had not been as fortunate as Ned Howarth.

'Very welcome, sir,' said Dorcas kindly, 'but you have been too long in coming. Is your son not with you?'

'For here's one of ours!' shouted Ned, jubilant, as Richard ran up and caught his father by the leg. 'And here's another!' For William was striding towards them, to shake the Scotsman by the hand, 'and here's our little lass!'

Charlotte smiled and curtseyed, then stood with her hands clasped shyly before her, fair skin flushed.

'Aye, you are rich indeed. Rich indeed,' said Jamie slowly, looking round.

'And how's it been wi' you?' Ned asked, troubled by the man's worn aspect.

'I have an old apology to make, Ned. I fetched the rinderpest to you, those many years since, though I did not know it until my beasts began to sicken, and we were well away by that time.'

'Take Mr Blair's horse, Tom,' said Ned quietly, then, 'That's never why you stayed away? Somebody's beasts gave it to yourn!'

'We reckoned so, for they were free of taint when we set out. No, Ned, I did not stay away. I was wiped out, my friend, and far from home, wi' not a penny in my pocket – and many a pound owing on the beasts. I had paid my debts and started again in a small way when the next cattle plague came, and that one stayed for three long years!'

They were walking towards the house, side by side, Jamie and Ned and Dorcas; and the children followed behind. They could hear the beasts being counted into the Ha'penny Field.

'Yan, teyan, tethera, lethera, dic . . .'

'We came into England, Dugald and I, to find work of any kind, for all of Scotland was a bare bone. We walked down to London, where there was a man who helped me once, and knew my worth. We could not find him, and we slept in evil places full of fever. Dugald died of it. He was but eighteen years old, and he took the greater part of me with him.'

'Yan-a-tic, teyan-a-tic . . .'

'I have followed the road all of my life,' said Jamie, 'and never knew it was the companion that makes the road sweet.'

'Sezar, laizar, catra, horna, tic . . .'

They had eaten hugely and well of roast mutton and red-currant jelly, potatoes and pease pudding. Now Betty made up the kitchen fire again, more stiffly than in former days for she was troubled by rheumatism. She set the poker in the red heart of the coals, and put a block of peat and a thick log atop (the one to burn slowly and the other to give a good flame). Nellie served out the ale. Tom and Billy had carried up the cask from the cellar.

The great kitchen could not have held one more listener. Ned sat in the inglenook opposite his honoured guest, but Dorcas stayed in the centre of the room among her servants and farm hands. Then all raised their drink and wished each other good health, and took a long sup, and waited in silence. They would play their parts well tonight, for much had happened and they had much to say.

'You have grown a wee bit, Billy!' said Jamie, as the man nodded to him.

They all laughed, and Betty cried, 'He's got six young 'uns down in Garth. He only came up this evening to see you, Mr Blair. He married Sallie, tha knows. The little wench. Nellie's sister!' And as he looked uncertain, though polite enough to dissemble his lack of memory, 'Nay, I'll be forgetting my own head next! They was only childer, then. Nellie and Sallie!'

It was then that Dorcas realised they had all been changed, and caught an answering emotion on Jamie's face, and snatched the moment up lest it tremble the evening down to its foundations. For they must not be sad tonight.

'You will have been a ways in the past few years, Mr Blair?'

Dorcas hinted.

Then the drover sat again at his ease, puffing his long pipe, thrusting out a leg, staring into the flames. And by the blue absorbed gleam beneath his eyelids, they knew that he was only waiting for the silence to last long enough. The story-teller was in their midst again, stretching and sighing and taking the stem of his pipe from between his lips, looking round at his audience in apparent surprise.

'Aye, aye,' he began softly, 'we have travelled a ways these last years, to more fairs in your English shires than you could count on all your hands, and seen more marvels in a twelve-month than most good men do in a lifetime . . .'

With him they travelled the road again, and looked for the clump of firs that they might put up for the night; and skirled the bagpipes so that the beasts might step out grandly; and ate from pies the size of cart-wheels at Brough Hill, with a rich wall of crust to them. They ferried the cattle over the roaring rivers, and let turkeys roost in trees for the night, and saw the geese shod for their long walk to Nottingham, and journeyed deep into the South of England. No man was their master, then. They followed an old call. But ahead of them rode a bonny lad upon a little pony, and they were never able to catch up with him.

'Father,' said William, 'Mr Blair says I might go with him for the rest of the way, and look to the cattle if they should lose a shoe. Then he will set me on the road home when he turns for Scotland. He will not be long. A month at most. And, oh, I should so like to go, father!'

'What dost think, Dorcas?'

She paused only for an instant.

'It would be good for both of them, I do believe,' said Dorcas, and was swept off her feet by her son's wild hugging.

She said nothing more just then, but they guessed that she would be in favour of the Scholeses of Birmingham. It had occurred to her that there were worse ways of losing a son than making him apprentice to a Dissenting blacksmith. And she had always been a little fond of Jamie Blair.

Dorcas's letter was answered by Bartholomew Scholes's wife, who addressed her bluntly as *Dorcas Howarth* and ended *Y^r friend in God, Ruth Scholes,* which Dorcas considered to be an extreme familiarity. Nevertheless, she found no fault with the intelligence and sympathetic tone of the letter, which divined her doubts and endeavoured to alleviate them even though they might not be dispelled. She suggested that Dorcas should visit them with William, and then they could make their separate decisions in full knowledge.

On the tide of events, Dorcas set out with her son for Birmingham. She had not been further than Kit's Hill from Millbridge since she first arrived there to live with Miss Wilde in 1757, and found that coaches and roads had improved tremendously. They took the journey very comfortably and quickly, staying overnight at Manchester. The broad highways, the stops for refreshment and a change of horses, the bustle of inns and ostlers and baggage and their fellow-passengers, delighted both travellers. The world outside Kit's Hill burst upon them. Their relationship was now most apparent: a quickness of tongue and thought, a brightness about them: blackbirds both, and in full flight.

On the evening of the second day they approached the city. For the first time in their lives they saw an industrial landscape in all its awesome grandeur. Like a preacher's vision of hell, the everlasting fires flushed the sky for miles around. Flames were vomited from a multitude of furnaces, and a constant dull roaring troubled the ears. Pale people hurried by, bent on some errand which wholly absorbed them. They seemed not to notice each other, but brushed and flitted past, faces averted, as though they had all been ghosts.

There were many shops here, displaying such a variety and abundance of goods that the onlooker was spoiled for nothing but lack of money. There were regiments of black brick houses, built in terraces, back to back, each bearing its little funnel of smoke, and they stretched as far as the eye could see. The air was hot and harsh, the sparse grass and laggard leaves were grimed. Yet the unceasing noise and energy of the place gave forth a spurious feeling of excitement and hope. For surely, in all this activity, some vast design was being accomplished, something marvellous was about to happen?

Bartholomew Scholes had sent his chief apprentice, the man whose place William would fill, to meet the travellers. William looked at this big fellow with deep respect: the omega to his alpha, the finished product. He was a quiet pleasant youth, who took off his hat to greet Dorcas and addressed her as 'Mrs Howarth' (which she found reassuring) and set them and their small trunk into a stout gig.

Other guests were staying with the Scholeses, from different branches of the firm, or from the Quaker assembly, and Dorcas very soon dropped polite conversation in favour of earnest debate. William had never seen his mother so animated, and ate his dinner in silence, quite astonished at the depth and forthrightness of her judgements.

Food and furnishings were simple but of the first quality. Hospitality was abundant without ever verging on extravagance. But it was the play of minds, the frankness of discussion, and the underlying steel of their honour which won Dorcas over.

That night she lay awake for hours, hearing the rumble of stage-coach wheels in her head, recalling points of the evening's argument, listening to the humming of the city's restless hive. William had not flinched as they drove into this modern Babylon. Country-bred though he was, those great fingers of brick pointing to heaven, those black canals and distant furnaces, those ceaseless machines, had exercised a profound influence upon him. He had come home in this wilderness, to the sight and sound and taste and touch and smell of iron; cold, incandescent god.

Dorcas missed the sleeping warmth of her husband. For the first time in seventeen years they were apart, and she was suddenly afraid of being alone. She comforted herself by speaking of him often.

'Oh, how your father would detest this place, William!'

And was reassured when the lad replied, much as his father would have done, 'Well, he is spared the sight of it!' with dry humour.

William's sewing was finished. His box was packed. Everyone had given his advice, unasked for and quickly forgotten. Then Ned took both box and son in Dorcas's trap, to catch the Yorkshire Coach from Millbridge. They were to breakfast with Miss Wilde, now in her seventy-ninth year and growing frailer and blinder with each birthday. But she had risen, at an hour unheard of in the genteel circles of the town, and was waiting for their arrival, with Agnes in close attendance, These days she tended to avoid irritations, and in order to bear with Ned had bestowed upon him the status of a gentleman landowner. Ned good-naturedly answered her when he had to, but otherwise kept silent (which suited her better for his replies were out of keeping).

'Good-day to you, William,' cried Miss Wilde, trying to focus him through her eye-glass.

He came up and made his bow, so she might see him properly, and kissed her frail light hand and her light dry cheek.

'And how are you, sir?' amiably to Ned, dropping the eye-glass that she might not notice. 'Dorcas tells me that the avenue at Kit's Hall is now cleared of trees. This should facilitate a splendid view from the house. Tell me, are you still troubled by unrest among your gardening staff?'

Ned cleared his throat, but Agnes had not yet brought in the hot dishes, so there was no help for him.

'Aye, we've tipped a couple of wagonloads of ash and grit onto t' track, to sop up the mud. And Eli grubbed up an old tree stump while we was at it. I had to sack Fred Bowker in the end. He were stirring up trouble. How are you keeping, ma'am?'

She looked puzzled, but replied, 'I keep very well, do I

not, Agnes?'

'Never better, ma'am,' said Agnes cheerfully, laden with good things. 'Now should I pour your chocolate out? Here it is, just by your right hand. Can you feel it? It's not too hot. Now, Mr Howarth, you'd rather have ale, wouldn't you, sir? And, Master William, you like chocolate with your aunt, don't you?'

'Have you given up drinking claret before breakfast, sir?' Miss Wilde enquired suddenly, confounding them all.

Ned looked round desperately, and finally said, 'Aye, I have!'

Which made Agnes hide a smile, and William shake with suppressed laughter.

'You are very wise, sir,' said Miss Wilde solemnly. 'My father was often plagued by the gout, on account of drinking claret before breakfast.'

She supplied the only touch of humour to the occasion. No one ate very much. Their throats were too full to swallow easily, and Agnes alternately wiped her eyes with her apron and urged food and drink upon the guests.

'Where is Dorcas, and Charlotte and Richard?" Miss Wilde asked, coming from whom knew what tomb of thought. 'Why are they not here with you?'

'You remember, ma'am,' said Agnes, soothing her. 'We all thought as it would be too much for you on Master William's last morning. Miss Dorcas'd be sad, and Miss Charlotte cries that easy, and then she sets the little lad off. Now ma'am, shall I fetch in what you said? I believe as Mr Howarth is anxious to be off.'

A brief and sorrowful silence fell until Agnes returned.

'Now, young sir,' cried Miss Wilde, re-animated, 'here is a guinea for you, but I dare say you expected that! Come closer and see what else I have for you. It is your great-grandfather's silver chain and watch. They are very old, even older than I! We sent the watch all the way to London, to the King's watchmaker, to be repaired. And he complimented me upon it, and said it will outlast your time.'

It ticked quietly and purposefully in William's palm, very fine and worn and beautiful. He was afraid lest he should weep, and he could not speak for he had recognised the watch as his own. So he hugged Miss Wilde very carefully, and his solitary tear touched an answering tear on her cheek, while the watch pulsed between them like a third heart.

'We must be gone, now,' said Ned kindly. 'It's very good of you, ma'am, to give our lad his great-grandad's time-piece. Dorcas and me appreciate it. Very kind! Very good!' He gave her hand a little shake which was both friendly and compassionate. 'Take care of thyself. Dorcas'll be coming to Millbridge a-Tuesday to see you, and bringing the childer wi' her.'

But Miss Wilde, exhausted and forgetful with the emotion of leave-taking, only answered, 'It is very old, even older than I, and we sent it to London to the King's watch-maker, for repair . . .'

'Is this the young gentleman as will be travelling on t' box wi' me?' asked the driver, resplendent in two great-coats and two mufflers, and so stout and scarlet that he could hardly move his chins.

'Oh, yes, if you please, sir!' cried William, temporarily restored.

It was cheaper to travel on top, and far more exciting.

'Up you get, then, lad!'

'Take care, Will,' cried Ned. 'Don't do owt as'd upset your mother. Say your prayers and work hard, and think on. Remember to give them new-laid eggs to Mrs Scholes, and the gingerbread as Betty baked, and pay them our respects, wilta? Tha'lt be home for Christmas, lad.'

Outside the Royal George the September morning was fine and cold, the horses fresh, the coach newly-cleaned, the overnight travellers from York restored. A couple of ostlers handed up the last of the luggage. The company wrapped rugs round their legs, and got out their foot-warmers. The ladies plunged hands into soft muffs.

'Is that the lot, Dick?' asked the driver comfortably. 'Hop up, then!'

The guard jumped aboard, horn at the ready. The ostlers whipped off the cloths. A moment of silent expectancy held horses, travellers and spectators in thrall. Then out rang the horn loud and true. The driver clicked his tongue and flourished his long whip. The horses started and pulled. The wheels began to roll.

'They're off!'

Over the cobbles and out of the inn yard. Handkerchiefs fluttering, hats waving, farewells echoing.

'Good-bye! God speed!'

Another stirring blast on the horn, and they were rattling down the High Street at a spanking trot, crossing Middletown Street (which used to be the Roman way), rolling along Lower Gate, over the Grand Canal bridge, and onto the King's Highway. The horn rang out one last time, the driver cracked his whip, crying, 'Let her go-o-o-o-o-o!' And they were off. Racing along, hedges flashing, voyagers on top laughing and holding their hats, mufflers flying. Down to the iron world and the iron towns, with the great high road opening out before them like a promise.

'Hast seen thy lad off to foreign parts, then, Ned?' asked a burly farmer, stopping by the motionless man.

'Aye, I have that,' said Ned, feeling strangely empty.

'Dost want a pint at The Red Lion? I'll treat thee, lad!'

But he wanted nothing except to go home to Dorcas, and comfort and be comforted. So he shook his head in thanks and apology, and turned away.

Chance-Child

Seventeen

1779

'Can I have a word wi' you, ma'am?' Nellie asked, coming in quietly just as Dorcas thought herself safe with the accounts for an hour.

'If it is necessary,' said Dorcas drily, then added in penitence, 'but I should not have said that, for you never waste my time as others do. Please to come in, Nellie!' And as the young woman closed the parlour door behind her, 'So the matter is very private?'

'Yes, ma'am. It's about Betty, ma'am. She's badly and she won't tell nobody, and she keeps after me like a blessed cow's tail for fear I'll say summat to you. There!' As a voice called her name from the kitchen, 'Hark!'

'Nellie! Nellie! How am I to manage this cauldron by myself?'

'Leave the door open, and I will watch her without seeming to. You did right to tell me. Go now, and help her, Nellie.'

The cauldron and its contents had never presented any problem to Betty before. Now, even with help, she winced as she lifted the handle, and her face was screwed with pain until the weighty object reached its destination. Then she sat down, saying in her usual aggravating manner, 'Well, there's no good keeping a dog and barking myself. You may as well start cooking, Nellie!'

As soon as the young woman's back was turned, Betty

eased off her clog and slid it under the table out of sight. She found two clean woollen rags in the table-drawer and, gasping with pain, wound them round the foot to replace the warmth and protection of the clog. She nursed her knee and smoothed her leg reflectively. She was trying to comfort herself. After a while she tested her weight on the foot, but still did not find it strong enough to bear her.

She called peremptorily to the little kitchen-maid, 'Fetch me a sup of small beer, Susan, and be quick about it. Do I have to think of every mortal thing myself?'

She drank down the beer and sat looking at the pewter mug as though it had betrayed her. She called for it to be filled with fresh water. Nor was this enough. She drank another mug, and another. Then, nature insisting on a vacuum here at least, she was brought again onto her feet.

'Shall I help you into t' yard, Miss Ackroyd?' Nellie asked, for she could no longer pretend to ignore the limp.

'No, you won't! There's enough for you to do without minding other folks's business,' said Betty unfairly. Then, in a voice of false surprise, knowing she had gone too far, she cried, 'Eh, this clog do pinch. I see what you mean, Nellie. I'm nigh on lame wi' it! I must see if I can find a nail poking up.'

'How long has this been so?' Dorcas asked, as Betty winced and panted towards Jericho, treating every cobble on the yard as though it were a boulder.

'Some weeks now, ma'am, and getting worse all the while, But you know what she's like!'

'Well, I will speak with her. Leave me alone with her in the kitchen, and see that no one disturbs us. She does not like to come into the parlour, and indeed I hesitate to ask her to take one more step than is necessary!'

'Wrong wi' me? There's nowt wrong wi' me,' said Betty with a short laugh, and she looked very hard at the cauldron as though it had called her a liar.

'Betty,' said Dorcas, sitting by her, 'you are in pain, and

limping.'

'Oh that's what's mithering you, is it?' cried Betty, apparently relieved by this nonsensical reason. 'I've gotten a nail in my clog. I said as I went out just now, "Eh Nellie, this clog do pinch!" I said . . .'

'Betty, you are in great pain, I can tell. I beg you to tell me the nature of your trouble, and then we can soothe and heal you.'

'It's the tugging and mauling as does it,' Betty cried, aggrieved. 'Them girls don't work like I used to. There's too much to do.'

'You know very well that you may have as many girls as you please, to help in the kitchen,' said Dorcas. 'You are evading me, Betty, and it is so foolish. A little matter can grow great for want of attention.'

Betty said, 'I don't like showing you, missis. You've got a fine nose.'

But she bent, holding her breath against the pain, and unwrapped the outer rags on her foot. Then she paused, probably eased for a moment by the lessening of pressure, and said heartily, 'Nay, it's nowt. I've getten a boil on my foot as has gone bad!'

'Then I can bruise and fry lovage leaves in hog's lard,' said Dorcas, 'and lay them against the boil and break it. Let me see, if you please.'

More and more slowly, wincing and afraid, Betty gradually exposed such a spectacle as Dorcas had never seen. The flesh was swollen, mottled and caked with dirt, red with inflammation. In one place, a soft black island fell away from the rest, ringed in pus and stinking sweet with corruption.

Dorcas could only say, 'How have you borne to stand upon it?'

'There's more,' Betty admitted, reading the verdict on her mistress's face. Then she unwrapped her leg, revealing three ulcers on the line of a vein. 'It is bad after all, ain't it, missis?' she asked humbly.

'I believe,' said Dorcas slowly, 'that we should ask

Dr Standish to call.'

'Nay,' cried Betty, scandalised, 'you're not throwing good money away on me. I can manage wi' the lovage leaves well enough. Else, another simple.'

'I must know the reason before I apply the remedy,' said Dorcas.

Then she flew into one of her inspired bursts of activity.

'Nellie! Susan! Please to help Betty to bed. Tom!' seeing him in the yard, 'Tom, where is Mr Howarth? And have you seen Richard? Oh! I would speak with my husband if he can spare me a moment, and as Richard is with you please to keep him there! And Tom, please to lend me the stable-lad and a horse for this morning. He must go to Millbridge and fetch Dr Standish. Betty is most unwell. Oh, and he must call at the rectory and give a message to Miss Jarrett. Oh, and to take a note to Agnes for my aunt. One moment, and I shall write it all down. No, Charlotte shall be my secretary while I see to Betty. Charlotte! Where is she? Susan, fill the kettle . . .'

A pair of hands caught her round the waist, and Ned cried, 'Now what's up, Dorcas?' his face changing as he heard the news, 'Aye send for t' doctor. She's worth a hatful of gold guineas is our Betty. Now, Lottie,' as his daughter appeared, book in hand, lost in her own world, 'write some notes and help your mother. Tom, saddle up the cob for young Luke. I dunnot want to lose a horse – or t' lad, come to that! Never fear, my lass, we'st be right!'

He provided, as always, an outer circle of security within which she could work the better. In a steadier mood. Dorcas ordered hot water, so that they might prepare Betty for her first encounter with a medical gentleman.

Nellie and Dorcas spent the whole of that summer afternoon, to the mournful accompaniment of Betty's plaint, in soaking and scraping from her body the accumulated dirt of years. They worked portion by portion, keeping the rest of her warmly covered. Susan fumigated and aired the straw mattress, and Dorcas supplied two of her old nightgowns when she discovered that Betty had none.

'For you can catch your death of cold taking your petticoat off!' cried Betty, aggrieved, as the greasy flannel was borne away to be burned.

'Why did I not look into this more closely?' Dorcas said privately to Nellie, as they met on the landing over yet another bowl of hot water. 'She has quite neglected herself. My aunt's maid, Agnes, is as scrupulous in her person as my aunt!'

Scrubbed and combed, savouring the luxury of clean linen and clean flesh, Betty supped a bowl of bread and milk with great contentment.

'And how do you feel now?' Dorcas enquired gravely, small and tired in her vast white apron.

'Like grand folks, missis,' said Betty. 'Eh, I feel grand, I do.'

She had found life a difficult business. Now she gave herself up to a disease, and to those who would fight it for her. Worn out, she could rest.

Dorcas considered that Dr Standish's worst fault was his discussing a poor person's condition as though that person did not exist. It was a fault shared by most of the medical profession, and would not be erased for a very long time. Fortunately, Betty was too awe-struck by the occasion to think of anything but the expense, and too ignorant to comprehend half his words.

'These people never consult a physician from when they are dragged into the world until they are dragged out of it! It is a common case with them, and indeed furnishes the hospitals with quite the best examples for dissection. I dare swear you have never consulted a physician before, have you, Betty?'

'No, sir. Thankee, sir,' said Betty, anxious to please him.

'Exactly. Well, Miss Dorcas, your good servant has a multiplicity of diseases. I believe her to be suffering from diabetes, though I have not yet got proof positive. Her eyes are failing. She has these ulcerous sores upon the limb, and one upon the foot is gangrenous. I can let six ounces of blood, which should relieve her somewhat. I can amputate the limb if the sores do not yield up to your simple remedies. I can cauterise. What do you wish?'

'That we endeavour to heal her, sir, before proceeding to more serious measures. At least, that would be my hope.'

'Very well, Miss Dorcas. She will be abed for a long while!' Significantly. Then to Betty, loud and cheerful as though she were both deaf and stupid. 'You will be abed for a long while, my good woman, and must be thankful for a kind mistress that will nurse you!'

'Thankful, sir,' cried Betty, afraid. 'I'm very thankful.'

Ascending the staircase, Matthew Standish said in a highly confidential manner, 'You are a sensible person, Miss Dorcas, so I will not conceal from you that you would be wasting my time and your substance if I was to call again. You have lost her services for good. That foot will rot as the disease progresses, I have seen it before. There is no cure for diabetes. Aretaeus named it "a passer through" since the body is merely a channel through which fluid runs. Feed her lightly – bread, broth and jelly and such. You can but ease, you cannot heal her. Cleanse the body from within, treat the sores without. Your homely simples are well enough for that. This will be an arduous task, Miss Dorcas, for her heart is strong and her constitution also. She will not let go until she must. I advise you to hire what servants you can, so that you are not wore out with attending to her wants. And towards the latter end,' he added thoughtfully, 'you may send to me for her relief. Write me her symptoms, and the progress of the disease, and I will prescribe an opiate.'

As they entered the kitchen, which seemed empty without Betty there, Matthew Standish cried, 'By the by, what age is your good servant?'

Ned, awaiting the verdict, looked steadily at him. 'She's a few year older than me. Nigh on sixty, I dare say. She's been with us since I were the size of this chap!'

And he caught Dick up to his broad chest and held him

there, both of them suddenly laughing as though they had done something clever. Then Ned sat with his son on his knee, and looked from Standish to Dorcas, and did not need to ask his question.

'A fair age,' cried Matthew, 'though I dare say you live longer up here. You are as strong as oxen in this pure air!'

'You need to be strong to draw it in!' said Ned with sober sarcasm. 'I've known more than one or two die of it! Still, we all come to that in the end, don't us?' His rough hand smoothed and smoothed Dick's bright hair. 'So our Betty's for her long home, then?' he remarked. 'Is there nowt you can do?' And as Matthew Standish shook his head, and looked about him somewhat impatiently for his horse, Ned set the little boy down again. 'Go and play thee,' he said gently, 'while tha can.'

So Dorcas enlarged her household to accommodate Betty as a long-term invalid, and her still-room became an apothecary's dispensary. Nellie took command of the kitchen in which she had served for nearly twenty years. Young Susan was elevated to position of house-maid; and two small creatures from Garth, red of nose and elbows, began training as scullery and laundry maids.

It was a good time of year for herbs, and Dorcas collected them fresh each morning, when the dew had evaporated from them, and closely studied her mother's receipts. She powdered the roots of bistort, measured a dram into a glass of water, and plunged a red-hot poker into the decoction until its heat was quenched. This Betty drank, making terrible faces, to purge her body of offensive humours. The ulcers were cleansed twice daily with briony juice, and soothed with poultices of yarrow, toadflax and pomatum; for a poultice of rotten apples was not to be obtained, though Dr Standish had said this was best. Each night Betty sipped an infusion of wild thyme leaves, to fight the disease and help her to sleep. The juice of horehound, mixed with honey and wine, was dropped into her blurred eyes once a day, and henbane leaves laid upon the lids for an hour to soothe them and clear them. Dorcas also bathed them with infusions of chickweed and eyebright.

As the weeks drew on, and Betty was troubled with bed sores in spite of this assiduous nursing, Dorcas beat up the white of an egg, stirred two large spoonfuls of spirits of wine into it, and applied the mixture with a goose-feather. Phoebe visited once a week, since Dorcas could not go to Millbridge, and made calves-foot jelly with her own hands. Charlotte sat for hours by Betty's bed, and read to her from a strange variety of books chosen by herself. Dorcas wondered what Betty made of this miscellany, and concluded that she simply enjoyed the girl's voice and company. William wrote a letter to Betty, which was read to her regularly after the morning routine had been accomplished, and kept beside her bed where she could admire it all day. So that Dorcas asked if he would write another. ('For this Excellent Essay I know by Heart, my dear Son, and though it is Most Interesting – still, I am Weary of it!')

For a time, Dorcas and her medicaments stayed the course of Betty's illness. Then gangrene spread to the other foot, and began to invade the ulcers and even the bed sores. Simple remedies were rendered useless in this onslaught, and Betty could no longer suppress her suffering. However carefully Dorcas and Nellie moved her, or changed the dressings, they caused her such agony that she would shriek out. Continual pain reduced both endurance and appetite. Betty could not eat, and would be waiting for the arrival of her nurses in dread. While they, gathering sufficient resolve to torment her with their healing, were filled with as much terror as the poor creature who begged them not to touch her. At night, Dorcas could hear her gasps and moans through the wall. She lived like a sick animal that would die quietly if it knew how, but could not. Her shrill weak screams crucified the household. So, one autumn morning, Dorcas packed Charlotte off to the rectory, and Dick off to join Mary Braithwaite-Wharmby's brood at Windygate, and sent an account of the disease and a plea for succour to Dr Standish.

That gentleman tapped his upper lip with his fingers. Then went to his cabinet and measured out ten grains of opium.

'Half a grain, twice a day, will relieve the poor creature somewhat,' he said to Ned, who had brought the message and now stood hat in hand, waiting for the reply. 'Tell your wife that if she must give more she is to increase the frequency of the dose, but not its amount. I will write that down for her. The patient is taking little nourishment? Ah, that should hurry matters along nicely. I have "naught for your comfort", Mr Howarth. Your good servant is at her latter end. Let us hope for her sake, and for those who care about her, that it is a speedy one. Tell your wife to take away the pillow at night. It will help the poor woman to go faster. The organism reaches its lowest ebb in the early hours of the morning.

'Mrs Howarth must rest. Let her take turn by turn with nursing. Have you brandy in the house? I advise a small glassful, now and again, diluted in an equal quantity of water and served by the spoonful, for the patient. Brandy has a soporific effect, and induces a mild euphoria,' and as Ned fetched out the half-guinea which Dorcas had specified for consultation, 'No, no, sir! We have done business together these many years. I am not so mean that I must charge you for your wife's nursing. But I will take for the opium. Good-day to you, Mr Howarth.'

Agreeably surprised, Ned went round to the Red Lion and purchased a bottle of brandy; of which he took a modest nip or two on the way home, the day being very cold.

'Eh missis,' said Betty, as she sipped obediently at the contents of the feeding cup, 'why do physic smell bad and taste worse?'

Though she herself stank worse than any physic.

Dorcas had attempted to disguise the opium in warm milk, but its peculiar odour and hot bitter tang rose above this mild solvent.

'I do not know,' said Dorcas gently. 'It is like many things we must endure, which we believe will help us. If I could sweeten it for you I would. A little later you shall have brandy mixed in hot water, which is most pleasant.'

After a few minutes Betty murmured. 'It takes the edge off the pain, missis, I'll say that for it.' Her eyes closed, and opened again. 'You've been very good to me, Mrs Howarth. I wish there was some way to make it up to you. But I don't know how.'

She slept all afternoon. The house was quiet, and Dorcas drowsed at her ease by Betty's bed and dreamed of her childhood. She had noticed, in times of deep trouble, that she returned to this source by way of sleep or vision or reflection, to replenish her vital self. So she woke first, and was ready with the brandy and water when Betty moaned her way back to consciousness.

'Yes,' said Betty, smacking her lips and continuing the conversation of three hours ago as though it had not been interrupted. 'I wish there was some way to make it up to you. Mrs Howarth, you'll find a stocking in the mattress full of shillings and a few sovereigns!' They had, and had carefully replaced them, after fumigating the stocking. 'It's what I've saved of my wages, over the years, and that's for our Lottie. My god-daughter. For her wedding day!' She was pleased with this, and traced a pattern on the coverlet for a few moments, thinking about it. Then she roused herself, and took more brandy. 'I've thought on about our Willie, but all I've got to give him is my receipt for the gingerbread, which is secret, but it's in my head and if you'll print it out for me I'll give it him, and put my cross at the bottom of the paper so's he'll know it for truth.* Likely he'll get his wife to bake it for him one day, when he's a man, and think on me!' She traced the pattern again, contented, and sipped again. 'I don't know as I mind if you print it in *your* receipt book,† neither,' she added, 'and hand it down to our Lottie, only don't let

* Betty's recipe for gingerbread, written out by Dorcas Howarth and signed with a cross, is among the papers of William Wilde Howarth the Iron Master, in Millbridge Museum.

† Dorcas Howarth's Receipt Book is in possession of the Longe Family of Millbridge.

nobody else have it. Keep it in the family! That's right!'

Another rumination, 'As for Nellie, if she can find owt of mine as she likes she can take it. I can't say fairer than that!' She looked shyly at Dorcas. 'And there's a little box as was bought at Millbridge Fair when I were young, wi' two-three trinkets in it. Some folks might call it rubbish, but I liked it well enough. Any road, it'll help you think on me nice-like, when I'm gone. That's for thee!' Dorcas put a warm hand over Betty's cold one. 'And, do you mind the night afore our Dick were born, when you ate that meat and pickle? I said I'd tell you summat someday. But I dunnot want you to tell Master. Can you listen and say nowt?'

'It is not of any hurt to him?' Dorcas asked anxiously.

'Nay. It'd hurt him to know it, though.'

'Then I will listen and say nothing, to him or to any living soul.'

'Right!' said Betty, satisfied. Then she yawned again, and said, 'I'm not sleeping, missis, just like shutting my eyes a bit!' And slept.

Years afterwards Dorcas would remember these last few days, with Betty stopping and starting her tale like some homely story-teller. Waking from or drifting into a drugged sleep, she would continue from the very point at which she had left off, as though it were printed upon the pages of her mind, and she turned back the page a moment to re-read the last few words.

'Now you've heard tell as Mrs Hetty Howarth fetched me out of Millbridge Orphanage? Well, that weren't the truth, but it kept folks's mouths shut at the time, and they didn't know no better as time went on!

'I were a chance-child, missis. But nobody left me on a doorsill. I knew who my parents was, and I lived with my Mam until I were near ten year old and then she died. She were a weaver's daughter near Millbridge, as had been orphaned herself. She were a good spinner, and lived in wi' another weaver's family, and they didn't turn her out when she was brought to bed wi' me. She were never a flighty lass, you see, missis. But she'd set her heart and mind on a grand gentleman was pledged already.

'He told her no lies, and he promised her nowt, but they was o'er fond of each other, and that was the way of it. But he'd given his word to this other, and he kept it. He couldn't do right by both, you see. Still, he were true to us in his fashion. He saw that we wanted for nowt, and helped us out wi' many a shilling, and he visited us regular, and he thought rarely of us. He never come to see us without I must put my hand in his pocket and find a fairing. Then he took me on his knee, and called me his little lass, his bonny little lass. It makes my heart ache to think of him, even now. He were a grand gentleman, and a man of his word, wi' a big laugh and a pleasant face.

('When's our Willie coming, missis? Is he coming soon? Eh, I should like to see the lad. I'm not long for this world.)

'He had other childer, but not by my Mam. There were never owt else between them, once he were wed, but he allus told her as he'd take care of me. When I were close on ten year old my Mam died of the spotted fever. He rode down on his horse to see that she were buried decent-like, not on t' parish. Then he told me to put my bits of things together. I made up a paper parcel. I had nowt else, saving the little box as he'd bought me once at Millbridge Fair. He set me afore him on his horse and took me home. There were nowhere else for me to go, excepting on t' parish – and the parish were cruel hard.

('Eh, missis, when this pain starts up it's like being laid between anvil and hammer!)

'My father were Richard Howarth of Kit's Hill. Aye, Richard Howarth. I hadn't known his name afore then, just called him 'father' like. Mrs Hetty were a proud woman. He told her the truth – he'd tell her no less, he were like the master. When she come down next morning she were a flintstone. I were feared and lonely and asking for my Mam. She took me into the parlour where we could be private. It were a store-room then. (That's why I never liked it, missis. I knew you thought I was agin you, but that room were hell's gate to me long after you made it look proper.)

'She told me who I were, and what I were, and what my Mam were. She said she would do her duty by me, but I must never call Mr Howarth 'father' nor think of him as that. I must never tell nobody nowt or she'd turn me out and I'd starve. She fed me and housed me and worked me. She shut me out in a way, for all that she took me in. I had nobody, and I were nobody. My father dursen't speak, and it hurt him. She punished him through me, you see, until he died. I cried myself to sleep many a hundred times, missis, but I kept my word even after she were dead, and I did my duty by her.

'I've kept it to myself all these years. I'm main fond of the master, and I wouldn't disgrace him. "What!" they'd say in Garth, "Owd Batty Ackroyd! That's a bit of a come-down for them high-and-mighty Howarths!" But I wanted you to know because you'll make it right for me somehow. I don't know how.* But dunnot tell the master. It'd break my heart if I thought you'd tell him.

('No, that's right. Just thee and me, missis. You've been very good to me. Godmother to our Lotta Sophy, and the run of the kitchen all these years. Very good. Very kind. I'll just close my eyes a minute or two, missis. I'm not asleep. Just having a chat wi' the world, as you might say . . .')

The doses of opium and brandy grew more frequent, the dressings were changed more rarely. Kit's Hill was waiting on this November night for Ned to return from Millbridge with both William and Charlotte, while Richard was brought over from the Braithwaites' farm on Windygate. Phoebe had fed her godson, the Birmingham traveller, and written a blotched

*Betty Ackroyd is buried among the Howarths in Garth Churchyard, and on the stone which bears her name and dates is chiselled, 'A true and faithful member of the family'.

letter to Dorcas (to say that she and her Papa would be praying for Betty's soul), and sent a bottle of currant wine to ease both nurse and patient. So Ned and the two youngsters drove home sombrely through the wet mist, and Nellie lit all the candles to welcome them. They sat in the kitchen in silence, Dick sucking his fingers because there was no one to chide him, until Dorcas came down.

She sat by the fire, warming her hands and thinking. Her greeting had been absent-minded, for the living could take care of themselves and she was concerned with the dying. Her mien was weary but composed.

'I have considered each of you children,' said Dorcas, into the flames, 'and none will be expected to do more than he or she is able. But Betty will be deeply hurt if she does not see you, and heaven knows she has suffered hurt enough. So, my dear William, you are to be your charming self: she does not want a long face at her bed. Charlotte, though you are sensitive, I forbid you to weep: you must find some way of thinking of Betty's comfort sooner than your distress. Come here, Richard Howarth, my little lad!' He whisked his fingers from his mouth and climbed on to her lap. 'Poor Betty is very sick, and like to die, and she looks but poorly now. Do not crawl upon the bed or touch her, for this gives her great pain, but smile and kiss her cheek. Ned, you could hold him – and then there is no accident!'

She handed him to his father and stood up, arching her neck to ease it, rubbing the small of her back.

'Betty has not long had her medicine, and this is the time when she is quiet in herself. She is very thin and white and small, and does not look like the Betty we knew. She can but whisper. She can hardly see. There is a bad odour when you come close to her, though I have disguised it as best I can with lavender. That is her sickness, and she cannot help it. Do not seem to notice. You need stay no more than a few moments. Speak to her about things that have pleased you of late. As though there were no difference between Betty well, and Betty ill. She is a part of us, not some diseased thing that can be cast off or shut out.'

She smoothed her hair and apron, holding out her hands to William and Charlotte, motioning the rest of the company to follow.

'Let us all visit Betty,' she said gently to the people of Kit's Hill, and beneath the gentleness lay an order like steel.

The stench of corruption was hardest to bear, catching the throat, making the eyes smart. But William stepped forward heartily, and kissed Betty's shrunken cheek and held her hand and said, 'I have come home to see you, Betty. All the way from Birmingham, in a fast coach. And I have made you this little cross, at the forge, and chose a chain to go with it – for your Christmas Box!'

'Eh, my lad,' Betty muttered. 'Eh, my dear lad.'

'I beat it out for you myself. Do you feel it in your hand? It is very small and fine. Can you feel it?'

'Aye, my lad. I can, that. It feels lovely.'

'And I have picked these violets for you, from Aunt Phoebe's garden, Betty,' said Charlotte. 'Can you smell them?'

'Aye. They smell right sweet.'

'And here's our Dick come to see thee!' cried Ned, lowering the boy to Betty's eye-level.

'I said he'd be good, missis, and not run about,' Betty murmured, animated by the child's blue and gold presence. 'Eh, Richard Howarth, I'm glad they let·thee come. Take him away now, master. I don't want him to be feared by me. I love that little lad, I do.'

She lay there quietly, smiling on the assembled company with such loving kindness that they came forward one by one, and touched her hand or kissed her cheek, and went silently out.

'I'll stay wi' her now, ma'am,' Nellie whispered. 'Go and rest you.'

But Betty called weakly, 'Dunnot leave me, missis. Sit wi' me a while longer. I'st be piking away, soon.'

So Dorcas sat again, administering brandy and water with a silver spoon, while Betty meandered back to her early years, returning occasionally to comment and amend. Ned came up with tea in a china cup, to tempt Dorcas to refresh herself, and sat sorrowfully for half an hour watching the awesome crossing from life into death. As Betty had grown weaker they had put a feather bed on top of the straw palliasse, but now they must move it lest it contained game or pigeon feathers – which would prolong the dying. So Ned crept softly out again and went to fetch Tom and Nellie and Susan. Then he noticed that the bed lay under a cross-beam, so they moved it out of range, and took away Betty's pillow and laid her down again.

She was going more quickly and more easily now. She flexed her hands and grasped the coverlet, drawing upon it as though it were a net full of fish that she must bring in. Her breath came infrequently. A pause, a long snoring inhalation, two short gasps, a longer pause.

Dorcas laid her fingers upon Betty's pulse, but the heart beat strongly still: the Howarth heart, steadfast in purpose, bringing her back to make amends.

'We stuck it out together, missis, to the end!' Then, seeing it was Dorcas, she added tenderly, 'Eh, I do like you!' and looked at her hands amazed, and fell asleep again. The independent fingers resumed their business with the net.

'She is going,' Dorcas announced to Ned.

Now Nellie's candle gleamed momentarily in every room at Kit's Hill, as she lifted it high. By her side, Tom Cartwright drew back iron bolts, turned iron keys in iron locks, opened doors and windows wide. The November fog drifted in, silent and lonely as the soul that was drifting out. The stable-lad came back from Garth with the new Parson. And still she could not die.

'Folk said she had a foul tongue!' Betty cried to some invisible accuser. 'But I never told them owt. I kept my word. It's best, that road.'

Then she came to, and smiled again most lovingly, and tried to reach Dorcas's hand in recognition.

'Give Betty that box,' she advised. 'It were the last thing

her father bought her afore she died.' Then, a shadow crossing her forehead, 'Tell her I didn't mean it.'

When or what or how long ago was not important. She had atoned for her shortcomings.

Josiah Sidebottom held his shabby hat to his breast, closed his eyes for a few moments in silent prayer, clasped the rope as though it were a capricious but beloved mistress, and began to toll the Passing Bell. Six solemn notes, to betoken the death of a woman. Sixty insistent ones to follow, being the busy years of her age. Then silence, which is the end of all things.

The scattered birds returned to their perch, and hunched disconsolately in the belfry. Down in Garth you could hardly see your hand before your face, but up on the fells the fog was clearing. They were closing the doors and windows now, at Kit's Hill, and dousing the lights – all but one. They would keep the death-watch, turn by turn through the night, by the corpse. And they would marvel at the change.

For this was not old Betty Ackroyd, long-time drudge and shrew, but some warrior queen wrought in marble. Her face was strong and resolute. Her peaceful hands folded in prayer. Dorcas had wound the small cross and chain between her fingers, and laid the spray of violets in tribute on her breast. And by her poor disfigured feet she placed the box of trinkets, bought long ago in Millbridge Fair, by a father, for his chance-child.

Warp and Weft

Eighteen

1781

The reckoning of Miss Wilde's long clock, which stands at the foot of the staircase in Thornton House, puts her age at four score years and three. The lady, having lived thirteen years beyond her alloted span, now holds on to life persistently, though she is almost blind and immobilised and bereft of many small pleasures. Still, within that aged shell the mind ticks and the spirit sparks. She demands the reading of her morning paper with zest, and comments upon international, national, and local affairs with her usual asperity; no doubt feeling that if only they would let her have the ruling of them folk would be better off! This idea has not occurred to King George the Third, nor to Lord North and his Tory cabinet, so England is in disarray both at home and abroad. Her American colonies have declared their independence, backed by the Dutch and the French who have made a nonsense of the English fleet. The previous year found London at the mercy of Lord George Gordon and his mob, screeching Protestantism and wreaking destruction, so that for some days the country seemed to tremble on the brink of civil war. National discontent is mounting, and so is the national debt. Even in the quiet valley of the Wynden a truly shocking event has occurred.

Phoebe Jarrett adjusted her spectacles, which tended to slip down her nose as she read, and folded *The Wyndendale Post* smaller that she might concentrate on it better. Miss Wilde sat in the window, with the sun warming her, one wrinkled hand grasping the silver head of her cane, and commented as she thought fit.

On Friday last, the spinning mill at Thornley Fold was most maliciously sacked and burned by a mob of working men. Mr Jonathan Brigge, of Brigge House, and various public-spirited gentlemen of Millbridge . . .

'They mean Lord Kersall and his impudent friends,' cried Miss Wilde, still incensed by his lordship's branch canal.

. . . had set up a fund, together with two Manchester businessmen, to build one of the new cotton-mills on Mr Brigge's land near Thornley. This mill, intended to bring employment and prosperity to the inhabitants of the Wyndendale valley, was to have been opened on 15 October next.

'Ah! I know who would have undertaken the employment,' said Miss Wilde, nodding her chin with considerable emphasis, 'and who would have enjoyed the prosperity! Kersall must have the editor in his pocket!'

The mill, some four storeys high, and handsomely proportioned, had been fitted with over one hundred water frames based on Mr Arkwright's patent.

'Aye, to draw off most of the Thornley Falls water!' cried Miss Wilde. 'Why, my Papa used to put me up on his shoulder when I was a child, to show me the waterfall, and now they would turn it to a dirty trickle!'

No one can tell who the offenders are, for the night watchman was overpowered immediately . . .

'And would have sense enough to keep his own counsel!'

. . . but it is presumed that the bulk of the agitators were workmen who feared a fall in their wages.

For cottage industries were enjoying a golden age and treasured their liberty and independence. A man could weave, his wife could spin, at home, with their children about them learning the easier and more tedious parts of the crafts. When it was wet they all stayed indoors and worked the spindle and loom. When it was fine they could cultivate their patch of ground and attend to the pig and hens. They were their own masters, or if the weaver was part of a group then he knew his master, and could change masters if that one did not suit. But this great building, as Jack Ackroyd of Millbridge had said to the collected people, was the work of the devil.

'Who owns it? That's what we want to know!' he cried to the assembly of grim faces and flaring torches.

Cambridge had modified his dialect, but the north spoke through his tongue. Mr Henry Tucker's prodigy had learned more than his letters, and had remembered that he was a weaver's son. He had been plucked from obscurity, drilled with education, forced into being, without thought for what he felt or needed or wanted. Now in his twenty-fifth year, without the background or connections required to keep him in an academic sphere, he was turning again to his kind in the only way he could use and serve them. Jack Ackroyd had been split in two, and would belong nowhere, by reason of educating himself above his origins. He was only the first of many generations to straddle this particular fence. Nothing was ever going to be the same again.

'I read the newspaper,' cried Jack Ackroyd, 'and that newspaper, which is supposed to tell me the truth, tells me a lie. *The Wyndendale Post* says that this mill is being put up for the benefit of the workers, to give them steady wages and full employment. I'll tell you what sort of employment you're likely to get. Slavery! Do you know who has the biggest interest in the mill? Lord Kersall and his friends! And do you know who owns *The Wyndendale Post*? The same little group!'

He was a good-looking fellow, sturdily built, of dark complexion, and his movements and voice were full of vitality.

'So why should they tell you the truth when it serves their pockets better to tell a damned lie?' he shouted, and the crowd stirred. 'Shall I tell you what they'll do with their mill? They'll use it to employ folk, men and women and little children, for low wages. Then they can sell cheaper, and undercut your present prices. If you don't like it you can get out, and you'll never get back – bad as it was. For they can fetch other folk in. Strangers so poor that they'll work for less than you would. You won't be workers, my friends, you'll be slaves! Slaves!'

His voice rose to a shout, and the crowd murmured.

'That's the truth of it. Starvation wages or starvation. But there's worse to come. Right now some of you work for yourselves, and some work for masters, but you've all got your bit of independence and self-respect. You know who you work for, too, and he knows you, but you're like as not never going to see the man who owns the mill. He won't be Bill Shawcross there, or Arthur Bowden here, he'll be Lord Kersall or Mr Brigge of Brigge House or Mr Rich of Manchester! And if you happen to set eyes on him you won't say, "Good-day to you, how's the wife?" you'll bow and scrape and crawl, and hope he doesn't give you a kick in the backside. Because you'll be one Nobody out of three hundred Nobodies at that mill!'

Now he was well away, and so were his listeners, and many began to talk at once, but the others hushed them, for Jack Ackroyd had not yet done.

'There's more to come,' he cried. 'You work long hours, I know. Aye, all the hours God sends. But you've got the right to go out and dig your patch of ground, or feed the pig or the hens, or chew a blade of grass and take a look at the day. If this mill opens, and you work there, you'll keep your eyes on those machines until they're red with tiredness. The same with your wife and your children. You'll be too damned tired when you get home at night to speak, and you can be sure they won't pay you enough to eat as well as you did. You'll work until you drop, and when you drop they'll fetch some other poor devil in who can't help himself any more than you could. Is that what you want?'

Then they all shouted 'No!' in a great voice, and he had them ready.

'Burn it! Aye, burn it down!'

The cry ran through the crowd, and the crowd once fetched into the mood became a mob. The torches were in their hands. The Constable was in his bed. Down in London the mob had shown them a thing or two not long since (though they were unsure as to the reason for the riots there, it was far off).

'Listen to me!' cried Jack, and various people repeated, 'Listen to him!' 'We'll need to march in order and keep quiet, or we'll be in trouble. So fall in, and not too much noise. It's a mile and a half to Thornley Fold.'

The meeting had been formed by a chain of messages. The place was well outside the town. Untroubled by those whom they were to trouble greatly, the men set forth in good order.

'Soon after two o'clock in the morning, one of the farmers on Thornley Fells who was tending a sick animal saw lights down in the valley,' Phoebe read, with mounting excitement, while Miss Wilde's frail hand gripped her silver-headed cane in anticipation.

'There it is! Aye, look at the size of it! Must be close on a hundred windows in it!'

'Ted!' called Jack Ackroyd. 'We shall have to break the door down. There'll be a night watchman, too, I dare say. Just tie him up. Don't hurt him.'

The mill rose before them like some strange brick palace, dwarfing the scatter of cottages at Thornley. The moon, sliding between the clouds on Thornley Fells, illumined her windows. From one of them a fat scared face stared down at the little army of weavers. He made no move, no cry, as they caught up a heavy post and formed themselves into a battering ram, but sank upon his aged knees and prayed for succour.

The door parted company with its hinges and fell. Then with shouts and yells they ran loose over it, and poured into the great building, torches held high.

'Take the top floor first!' shouted Jack. 'Or else someone'll get burned to death. All of you, now. The top floor.'

The wooden machines stood rank upon rank, from one end of the long room to the other, an inanimate regiment of new enemies. And the men fell upon them with a savagery that sprang from supreme fear, and smote them down and smashed them apart, and when they had done with the machines they set the first torch to the wooden floor, and cheered as the planks licked up the flame.

Still in order, under Jack Ackroyd's command, they made their way out again to safety, carrying the trussed night watchman with them. But three or four men stayed behind for a moment on each storey, to make sure the wood was well alight. They they crossed the River Wynden and huddled among the trees on the other side. All good folk were abed, and the farmer on the fells was a long way from the village. Only the sly fox, winking gold and ginger in the brightening fields, the night owl and slinking cat, were witness to the first cracking window of the mill. For a few minutes it seemed to the watchers that the fire was pitifully slow and feeble, and then suddenly it danced alight all at once and swept from end to end of the building. Windows burst open, and pennants of flame blew out. The roar was indescribable, and every floor crashed down its machines into the basement with abandonment and added to the noise and heat. So that people began to run out of their cottages, and light candles to see what was to do (though the light outside was better by far than their home-made tallow could be).

'Scatter about, and get back home as fast and safe as you can!' Jack ordered quietly, and the message was passed round swiftly and obeyed. 'As for you,' said Jack to the night watchman, 'you'll be found in the morning, and you'd best remember nothing. Say we gave you a tap on the head, or else you might get worse than that.' The man trembled, and swore silence. 'Aye,' Jack continued, staring at the conflagration, 'that should stop them – for a year or two!'

'Dreadful!' said Miss Wilde, with deep satisfaction.

Phoebe tutted, and took off her spectacles, and set the newspaper aside for soon Agnes would be bringing in their afternoon tea. She wished that Dorcas might have called, for she was their only entertainment nowadays, but she was busy with the harvest supper and would not see them before Tuesday at the earliest.

'I wish that Dorcas would call,' said Miss Wilde, echoing Phoebe's thoughts. 'I am very old, and the days seem so slow, and yet I am afraid they will pass too quick!'

Phoebe mused in the late sunlight on change and decay. For Mr Jarrett had gone to his Maker, and was no doubt attempting to mollify heaven. He had died as easily as he had lived, slipping out while writing a note to Phoebe about his dinner that coming day. They found him, head down on the paper, with a quizzical look on his countenance, and the three words 'My Dearest Daughter' under his cheek. He had meant, actually, to chide her on the similarity of menu, but Phoebe was always optimistic. She had assumed that he knew the Lord was at his elbow, and had sought to communicate a last loving message. This assumption had carried her through the shock of the death, and the discovery that he had left her well nigh penniless.

Dorcas had taken over. Dorcas took everything over nowadays, except for her husband, who resolutely continued to be himself however much he loved her. Dorcas had decided that Phoebe should live with Miss Wilde, and read her the morning newspaper, and eat four times a day, and sew while the old lady dozed. Miss Wilde was content, and Phoebe was grateful, and Agnes relieved. For poor Agnes had been greatly beset of late, not having the advantages of a good education, to cope with the written messages. So all was well, and once more Thornton House had its complement of maiden ladies. Miss Wilde was not too bad these days, realising that she lived on borrowed time and that death was a jealous thief. So they sat in peace together, in the late sun.

'Is it not strange,' said Miss Wilde, 'that poor Miss Spencer died only ten days after old Dr Standish?'

Again echoing Phoebe's thoughts, for the grim reaper had taken his toll of old Millbridge.

'He was a great consolation to her,' Phoebe suggested. 'Perhaps, ma'am, she could not live without him!'

'Oh stuff!' said Miss Wilde vigorously. 'He was a great consolation to me also, as was your dear father, Miss Jarrett. But I have not died.'

'You have other consolations, ma'am,' Phoebe reminded her.

Her busy Dorcas, her handsome William, her pretty Charlotte. Even Dick, though he reminded her too much of Ned to be anything of a favourite!

'To think of the mill burning!' said Phoebe skilfully diverting the old lady from her thoughts of death.

'Yes, indeed,' said Miss Wilde. 'We are most fortunate in our lives, do you not think, Miss Jarrett? For nothing ever happens to us.'

'Fortunate indeed, ma'am,' said Phoebe, 'and here is Agnes with the tea!'

Our Lass

Nineteen

1781

Dorcas's hair held an iron sheen these days, but her muslin cap was grand with lace, and Martha Glegg still starched it to perfection. Trim of figure, straight of back, her gaze as bright as ever, Dorcas ruled Kit's Hill and her family with a subtle resoluteness. 'Our missis!' the workmen would say to each other, with a knowing nod or a covert wink.

Ned had thickened and strengthened with the years like a true Howarth, like a sound tree. His fair hair had paled from wheat to ash. Age and patriarchy suited him. He was severe with liars, worked alongside his men in equal sweat and humour, dealt justly and acted mercifully.

'Our little lad' was everyone's favourite. Dick Howarth, now all of six years old, with his ready smile, lived and loved easily and naturally, taking life as it came. The wheaten-gold and blue livery of the Howarths shone in his hair and eyes. He was as durable as the millstone grit beneath his sturdy feet, as simple and frank as his father, and Dorcas doted on him.

Then there was 'our little lass', the royally-named Charlotte Sophia, very shy at growing out of her clothes so fast, and as graceful and delicate and silken-haired as a queen should be. Charlotte loved Dick passionately, as she loved her father and William. Between herself and Dorcas there was a natural affection, but no great closeness, for Dorcas's ambitions were invested in her sons. From birth, Charlotte had been dedicated to the opposite sex. Her gentleness, her thoughtful mien, her innate need to lean upon and cherish a man, made Dorcas fear for her. She wished that her daughter had inherited the strong vein of common sense and self-preservation which ran through the Wildes' female line. With Miss Wilde these qualities had rusted into suspicion, but nonetheless they enabled her to look after herself and her interests still.

'I am glad, and I also fear, that Charlotte is like my mother,' Dorcas said to Ned, in the familiar comfort of their four-poster bed. 'It is imperative that she marry the right man, or she is lost. She could never defend herself, and would be wretched with the wrong one.'

Ned did not dismiss her fears. They were his own. For he saw the girl as an extension of Dorcas without Dorcas's strength, and loved her so dearly that he could never bear to hear a voice raised against her.

'It is wise to have her marriage in mind,' Dorcas continued, thoughtful beneath her frilled nightcap. 'She is close on fifteen. Who, among our acquaintance, would make a husband for her in four years' time?'

'Bloody nobody!' cried Ned, with such emphasis that she was startled. He added furiously, 'The lads have started gawping at her already. I fetched one of them a smack across his head today. Standing there, gawping!'

At the immature breasts beneath the girl's cotton bodice, the thin young arms and sweet young face, and the long wheat-coloured hair.

'I fair made his head ring for him!' said Ned with satisfaction, and smote the coverlet in recollection.

Dorcas stared at him in amazement, merely remarking that she hoped he intended to let his daughter marry eventually!

He did not answer at once, brooding, then said, 'What about them Scholeses in Birmingham? They know more gentlefolk than us. Folk as'd see the quality of the lass and look after her. William might fetch a friend home. He's a smart lad. But then, they'd be Methodys or Quakers, Dorcas, and you wouldn't made up your mind to one of them, I reckon.'

'The Scholeses' connections in business and society are varied enough even to please me,' said Dorcas with serene irony, 'but I should have no difficulty in preferring a Quaker gentleman to (shall we say?) Abel Tunstall.'

Here Ned twitched slightly, and looked suspicious, for it was Abel's head that had been smacked so soundly, and Abel was a lusty eighteen. 'Still,' he replied, jerking his chin up and down sarcastically, 'I dare say you and our William have got somebody sorted out already, and I'm not to be told. For a surprise, like!'

'You are being very quarrelsome about Charlotte,' Dorcas remarked peaceably.

'She could allus stop at home, safe wi' us,' Ned suggested hopefully.

'But we shall not live for ever, my love.'

'Our Will'd give her a home, surely? Else our Dick. I think nowt of a man as canna take care of his sister!'

'They will have their own wives and children to care for, and I should not like Charlotte to be a dependant in another woman's household. Besides, what is all this pother about sisters? I have not ever met with yours!'

'Pair of vixens,' Ned grumbled. 'They live far enough off, and thank God for that. Don't you let them come to *my* funeral.'

Dorcas sat upright with astonishment on her pillows.

'Why, what has upset you so?' she cried. 'Young Abel Tunstall admiring your pretty daughter? He is a hulking fellow, I grant you, but his gaping is natural enough. I dare swear you looked (aye, and winked!) at many a pretty face in your youth, did you not?'

'Aye, I dare say. I canna remember them, any road. I just know as I won't have my lass leered at, and I won't have her feared.'

'Of what was she afraid?' Dorcas asked, attending him closely.

'She were picking flowers, unbeknowing, and he were skulking in t' hedge. Like a blasted fox watching a chicken. I went for him, and it made her jump and cry out, then she ran off into t' house. I asked her if he'd been looking at her afore, and she says as he hides in wait. He don't offer no hurt, nor so much as a word, but he follows her round, gawping.'

'Then it is time for me to speak with her,' said Dorcas decisively, 'and she must not go outside the garden by herself.'

Ned was not listening to her. He was still creeping up on Abel with cold anger in his heart. He smote fist into palm, remembering.

'I'll tell thee what,' he burst out, 'when I see that mucky gowk this afternoon I could have wiped every man off the face of the earth. Fox, I thought, and I thought right. "The little foxes, that spoil the vines," the Good Book says. How's any man better than a fox? Tearing and spoiling a woman for his pleasure, and the woman giving good for bad as like as not. Nay, I thought then, that Standish were right, for all his nosy manner. Eh, Dorcas, I've cared for thee and cared about thee, but never enough until this afternoon. It's hard to think how I set thee at risk, in more ways than one, and to reach five-and-fifty afore I knew it. A young chap's no wiser than what he's got in his breeches, and yet life lets him loose as if he knew what he were doing. As if he could ever put right what he did wrong.'

Dorcas clasped him to her, crying, 'But you were not like that. You were never like that,' and rocked him gently, as she would have rocked and soothed Dick, saying softly, 'you must not fret so about Charlotte. We shall find a good kind husband for her. All men are not thoughtless, and all women are not gentle,' and as his face began to lose its sorry aspect she added, 'think of your mother and sisters!'

'Eh, you're a sharp one,' he cried, grinning. He freed himself so that he might put an arm around her, and stroke the elegant fall of hair. 'Tha'rt growing grey, my queen.'

'And so are you, sir,' Dorcas replied, smiling.

'I like it, mind you,' he said hastily, lest he had hurt her. 'It's like all about thee, it seems right!' Smoothing away his cares on the steely silk. And as she kissed him full on the mouth he added, 'I tell thee what else I like about us getting on in years. We can pleasure us without worriting about having another babby!'

'Can we indeed, sir?' she cried, laughing into his face. 'Why you are a cunning fellow, sir, that attains his desires by way of regretting them!'

'Am I?' he replied, delighted by this cavalier portrait, and the coquettish way she sirrahed him. 'Give us another kiss, then. But Dorcas,' holding her away for a moment, 'Dorcas, I know as you weren't much for married life, the first year or two. But I weren't like Abel Tunstall with thee, were I?'

'Why, no, you were not,' said Dorcas mischievously, 'though it was a little like making love with a midden . . .'

'A midden? Nay, I were never as bad as that. I come up and washed myself afore I took thee the first time – aye, and you was watching me through your fingers, for all you was pretending to pray. I saw thee!'

'. . . and your hands were more like hand-saws,' she continued demurely, as though he had not spoken, enjoying his every change of colour and expression. 'My best night-gown was all drawn threadwork in the end!' He inspected the callouses on his hands. 'But now I do not mind them, and since you stopped eating raw onion for supper we have agreed pretty well.'

'Eh, tha wicked wench,' cried Ned, seeing by the twist of her mouth and the glimmer in the eyes that she teased him, 'I should've leathered thee years since. I'st tousle thee instead, my lass. My dear lass.'

Nevertheless, love-making and amicable discussion did not solve the problem of Charlotte. Her lungs were delicate, and every winter was spent indoors lest they become inflamed. Dr Standish had prophesied that she would grow out of these bouts of bronchitis and catarrh as she approached puberty, but even now a sharp gust of wind would set her coughing.

The fair skin of the male Howarths, inclined to redden and weather, was translated in Charlotte to an exquisite pallor. The inheritance of Dorcas's small bones, in her became fragile things finely enveloped in flesh. Her shoulder-blades, as a child particularly, stuck out like little wings Her form was slender, drooping.

'Let her exercise regularly in the fresh air on horseback,' Dr Standish ordered, 'for the great Dr Sydenham would have it that the lungs benefited from this. Let her ride as much as may be!'

Ned, delighted to serve and please the girl, found her the nicest pony he could see, with a white star on its forehead. Then Charlotte, warmly wrapped, would canter over the fells, side-saddle, in spring and summer. But the Nick was a funnel for bitter winter winds, and she could not withstand those, whether the riding would have benefited her or not. And now that Abel Tunstall, and the other young bucks on the fell farms, were sniffing around his daughter, Ned was afraid of letting her ride alone. But she was contented to read an endless variety of books, with her feet on the parlour fender all afternoon, and to match her knowledge against that of her mother. For she had learned both Latin and Greek, had a fairish grasp of mathematics and a love of history and geography, as well as all the ladylike accomplishments. Indeed, as even Dorcas waxed impatient at Dick's stumbling progress, Charlotte had taken him over with smiles and praises and was doing well enough. Though Dick showed more talent at drawing horses in his book, and otherwise stared through the window and hoped she would soon let him go.

'She would make an excellent governess,' cried Dorcas, inspired, 'for she has twice my patience, and is not so quick with her tongue.'

'She's doing no governessing,' said Ned firmly. 'She can stop home until she's wed. That's my final word, Dorcas, so think on!'

Then in the summer of 1781 a new form of education

came to Millbridge. The High Street had its full complement of maiden ladies, and among them were the middle-aged sisters of Mr Percival Whitehead. The Whiteheads were considered to be superior people, and many were the musical evenings which Dorcas had attended in her years with Miss Wilde, for both sisters played the harpsichord then (now they had a new Piano Forte) and Mr Percival warbled on his flute. So when the gentleman died of an apoplexy (for Miss Mary and Miss Frances tended to overfeed him) the ladies found Beech Grove House too large, and yet did not want to leave it. So they decided to open a highly select day school for young ladies, in order to fill their lives. Actually, Mr Percival's income had died with him and left them in straitened circumstances, but no one would have dreamed of saying so though everyone knew it.

Miss Mary and Miss Frances, with their talent for petit-point (shown in the drawing-room to great advantage), their musical accomplishments and sketching (a charming little depiction of the corn mill could be found in a dark corner of the hall) and their elegant letter-writing, were no worse equipped to educate young ladies than most other teachers. It was Dorcas, seizing upon their idea with a slight pang of envy (for how she would have loved to run an academy) who suggested that Charlotte might be an assistant.

'For she can live with my aunt and Phoebe,' said Dorcas to Ned, 'and the climate in Millbridge is so much milder than here. She will be home for the vacations, and will have the opportunity of meeting other young people. And the Misses Whitehead are dear quiet ladies who will not be harsh, or expect too much of Charlotte. For when we were taking tea with them, Miss Frances remarked on Charlotte's complexion, and said she should drink a glass of claret before retiring, and asked if she should not like to lie down for half an hour on the parlour sofa.'

'Oh, you've sorted it out already, have you?' said Ned, amused and exasperated. 'Are you asking me, or telling me, then?'

'I'm asking you to consider the advantages of such a post, Ned,' said Dorcas earnestly. 'The Misses Whitehead cannot afford to pay her very much, but it will be something towards her dress and her books.'

'Well,' he said reluctantly, 'if she wants to then I'm not agin it.'

Dorcas slipped her arm in his, and played with his hard fingers and watched his downcast face.

'They were going to name it "Miss Whitehead's School for Young Ladies", ' she observed with quiet pleasure, 'but I persuaded them that "Beech Grove Academy for Young Ladies" was far better.'

'Give them a chance, wilta?' said Ned humorously. 'They can only have one idea at a time, like the rest of us. It takes Dorcas Howarth to have two or three. King George should have thee in his parliament. It'd be petticoat tyranny!'

Then, fortuitously as it happened, sad though it was, poor Agnes fainted one afternoon while baking bread, and was found on the kitchen floor by Phoebe. Dr Standish went through his personal medical procedure, and pronounced her to be suffering from overwork and anxiety.

'For your good servant is in her middle sixties, ma'am,' he said to Miss Wilde, 'and has been endeavouring to accomplish the tasks of her youth. Her constitution is sound and whole, but she requires assistance. She can supervise, ma'am, but she cannot do it all.'

'But the whitster comes for the washing,' said Miss Wilde querulously, 'and a girl does the scrubbing once a week.'

'Yet there is more than cleanliness to running a household,' said Matthew Standish patiently. 'Your good woman needs a healthy young girl to live in, and to be trained to take her place when the time comes. We shall not live for ever, ma'am. Any of us!'

'I do not understand,' said Miss Wilde pitifully, 'for Agnes is younger than me. We must ask Dorcas, Miss Jarrett. Dorcas always knows what to do.'

Therefore, on a mild September morning which followed

the hottest summer they had enjoyed for years, Ned drove his daughter and the new maid to Millbridge. Billy Sidebottom's eldest girl, Sallie, was close on twelve years old and very excited at the prospect of a good position with grand folks. The whole of Garth had come to wave her off, for Sallie would be more fortunate than her aunt and her mother in many ways. Agnes was a kind creature, and Phoebe a soft one, and Miss Wilde too toothless to bite. Sallie's worldly property was contained in a paper parcel, and Ned gave her sixpence before he left, so this was a great day. While fifteen-year-old Charlotte, suddenly made free of Dorcas's old room, and in the whirl of Millbridge society, unpacked her clothes and admired her face in the looking-glass. An adventure had begun. She was to enter the world of the imagination for two beautiful years, unhampered by delicate lungs and the wild wind. Her tasks at the academy were so well within her capabilities that she would be able to continue her private studies. With her gentle nature and fragile prettiness she would be much admired, both in and out of the school. The joy of earning a little money, more often to be spent on gifts for others rather than luxuries for herself, was another facet of this new life. The freedom gained was perhaps the greatest benefit of all.

Therefore two girls blew out their candles that first night, beneath the roof of Thornton House, and lay between the linen sheets watching the play of light and shadow on the wall. And though one might be in a front bedroom, and the other in the garret, they fell asleep with the same feeling of wonder, with the same sense of life's sweetness.

Twenty

1783–1784

The summer of 1783 was disastrous. Ned and Dorcas watched storms beat down their crops and swill away the topsoil. The new Parson gave thanks to God at harvest-time more out of habit than conviction, and Garth faced a sad prospect of empty stomachs. Then the winter came upon them with such savage winds and snow, with such malignity, that Dorcas sent word to her daughter to stay where she was until the weather should be better. Ned struggled to Millbridge with a Christmas hamper and the message, and kissed his lovely child in sore disappointment, and struggled back with her tears and kisses on his own cheek. For Will would not be home until Easter this time, and only eight-year-old Dick remained to cheer them at a season when all families should rejoice together. Furthermore, he knew that Charlotte's Christmas threatened to be a dull one, for Miss Wilde spent much of her day abed, and Phoebe was not the liveliest of entertainers.

Yet as he drove miserably away from Millbridge, a gentleman was riding in from Preston who would shortly enliven the town.

Tobias Longe was a bachelor of some years' persuasion, since he found his professional career more fascinating than any woman he had met so far. Though just past thirty he seemed much younger, being lithely built and possessing an enthusiastic nature. His complexion was brown, his eyes tawny, and some personal vanity or flair bade him dress himself in autumnal shades, with linen of the whitest and crispest to offset them. So that folk remembered him as, and even dubbed him, 'the brown gentleman'. Immaculate, ebullient, friendly, he appeared at first sight to be the perfect companion, for he had the gift of making people feel unique. On meeting, for he never wasted time, they discovered that he held outrageous views on religion and politics and expected to make converts. On subsequent occasions someone was sure to pick a quarrel with him, which he obviously enjoyed: defending his views with erratic brilliance; wheedling, needling, delighting and infuriating, and generally making everybody animated.

Printer, publisher and bookseller, Toby Longe had inherited his father's business a few years previously, and while keeping its goodwill had soon extended its interests. The new held infinite appeal for him: new people, new places, new ideas. He lived over his bookshop in Fleet-Street, which was a meeting-house for intellectual Radicals and Dissenters. He was looked after by a succession of slatternly servants, for no housekeeper could ever be persuaded to stay in this haphazard establishment which ran according to Toby's whims. He did business in coffee-houses, dined in chophouses or the homes of his friends, and worked (sleeves rolled up, an apron protecting his shirt and breeches, his wig stuck on a peg) with a bottle of wine by his side, and a pie from the bakehouse for sustenance.

His kindness was spontaneous but not sustained. He would forget, simply because he was too busy or had become more interested in some other person or cause. His friends loved him dearly, but loved him longest and best when he was not too close. Business had brought him to Preston. A gentleman of radical persuasion and some literary ability had proposed to write a book which would set the Establishment by the ears. Longe could not resist the idea of publishing at risk. Since they were unmarried men, the two bachelors had planned to set the world to rights, and the book to a fine start, over plum pudding and goose at the festival. The bitter weather had not deterred Toby from travelling, and though the skies threatened further disaster he had even set out on his second errand.

Kindness fetched him to Millbridge. For many years the Reverend Walter Jarrett had done business with his father. The two old men had died within months of one another, and Toby felt it would be nice of him to call upon Miss Jarrett. It was the season of the year when the poor lady's thoughts would be returning to those days of modest glory at St Mark's rectory. He could offer and receive delayed condolences. He had also considered calling upon his other customer in these parts: Mrs Dorcas Howarth. But as the bleakness of the Pennines came upon him, and he realised that Kit's Hill might be more remote than he bargained for, he contented himself with charming the one lady and sending his compliments to the other.

So Phoebe was fluttered when Toby encountered her in the church, and dropped a branch of evergreen with which she was dressing the altar (this former service being kindly allowed by the present rector's wife). The lithe brown gentleman swept off his hat and bowed low, then kissed her hand and explained his presence. Caught up with her obvious pleasure, and his own persuasiveness, he spun quite a tale; until Phoebe saw her father as old Mr Longe's most distinguished and favoured client, and the fact that only money and books had been exchanged a mere irrelevancy. Here at last, Toby seemed to say, was the moment that the family firm had been waiting for: to meet Miss Jarrett decorating St Mark's church for Christmas in the year 1783.

Of course, she asked him if he were staying long in Millbridge; and upon discovering that he purposed to stay the night at The Royal George, was departing the next morning to rejoin his friend in Preston, and had come solely to meet her, invited him to sup with them that evening. Then hurried home to persuade Charlotte to act as mediator to the feast, and thus make it fit for a London gentleman. Miss Wilde being strict over the matter of male visitors, and suspicious of all strangers, it took Charlotte a good hour of talk to extract a bottle of Grandfather Wilde's claret from the cellar. But, this point gained, the rest was simple. Agnes and Sallie set the dining table with shining silver, and cut-glass goblets, and fetched out the best white damask napery. The ladies had formerly proposed to dine lightly upon a pair of roast fowls with egg sauce, followed by apple tart, and cream from Kit's Hill. Now Phoebe and Charlotte sat at the kitchen table, revising the menu. They were anxious that Mr Longe should not go hungry. So Agnes set about making a good soup of the giblets, and Sallie was sent to the bakehouse for mutton pies, Miss Jarrett fashioned a splendid jelly, and Charlotte brought forth a cheese from the hamper. Then Miss Wilde thumped her stick on the floor, and rang her bell, and suggested a bottle of port, and said that she would dine with them after all – which necessitated an extra place being laid at the table.

So it was that Tobias Longe, elegant in chocolate brown, with icy ruffles at his throat and wrists, found the ladies of Thornton House awaiting him with one of the grandest dinners a man could eat, and company to match. Phoebe, flattered and flustered, had donned her Sunday mourning of black silk and her mamma's onyx brooch and earrings. Miss Wilde, in crimson brocade, looked her most regal, and the new white powdered wig suited her better than the youthful black one. Perhaps her diamonds lent sight to her failing eyes, for she whipped up her lorgnette to scan Mr Longe's countenance, and seemed very satisfied with the result: taking one of her capricious fancies to him. Sallie curtseyed, very trim in her muslin cap and apron, and helped him off with his greatcoat. Agnes received his hat and cane Last of all, hanging shyly back so that she might view him without being noticed, came Charlotte: a slip of a girl with light hair and dark eyes, in a cinnamon velvet dress.

'Why, this is a household of flowers, madam,' Toby declared to Miss Wilde, bowing over her hand, 'and I, poor wretch, in very heaven to be among them!'

'You are welcome, sir,' cried Miss Wilde. 'We do not have so much company these days. You must excuse our shortcomings, being unused to gentlemen in the house. But we do not dine so badly, and I can still offer a good game of cards, and Charlotte has learned to play our new Piano Forte and she shall sing for you.'

'I should be happy, madam, were I but able to marvel from a distance!' and he parted his coat-skirts and sat down in Grandfather Wilde's armchair, smiling on them all.

'Well, we hope to do better than that, sir!' In high spirits. 'But you must tell us of London, if you please. Where do you live, sir?'

'Pray, have you seen the King and Queen, Mr Longe?' asked Phoebe.

'Or Dr Johnson, sir?' cried Charlotte.

'Excuse me, sir, but should you like a glass of sherry while you wait for supper?' Agnes demanded.

'Sir, I've took your coat into the kitchen to dry,' said Sallie, not to be left out, 'for it were wet through!'

The flatterer was flattered, the charmer was charmed. At his ease, Toby crossed his legs, sipped his sherry and gossiped in great good humour. He had the claret almost to himself at dinner, but insisted upon the ladies joining him in half a glass. He ate and praised heartily. He talked almost unceasingly, finding they preferred to hear of his rattle-trap existence rather than divulge their own quiet way of life. He was an instant, and a tremendous, success.

At a half past nine o'clock Miss Wilde was forced to retire, but begged him to stay another half hour and entertain Phoebe and Charlotte.

'For we are very dull here of an evening,' she said tremulously, 'and such a wag as you, sir, is a rare enough treat. But if you would stand upon the doorstep when you go, and hear the bolts drawn safe behind you, I should be much obliged. One cannot be too careful in these times.'

Then he stood respectfully, and inclined his neat wigged head, and assured her that all should be well, and kissed her frail hand and thanked her. Agnes came with the candle, and escorted her aged mistress upstairs to bed, with Sallie following. And Toby Longe continued to talk.

'So your respected mother is the lady who orders such advanced books, Miss Howarth? I wish it had been possible to meet with her. My father, years ago, thought her a most remarkable person. Do you share her interests?'

'In part, sir. My mother was the daughter of a clergyman in Gloucestershire, and more accustomed to learning than to farming. When she married my father she made intellect the servant of agriculture, but taught her children Greek and Latin!' She gave a little scared laugh as he raised his eyebrows, yet wine and company had warmed her and she hurried on. 'I love my home, sir, at Kit's Hill, but I have no gift for farming. My mother spoke for me with the Misses Whitehead, and I teach young ladies at the academy here. My health is better suited to the milder climate of this town.'

'And your inclination also, madam?'

Obedient to her father's love of the truth, she bowed her head.

'Are you of a literary turn of mind, perhaps, Miss Howarth?'

'I do not know, sir. I have never tried.'

'I think you should. Ladies and learning do not often go together, but I know one or two lady authors. Should you ever, by chance, be in London, I feel your preference for an intellectual climate would be well suited!'

But Phoebe, leaning forward in sudden fear, lest the gentleman be a loose-living creature after all, cried, 'That is not possible, sir. Charlotte remains with her family, here.'

'Then London shall be denied, madam!' Toby replied gaily, and raised his glass of port to them both. 'It was but a fanciful hope, after all.'

The clock struck ten, reminding him that he should be gone. Agnes and Sallie fetched his greatcoat, his hat and his cane. He smiled on them, and slipped a coin into each of their hands, murmuring something about a Christmas box. He kissed the ladies' hands, hovering no longer over Charlotte's than he did over Phoebe's, and bowed his way out. Snow was falling thickly, softly, and their gentle voices exclaimed over the distance he would have to walk to reach the inn (all of three hundred yards away).

'It is nothing, nothing,' he cried to the elements, exalted.

'You would not say so, sir, if you were on Garth fells,' said Charlotte seriously, and was stricken to think of her little household marooned.

'How will you return to Preston in this, sir?' Phoebe enquired, shivering in the cold air.

'Madam, I beg you to go into the warm. I shall find my way, I do assure you, and I thank you for one of the pleasantest evenings I ever have spent. Pray, ladies, retire – that I may hear the bolt drawn safely!'

Their light voices conferring, the harsh rasp of the bolt, the little cries of farewell, the covert laughter as they carried the candles down the hall, touched him. He dealt with the brilliant, the pretentious, the devious, the bogus, the anything but innocent. Tonight he had been shown a little world of kindness and humility. Yes, Toby Longe was deeply touched, and reflected that he must write them all a letter when he got back to London.

By what strange chances lives are forged together. Had Toby not been chivalrous he would never have come to Millbridge. Had Charlotte not been delicate she would have stayed at Kit's Hill. Had the weather been reasonable both would have parted the following morning, and probably never met again. But snow decreed otherwise: snow and fate, and imagination which heightens circumstances. So that all night Charlotte lay awake and wandered through the picture Toby had painted of his life in London, and was wistful for the pleasures and anxious to smooth away the pains. She had glimpsed another world from the genteel round of Millbridge, or the steadfast stones of Kit's Hill. In her mind she saw an earthly heaven, peopled by thousands of wigged ladies and gentlemen whose wit was as fine as their clothes.

She saw herself, forever clad in her best gown, writing important pamphlets for which Mr Longe waited impatiently: his printing press idle for want of her composition. She was, after all, only seventeen and very sheltered.

She woke in such a dazzling light that she knew, before Sallie drew back the curtains, that Millbridge was snowbound. She waited, letting Phoebe make all her own conjectures aloud, to hear that Toby could not get through to Preston that day. Even Miss Wilde, sipping hot chocolate from the cup so patiently held by Agnes, remarked that she thought the rascal would be back for another hand of cards. And so he was, and very merry over the prospect, with an invitation of his own to sup that evening (early, for the sake of Miss Wilde) at The Royal George. For it was Christmas Eve, he said, and he could not dine alone and sorrowfully at that time of the year.

'I cannot walk, good sir!' cried Miss Wilde, holding his hand and giving it a coquettish little shake. 'I could walk for miles when I was young, but now I can but hobble!'

'I have hired a sedan chair, dearest madam, to convey you ladies safely across the street. There, what of that?'

Then Charlotte surprised everyone, including herself, by saying shyly, 'Indeed, sir, you have hired *the* sedan chair. There is but one in all the town, and we shall be troubled to pack into it!'

'That is her mother's tongue!' cried Miss Wilde gleefully, and they all laughed together.

'Then you shall come, sweet ladies,' said Toby. 'We dine at seven!'

'But what of the Christmas Eve service?' Phoebe reminded them.

'We shall all go – unless Miss Wilde prefers to remain indoors, as I believe she should – after supper,' declared Toby, equal to anything.

'And what of Christmas Day, sir?' said Miss Wilde. 'For this snow will not be gone for a while. Shall you not join us? Charlotte's Papa has sent such a goose, and a great cheese (which you tasted last night), and fresh-killed pork, and butter, and cream you could stand a spoon in . . . why, what is the matter with Miss Jarrett?'

For Phoebe, remembering the Christmas of 1760, when Ned had ridden down to the rectory in just such another snow, was overcome by tears and had to be excused from the company for a while.

'She was wrapped up in her Papa,' said Miss Wilde to Toby confidentially, 'and is often reminded of him. Best let her be for a while. She will join us again later. Yes, Charlotte's father is a gentleman farmer, and they have an estate near Garth. Dorcas sends our hamper every Christmas, since Agnes grew less spry, and the produce is all their own. They had a housekeeper in the family for many years, that would not divulge the receipts until her death. Dorcas has them now. The plum pudding is very good . . .'

All this time Toby observed the expressive face of Charlotte, which had become pink and distressed as Miss Wilde embroidered her origins.

'. . . and there is a gingerbread, the like of which I dare swear you have not tasted before. Yes, it is a pity you shall not meet with Charlotte's parents, or see Kit's Hall . . .'

Then, as it was obvious that Miss Wilde would go on talking until she dozed away, and had no more heed of them than the silver head of her cane, Charlotte drew closer to Toby and whispered urgently.

'Sir, I should not like you to gain a false impression of me. My father's house is called Kit's Hill, and though the farm is a large and prosperous one it is no estate. We despise pretension, sir . . .'

Then he took both trembling hands in both of his, and said sincerely, 'Dear Miss Charlotte! Your countenance is truth itself, and would not let you lie. If it please the lady to colour matters, let her be. Life is hard and dull enough, God knows. Do not despise or reject those who must make it rosy, even though the truth is less so.'

'You are kind, sir,' said Charlotte, not knowing where to

look because his eyes were fixed upon her, and of a velvet brown with gold lights (she could not help noticing). 'Indeed, you are most perceptive. Only, I would have you know that I am the loving daughter, and the proud daughter, of a yeoman farmer. Nothing else, sir.'

Then Toby was moved again, and relinquished her hands, and smiled, and took his departure of Miss Wilde.

'Yes, you shall have Dorcas,' she was saying, blurred now with age and unaccustomed excitement, 'you are the very one I have looked for. I fear, otherwise, that she will marry beneath her . . .'

The trouble on Charlotte's face showed her love for her father. She looked pleadingly at Toby Longe, who with rare delicacy rang for Agnes and counselled that Miss Wilde should be helped to bed.

'Good-day, Miss Charlotte,' he said, bowing gravely.

She curtseyed, unable to answer, and shut herself away in her room until the evening, weeping and praying in such a tumult as had never previously disturbed a mild and affectionate nature.

But no one could cling to sorrow while Toby Longe was near. Before six o'clock the house was in a turmoil of curling irons and steamed velvet. Miss Wilde had slept all afternoon, and was so confused when she woke that they decided to leave her to the care of Agnes and Sallie, and sit turn by turn in the Millbridge sedan chair.

What a Christmas that was, in the harsh winter of 1783. A helter-skelter of the light and the sacred. The great candles burning in St Mark's church as the boys' voices rose fine as threads to the fan-vaulting, at the midnight service. The pure and creamy shell of snow in which a love affair blossomed. The laughter and nonsense of Christmas Day, when Toby rolled up his shirt-sleeves (having asked permission to remove his coat) and carved the goose; and the way Miss Wilde went on about her grandmother's receipt for apple sauce (which contained vinegar) and then refused it because it upset her stomach. The gifts which Toby managed to provide from nowhere: a bottle of fine old brandy for Miss Wilde; a recent English translation of *The Sorrows of Young Werther* for Phoebe; William Cowper's poems for Charlotte, with a Christmas rose (removed from a Millbridge garden, unbeknown to its owner) pressed between the pages. And Agnes had half a guinea, and Sallie a shilling.

How dull Thornton House was after he had gone. Miss Wilde complained about everything, and kept to her bed more and more. Phoebe wept at every allusion to her late father. Charlotte drooped, and found her lightest task a woeful burden. But Toby had not left unscathed, and, though popular fancy might suppose that he was caught by the shy beauty of an innocent girl, popular fancy did not know the full tale. For he could have thrown off the thralls of the flesh, or replaced them with something less demanding than love, but Charlotte's virginal mind held him completely captive.

He wrote letters: at first to them all, then exclusively to Charlotte. He sent books: alarming, fascinating, awakening books written by radicals and dissenters. He plied her with Rousseau, whose first London edition of *La Nouvelle Héloïse* was making such an impact on the novel-readers of the day. No idea was too advanced, no discussion too frank, no philosophy too revolutionary, to be reported by him. In return, he begged for her reactions, and was delighted when she set down the truth (however painful to her, however dearly bought with some old illusion, some frail dream, and hours of scared reflection). She missed his company, despite the correspondence, but he was very busy. So much was happening at that hub of the civilised world, so much purported to be afoot in other hubs (especially Paris). It was some months before they met again, and when he arrived on the doorstep of Thornton House she had elevated him to the status of her lover, while to him she was merely a dear friend.

Phoebe had encouraged Charlotte in this romance, and Miss Wilde had affected not to notice the volume of letters while secretly hoping a match might come of them. All three, in different ways and for different reasons, had nourished the relationship while keeping it from Kit's Hill. They must have felt that Mr Longe's courtship would not have been popular there, though they never touched upon the matter, and here again chance played a major part.

Astonished to find himself received at Thornton House as Charlotte's affianced husband; Toby beat a terrified retreat to The Royal George, where he ordered a bottle of indifferent claret and set about composing a letter to the girl. He would have liked to put matters back on the former footing of a sentimental friendship, but this was hardly possible since he had left the household in a ferment. He did not want to hurt her with the truth (that he was fond, but basically indifferent). So he hovered over the page, and wrote and crossed out, and wrote again, until he was in a thorough bad temper.

Meanwhile, Nemesis was driving into Millbridge, in the shape of Dorcas, who had been summoned fondly by Phoebe and Miss Wilde, in order to meet the fruit of their hopes for Charlotte. And while Toby drank, and kicked his hat around the best bedroom of The Royal George, a similar scene was being enacted over the street in Miss Wilde's parlour.

'It is obvious,' said Dorcas, biting off every word as though it were her aunt's white head, 'that you have succeeded in making a great deal of mischief. Let us hope that it is no more than that. Charlotte had always a tender heart. Pray God it is not broke!'

She was turning over the letters her sobbing daughter had thrust at her in explanation. They contained not one phrase which could have offended the girl's protectors, nor a single word of love. Their genuine interest, and Toby's enthusiasm, had been mistaken for passion.

'You knew that she was corresponding with him? Then why not ask to see the letters? They would have shown you well enough what he was about! Oh, I know these Ranters very well!' cried Dorcas, who knew nothing about them at all. 'They would overthrow both church and state. Did you not know his views? Phoebe, did you not know that the man was a Radical and a Dissenter?'

Phoebe shook her head and wept bitterly into her pocket-handkerchief. But Miss Wilde sat stoically beneath the hail of her niece's displeasure, cogitating on ways and means of bringing them all to heel.

'He is fond of the girl,' she said at last. 'A little manoeuvring would fetch him round. He comes of a respectable family. He has money of sorts, though I dare swear the scamp spends it as soon as he makes it! And all young men are full of wild notions until they marry, when they settle down at once and we hear no more of this and that idea.'

'I wish I could be of your persuasion,' said Dorcas, in cold anger, for she saw that her aunt was off on another of her fixations, and had undoubtedly planned the whole match. 'I had not noticed that Cromwell changed his beliefs when he married! And I could point you out a hundred other cases. What nonsense folk talk when they wish to have their own way at any cost!'

'Your Quakers are Dissenters,' Miss Wilde remarked, unkindly.

'I have no quarrel with the Scholes family,' said Dorcas. 'They argue peaceably and reason soundly, but these letters are full of insidious provocations. He has deliberately set about changing Charlotte's inmost beliefs, and I shall speak with him!' She said, 'Oh, I shall set about this puppy of a fellow!'

'Well, do not set him against her,' cried Miss Wilde peevishly, 'or you will spoil her chances with him, Dorcas. You was always headstrong!'

'Set him against her?' said Dorcas, in a voice so silken that even Ned looked chilled. 'What do you mean, aunt? I would not have this traitor marry my daughter, no, not if she were with child by him!'

At this they all sat aghast, but did not dare argue with her.

'I'll come wi' you, then,' said Ned firmly, 'and when you've had your say I'll have mine. It'll be simple enough. I shall say "Get gone!" And if he's not out of Millbridge afore tonight my name's not Ned Howarth!'

From such small beginnings great misunderstandings spring. Toby had been thrust too suddenly upon them, and in a role they could not be expected to accept. Charlotte was too involved, too inexperienced to take part in the confrontation. Ned, while assenting to his wife's version of the courtship, nevertheless believed the fellow had tried to seduce his daughter. Dorcas, seeing more clearly than any of them that Toby was innocent of such intentions, declared war upon his ideas and his irresponsibility. Had she shared a sociable discussion she would have seen much in his arguments with which to agree: as she had been persuaded to think quite kindly of Quakerism, by way of knowing good Quakers. Instead, she planted horns upon his head and then called him the devil. Routed from Millbridge, with such phrases in his ears as would be ever remembered at inopportune moments, Toby was shocked into the knowledge of Charlotte's importance to him. When his vanity had been assuaged he returned to thoughts of her, and was sorry and piqued at once. He wrote her a letter, explaining (while trying not to offend her sensibilities) his version of the affair. He sent it via Miss Wilde, to observe the proprieties.

Having read it, and watered it with tears, Charlotte sat down and wrote a reply which he kept to the end of his brief life. The letter was a summary of a girl's hopes and fears, in a world which was guided by men and by the necessity of making a good marriage.* Correspondence with him had taught her to write openly. Her upbringing had made sure that what she wrote was the truth as she knew it. Impressed, Toby replied, again through Miss Wilde.

Miss Wilde preserved her role as chaperone impeccably, while allowing reconciliation to take place. Again, she did not inform Dorcas. Some old desire, or grudge, was being played out in the dark of her mind. Some power was being

* This letter has been preserved in the correspondence of the late Charlotte Longe.

wielded now, which had been overthrown by a will as strong as her own. Some obscure satisfaction would be reaped from Charlotte's harvest.

On the last day of the school term Charlotte bade her pupils a merry Christmas, and made her way up the High Street to Thornton House. She was a grave eighteen, slender and of an exquisite pallor still, and full of purpose. Did Miss Wilde know, as her great-niece kissed her even more tenderly than usual, that this would be a farewell? Phoebe, less observant and always obedient, had long since lost hope of Mr Longe's return to Millbridge. Did Agnes not realise that her god-daughter had made an irrevocable decision? Possibly only Sallie, who helped her pack and saw the front door safely barred behind her, had been let into the secret.

At The Royal George waited a gentleman dressed in golden-brown, with icy ruffles at his throat and wrists, and a hired post-chaise which was to drive through the night, hastening towards London and the rooms over the bookshop in Fleet-Street.

And what of eighteen years of love and devotion, of the lakes of salt tears shed when William left home, of the young-mothering of golden Dick, of the fortress of Ned's arms and the soft embrace of Dorcas? Not gone, but put aside for the moment, and that moment was to change them for ever. Charlotte wrote, in her first happiness, to reassure them of her husband's goodwill; for she was not to know until later that great decisions made great divisions, only to hope that the letter would link them all together again.

. . . and on the morrow we walked across the fields to our little church, which is as pretty as you could wish, and there is much of countryside in London. We had two strangers for witnesses, but I so thought of you that I felt you were with me at that solemn hour of my life, and the strangers seemed like friends.

Dorcas let the note fall in her lap, and two tears slid down her face. She saw her daughter walking arm-in-arm with her new husband across the London fields. It was as though she walked out of their very lives, growing smaller and smaller in the distance until she vanished quite away.

Journeyman

Twenty-One

1785

In the late summer of 1785 a stalwart young man on a great bay horse was picking his way down the track from Kit's Hill. The horse, powerful and clean-legged, with a white star on the forehead, was a gift from his father on his coming of age. His black felt tricorne hat, his white stock fashionably tied, his plum-coloured coat and breeches, were a present from his mother. William Wilde Howarth, journeyman, was taking a holiday with his parents before starting work for Caleb Scholes, iron master, in Warwickshire. His ambition ran silent and deep as ever. He had accepted praise with modest forebearance, though knowing it to be well-earned. He aimed for first place, and was quick to congratulate those who had gained second and third places. Built like a blacksmith, dressed like a gentleman, William moved in society easily whether it was high or low. Dorcas had questioned him anxiously about religious principles. He could answer her honestly, that he had not become a Dissenter. Had he been more honest he would have added that the established church meant as little to him. That he paid lip-service, while holding his own code of ethics. But he knew that this would only hurt his mother, who had grieved since Charlotte married and was afraid to open her letters (though waiting for them all the while) lest some fresh radical opinion chill and estrange her further. So he said nothing, and apart from an increase in height and girth, William was the same William who had once stolen away to the smithy at Flawnes Green. He still did what he wished. This bright morning he was on his way to see Aaron Helm again, and bearing provisions from Dorcas's kitchen since the blacksmith was a bachelor.

In Garth village the people looked more pinched and poor than ever, for the bad summer, two years ago, had taken its toll. King George's men had at last penetrated the stronghold of the Wyndendale Valley with their enclosure orders. True, they could not hope to reap the riches of southern England and the fertile valleys of warmer regions, but there were humble parcels of common land in the north still, scattered outside the industrial areas. From Garth to Flawnes Green there was not now one village which had common fields on which to keep its geese, collect its brushwood, graze its lean cattle. The poor, stripped of this last defence against hunger, were wholly reliant on their employers and the parish. The enclosure order had begun with Malachi Glegg standing up at the back of Garth church, and cursing King and Parson and crying revolution until he was dragged out, shouting that the common man would rise against his masters. It ended by Harry Sowerbutt grumbling in The Woolpack that every lazy bugger in Garth were on t' parish, and he and the other yeoman farmers were paying for the privilege of keeping them idle! The poor looked anywhere for work, and the answer came in the shape of another mill twice as large as its predecessor. This time it was not burned, and six hundred men poured into its doors, glad of low wages.

So William rode slowly through Garth, exchanging greetings with gaunt men who had once played marbles with him, and knew that they were trapped as he was not. The valley was changing. Coal had been discovered on Swarth Moor, between Childwell and Whinfold, and Farmer Letherbarrow sold the land at a high price. At least, it seemed a high price then, but as the seam was deep and produced good coal the bidder had made the best bargain. At Thornley Fold the mill was working full blast, and the village huddled at its flank like a submissive infant at its mother's skirt. Jonathan Brigge of Brigge House must have been doing well, because he was re-building the old manor and adding another wing. The hamlets seemed to be losing their identity, merging one into the other, as extra cottages and houses were built for managers and overseers of the new industries. Yet to William, whose eyes and ears were accustòmed to the grime and roar of Birmingham, this countryside was green and pleasing still.

He turned down the lane to the smithy, very proud and glad to be able to display himself in his manhood, to call himself 'journeyman'. But instead of the blacksmith, standing four-square before his open door, arms akimbo, there was but one little lad plying the bellows to a dull forge. William reined in his horse, and sat at his ease in the saddle, peering into the dark shop.

'Ho, there!' he called, and the lad jumped and came running, wiping his hands on his apron (which hung nearly to the ground).

'Sir?' he said respectfully, pulling a lick of hair that straggled over his forehead. 'Has lost a shoe, or what?'

'I seem to have lost a man by the name of Aaron Helm,' said William, smiling, 'unless he's shrunk to your size, lad.'

'He's but poorly,' said the lad, rubbing his mouth nervously. 'He's laying in the back yonder. I'm looking after t' shop. Sir.'

William got down, and tied the horse to a stump on the green. He nodded humorously at the jewel patch of grass, the little duck-pond, and the children bowling hoops from a broken barrel.

'They haven't enclosed that, then?' he cried, grinning, but there was no humour in the lad, who looked at him, half-afraid. 'Show us inside, then,' said William. 'I haven't seen him in a long while.'

The close air of the room, sweet and stuffy, smelled of sickness. The blacksmith lay at the far corner under the small window, his back humped towards them. He seemed to have been washed up onto the narrow bed, to be lying there stranded, like an old dark wreck plundered of its riches.

'Aaron Helm!' said William, and again, 'Aaron Helm!' as though calling him from another shore.

The hulk stirred feebly, and managed to turn upon its side, groaning. The blacksmith's face had sunk into his beard, which held more grey than black. His eyes were tired of pain. Then, as they focused, a brightness came upon him, and he put out his hand, saying, 'Is it Will, then? Come back from Parliament or summat?' Looking at the plum-coloured coat, the white stock.

'Will, come back from Birmingham more like,' said William, smiling, but Aaron's appearance shocked him. 'What's to do?'

'Summat and nowt,' said Aaron steadfastly. 'Good days and bad, tha knows. The good Lord never meant us to live for ever. I'm slowing down, I reckon. Aye,' comforting himself and the young man, 'that's about the size of it, Will. I need to take things a bit easier, and this is the Lord's way of making me!'

The lad hovered in the doorway, waiting for orders.

'Is he doing owt?' Aaron asked, without much hope.

'He's mending the forge fire.'

'Here, Stephen, fetch us a tankard apiece, wilta? You may as well earn your keep. He's been mending that fire for two days, and doing nowt else!' As the lad scurried out. 'Were he feared when you turned up? He won't lift a hammer without I'm behind him, watching.'

'He's only two ha'porth of copper,' said William kindly. 'How old is he?'

'Nigh on fifteen. He don't look it, I'll give you that.'

'Where's the other apprentice, then? You can't run a smithy with one little lad. I wouldn't ask him to hold my horse!'

'I've been ailing,' said Aaron. 'The one as I took on, as should have been you, he left this Easter. The other had gone the year afore that, and Stephen took his place. I couldna face taking a new lad on again.'

'I'm not surprised,' said William truthfully. 'It'd be more like minding a nursery!' They both smiled. 'Well, I've got nothing better to do,' William continued, taking off his hat and coat and hanging them on a peg, 'I may as well sort up for you a bit. I know where everything is, I reckon.'

The sudden life in Aaron's face made the young man pause.

'It's been going downhill,' said the blacksmith. 'I've lain here like a babby and cried at times. Watching it go, after I'd built it up from nowt. They knew me in this valley from end to end. Aaron Helm, the Methody farrier. I think they must be taking their trade elsewhere, Will.'

'Then they'd best fetch it back again!' Stripping off his fine shirt.

'Here, if you're stopping,' said Aaron, 'put a pair of my old breeches on. They'd fit thee now, I reckon. You'll only muck them good 'uns up. Rummage in that chest over there.'

'Does nobody do for you, then?' William asked. 'There was a woman that came in to do a bit of cleaning and cooking. Where's she?'

'You're a year or two behind the times, lad,' said Aaron. 'She died of the spotted fever. I tell thee, since I started being poorly, twelvemonth since, the whole shop's gone downhill and me wi' it, and all!'

William looked at him sharply, and wished that Dorcas was there to diagnose and organise. So he questioned him as to his condition, and thought he would ask his mother when he returned home.

'And what are you doing now, Will?' asked Aaron, cheering up considerably.

'I'm having a bit of a holiday up at Garth, and a friend of mine is coming to stay. Caleb Scholes. He's the eldest son of Caleb Scholes the iron master, and his father put him to an apprenticeship with Bartholomew. I tell thee what,' said William, lapsing completely into his old easy tongue with the blacksmith, 'I'll fetch him along here, and we'll run it between us for a week or two until you're on your feet again. It'll be good practice for the pair of us. We won't ruin thee!'

Grinning, as he pulled on Aaron's old breeches, and tied the leather apron round his middle.

'And then what?' asked Aaron, smoothing the coverlet, pleased and sorry at once. 'Where do you go then, Will?'

'Caleb's father's going to find a use for me. I'm going to learn a few things besides smith-ing.'

Aaron's face had sunk into its pain again. He fingered the covers, as a woman fingers them: slowly and lightly, touching her thoughts into them.

'Aye, you'll go a long way,' he said, attempting to speak heartily. 'I told your father as much, eight year since. You'll go a long way, Will.'

'Caleb and me are going to set up business together someday,' said William, completing his change of costume. 'He's a year younger than me. We get on a treat, him and me. I'll be proud for you to meet one another.'

'Eh, my lad,' said Aaron, 'I've looked for'ard to the day when you come back to see me, and us with so much to say to one another that we couldna start. And I saw us sitting together, in my mind like, talking into the night, and supping ale. And now it's different.'

'Where's that lad got to?' William asked briskly, to change the blacksmith's course of thought.

'Give him a shout,' said Aaron philosophically. 'That's all he's good for. A shout and a clout and a kick up the backside!'

William accomplished all three within half a minute, and brought the lad into the smithy by his ear. He pointed to the dying fire.

'You see that?' he cried, grinning. 'If it isn't burning up afore I've drunk my ale I'll lay you across it and roast you!'

'Aye, master,' said Stephen, and set to with the bellows as though Satan himself had ordered the flames to burn more bright.

'And severe abdominal pain?' Dorcas enquired, hooking her spectacles into the thick part of her piled hair. 'And he has lost strength and weight, you say?' She pondered her little list of symptoms. 'He should consult with Dr Standish,' she said firmly.

'My dear mother,' said William tenderly, 'your faith in Dr Standish is sublime, but Aaron Helm is a plain man who would not trouble so much as an apothecary. He believes that God has sent him this affliction, and he must fast and pray until it is better.'

'He will not get better,' said Dorcas. 'If I am right in my assumptions he has a disease which cannot be cured, no, not even by surgery. Alleviation, patience, and no hope, William. That is my diagnosis.'

The look on her son's face caused her to clasp his hand momentarily, saying, 'I shall send him some of my medicaments to ease him!' Had she known all that was in his mind she would have cried folly, but still not changed him.

So William rode forth daily, now plainly clad, and carrying various homely remedies and comforts with him. He was soon joined by Caleb Scholes. And now the wound in Dorcas's heart was opened afresh, for Caleb would have been the husband for Charlotte. He was a quiet young man with a solemn face, long-nosed and droll-eyed, and a tremendous sense of humour. Powerfully built, but not as big as William, he would shout and tumble Dick into the hay with a vast pretence of punching him to death. Dick adored him as much as William, and without their employment at Flawnes Green the two young men would have been bored to death by the lad's attendance. But off they went, rain or shine, from first light to last, and now the anvil rang again and the customers were coming back, and Stephen was kept busy with the bellows.

Occasionally, Aaron would wrap a fustian blanket round himself and feel his way into the shop to watch. His eyes went from one to the other man, seeing their broad chests marked with the spat of flying sparks, their arms shining with sweat, and the swing of hammer and sledge, and the incandescent irons in the fire. Then he would bow his head in acceptance that the glory was passing, and make his way back, to lie facing the small window and see the last of summer.

'The Lord giveth, and the Lord taketh away,' he would say steadfastly. 'Blessed be the name of the Lord!' Watching the light on the leaves, hearing a blackbird give praise.

'It is one blow upon another,' cried Dorcas passionately. 'Why must my children throw away their chances? What will Aunt Wilde say to this wicked waste of opportunity? She was to have given you a hundred gold guineas when you finished your apprenticeship. Oh, she did not mind your working for a gentleman of Mr Caleb Scholes's quality, for he is well known and much respected . . .'

'And very rich,' William added slyly, waiting for his mother's rage to blow itself out, for he accepted that she would be very angry.

'What matter?' cried Dorcas, pacing her little parlour. 'It is the quality of folk that counts, not their money. If he made money, well and good. If he did not, still the way that he works and looks after his people, and endeavours always to improve their lot and his, that is what counts.'

Ned, sitting side by side with his son (he had warned him to stand fast, for they must see this storm out together) said, 'Well, our lad has quality, Dorcas. You canna deny that. And I don't know as he's throwing away an opportunity. I've seen and spoken to Aaron Helm and he wants the lad to have the smithy when he's gone. It's a good little smithy. You should go and see it. Go and see poor Aaron, and all. He could do wi' a bit of comfort.'

Dorcas stood very still, and thought to herself, breathing as though that were all she had the strength to do.

'I have a great respect for Mr Helm,' she said, 'and I was willing, as you know, for William to be his apprentice. But now William has the chance of working with one of the first gentleman iron masters in the land, and he throws it away for the sake of Flawnes Green Forge!'

'You see, mother,' cried William, strong in his conviction,

'you will not look further than one step ahead. If that step does not suit then you believe all is lost. The forge is the beginning, not the end. I am but one and twenty. Who is to say what I shall be or do when I am one and forty?'

'I shall not be here to see it!' Dorcas cried, and wept bitterly.

'Now, now, now,' said Ned, putting his arms round her and winking at William to hold his peace. 'You've got yourself worked up again over nowt. Of course you'll be here to see it. I might not! Why, what age is that old bugger in Millbridge, eh?' This made Dorcas sob and laugh in spite of herself. 'Aye, she must be close on ninety, and still holding on. Our Will'll be tottering in to tell you how well he's done, and you'll still be a young lass. That's better. Here, Will, tell our Nellie to make the missis a pot of tea! And then you'd best be off, hadn't you, lad? There'll be one or two things to see to at Flawnes Green, if Aaron's making his Will.' Then he concentrated on healing Dorcas. 'Now listen, my lass,' he said, 'our lad's a man, and he knows his own mind. If you try to make his mind up different he'll stay away. The same wi' our Dick. You've got to let be, Dorcas. Besides, our Will'll only be a few miles off. You'll see a sight more of him than you would if he was in Warwickshire.'

Gradually, she came round, but had been wounded through her children. Charlotte's letters were bright and defiant, so that Dorcas dreaded to read them. She sensed unhappiness between the lines, and the fact that her daughter had not been home, in spite of many invitations to them both, distressed her. She would have liked to see her first grandchild too, due to be born in November, but her offer to come to London had been evaded. Charlotte's friends, of whom she seemed to have an unaccountable number, were looking after everything. At every turn Dorcas saw a forbidding hand, whether that of Charlotte or Toby Longe she was not sure, but the answer to any question was always in the negative. They had cut themselves off from the family, and she must content herself with recounting daily news and hoping they might meet again sometime.

Towards Christmas Aaron became worse, and Dorcas drove over to Flawnes Green to sit by the bed and dose him with opium, as she had dosed Betty, into a kinder world. She had no quarrel with the blacksmith, and he was entirely unaware of the struggles he had caused her, being a simple man. Besides, Dorcas was now resigned to the fact that her working life seemed to be over. Dick was his father's companion, not her baby. Kit's Hill had been brought to a peak of efficiency. Even fringe dependants were settled. What more was left but to preside over Ned's table, and drive the trap to market, and make herself useful when she was needed – as she was needed now for this poor man, who groaned out the praises of the Lord even in his semi-coma, and ventured to sing a hymn in a voice so frail that the thread of it broke halfway. So she sat and mused, for she was healthy and full of spirit, and though not young at fifty, still far from old.

Perhaps she should set up a school? She had always thought it a failing in Mrs Redfern (poor soul, dead, years since!) that she did not try harder with the village children.

Later she peeped in at the forge and saw her son, in the first flush and prime of manhood, working the white iron: a handsome Vulcan, with his black hair tied at the nape of his neck, his brown flesh glistening. He was singing as he hammered, rapt in some world of his own, utterly content. The smell of singed hair and roast hoof offended her nostrils, and she let the curtain drop.

Aaron's eyes half-closed, his mouth half-open, alerted her. She moved softly and rapidly to his side, felt his pulse, listened to his breathing, then called William, for the end was near.

They sat together, mother and son, in perfect tranquillity. The young man's beauty was stern now, watching his friend's crossing; but Dorcas's fine-boned face beneath the steely hair was lovely in its contemplation.

'He is not in pain, is he?' William whispered, for now and then a movement seemed restless, almost pettish.

'We cannot tell. We can only hope. He has had opium enough to quiet three men – but he is very strong.'

There was a struggle, followed by a long pause. They could see him falling away, very light and quick like a leaf in the wind. Then he came back, as people do and must, since life holds fast even when the pain of it is sharpest. For sharper still comes the pain of losing it. Aaron opened his eyes fully, and in full consciousness, and William held his hand very hard.

'In a barrel,' said Aaron, labouring over every word. Then he smiled most beautifully, and said without any trouble at all, 'and shouting Glory through the bung-hole!'

Piking Away

Twenty-Two

January 1793

My Dear Mother,

This letter will reach you far Sooner than Me, for the Business with Farmer Cotrell is now Afoot. Though it has been some little While since I saw you and Father y[r] Patience shall be well Rewarded, for Caleb and I should soon be Joint Owners of that Land called Belbrook in the sneck of the River near Childwell. It is Well Placed, being opposite the Coalfields on Swarth Moor and provided with Water Power from the Brook. The Ironworks will take Time to Build & we shall begin with a Back Shop, Foundry, Forge and Wheelhouse. As the Foundry grows we shall Provide terraced Cottages for our Workmen – but now I talk of Years hence, whereas I shall see you ere long. We shall Keep the Forge at Flawnes Green and take on a Journeyman and an Apprentice. Caleb thought to Name our Firstborn 'The Howarth-Scholes Ironworks' but I Persuaded him that 'Belbrook Iron Foundry' had a more Splendid Ring to it! How proud my Great-aunt Wilde w[d] have been over Belbrook, and already Naming me an Iron Master all round Millbridge! Do you not remember how she baptised our Home – Kit's Hall? Ah, how I rattle on while my Heart beats out the one word *Belbrook*! There, now I have wrote a Book and did but mean to pen a Letter. God bless and keep you, Dearest Mother. Soon we shall Talk to our Mutual Content. So Promises y[r] Affectionate Son. William.

Yes, Miss Wilde had been reaped in the night: a grisly little harvest. She had made her Will once a week for the last year of her life: asking young Mr Hurst (grandson of her late solicitor) to step round of a Friday evening and take a glass of claret while he wrote out the codicils. He was a humorous fellow and became quite a favourite with the old lady: steering her away from fits of temper with her beneficiaries, checking with Phoebe that she possessed such-and-such and had not fished it from the past, and generally behaving as a friend of the family.

The final result bore a close resemblance to the original document. She left Thornton House and a handsome income to Dorcas, together with her jewels and the contents of the household, provided that her niece did not re-marry. This caused some amusement, even in the midst of mourning, for Miss Wilde had still thought of Dorcas as an impulsive girl. Yet the vagaries of old age were able to picture William, to whom she left one thousand pounds, thus enabling him to buy Belbrook; to tie Charlotte's inheritance up so that it would trickle steadily forth, and Toby could not whim it all away; to give Dick five hundred pounds, since she liked him only half as much as William; to ensure a small pension for Phoebe while she lived, and a place at Thornton House; to duplicate that home and pension for Agnes; and finally, among the bric-à-brac of gifts to friends and neighbours, to leave Ned the contents of Grandfather Wilde's wardrobe. They found it in an astonishingly good state of preservation, and the funeral party ended in a round of laughter when Ned brought out a full-bottomed wig and stared at it, perplexed. He decided that Miss Wilde was suffering from a softening of the brain, but Dorcas and William privately agreed that the old lady was playing a final joke on him. The clothes were eminently suited to the role of a gentleman landowner.

Charlotte had not been able to come to the funeral. She was seldom able to leave London, and the family contented itself with seeing her and the children once a year in the summer, when flies and heat made the city unhealthy. She had changed from a shy tender girl to a thin dedicated woman, who spoke of her husband in a wry affectionate manner as mothers speak of wayward sons. Serious subjects were not discussed, since the Longes' views were diametrically opposed to the Howarths'. The French Revolution had found Toby printing pamphlets of praise, for he considered the débâcle a necessary beginning to a new world. Three years later, ominous events wrought changes in his opinion, but still he chose to see for himself and make his own judgement.

January 1793

My Dear Mother,
I do not know if the Shocking News has yet reached you, but all of us here are Aghast at knowing that King Louis of France has been Executed. Toby has been Greatly Concerned since the September Massacres and shortly after Christmas he set sail for Calais. Unfortunately he left us Little Money, thinking to be soon Home again, and I do not like to ask our Friends. W^d^ it be possible for Mr Hurst to forward my Allowance a little Earlier than is his Wont? For we Require a number of Things, and I am Fretted to find them. This is wrote in Haste but I shall send you a Longer Letter after this one. Pray Forgive me my Importunity and Believe me to be

Y^r^ Affectionate Daughter. Charlotte.

March 1793

The mail-coach dashed up Millbridge High Street in a fine flurry of hooves, a sounding of horns, and a general air of muddy importance. Adventure was afoot in The Royal George yard as usual. Ostlers ran forward to unhitch the weary steeds, whose rapid breath was hanging on the frosty air. Passengers alighted with the worldly appearance of seasoned travellers. People came to greet them with cries of excitement and recognition. Parcels, baggage and mail were handed down. The driver sat on his perch, monarch of the road, accepting all the excitement and commotion as homage. And Ned Howarth gripped his felt hat to his chest and peered into the throng.

A tall young woman in a shabby but fashionably-cut travelling costume stepped lightly to the ground, and turned to help her children out. Down scrambled and jumped a little fellow, some seven years old, who wore a cockade in his top hat and looked boldly about him. And then a pretty child of five, still half-asleep with hot flushed cheeks, a miniature fashion-plate of her mother.

Tears of relief started to Ned's eyes and he wiped them fiercely away, crying, 'Charlotte! Here I am, lass!'

She smiled, looking suddenly younger, and hurried towards him clasping the children by the hand. They all met in a laughing embrace, and Ned kissed his daughter soundly. Her chin trembled for a moment, then she smiled again as he swung first Ambrose and then Cicely up into the air.

'Your mother wanted to come wi' me,' said Ned to Charlotte, 'but I wouldn't let her. She could have catched her death of cold, and by Gow it is cold and all. Let's have your baggage, then, and see you settled. Is this all you've brought? It don't seem much.'

'It is all we have,' said Charlotte drily. 'The furniture was sold to pay the rent. At least we owe nothing. But the shop has gone, and the printing press. Toby had plans which did not come to fruition, you see. Poor Toby.'

'Ah well,' said Ned grimly, 'we'll not speak ill of the dead.'

For Toby's love of the new, and his insatiable curiosity, had drawn him to Paris at the height of the Terror, and he had been shot in the street quite by accident. He died as haphazardly as he had lived, leaving behind him a wife and two children whom he had loved in his way. So Charlotte was coming back to the shelter of Thornton House. The little boy trotted along by Ned's side, holding his sleeve and chattering about the journey. On Ned's shoulder the little girl lay and sucked her fingers wistfully, staring into his weathered countenance.

'So we're at war wi' the French again, are we, lass?' said Ned. 'They've been nowt but trouble and grief to us all along. Let's hope it'll soon be over. I wonder if they'll take either of our two lads? Still, Dick's running the farm for me, nigh on, these days. And our Will's got his ironworks coming up. They're more use at home, I reckon.'

Charlotte was silent. She had learned to live inside herself.

'Your Aunt Phoebe's been in a right taking ever since your mother decided to send for you,' Ned continued, changing the conversation. 'Agnes isn't up to much these days, but Sallie's been cooking since last Monday. It'll bring a bit of life to the house, having the childer there, and you can rest you.'

'Yes,' Charlotte said, 'it will be good to rest.'

'Your mother'll be along to see you as soon as the weather lets up a bit. I shan't have her coming if it's icy underfoot, so don't go blaming her, blame me! I have a rare tussle to stop her. You know what she's like, and no younger than she used to be – not that I durst say that!'

His own head was white, his shoulders faintly bowed, but he stood on the doorstep of Thornton House, stalwart and unperturbed, and sounded the brass knocker. A shadow crossed Charlotte's face. No man had cared as much for her and about her. She knew how to deal with a bailiff, how to beg and borrow food and money for the children, how to earn a little by her pen. She could discuss, argue, coax, take and give criticism, avoid trouble; but of how to love freely, and to receive a dependable love in return, she knew nothing.

Sallie, now châtelaine of Thornton House, flung open the door in delight: a strapping wench of twenty-two, and in no hurry to get married. Behind her hovered Phoebe, very small and grey, and Charlotte seemed to open the chilled flower of herself to this warm welcome.

'Oh, Ambrose is the image of his dear Papa!' cried Phoebe tremulously, of the brave fellow wearing his cockade.

Then suddenly she and Charlotte embraced and wept, for

only here was Toby loved and forgiven, and only here could Charlotte regain the peace of mind that Toby had taken away. Later, when they had all dined, and Ned was gone and the children abed, they would talk of the brown gentleman and make free of a happier past.

Ned lit the candle in his lantern and put it on the saddle-stick. He liked the old leisurely way of doing things, the silent pleasure of accomplishment. Once he could have ridden home without meeting more than a poacher or a passing fox. Now the valley seemed to be lit from end to side, and to work half the night.

A worsted mill had been built just outside the town, and weaving sheds huddled round it. Folk reckoned it would sort out and comb nigh on three thousand packs of wool a year. The Council had paid high prices for the long gardens at the back of the High Street houses, and given no choice to the occupants who were now left with a handkerchief of lawn and border beds. Then they had built a terrace of workers' homes by the side of the branch canal, so that a lady could no longer stroll among her few flowers of a summer evening without some rough fellow staring over her hedge, smoking his pipe. The rectory had lost its little wood, and the rural aspect of its lane, and stood in isolated beauty between rows of brick-built houses. Already the original Millbridge was dubbed 'the old town', for a new town was sprawling almost to Flawnes Green.

And this hamlet, formerly composed of two farms and nine cottages, now boasted a Methodist Chapel and nearly a thousand inhabitants. It straggled greyly down to Brigge House, which was treading on the heels of Thornley, and there was the resurrected spinning mill, six storeys high and working from five in the morning to nine at night. It shone out over the countryside, humming like some vast lighted hive, with Whinfold hamlet spreading around and beyond it merging into the coal-mining area which had swallowed Childwell.

The road had been mended and widened from this point,

to allow the wagons of coal to pass. A series of shafts were sunk, and miners worked each seam until it was exhausted and then moved on to the next shaft. The sound of blasting. of the steam winding engine, of sledges drawn over wooden rails, had driven away the birds. Once countryfolk had dubbed this lane 'Childwell Way' but now they called it 'The Black Road'. And over the river was Will's ironworks, or would be. They had carted a load of bricks there already, to start the foundry. Belbrook. Ned remembered lads fishing there, not six months ago. There wouldn't be much of a brook left by the time it had been harnessed, and no fish. The dyeing-house near Medlar poured all its filth into the stream, and nothing could live in those fouled empurpled waters. Once you could smell a hundred subtle scents, and now one great stink overcame them all.

But Coldcote hadn't been touched yet, and Jacob Grundy's son made saddles as well as his father had done. Coldcote was almost dark. Thank God for the kindly dark and quietness. You got weary of light and noise. And here was Garth coming up, small and pinched as ever, with St John's in its midst. At the south-west corner of the churchyard, where the sun came in sweetly of a late afternoon, the Howarths lay rank on rank with Betty Ackroyd among them. Only the dead were safe, nowadays. Which reminded him that he must make a new Will. Oh, he was hale and hearty, good for many a long year yet. But, on the other hand, he was sixty-eight.

He turned up the track and the horse slowed down from habit. You needed a lantern here all right. Black as pitch and wild as the devil. Then his heart swelled with joy because he could see the candles shining in every window facing the lane. Kit's Hill. As he clattered into the yard another lantern bobbed towards him on the frosty air.

'Is that you, Tom?' called Ned, swinging down from the saddle.

'No, it's me, father,' said Dick, emerging from the stables, grinning.

'Nay, you should have stopped indoors, lad. I could have

rubbed horse down myself.'

'They've come, then?' said Dick, asking an important question, fair head held a little to one side, blue eyes intent.

'Aye, right as ninepence, and settled in a treat,' Ned answered cheerfully. 'The little 'uns were as good as gold, and our Charlotte'll be all right when she's had a bit of a rest. Little lass looks just like her! Aye, and for all that Phoebe says the lad is like his father, I don't see it!' All the while unsaddling the horse. 'Nay, there's a touch of the Wildes about that lad. I'd say he probably took after the grandfather, myself . . .'

The door of the house opened and Dorcas stood there, a fine wool shawl drawn round her shoulders for warmth.

'Go on back!' Ned ordered, striding towards her. 'That Standish says as you should keep out of the night air, don't he?' Holding her tenderly while he scolded her. 'I shan't allus be here to take care of you!' he warned terribly.

In the name of God, Amen. I, Edward Howarth of Kit's Hill, Garth, in the County of Lancashire, being of sound mind and understanding, praise be God, hereby bequeath my entire property to my wife Dorcas Cicely Howarth, to be held in her custody until my second son, Richard Edward Howarth attains the five-and-twentieth year of his age. This being . . .

'Now, you've got Thornton House,' said Ned, as Dorcas read through the draft document, pointing out minor errors, 'and more than enough money to live on. So when our Dick's five-and-twenty you should go there, and leave him to it. I've reckoned out he should be old enough by then. Our Will makes his own way, so he needs nowt from me bar a blessing. Our Charlotte'll have a roof over her head, and that bit of income from your auntie. So I'm giving our Dick Kit's Hill and my money, outright. What you do wi' your property is up to you. I know as you'll see everybody has a fair share.'

Dorcas laid down the paper abstractedly.

'There are always women at Thornton House,' she said to

herself. 'That house is always full of women.'

'Now don't try marrying any of our childer off!' Ned warned. 'Neither of the lads'll be told what to do, and our Charlotte's had enough trouble for the time being. So let be, or you'll only set them agin you, and I shan't be there to sort it all out!'

A half-smile on her mouth stopped him, and he took her hand and fondled it.

'I'm only saying it for your own good,' he apologised.

'Oh, I have grown so used to you,' said Dorcas, musing, 'that I cannot imagine life without you, Ned. Nor life without Kit's Hill. But I shall do as you say, of course. For that is right. I know that you are right.'

'Eh, we'll do many a year together yet, my lass. Only I must see to everybody afore I pike away.'

They sat in companionable silence together in Dorcas's little parlour, he smoking his pipe and talking of Charlotte and the War and the Valley. She speculated on the rise in food prices, he on the changing values. In the kitchen Tom sat and talked to Nellie, who was stirring frumenty for Lent. Outside on Garth fells Jonas Cartwright brought forth the first lamb of the season, and saw it suckling before he strode on to the next pasture. And Kit's Hill stood unmoved by the gathering wind which came down the Nick o' Garth and tuned up an orchestra of threatening sounds. Time was of small consequence here, and life still simple. A man woke with the coming of day, and stopped work at twilight. When he was hungry or thirsty he ate and drank. When he was tired he slept. And when he loved, as Ned Howarth had loved, he won his lady and began a new dynasty.